FAREWELL, THRUSH GREEN

FAREWELL, THRUSH GREEN

An omnibus volume containing

Extracts from THE WORLD OF THRUSH GREEN
CELEBRATIONS AT THRUSH GREEN
THE YEAR AT THRUSH GREEN

Miss Read

ILLUSTRATED BY JOHN S. GOODALL

MICHAEL JOSEPH
LONDON

MICHAEL JOSEPH

Published by the Penguin Group
Penguin Books Ltd, 27 Wrights Lane, London w8 5tz, England
Penguin Putnam Inc., 375 Hudson Street, New York, New York 10014, USA
Penguin Books Australia Ltd, Ringwood, Victoria, Australia
Penguin Books Canada Ltd, 10 Alcorn Avenue, Toronto, Ontario, Canada m4v 3b2 Penguin Books
India (P) Ltd, 11 Community Centre,
Panchsheel Park, New Delhi – 110 017, India
Penguin Books (NZ) Ltd, Cnr Rosedale and Airborne Roads, Albany, Auckland, New Zealand
Penguin Books (South Africa) (Pty) Ltd, 5 Watkins Street,
Denver Ext 4, Johannesburg 2094, South Africa

Penguin Books Ltd, Registered Offices: Harmondsworth, Middlesex, England

The World of Thrush Green first published by Michael Joseph 1988
copyright © Miss Read 1988; revisions 2000
Celebrations at Thrush Green first published by Michael Joseph 1992
copyright © Miss Read 1992
The Year at Thrush Green first published by Michael Joseph 1995
copyright © Miss Read 1995

First published in one volume as *Farewell, Thrush Green* by Michael Joseph 2000
1

Copyright © Miss Read, 2000
Illustrations copyright © John S. Goodall 1988, 1992, 1995

The moral right of the author has been asserted

Set in 11.5/13.5 pt Monotype Garamond
Typeset by Rowland Phototypesetting Ltd,
Bury St Edmunds, Suffolk
Printed in England by Clays Ltd, St Ives plc

A CIP catalogue record for this book is available from the British Library

ISBN 0-718-14469-4

Contents

From

THE WORLD OF THRUSH GREEN

The World of Thrush Green

I never made any secret of the fact that the village of Thrush Green was based, outrageously loosely, on Wood Green at the northern end of the Oxfordshire town of Witney (which I called Lulling in the books). Here I spent most of the war years from the winter of 1940 to that of 1945. I use the expression 'outrageously loosely' because I took great liberties with the place, erecting a monument to a fictitious Victorian missionary called Nathaniel Patten, depositing a village school where there is none, and adding a rectory at the southern end of the green which I greatly enjoyed burning down in a later book. There is a touch of the arsonist in us all, I suspect, and anyway it was a hideous building to find in such a delectable Cotswold setting.

How I came to light upon Wood Green as a background for the Thrush Green books might be of interest to those who like to know how a writer's mind works. By 1958 I had written three novels in quick succession about the quite imaginary village of Fairacre. These all used the village schoolmistress, Miss Read, as their narrator, but I found writing in the first person was irksome. Also, I was getting rather tired of those characters, and if anyone had told me that I should write a good many more stories about Fairacre, its school and its inhabitants – in fact, eighteen in all – I should have been profoundly surprised.

I think it was J. B. Priestley who said that there was no need to pity the novelists as 'they are only playing with their dolls'. The time had come to find a new set of dolls for me to play with, and this time I was determined to write in the third person. It is advice I give to all budding authors of fiction. Trying to observe the verities of time and place, when acting as a narrator, can be a most traumatic experience, take my word for it.

So where should I play this time? I wanted a village. I wanted a few well-defined characters. What did Jane Austen advise her niece Anna when the girl was embarking on her first novel?

'You are now collecting your People delightfully,' she wrote, 'getting them exactly into such a spot as is the delight of my life; three or four Families in a Country Village is the very thing to work on.'

No one could give better guidance. Although I was lucky enough to have been brought up in a Kentish village, Wood Green was closer to me in time and place, and I had spent five amazingly happy years there considering that it was war-time and that my husband was busy in the RAF on flying duties. Our daughter Jill had been born during that time, and almost every day I pushed the pram up the steep hill that led to Wood Green from Witney. I saw those lovely Cotswold houses in sunshine and shower, while bombers lurched back to air bases nearby and army convoys thundered south from the Midlands.

It was a strange world, and one's senses were made more acute by the times. There were several of us young mothers, far from home, wheeling our babies in Witney and Wood Green, and friendships were forged then that have lasted a lifetime. And the people of Witney were outstandingly kind and welcoming to the strangers in their midst. Scarcity of housing, of food, of clothing, and of all the other necessities of living did not quench their generosity and I hope we showed that we were grateful.

And so, in 1958, it was to Wood Green that I returned in spirit. I had long wanted to write a book wherein all the happenings take place in one day. It is a great challenge, and now that I was freed from that wretched first person as narrator I felt that I could try my luck on this new project.

Thus 'Thrush Green' was born. It seemed a good idea to make that one day a particularly interesting one, and so I decided to have Mrs Curdle's fair on 1 May.

Witney has a splendid annual Mop Fair in September, but that is held on a larger green, the Leys, at the other end of the town. For my purpose, the smaller affair at Thrush Green fitted very well, and I began my book: 'Thrush Green Chapter One. The Day Begins.'

When I wrote my novels, the place came first, the people second. In this case, Wood Green was there, already laid out, and it only remained for me to people the houses. I can truthfully say that every one of the Thrush Green characters is of my creation. The nearest I came to reality was to have Dr Bailey and his wife living in a house very close to that of the doctor whom I knew during the war. But the latter's surgery was in the High Street of Witney, and I was obliged to build a surgery for Dr Bailey beside the house.

Much has happened to Witney and its neighbourhood over the last forty-plus years. The path down which I used to push my daughter in her pram and which I made into the path beside Albert Piggott's cottage led to open fields and the imaginary Lulling Woods, but now leads to a housing estate. More houses have been built along the New Yatt Road, and between that road and the larger Woodstock Road. Witney itself is greatly altered with at least two important roads leading from the High Street, where once were large gardens or paddocks.

But Wood Green itself is little changed, and when it was filmed for a short television programme about Thrush Green, it warmed my heart to see it so close to my memories of it.

Long may it remain so!

When I began to write about Thrush Green in 1958, I described it in the first few pages of that first book, Thrush Green.

Thrush Green stood on high ground at the northerly end of Lulling, a small sleepy prosperous town, which had been famous in the days of the wool trade.

The town itself lay some half a mile distant, its gentle grey houses clustered in a hollow on each side of the twining silver river, like a flock of drowsy sheep. The streets curved and twisted as pleasantly as the river, but were shaded by fine lime trees instead of willows.

The High Street tilted abruptly to rise to Thrush Green. It was a short sharp hill, 'a real head-thumper of a hill' in hot weather, as old Mr Piggott, sexton of St Andrew's, often said. In the grip of winter's ice, the same hill was feared by riders, drivers, and those on foot. The green itself was triangular, with the church of St Andrew standing at the southerly point. The main road from Lulling to its nearest neighbouring Cotswold town ran along one side of the green, and a less important lane threading its way to half a dozen or so sleepy little hamlets skirted the other. Across the base of the triangle at the northern end ran a fine avenue of horse chestnut trees, linking the two roads and, behind them, facing towards St Andrew's across the green, stood five sturdy old houses, built of that pleasantly sunny Cotswold stone which reminds one of honeycombs, golden afternoons and mellow bliss.

Wood Green on which I based my Thrush Green was naturally the focal point of the village and, over the years, the dozen or so habitations and their inmates gradually took over from reality, and became very dear to me. The majority of the books' main characters lived in houses set round the green.

Joan and Edward Young's house was certainly the largest and one of the oldest. Travelling clockwise round the green, their house stood at twelve o'clock, at the far end of the green from St Andrew's church, a dominant position well suited to its size and dignity.

Joan Young, her architect husband Edward, and their young son Paul, grew clearer to me with every Thrush Green book that emerged. When the Victorian vicarage at Thrush Green burnt down, it was replaced by a set of one-storey retirement homes for old people. Edward was given the contract and threw himself into it with vigour, aided no doubt by his life-long abhorrence of the building which he was about to replace. Everyone agreed that the result was most successful. It was practical and in harmony with the surroundings.

Within fifty yards of the Youngs' home, across the road which led northwards to the Midlands, stood the house called Tullivers at one on our imaginary clock. Tullivers had been empty for some years when a stranger arrived in a red Mini and proceeded to look round. This turned out to be a young married woman called Phyllida Prior, who had a small son Jeremy to keep her company. But, to the great interest of all at Thrush Green, no husband was to be seen when she moved in.

Phyllida and Jeremy soon became friendly with the older residents of Thrush Green. The girl's solitary state occasioned a good deal of sympathy and, in some cases, even stronger feelings. There were many who admired her efforts to make a little money by freelance writing, whilst awaiting a divorce from the husband who had deserted her. Phil found a market for her work with an editor called Frank Hurst whom she was later to marry.

Dr Bailey and his wife Winnie lived next door to Tullivers, at two o'clock on the green, in just such a position that the doctor who attended us at Wood Green lived. This real doctor was a much younger man than the Dr Bailey I created, and at the time of the first book, *Thrush Green*, he was an elderly man contemplating retirement. Already much of his work had been taken over by the newly appointed Dr John Lovell who worked alongside him.

In fact, the good Dr Bailey only had a few months of his life left and, after his death, his widow Winnie did her best to come to terms with her new and sad circumstances. She was understandably nervous about living alone, until one happy day when Jenny, her friend and daily help, came to live with her. Here she rejoiced in her new flat and the modern kitchen where she had full scope for her passion for cooking.

If you walk up the steep hill from Witney to Wood Green on the main Woodstock road, on your right you will notice an attractive building on a high bank. It was once the Friends' Meeting House and here, during the war, a nursery playgroup met one or two mornings a week. Accompanied by Jill, our daughter, I spent many happy hours helping there. It was a lively place and did good work. I always felt that it was typical of the Quakers' practical Christianity to allow their building to be so used.

It was near here, at roughly four o'clock on the green, that

I placed the small house where the two friends Ella Bembridge and Dimity Dean lived amicably together for a number of years. Although it was generally believed in Thrush Green that 'poor Dimity was put upon by Ella', it was not the case. It was true that Dimity appeared to fall in readily with any of Ella's demands, but if it came to a matter of principle, then Dimity was unshaken.

This Ella knew. Her gruff mannish exterior hid a sensitive and complex nature. Those large and lumpish hands could produce exquisitely fine work when required. Doggedness was one of the virtues which Ella prized. Loyalty was another. It came to the fore most strongly when she faced the fact that one day Dimity might marry. It was Harold Shoosmith she had in mind then, mistakenly thinking that Dimity was attracted to him.

In due course, Dimity did indeed receive the proposal of marriage which was to change her life. But it was not Harold Shoosmith who put the question, but Thrush Green's rector, Charles Henstock.

After Dimity's marriage to the rector, Ella continued to live in her snug cottage, on her own now but still near her old friend in the rectory.

The rectory was a high Victorian monstrosity, facing north and perched on a small mound, the better to catch the chilly winds of the Cotswold country. Unlike its neighbours which were built of local stone, the rectory had been encased in stucco early in its life. The ravages of time had caused pieces to break away here and there, so that newer patches of different grey made the whole affair appear shabbier than ever.

Charles Henstock had lived alone here for several years, in appalling conditions of cold and discomfort; it was indeed fortunate that he cared little for creature comforts. The rectory became Charles and Dimity's first home and here they settled very happily – apart from the draughts.

The ugly rectory is a figment of my imagination, for there

was never such a building on Wood Green. However, I quite enjoyed describing the horrors of my creation, and share with Edward Young, the architect, his revulsion for the hideous house, covered in peeling stucco, as chilling within as without. The rectory stood at six o'clock on our clock, dead opposite the Youngs across Thrush Green, and was consequently a source of continuous irritation to Edward who could see it from every south-facing window of his house.

It was with great relish that I prepared to burn down the rectory – while Charles and Dimity were conveniently away for a few days. Harold Shoosmith undertook the unenviable task of ringing them in Yorkshire, and breaking the news to them. Of course, all their Thrush Green friends rallied round them, and Joan and Edward Young gave them comfort and supper on the evening of their return.

The Henstocks were lucky enough to find lodgings in the village while they awaited a new home. Fortune favoured them when, a little later, Charles was summoned to a meeting with his Bishop to discuss his future.

Wood Green stands at the northern end of Witney. Better known is the larger Church Green which is at the southern end and which is dominated by the fine church of St Mary the Virgin. When I began writing the Thrush Green books, I changed the name of St Mary's of Witney to St John's of Lulling, and here Charles Henstock became vicar after the fire at Thrush Green, he and Dimity settling happily into the comfortable vicarage nearby.

Charles was priest in charge of Lulling, Thrush Green, Nidden and Lulling Woods. The churches at Nidden and Lulling Woods are scarcely mentioned, but the one at Thrush Green, which I named St Andrew's, figures largely in the novels. In reality, there is a church called Holy Trinity on Wood Green. It is the only building to stand on the green itself. The houses, both real and imaginary, stand on the road which surrounds the green.

Holy Trinity is a sturdy Victorian building with a well-kept graveyard. The grass is mown regularly, the graves well cared for. It is not a bit like the imaginary churchyard of St Andrew's which is sadly neglected by Albert Piggott, sexton and general factotum.

It was Harold Shoosmith who took Charles Henstock to see a churchyard which had been tidied and made easier to keep neat. He had come across it when he stopped for tea on one of his afternoon drives in the Cotswolds. Charles was much taken with the idea that modern graves should be placed in a new burial ground somewhere else in the village, and the existing gravestones could be placed against the wall around the edge. Despite Charles's enthusiasm, Harold suspected there would be quite a few battles before they attained such a peaceful churchyard.

As it happened, Harold's fears were realised. It was plain to him that there was bound to be some hostility to the idea. Any disturbance to the churchyard would be looked upon as a desecration by some of Charles's parishioners and, indeed, the trouble began when the item on the Parochial Church Council's agenda, 'The Future of the Churchyard', was reached. Members of the PCC listened attentively but the battles raged beyond the confines of the council.

Poor Charles Henstock suffered greatly in the months that followed. It grieved him much to see the warfare among his parishioners, and it was even more difficult to bear when he knew that he was the cause of such bitterness. However, as time passed, he was able to persuade the objectors to with-draw their criticisms and, in due course, St Andrew's church-yard was cleared, and Albert Piggott's mowing chores greatly eased.

Charles Henstock has always been one of my favourite characters, a kindly modest man who took all his parishioners' troubles to heart. The fact that I had shifted him to Lulling did not remove him from Thrush Green for he was still rector of that parish. Always a conscientious pastor, he took particular interest in the old people who lived in the new Rectory Cottages,

built on the site of his old home, and designed by Edward
Young.

Albert Piggott's cottage stood at seven o'clock. It was even
closer to St Andrew's church than the rectory, which was useful
in view of Albert's duties as sexton and general caretaker to
the building and the churchyard. Not that this Pooh-Bah of a
person let his duties worry him, even though they were within
his sight at all hours. When his first wife died, he was content
to live in squalor, taking most of his refreshment next door at
the Two Pheasants to save cooking. Dr Bailey, and later Dr
Lovell, remonstrated in vain about a diet of beer, pickled
onions, pork pie and cold sausages, occasionally varied, when
the spirit moved Albert, by his own cooking, in a disgusting
frying pan.

The arrival of Nelly Tilling, an old school friend, soon altered
the interior of Albert's abode. She called frequently at the house
and enjoyed cleaning up the place and cooking her old friend
a meal. In due course, Nelly Tilling became his wife. She
cleaned his previously grubby house, and cooked him meals
which were far too rich for his sorely-tried stomach.

It was hardly surprising that his habitual gloominess was
increased by an incipient ulcer, and that Nelly grew more and
more impatient with his grumblings. The attentions of the
visiting oilman who called every Tuesday at Thrush Green were
of great comfort to Nelly at this time, and it was not long
before Albert put two and two together. His suspicions grew
stronger the more he thought about the oilman. Nelly certainly
seemed unusually happy on Tuesdays. There had to be some
connection.

Albert challenged his wife when she returned home one
evening and a fearful row ensued, ending with Nelly flouncing
off upstairs. Ominous thumps and door-bangings proclaimed
that she was active and when at length she reappeared, she was
dressed in her best hat and coat, and was carrying a large

suitcase. She was off, and after her departure, Albert had to muddle through on his own, although his daughter, Molly, was able to help out a little.

Far away, however, Nelly Piggott was discovering that Charlie, the oilman, was not only mean with money but also unfaithful. With some trepidation, she decided to return to Albert and life at Thrush Green. The two settled down together in a state of armed neutrality. It suited Nelly and it suited Albert up to a point. At least he did not have to bother about the house and feeding the cat, or locking up at night. Not that he had taken any of these duties even perfunctorily in Nelly's absence, but he knew she would cope with all the domestic arrangements, leaving him to grumble about his work for the church across the road.

It was not long before Nelly decided that she wanted a job. She needed the interest as well as the money. For a time she had cleaned Thrush Green school but then she heard that there was a post vacant at the Misses Lovelock. However, the job with the Lovelock sisters proved most unsatisfactory, as Nelly found out after only a few days had passed.

She completed her time in the Lovelocks' employment and later found her true vocation next door at the Fuchsia Bush. It came about because of an accident to Mrs Jefferson, an old-timer there. Mrs Peters, who owned the restaurant, told Ella Bembridge and Dimity Henstock the sad tale, and it was they who suggested that Nelly might help. Having this employment made all the difference to her. She enjoyed the company at the Fuchsia Bush and the knowledge that her skills were appreciated. Also she liked earning money of her own. When Mrs Peters went down with influenza one bitter winter, Nelly proved she was quite capable of running the restaurant on her own.

Almost next door to the Piggotts was the Two Pheasants, at eight o'clock on our time-piece. It was a snug little inn,

well furnished with beams and cushioned settles. Mr Jones
the landlord and his wife lived in comfort above the two bars,
and were as cheerful and welcoming as the best hosts should
be.

In real life, a trim public house called the Three Pigeons
stands on this spot on Wood Green, and the host and his wife
are ever-welcoming, as I can testify. Mr Jones in the Thrush
Green books is equally zealous in his work, and discreet in his
dealings with all and sundry.

There is certainly a public house at Wood Green, but there
is no village school. However, I remedied this defect when I
started the Thrush Green novels, and inserted the school and
schoolhouse between the Two Pheasants and Harold Shoosmith's abode.

I set the school, a sturdy one-storey building of Cotswold
stone, in a playground of generous proportions. There were
two classrooms, one occupied by Miss Dorothy Watson, the
headmistress, and the other by the teacher in charge of the
lower juniors. Miss Agnes Fogerty was the infants' teacher in a
temporary building across the playground.

The schoolhouse, standing at ten o'clock, was a small Victorian building, erected at the same time as Thrush Green
school. It was a pleasant two-bedroomed house with a long
garden running between the school playground and Harold
Shoosmith's garden next door.

Some of the most exciting events occurred in this imaginary
place, and I am always disappointed when I visit Wood Green
to find that no school, no schoolhouse, no children and, above
all, no Miss Watson or Miss Fogerty are to be seen. As the
Thrush Green series progressed, I became increasingly fond of
them.

When we first meet them, Dorothy was living alone in the
schoolhouse and Agnes was in lodgings. Some time later,
however, Dorothy suffered a severe accident and broke a hip.

She invited Agnes to share the schoolhouse with her, and the two settled down together very happily. Agnes had no relations, and relished the companionship of her headmistress. The two friends continued to live in harmony and, for Agnes in particular, the change from her lodgings was a lasting joy.

A great many things happened here – not only were school activities discussed but the usual domestic problems occurred as they would anywhere. Towards the end of the Thrush Green books, the two friends made plans to retire together. As anyone who has been house-hunting will know, there were months of anxiety and frustration. Both ladies found the inevitable clearing up, the farewell ceremonies and the general upheaval profoundly exhausting. At last the two friends set off to the house of their choice at Barton-on-Sea.

Everyone in Thrush Green awaited the new headmaster of the school with bated breath. Whoever arrived would be thoroughly scrutinized, his history known, his family background explored, his character and his earnings discussed, in the time-honoured tradition of all country communities. The new headmaster was Alan Lester, who arrived with his wife Margaret. Dorothy Watson gradually came to accept the fact that her school was safe in his hands.

Next door to the schoolhouse, at eleven o'clock, stood a fine Edwardian house which for many years was called Quetta. When we first hear of it, the house had been empty for some time. Fortunately, Quetta was bought a few months later by a retired man, Harold Shoosmith. Conjectures about the newcomer were many and varied. It was not long though before Harold met his future wife.

Isobel Fletcher was an old friend of Agnes Fogerty from college days. The two had always kept in touch but rarely met after Isobel had married and settled in Sussex, and had had a family to rear. After the death of her husband, and when her children were out in the world, Isobel decided to return to the Cotswolds where she had been brought up.

She stayed with Ella for a time while she was house-hunting, and it was then that she met Harold Shoosmith. Over the months that followed, Harold assisted with the exhausting job of looking at houses. When Isobel returned to Sussex, Harold found he missed her sorely. The weeks seemed to pass very slowly, and it was July before she returned to continue house-hunting.

This time, Isobel stayed at Tullivers, next door to Winnie Bailey, for Phyllida and Frank Hurst were in America and had offered her the house in their absence. It was here that Harold called on her again. He found her in a despondent mood at her lack of success in finding a house. Harold proposed marriage to her, an action which would solve both the problems of her finding a house, and his aching heart. She promised she would consider his proposal very carefully and the inhabitants of Thrush Green awaited the outcome with great interest.

The marriage, which duly took place, proved to be a happy one, and Harold Shoosmith and his wife were particularly popular in Thrush Green. They were on excellent terms with their next-door neighbours, Dorothy and Agnes, and were very sad when the two teachers announced their retirement and departure to Barton-on-Sea.

And this brings us to the end of our clockwise tour of Thrush Green and our meetings with the chief inhabitants. But there are two more establishments, a little farther away, whose inmates play their parts in the everyday dramas of Thrush Green.

Dotty Harmer, a spinster and stout friend of all animals, lived some quarter of a mile away, just a few minutes from Thrush Green. The narrow footpath beside Albert Piggott's cottage led across buttercup fields to Lulling Woods, and on the left-hand side was Dotty's cottage, sitting as snug and four-square as a cat, in a slight dell. As I remember that area during the war, there was no such cottage to be seen if you walked down that footpath, but there were certainly fields, and buttercups grew there at the right and proper time.

Dotty Harmer is one of my favourite dolls. She is, despite her idiosyncrasies, brave, honest and a great lover of animals. She is also unpredictable and pig-headed, and her friends were pleased when her sensible niece Connie with her husband Kit Armitage moved in to live with the old lady, and look after her.

The second establishment was located halfway down Lulling High Street and was occupied by the Misses Lovelock – Ada, Bertha and Violet. It was a handsome Georgian house, with a white-painted front door, approached by three steps and two elegantly curved iron handrails.

Among my dolls, the three Miss Lovelocks are especially loved. I think that most of us have our own particular streak of parsimony, hoarding lengths of string, storing the wrappings of butter ready to grease baking tins, cherishing chipped dishes which 'might come in useful', but never do. The Misses Lovelock tuned this art to perfection.

And so, from 1958 onwards, these characters became my dolls, and their way of life and the houses they inhabited became so real to me that it was quite a shock when I occasionally returned to the place which had started it all, Wood Green near Witney. Where was the village school? Why had Witney Urban District Council taken over Harold Shoosmith's house? Where was the statue to Nathaniel Patten which had caused such consternation at Thrush Green? And how had my chestnut avenue suddenly dwindled to one or two trees?

This clash of reality and imagination was disturbing. I had no such problem with the other village about which I wrote, Fairacre, for that was entirely my own creation. Nevertheless, I grew fonder of Thrush Green with every book I wrote about it, and I liked the characters as they developed.

I found it interesting to take one person, say the rector, Charles Henstock, and make him the chief character in one book and follow his fortunes. Naturally, the other villagers appeared and something would often crop up which made me plan to give their adventures an airing in a future book. Thus it was that I decided to give Edward Young a greater part to play in *At Home in Thrush Green* for, having burnt down the rectory in an earlier book, it seemed only right that I should hand over the job of replacing my act of arson to the architect I had created.

Now that I had my dolls and their dolls' houses, I set about playing with them with the greatest pleasure, and when I visited Wood Green I shut my eyes to some of the realities. I didn't look down the footpath which led to the buttercup fields where Dotty Harmer lived, for they were there no more, and I ignored the traffic which came down the New Yatt Road.

But there was still enough to enchant me. The Three Pigeons

stood as comfortably as the Two Pheasants, and the major houses round the green endured in all their Cotswold serenity. There was no doubt about it: Thrush Green was an ideal place to play, and I loved moving my dolls along their allotted paths during the next thirty-five years.

The final two books in the series, which follow now, will bring you the final episode of life at Thrush Green. What pleases me is that, since I decided to lay down my pen after *A Peaceful Retirement* – the last of the Fairacre series – in 1995, both Thrush Green and Fairacre have been frozen in time. They have been spared possible interruptions and spoliations such as a new bypass, the infilling of every nook and cranny with unattractive box-like houses or, worst of all, the closure of the school.

Here at Thrush Green, church services will continue to be taken by Charles Henstock, Nelly Piggott will reign supreme at the Fuchsia Bush, her husband Albert will continue to grouse about the upkeep of the churchyard, and Dotty Harmer will still mix her noxious potions without bringing harm to anyone. Long may they live!

CELEBRATIONS AT
THRUSH GREEN

To Babs
with love

1. One Wet Day

One wet November morning, Winnie Bailey stood at her bedroom window and surveyed the rain-drenched view of Thrush Green.

Usually at this time of the morning, a little past nine o'clock, things were stirring. One or two late arrivals at the school across the green would be running in breathlessly. Percy Hodge's milk float would be making its slow way from house to house. A few housewives would be hurrying downhill to the shops in Lulling, baskets in hand.

But today there was little movement. A wet umbrella passed below, its carrier hidden from Winnie's view. A duster flapped from an upstairs window of the Two Pheasants across the green, hard by the school, and two excited dogs cavorted by the deserted and dripping children's play area.

Winnie Bailey had lived at Thrush Green for over fifty years, ever since she arrived as the bride of young Dr Bailey. He had died some years before, but Winnie stayed on in the house she loved, sharing it with Jenny, her friend, companion and maid.

She could hear Jenny now, singing some unrecognizable tune as she washed up the breakfast things. And here she was, Winnie told herself briskly, supposed to be dusting bedrooms, and instead she was idling her time away gazing at the rain!

She was about to turn to her duties when she saw a small black car moving decorously along the road opposite, skirting the Two Pheasants and the school and finally drawing up outside Harold Shoosmith's house.

Surely, it was the rector's car, thought Winnie, peering again through the rain-spotted window, dusting forgotten.

A small chubby man emerged from the driver's seat and hurried through the downpour to the shelter of the Shoosmiths' porch.

The Reverend Charles Henstock, rector of Thrush Green and vicar of Lulling, was paying an early morning call on his old friend.

Winnie took up her duster again, and speculated.

'Come in! Come in!' cried Harold. 'Good grief, man, haven't you got a raincoat?'

'I didn't think I'd need it,' replied Charles.

'Let's have your jacket,' said his host, stripping it from the rector's back and shaking it energetically.

'Isobel's away for two nights, in Sussex. Come into the kitchen, it's warmer.'

The two men settled at the kitchen table. Outside the rain lashed at the window, and gurgled in the gutter. A pigeon sat hunched on the bird-table, presumably seeking shelter rather than food, raindrops dripping from the little roof above it.

'Coffee?' asked Harold.

The rector shook his head. He had turned round to try to extricate an envelope from the inside pocket of his wet jacket.

'Such a strange letter,' he said, puffing slightly as he pulled it free. 'It arrived yesterday but I didn't have a chance to get in touch with you.'

He handed it to Harold and sat back to watch his friend's reaction as he read.

Harold skipped the preliminaries and perused the second paragraph onward with growing concentration. He read:

I have been clearing up my late aunt's effects recently, and came across some letters and a diary among her papers. The letters are from one Nathaniel Patten and are addressed to the Reverend Octavius Fennel of Thrush Green. The diary, which also appears to be an account book, is that of Mr Fennel.

I have no idea how these papers came into my aunt's possession, but she lived for a time near Thrush Green, and only moved here to the Lake District a few years ago to be near her daughter, as she was becoming infirm.

It seems right to me that these papers should be returned to the church, and I shall be pleased to let you have them if you send word.

Harold peered closely at the signature. 'Can't make out the chap's name. "Wellbeloved"? "Wobblefoot"?'

'Wilberforce,' said the rector. 'And isn't it extraordinary?'

'It is indeed,' agreed Harold warmly. 'We must get hold of these letters. To think that we shall see Nathaniel's actual handwriting after all this time.'

The rector smiled indulgently upon his friend. He knew how much Nathaniel Patten meant to him.

Nathaniel had been a Thrush Green boy born and bred in Queen Victoria's reign, and had travelled to Africa as a missionary. There Nathaniel had set up a church, a mission hall, a school and the beginnings of a medical centre.

His project flourished, and Nathaniel Patten was greatly loved by the people he cared for.

His reputation grew over the years. His devotion, wisdom and sound common sense were widely recognized for miles around his settlement, but those in Thrush Green had forgotten the young man who had left his home.

He never in his lifetime returned. His duties and shortage of funds kept him at his post. But at his death his body was returned, at the express wish and expense of the Reverend Octavius Fennel, who himself conducted the funeral service.

Elderly inhabitants of Thrush Green and Lulling had memories of their parents' respect for the former rector. The Reverend Octavius Fennel had befriended the young Nathaniel, encouraging him in his missionary work and helping, it was believed, with financial support.

It was known that Octavius dearly wished Nathaniel to take Holy Orders, but the strongly evangelical nature of the younger man would not allow him to accept all the tenets of the established Church of England, and he was never ordained.

Over the years, Nathaniel was forgotten by Thrush Green. It was not until Harold Shoosmith had arrived some years before that Thrush Green folk became aware that it was the birthplace of their most distinguished son.

In a strange way it was Nathaniel Patten who had brought Harold Shoosmith to Thrush Green. Harold had lived near the community in Africa where the Victorian missionary had worked, bringing spiritual comfort and practical help to hundreds of his flock. By the time Harold was there, Nathaniel was dead, but his work still thrived and the small stone cross which was his memorial was kept immaculate with lime-wash, and flowers always lay at its foot.

The tales of the villagers about their hero moved Harold deeply, and when he had decided to retire he was excited to find that a house in Nathaniel's birthplace was on the market.

It suited him well, and he had become one of Thrush Green's most active and well-liked residents.

It was something of a shock to him to realize that Nathaniel meant nothing to his neighbours. His tombstone was overgrown, the inscription indecipherable. No one, it seemed, had heard of him. The parish register noted his birth and burial, and that seemed to be the only mention of the great man.

Harold set about remedying this matter, and was instrumental in getting a statue put up on the green on the occasion of the hundredth anniversary of Nathaniel's birth. It now stood, a matter of pride and affection, and Nathaniel had been restored to the hearts of those in Thrush Green.

Harold and the rector had worked hard to trace any descendants of Nathaniel when the business of the memorial statue was afoot. Evidently he had married whilst abroad. His wife, debilitated by the rigours of the climate, had died giving birth to a daughter.

When the child was old enough, she had been sent to friends in Yorkshire to be housed and educated. She had married a man called Michael Mulloy, borne a son and daughter, and the family had moved to Pembrokeshire to work on a farm.

Times were hard in the 1930s, and the Mulloys lived in poverty. The son, William, grew up to be a wild youth. The daughter, Mary, never married.

William married in the 1950s and his wife soon discovered that she had made a serious mistake. He was a drunkard, and violent when in his cups. She lived in daily fear of his attacks upon her and upon their young daughter Dulcie, named after Nathaniel's daughter.

Fortunately, his sister Mary, who lived near by, was a strong character who had no time for William, but gave support to his wife and child. It was she who had kept Nathaniel's letters to her mother, and who told Dulcie of the wonderful work he had done. Mary had died when Dulcie was a grown woman.

Harold and Charles had met William briefly in Wales where he farmed a few acres. He was a dissolute uncouth fellow who had no time for Nathaniel's memory. At the time of their meeting he had left his wife and daughter, Dulcie, and was living with a woman near by.

What had happened to William Mulloy, his poor wife and little Dulcie? the kind-hearted rector often wondered. Harold, of sterner stuff, did not waste his energies in thinking about them.

Harold continued to hold the letter, his face alight with enthusiasm. 'I can't believe it!'

'I thought I would reply to Mr Wilberforce today,' said Charles, 'and say how glad we would be to have these papers, and perhaps he would be kind enough to post them to us.'

'*Post!*' cried Harold. 'Dear old Nathaniel's letters? I wouldn't trust those to the *post*!'

'Oh, come,' responded the rector. 'Do be fair. How often does the post go astray?'

'When the post *does* go astray,' replied his friend forcefully, 'I don't know about it, do I? No, I'm not risking this lot to the post. If it comes to that I'll go up myself and fetch them.'

'Then what do you suggest I write?'

'Don't write. Telephone. Let's do it now.'

'But it's scarcely nine thirty! He'll be at work.'

'Then we'll ring him at work.'

Charles felt helpless in the face of such ruthlessness. He watched Harold lift a hand telephone from its bracket and settle down at the kitchen table.

'I'll get through, then pass it over,' he told Charles. 'It's an Ambleside number.'

Charles watched him pressing buttons on this new contraption. At Lulling's vicarage no such modern equipment was in use. A venerable instrument stood on the chest in the hall, and when it rang one simply hurried to it from the bedroom, the kitchen or the garden and announced oneself with as much breath as was left.

'Can I speak to Mr Wilberforce?' said Harold, and handed the telephone to Charles.

A woman was speaking. 'At work,' said the voice, 'but if it is urgent I could give you his number at the office, or I can leave a message for him.'

'Get the number,' whispered Harold.

'If you would be kind enough to give us his office number,' said the rector diffidently, 'if you think he will be free, of course. I should not like to interrupt any business matters he may be engaged upon, but it really is rather urgent.'

Harold was drumming his fingers on the table, but stopped as Charles wrote the number at the head of the letter in front of him.

'Most kind, most kind, Mrs Wilberforce,' he said. Something was said at the other end, and Charles's chubby face grew pink.

'I apologize, Mrs Er – er –' he said. 'And many thanks again.'

'Who was it?'

'His housekeeper. I didn't catch her name. Shall we try the office?'

'Certainly. I'll get it, shall I?'

'Please do. I don't think I have quite mastered it.'

He watched Harold as he tapped briskly at the buttons, then took the telephone from his hand.

'Is Mr Wilberforce free?' he began. 'My name is Charles Henstock, and I am the rector of Thrush Green. He wrote to me about some documents of his aunt's.'

There was a pause.

'He's coming,' Charles whispered excitedly. He held up a hand as a voice spoke at the other end.

'I must apologize for troubling you at work,' began the rector, but then became silent and attentive. 'That would be most kind. Yes, the post *can* be a little unreliable. In that case, perhaps after your meeting? For dinner, say? We can easily put you up overnight. I can't tell you how much this means to us. I will give you my telephone number, and look forward to hearing from you this evening.'

When Charles had finished he was smiling. Harold was fidgeting with impatience.

'Sounds a very sensible chap,' said Charles. 'He has to come to Ealing some time on business, and will bring the papers with him. He promises to deliver them to me personally, as he can come via Thrush Green. He doesn't seem to rely on the post.'

Harold forbore to remark that most people, less trusting than the good rector, felt the same.

'I shall know when he's coming this evening,' continued Charles. 'He is making arrangements, so I'll be in touch with you as soon as I've heard from him.'

'Marvellous!' said Harold. 'I can't wait to get my hands on all this material. We shall have to find a very safe place to store it.'

'I've no doubt that this house would provide the best possible shelter,' said Charles, 'and the most loving care.'

'You can be assured of that,' agreed Harold.

When his wife Isobel returned from her visit to Sussex Harold told her the great news even before she had put the kettle on for a reviving cup of tea.

Weary though she was from her long drive, she did her best

to match his enthusiasm. 'What will you do with the letters?' she enquired.

'Put them in our safe,' he replied.

'No, I meant permanently. Will you give them to the county archives?'

Harold looked dismayed. 'I can't say I'd got that far.' A note of doubt became evident in his speech. 'I suppose that would be the correct thing to do, but I'm jolly well going to keep them here at Thrush Green for as long as I can.'

'And why not?' agreed Isobel, pouring boiling water into the teapot. 'After all, without you Thrush Green would have remained completely ignorant of Nathaniel.'

Harold carried the tea tray into the sitting-room, followed by Isobel. Outside the rain still fell relentlessly, but it was snug by the fire, and soon they would draw the curtains against the unkind world outside.

It was beginning to grow dark but the bronze statue of Harold's hero was discernible through the window. Drops dripped from the Bible which Nathaniel held before him, and there was a steady trickle from his frock-coat tails. An impertinent sparrow was perched upon his shining head, but Nathaniel continued to smile benignly upon the rain-lashed scene of his birth.

'Will you meet this Mr Wilberforce?' asked Isobel.

'I intend to,' replied Harold. 'He sounds a very public-spirited sort of chap. After all, most people would have thrown the stuff away, and not bothered to get in touch with the rector.'

'How did he know about the rector?'

'Well, the letters were addressed to this fellow Octavius Fennel who was rector here when Nathaniel went away, so Wilberforce simply wrote to the present rector of Thrush Green, and our postman Willie Marchant took it up to Lulling, and that's that.'

'What excitement!'

'We shall have to have a celebration of some kind.'

Isobel refilled her husband's cup. 'Let's get the letters first,' she advised.

Winnie Bailey, on the other side of Thrush Green, did not see the rector hurry to his car through the driving rain to return to his vicarage a mile away in Lulling. Charles Henstock served several parishes, but he lived in a beautiful house close by the magnificent church of St John's in the little town, with his wife Dimity.

She had lived in Thrush Green for several years with her old friend Ella Bembridge, and the two spinsters had been very busy and happy. Dimity's marriage to the widowed rector left Ella alone at Thrush Green, but the two remained close friends and met often.

On this particular morning of portentous news, Ella had called at Winnie's to return a library book.

'Thought I'd better do it while I remembered,' she explained, when Winnie remonstrated with her about venturing forth in such weather. 'Don't want to let you in for a hefty fine.'

She followed Winnie into the kitchen and greeted Jenny who was chopping up onions.

'By the way, Jenny,' she added, 'did you go to Thrush Green school as a child?'

'I did indeed,' said Jenny.

'Then you know it's a hundred years old next year?'

'Never!' said Jenny.

'So there'll be some high jinks, I gather. I saw the headmaster at the newsagent's yesterday, and he told me.'

'I wonder what they'll do?' said Jenny, scraping the chopped onion into a neat pile with her knife.

'A party, I expect,' said Winnie. 'We'll probably have to make a cake.'

'I'm quite happy to make a cake,' replied Ella. 'Anything

rather than sitting through a concert on those uncomfortable chairs.'

'Perhaps they'll have both,' said Jenny. 'A hundred years is quite something, isn't it? I wonder if Miss Watson and Miss Fogerty will come back for all the fun?'

'I'm sure they will,' said Ella. 'Mr Lester said as much yesterday. They taught here for so long.'

'I can see some excitement in our midst,' commented Winnie. 'Coffee, Ella?'

But she refused, saying that she had left a piece of gammon simmering, and by now it was probably splashing all over the stove.

She plunged homeward through the rain.

As the day ended, the rain began to die away, but little rivulets continued to trickle down the sides of the hill leading down to the town of Lulling, and on roads around Thrush Green vast puddles caught the light of the rising moon.

Winnie Bailey, early in bed, was glad to rest. Although she had not ventured out for her usual afternoon walk, she felt as though she had been buffeted by the wind which had rattled round the house all day.

Tomorrow, she told herself, she would do some gardening and take a walk. It was time she went to see her old friend Dotty Harmer who lived near Lulling Woods some half-mile distant.

Ella Bembridge, a hundred yards from Winnie Bailey, was still up and about. She leant across the windowsill and breathed in the fragrance of wet earth. Across the green she could see the shape of the school with the schoolhouse beside it. She liked Alan Lester, the new headmaster, and his wife, but missed Dorothy Watson, the former head teacher, and her friend and colleague Agnes Fogerty.

Well, she hoped they would come to all the jollifications that appeared to be looming for next year.

The moon appeared briefly between ragged clouds, and Ella shut the window against the chill of a November night.

At the schoolhouse Alan Lester was carrying a tray bearing two mugs of hot milk and some digestive biscuits into the sitting-room, where his wife Margaret was busy counting stitches on her knitting needle.

'A hundred and four last time, and a hundred and six this,' she told her husband. 'I wonder which is right?'

'What's it supposed to be?' he enquired, putting down the tray.

'A hundred and four.'

'Forget the second count,' said Alan.

'I think I shall. Has it stopped raining?'

'Yes, and the wind's dropped. At least the children will be able to go out and play tomorrow.'

They sipped their milk in companionable silence, and half an hour later were in bed.

Next door Harold Shoosmith and his wife were also abed. Isobel fell asleep quickly, tired after her journey, but Harold was too excited by the prospect of seeing his hero's letters to follow his wife'e example.

He crept out of bed and went to look at the sleeping world of Thrush Green. Clouds scudded across the moon's face, but it was light enough to see Nathaniel Patten's figure on the grass before him.

What news! What a day! He remained at the window, relishing his happiness, until the winter's cold brought goose-pimples to his arms, and his feet grew stone-cold.

Sighing happily, he sought the comfort of his bed.

*

A mile away at Lulling vicarage, Charles Henstock, too, was sleepless beside his slumbering wife.

The expected telephone call had not come until almost ten o'clock, and the good rector had decided to ring Harold in the morning rather than at that late hour.

It seemed that Mr Wilberforce came about once a quarter to Ealing on business, and could bring the documents in about a month's time. Yes, he had said, he usually stayed overnight, and sometimes two nights, when he was down, and would be delighted to accept the rector's kind invitation.

They agreed a date together, and Charles was already making plans for Harold and Isobel to meet him.

It was all very satisfactory, thought Charles, as St John's church clock struck twelve silvery chimes. There would be no more chimes until seven the next morning, for the clock had been subdued to silence, by common consent, during the small hours.

Tomorrow, Charles told himself, he would have the pleasure of telling Harold all about it.

He turned his head more comfortably into his pillow and fell asleep.

2. The Search Begins

The fact that Thrush Green school would soon be a hundred years old had not escaped the notice of Dorothy Watson and Agnes Fogerty, although they were far away.

The two friends had retired from teaching at Thrush Green some years earlier, and now shared a bungalow at Barton-on-Sea. Here they enjoyed the sea air, the gentle countryside around, new friends, and above all, each other's company. Dorothy, who had been the headmistress, took most of the decisions, but Agnes, who had been in charge of the infants' department, although acquiescent nine times out of ten, occasionally overruled her friend.

The subject of Thrush Green's anniversary had cropped up as the result of a telephone conversation the night before. Isobel Shoosmith rang frequently, for she missed her old neighbours and was particularly attached to little Agnes Fogerty, for they had attended the same teachers' training college many years before, and had always kept in touch.

It was Isobel who had said that Alan Lester was already thinking about a celebration at the school, and the two friends had naturally been much interested.

'No doubt we shall get an invitation,' announced Dorothy

as they washed up the breakfast things. 'I must admit that I can't recall just when the school opened. Was it in the summer, do you think?'

'I have a feeling that it was earlier in the year,' said Agnes, twirling her teacloth inside a tumbler.

'I don't think you are right,' said Dorothy firmly.

'Maybe not,' agreed Agnes equably, 'but in any case it will be in the appropriate log book and Alan Lester can look it up.'

'Well, I only hope he does something suitable, and within the scope of the children and the school building. Some of these young men will try to be too ambitious. Do you remember that disastrous grammar school concert in Lulling where massed recorders waffled away at a piece by Haydn, and all at sixes and sevens?'

'I shall never forget it.'

Dorothy paused in her washing-up operations and gazed thoughtfully through the kitchen window above the sink. 'I wonder,' she mused, 'if it would be a good idea to have a word with Alan Lester. He might be glad of a little advice from an old hand.'

'It would be quite out of the question,' said Agnes. 'It is *his* school now, you know.'

Dorothy sighed. 'I suppose so. Nevertheless —'

Her voice trailed away, and Agnes, who knew her friend better than that lady knew herself, realized that the danger of Dorothy blundering into matters which were not her concern still hung over them.

As it happened, Alan Lester had temporarily shelved the matter of Thrush Green's celebrations.

The end of the winter term was looming, and Christmas with all its attendant distractions had to be faced before the anniversary year began.

He was a conscientious head teacher, and enjoyed the post he had taken up at Thrush Green some years earlier, although his first year had been fraught with anxiety about his wife Margaret, whose health had never been robust, and who had taken to secret drinking with alarming consequences. This addiction she had bravely overcome, and now all went well, but there was now no alcohol in the Lesters' home, and Alan was extra careful of his wife's frailty.

He had taken over a well-run school from Dorothy Watson, and was wise enough to follow much the same paths, only gently introducing some of his more modern methods as time passed.

He also inherited Miss Robinson, a cheerful young woman, who took over the infants' department from Agnes Fogerty. The third member of staff was also young, only just out from college, and still trailing the clouds of child psychology, pastoral care, and the perils of damaging infant sensibilities, but the day-to-day reality of the classroom would soon clear those in time, Alan Lester surmised correctly.

The three worked well together and the inhabitants of Thrush Green, whether parents of pupils or not, were proud of their school.

Alan Lester had no doubt that its hundredth birthday would be celebrated in fine style.

But meanwhile, there was Christmas . . .

But Harold Shoosmith had more urgent things than Christmas to occupy him.

The rector's invitation to dinner in mid-December to meet Robert Wilberforce was enthusiastically accepted by Harold and Isobel, and it was only a few hours later that Harold had been struck by a stupendous idea.

'Why not get in touch with Nathaniel's grandson again, or perhaps his wife and daughter?' he enthused to Isobel.

'But surely,' she pointed out, 'that man – Mulloy, wasn't it – was completely non-cooperative last time?'

Somewhat dashed, Harold was forced to agree. 'But his wife was helpful. And Nathaniel's great-granddaughter must now be grown up. I wonder if they would consider it?'

It was quite clear to Isobel that her husband would cling to this idea as resolutely as a terrier with a rat. 'You should have a word with Charles,' she advised. 'I imagine you are thinking of getting these people an invitation to the dinner party. I think Dimity and Charles should be told about your scheme. If the Mulloys are coming from Wales, they would need to stay overnight.'

'You are quite right,' agreed Harold. 'I get carried away. I will see how Charles feels about it.'

Later that day he rang the rector, who said he would consult his wife.

'After all,' Charles said, 'it is Dimity who has to provide the meal, and I do just wonder if Wilberforce would be at all interested in meeting the Mulloys. In any case, I must say at the outset, Harold, that I utterly refuse to have that dissolute fellow we met in Wales at my table.'

'Fair enough,' said Harold. 'I didn't propose to approach him. But the little girl we met –'

'Dulcie,' said the rector.

'That's right! Named after Nathaniel's daughter, her grand-mother. She might be available. Shall I try to find out? I'll report back, and you and Dimity can decide the next step.'

The rector agreed, unable to bring himself to discourage his enthusiastic friend, despite certain reservations about approaching the Mulloy ladies. Nathaniel Patten would have been a most welcome addition to a party at Lulling vicarage, but his descendants might not be such good company, thought Charles. He awaited developments.

Although it was some twenty years since the two men had

been in touch with Nathaniel's descendants, Harold set about the task of tracing them again the next morning with his usual energy and common sense.

He remembered the name of the Welsh village, and found the number of the local post office. If anyone could tell him about the family, it would be the local postmaster or mistress.

A woman answered in a lilting Welsh voice. 'I have to tell you that Mrs Mulloy died two or three years ago, and we heard of her husband's death before that, but Miss Dulcie is in London. They moved up there about eight years since. Dulcie's doing well. She was always bright, you know.'

A vision of a diminutive child briskly cutting up cabbage with a fearsome kitchen knife returned to Harold over the years. Yes, he thought, she had looked a competent little thing even then.

'And you have her address?'

'That I have. Letters still come now and again. Reunions at the girls' grammar school and that. I send them on.'

'Could you let me have it? And her telephone number?'

There was the sound of rustling paper, then she spoke again. 'I've no telephone number for her, but this is her address.'

She read it carefully, repeating each line with much emphasis, to Harold's amusement.

The young lady lived in a flat in north London evidently.

'But she works in a big office in London. Insurance, I think, but I don't know that address. Is it urgent?'

'No, no indeed,' Harold assured her. 'A friend and I met her when she was a child, and it is simply a little family matter we thought she might like to know about.'

'Money, is it? Left to her, I mean?'

'No, nothing like that.'

'Pity. She could do with it, I don't doubt, in spite of this fine job she's got. But there, we could all do with some more, couldn't we?'

Harold agreed, thanked her warmly for her help, and went to tell Isobel.

At the time when Harold was intent on tracking down Dulcie Mulloy, great-granddaughter of his hero, Winnie Bailey had decided to call on her old friend Dotty Harmer who lived some half-mile away to the west.

She took with her some magazines and a pot of honey, food for mind and body. Not that Dotty's mind really needed stimulation, if anything it needed slowing down, thought Winnie, remembering the way Dotty flitted from subject to subject with the most extraordinary mental agility for one of her advanced years. Winnie had heard her hold forth on animal welfare (Dotty's chief concern), modern education, the deterioration in public speaking, the shortcomings of the Church of England, the proliferation of caterpillars in this year's cauliflowers, all within the space of five minutes.

Dotty's father had taught at Lulling Grammar School for many years, and the remembrance of his punishments still caused strong men of Lulling to blench.

His sons had left home as soon as they could, but Dotty, who had never married, kept house for him until he died. She admired his undoubted brilliance of mind, his high principles and his physical bravery. She had seen him tackle a runaway horse careering down the steep hill from Thrush Green to Lulling, when he was in his sixties, whilst younger men stood gaping and too shocked to stir themselves to action.

On his death she had moved to a small cottage set among fields, where she had spent her time happily alone, surrounded by all kinds of animals from bantams to stray dogs and cats, not to mention goats for which she had a particular fondness, and two tortoises who were probably older than Dotty and to whom she bore a strong facial resemblance.

She delighted in collecting the harvest of the hedgerows and meadows and made preserves which she pressed upon her many friends with dire effect. 'Dotty's Collywobbles' was a local internal complaint known to Lulling and Thrush Green residents, and newcomers were warned about accepting Dotty's largesse.

Her contented solitude had to end when she became infirm, and her niece Connie and her husband Kit came to live with her at the cottage which had been sympathetically enlarged some years before.

Winnie always enjoyed visiting Dotty. Her kitchen remained the same chaotic muddle she had always known. Connie, very wisely, had an adjoining kitchen, where the real business of cooking was done.

As Winnie crossed the green to take the path to Lulling Woods, she met Albert Piggott emerging from his cottage opposite the church.

'Nice day, Albert,' said Winnie, as he paused on his doorstep.

'Bound to rain later,' said Albert morosely.

Typical of Albert, thought Winnie, with some amusement. Nothing pleased the surly old scoundrel. He had been sexton of Thrush Green church and an occasional jobbing gardener to whomsoever would employ him for as many years as Winnie could recall, but she had never seen him in a happy mood. He was lucky to have his buxom wife Nelly to look after him. She was the best cook in the district, and spent most of her time and energy in the kitchen of the Fuchsia Bush, a renowned restaurant in Lulling High Street, where her skills were much appreciated by her partner there, Mrs Peters.

'Well,' said Winnie, 'I hope the rain holds off until I get home again. I'm just off to see Miss Harmer.'

Albert's glum countenance lightened a little. He liked old Dotty! 'Ah!' said Albert, nodding.

Winnie moved on, leaving Albert still standing equidistant between the church and the Two Pheasants.

Which, wondered Winnie, taking the path through the fields, would Albert visit first?

She found Dotty at her kitchen table, not making chutney, jam or bottling some fearsome fungi she had come across on her travels, but plying a pen.

She rose to greet Winnie affectionately. 'Just in time,' she cried. 'How do you spell "benefited"? One "t" or two?'

'You've got me there,' confessed Winnie. 'I know if I'm not asked, but the same awful doubt arises as when one is asked if it's the sixteenth or seventeenth of the month. I think it must be one "t".'

'Good!' said Dotty. 'I'm just describing my father's gastro-enteritis.'

She held up an exercise book which had a shiny mottled cover. It brought back memories to Winnie of a science exercise book she had used as a schoolgirl. She could even recall the laboriously drawn illustration of a copper ball suspended over a tripod. Something to do with heat expansion, she remembered, through the mists of time.

'But what are you doing, Dotty?' she asked.

'I'm writing a biography of my father. So many people have memories of him, and I thought it would be so nice to have these recollections recorded. After all, he made a deep impression on his pupils.'

Physical as well as mental, thought Winnie, but forbore to comment.

'And I was just explaining how his gastroenteritis *benefited* from a draught of parsley and woundwort I used to make for him to drink last thing at night. As a matter of fact, I was wondering if I should include the recipe. Some readers might be grateful, don't you think?'

'It would certainly fill up half a page,' agreed Winnie diplomatically. 'You're bound to need a lot of material for a full-scale biography.'

'Oh, I don't envisage a really *long* book! Not Charles Dickens length. Something more in the way of a *vignette*. A slim volume, you know. Which publisher, do you think, should have it? It might well be a bestseller. Several people have said they will buy a copy, and there are hundreds of libraries who will want copies, I'm sure.'

She patted the mottled cover lovingly as if it were one of her many pets.

'Of course, I could do a *separate* cookery book. I've dozens of recipes, and the interest in herbs and their beneficial properties has increased enormously lately.'

'Quite an idea,' said Winnie.

'And I could have something in hand for the publishers when they had got out the first book. I believe that most writers have another book waiting to follow on the first.' Dotty's eyes were bright with enthusiasm behind her spectacles.

Winnie changed the subject. 'There is an interesting article about Gerard the herbalist in this magazine,' she said, putting it on the table, 'and some splendid photographs of Blenheim. I thought you'd be interested.'

'Harold and Isobel took me there a month or two ago,' said Dotty. 'Fascinating place, though I found the architecture somewhat grandiose. But have you heard Harold's news about Nathaniel Patten?'

'No. Tell me more.'

'Betty Bell told me. I don't know what I'd do without Betty to keep me in touch.'

Betty Bell was the exuberant woman who did her best to keep Dotty's domestic conditions in order. She also worked at the Shoosmiths' and was a source of much local information.

'Someone has found some letters written by Nathaniel, and sent word about them to Charles, and he wants Harold to see them.'

'How exciting!'

'Harold can't wait to read them. Betty says he's like a cat on hot bricks. Such a *cruel* expression if you dwell on it. I wonder why some people are so vindictive towards cats? That dreadful phrase about more ways of killing them than by choking them with cream, for instance. So *sadistic*!'

'Well, I'm delighted for Harold's sake,' said Winnie briskly.

She lifted the pot of honey from her basket, and put it by the magazines and Dotty's manuscript.

Dotty picked it up in her scrawny hands. She certainly could do with a little added flesh on those old bones, thought Winnie. Mentally, she had plenty of nourishment about her.

'How kind! So sweet and pure! A true natural comfort,' cried Dotty.

She put it down by the mottled exercise book, and patted the latter with proprietory affection again.

'I wonder if my little work will occasion as much pleasure one day,' she mused.

'I'm sure of it,' said Winnie. 'I shall leave you to carry on with your work.'

She saw herself out, and as she passed the kitchen window she saw that Dotty had taken up her pen again, and was immersed in her memories.

News of the existence of some letters written by Nathaniel Patten soon spread among the inhabitants of Thrush Green and Lulling.

Charles had told his wife Dimity about them, as a matter of course, and she, as a good clergyman's wife, had been as discreet as ever about the news.

Harold and Isobel knew, and were eagerly looking forward to meeting Robert Wilberforce and studying the letters he was about to bring to them.

But now, it seemed, everyone knew about this exciting find. How *did* the news get around so quickly, wondered Winnie as she retraced her steps?

It was like seed dispersal, she told herself, ancient memories of botany lessons stirred again by that glimpse of Dotty's exercise book so like her own Elementary Science notebook of years ago. Seeds were dispersed by wind, as in the case of thistledown, or by birds eating berries, or even by water. Winnie had some faint recollection of coconuts floating in Pacific seas and germinating on island shores.

Yes, it must be *wind* dispersal in this case. The news seemed to be airborne. It was unlikely that Harold had discussed the matter with Betty Bell, yet she knew. No doubt Albert Piggott knew as well, thought Winnie, catching sight of him wielding a besom broom by the church porch. Obviously he had already called at the Two Pheasants, for the door of the inn stood open hospitably, and his movements were unusually brisk.

She crossed the grass to her own house and found Jenny

brushing down the stairs with considerably more vigour than Albert Piggott's efforts across the way.

She stopped when she saw Winnie. 'Rector's been in and says can he count on you to do the crib with Miss Bembridge and his wife as usual this Christmas? And have we got any jumble for the scouts, and don't forget they're collecting for the Deanery Christmas Bazaar's produce stall.'

'Good heavens,' cried Winnie. 'What a lot to remember!'

Jenny put down her brush. 'And talking of remembering, we're too late to post surface mail to Australia. Christmas things will have to be air mail now to your cousins.'

'It happens every year,' sighed Winnie.

'Mind you,' said Jenny kindly, 'you're still all right for America, and Europe's not so bad.'

'That's a change,' remarked Winnie tartly. 'Europe these days can be most awkward.'

She made her way to the kitchen to make coffee.

Over their steaming cups ten minutes later, Jenny spoke again. 'And there's more news. They've found some letters that Nathaniel Whatsit wrote years ago. Should be a thrill for Mr Shoosmith.'

Definitely wind dispersal thought Winnie, draining her cup.

Charles Henstock wrote to the address of Dulcie Mulloy which Harold had obtained from the obliging Welsh postmistress, but the days passed, and he had no reply.

Secretly, he rather hoped that the young lady would not be able to come. Harold's enthusiasm swept one along, he mused. It would really be more circumspect just to entertain Robert Wilberforce, for Dulcie Mulloy was an unknown quantity and might not fit in with Harold and their new acquaintance. Harold seemed to think that she was a successful business woman, and Charles felt apprehensive. Would she be *bossy*? Would she be completely dismissive of Nathaniel's memory, as her deplorable father had been? Would she and Robert Wilberforce, who sounded such a quiet fellow on the telephone, take a dislike to each other? Would she demand Nathaniel's letters for herself as one of the family?

With such conjectures poor Charles tortured himself until Dimity, ever solicitous, asked him outright what was troubling him.

After some hesitation Charles admitted that he had one or two qualms about the proposed dinner party.

Dimity, always practical, tried to put his mind at ease. 'Well, it's all arranged now, whether she comes or not, and really one must consider Harold's feelings. He would love to meet Dulcie, if that turns out to be possible, and both she and Mr Wilberforce are bound to be civilized people and won't make trouble under our roof. Do stop worrying, Charles dear. I'm sure it will be a very cheerful little party.'

'I do wish she would reply,' said Charles, only partially content.

'She may have moved from that address,' said Dimity, 'or be ill, or looking after someone else.'

'I realize that,' nodded Charles, 'but I just wish we had *heard*,' he added piteously.

That same evening the telephone rang as he and Dimity were finishing a modest supper of cauliflower cheese.

Charles went to the hall to answer it, and took a long time in doing so.

Dimity stacked the dishes in the sink, set out two coffee cups, then settled herself at the kitchen table. She only hoped that the caller was not some troubled parishioner who was demanding Charles's immediate support and comfort. If so, she knew Charles would go at once to offer succour.

He returned beaming, and Dimity felt relief. At least he had not been called upon to take himself out into the dismal November night. She began to make the coffee.

'It was Dulcie Mulloy. Very apologetic for not getting in touch before, but she's been abroad on business. Hamburg or Frankfurt – one of those edible German towns – and she only got back today to find our letter.'

'And can she come?'

'She said she'd love to. She is going on to stay with friends in Wiltshire that night, but can come to dinner.'

'That is good news,' said Dimity, noticing the pleased expression on her husband's face.

'She sounds quite charming,' said Charles. 'Very soft voice. Very ladylike.'

Dimity hid her amusement. How often, these days, did you hear of anyone being 'ladylike'?

But then Charles was not of these days, she thought thankfully. 'So now you are happy?' she said, putting his coffee before him.

'I'm always happy with you,' said Charles.

3. A Memorable Evening

The Christmas street decorations began to go up in Lulling High Street at the start of December. Council men, perched on ladders, strung electric bulbs among the lime trees, and banners across the highway, causing even more traffic chaos than usual, and a number of distinctly unchristian comments from pedestrians stepping round bags of tools and coils of electric flex.

The shops were decking their windows with seasonal themes. Reindeer romped improbably round the Lulling Gas offices among refrigerators and ovens. Father Christmas sat on his sleigh amidst satin underwear and flimsy nightgowns in the window of Lulling's most prestigious draper's shop, and at the new florist's a gigantic silver and white arrangement of honesty, silvered pine cones and white Christmas roses evoked much admiration from the passers-by.

At the Fuchsia Bush, Nelly Piggott and her staff had been busy preparing Christmas cakes and the results of their skill stood proudly in the window of that establishment. Fringed collars of scarlet and gold encircled the snowy wares, and red satin ribbon was draped tastefully across the windowpane to add even more attraction to the goods on display.

The scene at Thrush Green was much less colourful, although Mr Jones, the landlord of the Two Pheasants, had a Christmas tree standing in a tub outside the door of his hostelry, and this was decked with miniature light bulbs which made a brave show after dark.

But in all the houses around the green preparations were going on with increasing fervour as the December days were torn from the calendar.

Winnie Bailey was debating whether to send tights or hankies to her Australian cousins, mindful of postage expense.

Ella Bembridge was hand-blocking some material, which was destined to be made into ties for her unlucky male relations. The recipients, however, were quite used to these annual gifts, and passed them on, after a decent interval, to bazaars some distance from Thrush Green.

Nelly Piggott had cleared away the supper dishes, and was settling down at the table to write Christmas cards. Albert was next door at the Two Pheasants, and Nelly had time to sort robins from snowy churches, cats in bobble-hats from reindeer, in readiness for posting to friends and relations.

Joan and Edward Young, the local architect, who lived in the finest of all the Cotswold houses on the green, were planning a Christmas party for their schoolboy son, and Harold and Isobel Shoosmith were sorting out their bottles of wine and making a list for more.

But it was at Thrush Green school that the most intense of Christmas preparations were in force.

Alan Lester had decided to keep things as simple as possible. The decorating of the three classrooms would be left to the care of the teacher in charge, and Miss Robinson, across the playground in the infants' room, was already supervising the construction of yards of paperchains, a Christmas frieze to encircle the walls, and some individual cracker cases, destined for unsuspecting parents, and waiting to be filled with wrapped boiled sweets generously supplied by the enthusiastic Miss Robinson.

The paperchains and frieze were roaring ahead with little difficulty, but the cracker cases were decidedly less simple than *The Teachers' World* diagram had shown, and infant tears had spotted many a piece of scarlet crêpe paper. In fact, Miss Robinson had almost decided to scrap that particular project and substitute nice plain squares of red paper which could be drawn up round the sweets and turned into a neat dolly bag with the aid of sensible and obliging wire tie closures.

The young probationer in the room next to Alan's had also embarked on an ambitious frieze showing angels with detachable wings which, in theory, fluttered in any light breeze available. It was a pretty notion on paper, but when transposed to practical hand work was far from successful. The Cotswold winds in winter are rough and rude, and at every opening of the classroom door the wings fell to the floor like confetti.

When Alan Lester discovered his assistant one playtime tearfully trying to stick back the recalcitrant wings, he suggested that these tiresome appendages should go into the wastepaper basket, and that wings could be added on each side of the figures quite effectively by drawing on the black background with white chalk.

'*Much* better,' agreed the girl, cheering up.

'You don't want to be too ambitious,' said Alan kindly.

'I thought of making some paper bells but they look rather tricky,' she admitted.

'What about paperchains?'

'But they *always* have paperchains!' protested the innovator.

'That's why they like them,' Alan assured her.

His own classroom was adorned with cardboard models of Father Christmas in his sleigh with rather weak-kneed reindeer pulling it. But beauty is in the eye of the beholder, and the children were enchanted with their efforts. Here, too, paperchains stretched overhead, and when a link occasionally gave way and there was a cascade of bright chains upon the heads beneath, it all added to the festive spirit.

The two older classes combined to practise carols, for it was in the school's tradition to take part in a carol service at St Andrew's on the green close by. The infants were exempt from this event, as excitement and nervousness had often brought tears, or worse, to the occasion, to the embarrassment of all present. They had a story read to them in the familiar comfort of their own classroom, while their elders fulfilled their public duties.

Alan Lester's two daughters were among his pupils, and were some of the keenest workers at the Christmas decorations. At home they continued their labours enthusiastically, and Alan found the schoolhouse as lavishly festooned in paperchains as the school itself.

'You know,' commented Alan to his wife Margaret when the little girls were safely in bed, 'I am a true lover of Christmas, but I do get a little tired of these ubiquitous paperchains.'

'Never mind,' said his wife consolingly. 'You know what Eeyore said about birthdays? "Here today, and gone tomorrow." Well, Christmas is much the same!'

'Ah!' replied Alan, 'but these things stay up until Twelfth Night. However, if the girls like them . . .'

'They do,' said Margaret; and there the matter was left.

Meanwhile, at the vicarage in Lulling, preparations for the dinner party were already going ahead.

Dimity, whose confidence in her ability to cook had grown since her marriage, was quite enjoying making lists of possible menus for the great occasion. She consulted Charles earnestly about his opinion, but always received the same unhelpful response: 'I'm sure that would be very nice, Dimity. Very nice indeed.'

Food meant little to Charles, and Dimity often wondered if he would patiently wade through a stewed boot or bread soaked in hot water if put before him. He would certainly not question such a meal, and probably compliment her when his plate was clean.

She remembered his angelic forbearance with the appalling meals his housekeeper had dished up, when Charles was a lone widower at Thrush Green years earlier. She and Ella had often taken pity on him, and invited him to lunch. He had always been excessively grateful, Dimity recalled, but now, after years of marriage and supplying him with meals, she wondered if perhaps she and Ella had been more satisfied then with their entertaining than their polite guest.

In the end Dimity had devised a main course which would survive in the oven should the guests be late in arriving. Chicken breasts in a creamy sauce in a casserole, accompanied by jacket potatoes, runner beans grown in the vicarage garden and taken from the freezer, and fresh carrots for a splash of colour should prove adequate. The problems of starters and puddings to augment the chicken kept Dimity engrossed happily for days beforehand.

Charles would be in charge of the wine throughout the evening, and here he took more interest and was quite knowledgeable. Dimity was content to leave things to him.

There would only be six at the table, but the plethora of dishes were to be tackled in the kitchen, while coffee was being taken in the vicarage's elegant drawing-room, by the stalwart daily help who usually came to give a hand with the housework on two mornings a week.

The warmest of the three spare bedrooms was to house Mr Wilberforce overnight, and Dimity was already planning the best arrangement of his bedside lighting and reading matter. With such domestic matters Dimity was happily occupied, while Charles thought only of the pleasure of seeing and handling the letters written so long ago by Nathaniel, and the diary kept by the Reverend Octavius Fennel who had once walked the streets of Lulling and Thrush Green to meet his parishioners, just as Charles himself did today.

At Thrush Green Harold Shoosmith looked forward to the evening with even greater excitement.

They were invited to the vicarage at seven o'clock to meet the other guests, and fortunately the night was clear.

Fog had shrouded the Cotswolds for two days, causing traffic to progress at a walking pace in the towns, and making it necessary to have lights on all day in offices, shops and homes.

A breeze had sprung up in the late afternoon, swirling the mist away in long veils. By the time early dusk had fallen over Lulling, the Christmas lights were shining as brightly as ever, and there was general relief, as the Shoosmiths set out.

The vicarage hall was also bright with extra polishing by Gladys, a splendid azalea on the hall table, and a Christmas tree standing in the corner.

Dimity, flushed with her culinary efforts, greeted Isobel and Harold affectionately and ushered them into the drawing-room where Robert Wilberforce was standing.

He was tall and dark, aged about forty, and looked remarkably healthy, as if he might well take a brisk walk daily over his native fells. He was not handsome, Isobel decided as they were introduced, but attractive in a rugged open-air way. His voice was low with a north-country burr about it, and Harold, who would have liked the biggest villain on earth as carrier of Nathaniel Patten's letters, took to this amiable stranger at once.

The rector poured drinks and Robert's journey and the providential dispersal of the fog kept the conversation going. A briefcase stood by Robert's chair and Harold was longing to see it opened.

A few minutes later the door bell rang and Charles hastened to answer it.

'That will be Miss Mulloy,' cried Dimity. 'I do so hope she had an easy journey.'

The latest guest came in shyly, warmly greeted by Dimity who led her to the fire and began introductions.

She was a small woman with soft fair hair, and was clad in a coral-pink jersey suit. Harold thought how pretty she was, this great-granddaughter of Nathaniel's, and remembered the gross unkempt man who was her father. Certainly this fragile-looking girl, whose small cold hand he held, did not take after her paternal parent.

Over their drinks she grew less shy and told them about her position in an insurance firm in the City, and how she went daily by Tube from her flat. Robert knew some of the directors of the company, and the conversation flowed easily.

Dimity hurried out to the kitchen to supervise the dishing-up operations, and while she was absent the rector said gently how sorry he was to learn that her mother had died, and how they remembered her kindness to them in Wales so long ago.

The girl looked down at the glass in her hand, and Charles wondered if he had been wrong to mention the subject, but Dulcie spoke calmly.

'We had two lovely years together in my flat,' she said, 'before she fell ill. I think they were the happiest years of both our lives.'

'So you live alone now?'

'At the moment. I suppose it would be sensible to get a friend to share with me, but I'm rather enjoying being on my own.'

'A lot to be said for it,' agreed Robert Wilberforce, 'but who looks after you?'

Dulcie looked bewildered. 'I look after myself.'

'But when you get home,' insisted Robert, 'who cooks a meal and so on?'

'Why, I do. It's no bother.'

Robert laughed. 'I suppose I'm spoilt. My housekeeper, Mrs Tanner, cooks and washes and does everything in the house for me. She's a Yorkshire lass and everything's kept at a pretty high standard. I have to leave muddy shoes in the porch.'

At this point, Dimity summoned them to the dining-room. Over the meal Charles enlarged on the excitement that had been engendered by Robert's gift of the letters to Thrush Green.

'Well, I must confess I had never heard of him until I went through my aunt's papers.'

'You're not the only one,' commented Harold. 'The name of Nathaniel Patten didn't seem to be known when I arrived here some years ago.'

'Now, come!' protested Charles, 'we knew he was buried in the churchyard, but we had no idea he was such a great man.'

'My Aunt Mary could have told you,' broke in Dulcie. 'She had a great many of his qualities, and she often quoted him to me as a good example. I'm afraid my father had no time for his memory.'

She said this with an apologetic smile towards Charles and Harold, and they realized, with some relief, that she had become quite reconciled to the memory of a far from satisfactory father.

Dimity's dinner was much enjoyed, although Harold was secretly so anxious to get hold of the contents of Robert's briefcase that he was scarcely aware of what was put before him.

When they were back at last in the drawing-room with coffee at their sides the great moment arrived, and Robert unclicked his case.

He handed a large envelope to Charles, and they all sat back to watch the rector open the treasure. A smaller envelope revealed a hardbacked diary, spotted with age, with a brittle silk ribbon marking a page.

'There's not a lot in the diary part,' said Robert, bending forward, 'but he seems to have kept his accounts in the latter half, and they look particularly interesting.'

'May I see?' burst from Harold, and Charles hastily handed the little volume to his anxious friend. A bundle of yellowing letters was next withdrawn from the envelope and Charles's chubby face grew pink with pleasure.

'I really feel,' he said, turning to Dulcie, 'that you should see them first as a direct descendant.'

But Dulcie would not hear of it, so Charles undid the string which held them, and looked at the first letter. The paper was brittle and so fragile that Dulcie thought of the paper burnt on a bonfire that turns to gossamer thinness before the wind shatters it.

The rector peered closely at the faded writing. 'It's dated 1892,' he told them. 'I can't see if it is January or July. He just puts "Jy". Let me see if I can make out the text.'

He adjusted the gold-rimmed spectacles on his snub nose, and cleared his throat.

It is now almost eight months since I said farewell to you at Bristol, and I write to tell you of the safety of our journey, and the beginnings of my endeavours which, with God's help and your prayers and inestimable support, I trust will be successful.

I have not yet met Dr Maurice as he is ministering to sufferers at a settlement up-river, but kind messages were waiting here from him on my arrival.

My faithful servant, already dedicated to Christ, awaits the conclusion of this letter, and will take it downstream some thirty miles to our nearest township where (Deo volente) *it will go by the next ship to England.*

My prayers, my thanks, and my whole heart go with this letter to one whose faith and bounty have inspired my life.

The rector's voice was husky with emotion as he read the words, written so long ago in the cruel heat of Africa, to one long dead. Both writer and first reader had loved Thrush Green, thought Charles, as he and the local friends with him did now.

There was a short silence, then Robert Wilberforce spoke. 'I find that very moving,' he said. 'And I think the date must be January. If you look in Octavius's diary you will see that he notes that a letter from Nathaniel arrived that summer. I imagine that fits.'

The rest of the company were as moved as Robert was, and longed to hear more.

'I shall spread them out,' decided Charles, 'on this side table, so that we can all see them easily. Somehow I don't think they'll stand much handling.'

They all helped to clear a space, and soon the fragile pages lay open to their gaze.

After some time, Dimity recalled them to the present by offering more coffee, and the company moved back to their chairs by the fire.

'They are not all dated,' said Harold. 'I wonder if we can get them into chronological order.'

'That's where the diary helps,' Robert told him. 'As far as I could make out, Octavius supplied the funds for this venture, and he seems to have put regular sums into an account at Coutts bank to support the mission.'

'But I don't think Nathaniel was backed by the Church,' said Charles. 'I wonder why Octavius was so generous? I know from records that he was a bachelor and a rich man, but it seems odd that as a churchman he should give so much to Nathaniel.'

'Reading between the lines,' replied Robert, 'I think he looked upon Nathaniel as a son. He mentions several times in the diary his sorrow that Nathaniel refused to take Holy Orders. Evidently the young man could not believe in all the tenets of the church, evangelical soul that he was, but had this burning missionary zeal with which Octavius had to be content.'

'We must try to find out more about Octavius,' mused Charles. 'He sounds a remarkable man.'

'There is possibly a full obituary in the back numbers of local papers,' said Harold. 'I'll look into it, shall I?'

And so it was agreed. Later the papers were carefully packed into a large folder from the rector's study to save them from being folded again, and they were given into the welcoming hands of Harold Shoosmith.

'This must be a particularly important occasion for you,' said Charles kindly to Dulcie. 'You had a wonderful forebear.'

'I know,' replied the girl. 'I only wish my mother and my Aunt Mary were alive to rejoice with me. Aunt Mary spoke of him often, although of course she had never met him.' She looked at the clock. 'I'm afraid I ought to be on my way. My friends expect me soon after ten. It's been such a wonderful evening for me.'

She said goodbye to the Shoosmiths, then to Robert Wilberforce.

'I hope we shall meet again,' he said. 'Do you ever visit the Lake District?'

'I may be going there next spring,' she told him, 'to see old friends.'

'Then perhaps you would come and have lunch with me?'

'I should very much like to.'

She went out to the car, accompanied by Charles and Dimity.

'It's a fine clear night,' said Charles, when they returned to warm their hands at the fire. 'What a charming girl she is.'

'Has she far to go?' asked Robert.

'Only half an hour's drive, she said.'

'I never like the idea of women driving alone after dark,' said Robert. 'A friend of mine was foolish enough to give a wretched fellow a lift, and he knocked her about pretty badly.'

'Oh, I don't think Dulcie Mulloy would be so silly,' said Isobel comfortingly. 'I thought she seemed a very sensible young woman, and obviously she was as thrilled as we all are with your wonderful discovery.'

'It's been an amazing evening,' agreed Harold. 'A thousand thanks for everything,' he added, kissing Dimity's cheek.

'And now we must think about bed,' said Dimity when Charles returned from seeing them off. 'I'm sure you must be tired after a day's business, and then all this excitement.'

'I have enjoyed every minute,' Robert assured her.

*

'What nice old-fashioned manners Robert Wilberforce has,' commented Isobel, as they drove down Lulling High Street towards home. 'I'm sure there aren't many men these days who worry about women driving alone after dark.'

'I do about you,' Harold told her. 'You're quite soft-hearted enough to give some plausible bounder a lift.'

Isobel seemed not to hear. She was immersed in her own thoughts. 'Perhaps he's slightly smitten,' she said dreamily.

'Oh, rubbish!' said Harold, swinging round Thrush Green. 'There was absolutely no sign of any nonsense like that. You women are all alike, scenting romance where there's nothing.'

'Maybe,' agreed Isobel equably.

4. Harold Is On The Trail

The last day of the term at Thrush Green school had gone without a hitch. The older children, hair brushed and coats neatly buttoned against the cold of the Cotswold winds outside and the Victorian chill of St Andrew's interior, filed decorously into their pews at the front of the church, and took part in the carol service conducted by the Reverend Charles Henstock.

The crib glowed at the side of the chancel steps, and piles of ivy and other evergreens waited in readiness for the ladies of the parish to put the final touches to the Christmas decorations in the next day or two.

The paperchains and friezes had been taken down and put into bin liners to await recycling. In the denuded infants' classroom, the last hours of term were devoted to stories, singing and such age-old games as 'I spy' which needed no apparatus, while their elders were at the carol service.

Alan Lester felt very proud of his little flock as they filed into the church, and ignored Albert Piggott who had stationed himself by the porch in order to cast a malevolent eye on those who omitted to use the doormat with suitable energy.

Margaret Lester sat by her husband, and he thought how lucky he was to have a wife who was healthy again, and a job which gave him satisfaction. As he looked fondly at the glossy heads of Kate and Alison Lester, just in front of their parents, Alan counted himself a fortunate man indeed.

Winnie Bailey had enjoyed setting up the crib at the chancel steps on the day before the carol service. She had performed this pleasant duty for more years than she could remember, usually in the company of Ella Bembridge and Dimity, but sometimes alone.

To tell the truth, she really preferred to go about her task alone. There was something very soothing about working in the solitude of the church. It was not an old building, as churches go. It did not have the ancient splendour of St John's in Lulling, a wool church of dignity and beauty as great as those at Burford or Lechlade or Fairford not very far away. St Andrew's was Victorian with over-elaborate stained-glass windows, a fussy reredos and some deplorable encaustic tiles which succeeded in distracting the attention of communicants as they knelt at the altar rail.

But its smallness gave it a homeliness which Thrush Green

folk liked, and in much the same way that Winnie had become accustomed to – even fond of – the crack in her bedroom ceiling, and the wardrobe door which swung open at odd times, so she felt affection for the shortcomings of her church's fabric.

On this particular occasion she was not alone for long. She had relished her solitary silence for a quarter of an hour, and felt refreshed in spirit, when Ella and Dimity joined her.

There was not a great deal to do, for the ladies were used to setting up the crib, making sure that the dim electric bulb which lit it was safely away from straw and hangings, and that the doll-child was easily visible to those passing the crib.

After ten minutes or so Ella returned from the vestry with dustpan and brush, and began to tidy up the wisps of straw and greenery.

'Perishing cold out,' she remarked to her companions, in what Winnie felt was much too loud a voice for a sacred place. At least, she told herself charitably, Ella was not smoking – a laudable tribute to holiness.

'I've put the kettle ready,' went on Ella, brushing lustily. 'Need a cuppa after this. Bit dusty in here, isn't it? And that brass lectern could do with a rub.'

'Mrs Bates is going to do the brights ready for the carol service,' explained Dimity, 'and yes, please, I'm sure we could both do with tea.'

Half an hour later, the three friends sat by Ella's fire enjoying tea and anchovy toast, and the talk was of Harold Shoosmith's delight over the discovery of Nathaniel's letters.

'He's going along to the newspaper people,' Dimity told them, 'to see if he can find out more about Nathaniel, and about Octavius Fennel, too. Everyone knew he was a good man, but it doesn't seem to be generally known how much he did for Nathaniel out in Africa.'

'The Lovelock girls might know,' said Ella.

'The Lovelocks?' queried Dimity. 'But even they wouldn't remember Octavius!'

The Lovelock girls were now, all three of them, around eighty years old, and lived in a pretty Georgian house in Lulling High Street, next door to the Fuchsia Bush. They had lived there all their lives, and were renowned for their excessive gentility and parsimony. Friends invited to a meal there usually stoked up beforehand with a slice of cake or a sandwich, whilst getting ready. Such a prerequisite of lunch at the Lovelocks' might not fully compensate for the paucity of the provender supplied but at least it mitigated the noise of tummy-rumbles.

'Oh, not the girls themselves,' said Ella, beginning to roll one of her untidy cigarettes, 'but I think their father knew Octavius Fennel. I'm sure I've heard them speak of him.'

There was a gasp from Winnie, and she replaced her cup on its saucer with a great clatter. She fell back in the chair with her eyes closed.

Dimity and Ella sprang to her side, Ella's cigarette-making equipment crashing into the hearth.

'Winnie, Winnie! What is it?'

After a few deep breaths, Winnie opened her eyes. 'Sorry about that. Better now,' she whispered.

'But what's hurting you? Shall I get John Lovell?'

'Heavens, no!' said Winnie, struggling upright. 'I'm fine now. I just occasionally get this pain on my right side. It goes within a minute. Nothing to worry a doctor about.'

'I think it is,' said Dimity roundly. 'Suppose you were taken ill in the street? Crossing the road? Going down steps, say?'

Winnie laughed tremulously. 'Don't worry about it. If it does get worse I will have a word with John, but I really can't face going back and forth to the county hospital for tests and things. Particularly just before Christmas.'

'Well, let me give you more tea. That must be cold.'

Winnie accepted the fresh cup, and conversation was resumed, but the subject of the Lovelock girls' father and his friendship with Octavius was forgotten.

Ella insisted on accompanying Winnie on the few yards' walk to her own home, and when Winnie was safely back in her armchair, she spoke to Jenny before she left.

'I know,' said Jenny soberly. 'I'm watching things, don't you worry, and if she gets many more of these spasms I'm telling Dr Lovell myself, come what may!'

A little easier in her mind about her old friend, Ella returned home.

Meanwhile, Harold had been tireless in his researches.

The editor of the local paper let him go through the files for 1912 when Octavius Fennel had died, but after a short and rather flowery obituary, the account of the actual funeral was taken up largely by a list of local dignitaries attending the service.

The county paper was more helpful, mentioning the generosity of the deceased and in particular his interest in missionary work. To Harold's great joy Nathaniel Patten was mentioned, and the date 1892 given as the year when his African mission settlement was officially opened.

Hot on the trail, Harold ploughed his way zealously through the weekly issues for that year, but was beginning to despair of finding any notice of Nathaniel's mission. By the time he had turned over the yellowing and musty pages of the summer weeks of 1892 showing photographs of ladies in ankle-length skirts and unwieldy hats at garden parties, race meetings, fêtes and the like, he was almost ready to give up.

However, he determined to struggle on, and noted the change of attire in the ladies' fashions as the shooting season began. Wild duck, partridge, grouse, snipe, teal, hares and geese, all it seemed should be wary of men with guns as autumn loomed, and the silk skirts changed to tweed and the pale kid boots to glossy leather.

On 1 October, Harold read, pheasants, too, would have to watch out, and the issue of 26 October gave not only a fearsome photograph of a score of tweed-clad gentlemen sitting behind rows of birds' corpses, but also a short paragraph saying that word had been received by the Reverend Octavius Fennel from Mr Nathaniel Patten that the latter's mission station and school had been officially declared open on 1 October.

Harold leafed through the rest of that year's copy, but there was nothing more to interest him.

He shut the great book, sneezed as the dust of ages began to settle, and sat back well content.

October the first 1892!

Excitement engulfed him. Why, next year it would be a hundred years since that great day! Here was a sound reason for rejoicing, he told himself.

He must get in touch with Charles at once.

This certainly called for a special celebration at Thrush Green.

The news that Winnie Bailey's health was not quite as it should be soon flashed around Thrush Green.

Naturally, Winnie's uncomfortable twinges at Ella's were translated into more dramatic form.

Albert Piggott told his old friend Percy Hodge that she had been 'took bad with the gastric', and he had seen her being helped back to her own home by Ella Bembridge.

Betty Bell told the Shoosmiths that Mrs Bailey had 'had a turn', much to their dismay.

Mr Jones of the Two Pheasants, usually the soul of discretion in his capacity as local landlord, rashly said that it was no wonder poor old Mrs Bailey had caught a chill working in that church which was as cold as the tomb. Albert Piggott, within earshot, took umbrage at this slight on his efficiency as church caretaker, and stalked out, but not before he had drained the last of his half-pint.

Winnie, of course, knew nothing of these rumours which were floating about, and as she appeared as healthy as ever to her friends, they began to think that their informants had been over-egging the pudding as usual, and indulging in the common practice of gross exaggeration.

But Isobel Shoosmith, on her way to the postbox on the corner of Thrush Green, did ask Ella, on the same errand, if Winnie was really in good health.

Ella looked troubled. 'She makes very light of it, but she had a nasty spasm after we'd been doing the crib. Mind you, it was devilish cold in there. May have been that, of course, but I was just telling her about Octavius Fennel when she keeled over.'

'Has she seen John Lovell?'

'She's dead against it, but I reckon Jenny will fetch him pretty swiftly, if she sees any symptoms. Winnie says the pain is only momentary, and nothing to worry about.'

'It worries *me*,' responded Isobel, dropping her bundle of envelopes into the box. 'I wonder if I ought to call?'

'I shouldn't,' advised Ella. 'Winnie's got plenty of sense, and if she gets any more pain she'll have a word with John.'

The ladies parted, and Isobel crossed the green to her home. Concern for Winnie occupied the larger part of her mind, but a phrase of Ella's niggled in one corner: 'I was just telling her about Octavius Fennel.' That would interest Harold, she knew.

She quickened her pace to tell her husband that Ella seemed to have something to add to his researches.

As she guessed, Harold was greatly intrigued and was about to hasten across to Ella's house, but was restrained by his wife.

'She was making for Nidden,' she told him. 'Do be patient. Give her a ring later.'

And with that Harold had to be content.

*

As for Winnie Bailey herself, all unsuspecting of the rumours flying around the neighbourhood, she was busy with her Christmas arrangements, in common with the rest of the community. She was honest enough to admit secretly to feeling tired and uneasy, but was determined to postpone any visits to the doctor until the festivities were over.

Her nephew Richard, his wife and two young children were coming to lunch on Boxing Day, and she and Jenny had planned to spend Christmas Day quietly together.

It was at times like this that Winnie realized how old she was getting. In the old days, a visit from Richard and his family would have been taken in her stride. Now she faced the fact that the extra work, the noise of two small children, the entertainment of her guests and the general disruption of her usual ordered routine all combined to dismay her.

Two days before Christmas Richard telephoned to tell her that the older child was in bed with measles, and the younger one seemed to be sickening for it. They were all terribly sorry, but their visit would have to be postponed.

Winnie was genuinely sad to hear the news, and said so, but was rather ashamed, as she put down the receiver, at the relief which flooded her.

A stab of pain made her sit down for a few minutes before she went to apprise Jenny about the change of plan.

'Well, I'm sorry for the poor mites,' said Jenny forthrightly, 'but to my mind it's a blessing in disguise for you just now.'

Harold's call to Ella had resulted in his being told that it was the Lovelocks who might know more about the deceased rector of Thrush Green; she herself knew nothing.

'You can't possibly go down to the Lovelocks', pen and pad in hand, on Christmas Eve,' Isobel told him. 'Do be sensible. All this has waited for a century; a few more days won't hurt.'

With commendable self-control Harold put aside his researches and joined in the celebration of Christmas with the rest of his neighbours, but before the year was out he rang the Misses Lovelock's house, and was lucky enough to get the youngest one, Violet, at the other end of the line. Violet, although almost eighty, was rather more practical than her sisters, and her memory was decidedly better.

'I'm sure we have some papers of Papa's about Octavius Fennel, but I have a funny feeling that we got one of the young men from the choir to put a trunkful of that sort of thing in the loft. I will check with Ada and Bertha and ring you back.'

For the next hour Harold paced about the house within earshot of the telephone, doing his best to be patient.

Just as he and Isobel and Betty Bell, their daily help, were sitting down to their morning coffee in the kitchen, Violet Lovelock rang him.

'Yes, indeed. Bertha clearly remembers the trunk going up into the loft. And I have recalled the article that Papa wrote. It was one of a series about local people who had contributed to Lulling and Thrush Green in one way or another. Quite short, you understand. I believe the series first appeared in the church magazine, and Papa had them put together in a little leaflet.'

'Wonderful!' cried Harold. 'When may I fetch them?'

'Well, today we are turning out the spare room, and tomorrow is bathroom-cleaning day, so what about Friday morning?'

Harold agreed readily. Secretly he wondered why the attentions to the Lovelocks' spare bedroom and bathroom forbade his picking up a leaflet from the ladies, but Violet's further explanation threw some light on the matter.

'I'm afraid we'll have to send you up into the loft to fetch the papers,' said Violet. 'We are now past coping with the little folding ladder.'

'No bother at all,' Harold assured her. 'I will look forward to seeing you at about ten, if that is convenient?'

'Perfectly,' said Violet, and rang off.

Charles Henstock, of course, had been kept informed of every step taken by Harold in his quest for details about Nathaniel and Octavius.

The discovery of a firm date for the official opening of Nathaniel's mission gave both men great satisfaction and they were in entire agreement that something must be done to note the occasion in October next.

'I hope it won't clash with the school's centenary,' Charles said. 'I know that Alan Lester is keen to mark that. It's quite extraordinary how one's calendar fills up for months in advance, what with church festivals, and visiting clergy, and the dentist.'

'I don't have to worry too much about your first two,' admitted Harold, 'but the dentist certainly seems to figure in my diary far too frequently.'

'By the way,' continued Charles, 'we had a charming letter from Robert Wilberforce after his visit. He hopes that we will see him if ever we go his way. And he wanted Dulcie Mulloy's telephone number. I think he means to get in touch when he comes south next time.'

'Good!' said Harold. Could Isobel be right about Wilberforce's interest in Nathaniel's descendant, he wondered? He dismissed the thought immediately. He was getting as bad as the rest of Thrush Green!

Friday came at last and Harold set out for Lulling High Street on foot. He carried with him a small case, notepad and pen.

'You look as though you are going for the weekend,' Isobel said.

'Well, heaven knows how much stuff I may find in that loft. I'm going prepared.'

He was greeted effusively by the three sisters who fluttered about him, pressing him to take coffee with them.

Harold managed to excuse himself, and was taken up two flights of stairs by Violet to what must once have been the servants' quarters. On the landing he espied a trap door above him which gave access to the loft and, he hoped, the treasure he was seeking.

Violet showed him how it opened and let down a metal ladder. It looked remarkably wobbly to Harold, who was a large and heavy man, but he hoped for the best. Violet pressed a light switch on the landing wall, and a dim glow filled the square above their heads.

'Now, will you be all right?' asked Violet. 'There is a torch up there, I believe, though the battery may have gone. And I hope you don't mind mice. We hear them scampering about at night, dear little things. We none of us have the heart to trap them.'

She scurried away and Harold mounted the steps gingerly.

He was relieved to find that the entire loft floor was boarded, and stood for a few moments trying to get accustomed to the dim light.

The sight that met his eyes was a revelation. The place was crammed with Victorian and Edwardian relics which would have delighted an antique dealer's heart.

There were two enormous hip baths, three wooden towel rails, and a fireguard which had probably been in use some seventy or eighty years earlier in the girls' nursery. There were several dismantled iron bedsteads stacked against one wall, the legacy probably of servants long-dead, and a pile of circular hat boxes towering over a wicker chair with a dilapidated cushion showing signs of mouse occupancy.

Tennis racquets of antique design, skating boots, skis and a wooden sledge were propped in one corner beside a box of toys. In it Harold saw a diabolo set, a Russian egg, several jigsaw puzzles, a clockwork train, and a dolls' teaset. Hard by stood a dusty dolls' house, a replica of the one in which he now stood, down to the three front doorsteps and the brass knocker.

The Misses Lovelock must have been very fortunate little girls, thought Harold, stepping past these relics to half a dozen trunks which occupied the main part of the floor space.

To his relief, he saw that each bore a label written in a fair copperplate style, but faded and grimy with years. The largest bore the inscription 'APPARATUS – PHOTOGRAPHY AND ASTRONOMY'. The next in size said 'MAMA'S, AND OTHER FAMILY PICTURES'.

Harold turned his attention to the smallest case of the collection, a brown tin object bearing a label which seemed hopeful: 'PERSONAL PAPERS'.

The little trunk was unlocked, but the lid was difficult to lift.

When at last he had forced it open, Harold saw neatly packed bundles of letters, notebooks and some cardboard-covered pamphlets. He tackled these first, squatting on the dusty floor, peering closely in the dim light from the naked electric bulb above him. The torch, as Violet had indicated, was useless, and Harold intended to take it down with him when he descended.

The bundle of leaflets was tied with fine string, and they appeared to be written either by the Lovelocks' father himself or by some of his friends.

Harold turned them in his now filthy hands. They dealt with such subjects as 'Spirit Manifestations', 'Electrical Phenomena', 'Scientific Experiments' and 'Astronomical Data'. He was almost at the end of the collection when he came across one with the title 'Local Benefactors' and his heart leapt. Could this be the series which first appeared in the local parish magazine?

He stood up to get nearer to the light, and studied the index. Yes, here was something! 'The Reverend Octavius Fennel 1842–1912.'

The print was small and Harold had difficulty in reading it. He put it aside with the torch, and delved again into the papers.

After an hour's search, he decided that this was really all that was relevant to his present endeavours, and he closed the lid, looked once more upon the dusty quietness of long ago, and retraced his steps.

'I am so very grateful,' he told Violet, as he washed the grime of ages from his hands at the kitchen sink. 'I will let you have this back as soon as I have copied out the important pieces, and I will also put a new battery in the torch, as a very small thank-you.'

He was in buoyant mood as he climbed the hill to Thrush Green. To be sure, the case he carried had only one small leaflet, and an ancient torch to keep it company, but Harold foresaw many happy hours ahead with this treasure from the Lovelocks' attic.

5. New Light On Old Times

The first days of the New Year were mild and still. The naked trees stood motionless against a grey sky, and the hedgerows were spangled with drops from morn until evening.

In the gardens a few hardy flowers showed a little colour. Tough marigolds, brave pansies and here and there a pink, all somewhat bedraggled, nevertheless were tattered reminders of the summer long past.

Bright berries of pyracantha and cotoneaster glowed against the Cotswold stone, providing cheer for passers-by and the hungry birds.

Indoors bowls of hyacinths and tulips gave hope of spring to come, sharing the tables and windowsills with the azaleas and poinsettias of Christmas.

It was a time to relish one's home. In the dark of the year, when curtains were drawn between four and five, and the long evening stretched ahead, the people of Thrush Green turned to their fires, books, knitting, needlework and, sometimes, television to amuse themselves. Domestic comforts became doubly precious: a warm bed, a hot drink, the snugness of curtains shut against the night's chill, all brought comfort in the dismal days of January.

Even Charles Henstock, who thought little about creature comforts, enjoyed these simple pleasures at Lulling vicarage, and occasionally thought about his former house at Thrush Green which had been burnt down some years earlier. On that site there were now some homes for old people, one-storey pleasant places designed by Edward Young, the local architect.

Edward had always thought that Thrush Green rectory was an abomination, and had pitied Charles and Dimity, obliged to live in a tall bleak house entirely out of keeping with the Cotswold architecture around it. It faced north-east, and the front door opened on to a long passage which ran the length of the house forming a wicked wind-tunnel whenever one or the other door was opened. The ceilings were lofty, the windows badly fitting, there was no central heating and, even in summer, the interior was chilly.

When at last it vanished and the ashes and debris had gone, and Dimity and Charles had moved to Lulling vicarage, no one was more delighted than Edward; and to be asked to design the new buildings to take its place gave him enormous satisfaction.

Phoenix-like, the present homes had risen from the ashes, and everyone, even dear uncomplaining Charles who had grieved at the loss of his old home, agreed that Thrush Green had been much improved by Edward's endeavours.

It was at the old people's home, called Rectory Cottages in tribute to the former residence, that a coffee morning was held on one of the quiet cold days of January.

Thrush Green was particularly fond of coffee mornings to raise funds for whichever good cause was in need. Usually the posters proclaimed that those perennials, the church roof or the organ, were pleading for help. But sometimes the posters exhorted all folk of good will to save the children, or rain forests or whales.

On the whole these occasions were looked upon as a pleasant way of meeting friends and catching up with the local gossip, both laudable and necessary in a small community. The aim of raising money really took a lesser place of importance, although when the proceeds were counted, among the unwashed coffee cups and cake plates when the public had departed, it was usually found that the local good causes – Church Roof and/ or Organ Fund – did rather better than Ethiopian Famine or Brazilian Earthquake.

'Which really,' said Winnie Bailey, seated in the warden's office at Rectory Cottages, 'is as it should be, I suppose. After all, charity should begin at home, and although we see all the dreadful things that are happening worldwide on telly, it's not quite the same as hearing the organ wheezing badly at Matins or watching a steady drip in the chancel.'

Jane Cartwright, the warden, agreed. 'I make it sixteen pounds forty-five,' she said, dropping piles of coins into plastic bags. 'That's all from the Bring and Buy stall. Nelly Piggott's seed cakes accounted for half that.'

'I can't understand this revival of popularity for *seed cake*,' mused Winnie. 'Frankly, I find it abhorrent.'

'All my old dears love it,' Jane told her. 'Takes them back to their childhood.' She turned again to her accounts, brow furrowed. 'So this can be added to the raffle money. That brought in five pounds and four pence, though how we managed to get *four pence* when the tickets were ten pence each, I can't imagine.'

'Poor sight,' said Winnie kindly. 'Mistaking a two-pence piece for a ten-pence one.'

'I thought it was uncommonly generous of the Lovelocks to give that rather nice cushion as a prize. I mean, it's usually impossible to get them to part with anything.'

'They probably disliked it,' replied Winnie. 'As a matter of fact, I gave it to them last Christmas.'

'Oh dear,' cried Jane, 'I hope you don't mind?'

'Not in the least. I'm all in favour of recycling. Actually, the tray I put in was one they had given me years ago, so I suppose we are quits.'

The two ladies put the proceeds into a cash box ready for the bank, and Jane helped Winnie into her coat.

Winnie suddenly gave a little cry, rocked unsteadily, then sat down on the chair she had just vacated. Her face was white, her eyes screwed up in pain.

Jane, who had been a nurse, loosened the fastening of the coat she had just put on, and took hold of Winnie's hand.

'I'll ring the doctor,' she said.

'No,' gasped Winnie. 'Don't bother him now. In any case, he's probably on his rounds.'

'What is it? Has this happened before?'

'Too often for my liking,' confessed Winnie. 'That's the second time within twelve hours.'

'You simply must see John Lovell,' urged Jane.

'I shall go this evening,' Winnie promised her. 'I've been putting it off for weeks. They say that doctors' relations are always the most procrastinating, but I really will go tonight.'

'I hope it isn't anything you've eaten here,' said Jane, much perturbed.

'I assure you it wasn't seed cake,' replied Winnie. 'And now I'm quite all right again, and will go home.'

But Jane insisted on taking her the short distance to her gate, before returning, very worried, to her warden's duties.

Later that day Winnie submitted to John Lovell's probings and pressings and innumerable questions.

'I'm going to send you on to Dickie's,' he told her, naming St Richard's, the large county hospital. 'You'll need X-rays and some pretty painless tests, and then you'll probably be forwarded quite quickly to the consultant, Carter. I know him well.'

'Is he good?' asked Winnie nervously.

'Good? Of course, he's good,' responded John Lovell. 'He's a St Thomas's man!'

As John Lovell was himself a St Thomas's man, Winnie said no more.

'It sounds like the gall bladder,' said the doctor. 'Much easier to cope with these days. Very often no surgery is needed at all. I'll give you a prescription, and just cut out fat in your diet. I'll see that you get looked at quite quickly.'

'And you think I may not need surgery? I must admit that I have a horror of the knife.'

'Now don't worry. The chances are that if there are any stones there they can be dispersed, and if it comes to surgery Philip Paterson is the real expert at Dickie's, and he's a St Thomas's man, too. You'll be in safe hands.'

'Well,' said Jenny when Winnie returned, 'what did Dr Lovell say?'

Winnie told her.

'Are there any other doctors at Dickie's? I mean, who haven't trained at St Thomas's?'

'Not worth mentioning, according to John Lovell,' Winnie said.

Now that term was well on the way, Alan Lester set about looking for more details about the opening of Thrush Green school in 1892.

Unlike his neighbour, Harold Shoosmith, he did not have to search through contemporary local newspapers for his researches. Three stout log books, with mottled leather-edged covers, were carefully stored in the bottom drawer of his school desk, and in the oldest of these Alan found all that he needed.

The first entry was for 15 August, inscribed in a firm copper-plate hand. The ink had turned brown with age but the entry was clear:

> *Harvest now safely garnered, so that pupils could be admitted.*
> *Sixty-two enrolled. Some twenty still hop-picking in Hampshire, and returning before the month's end.*
> *Miss Mackintosh in charge of Infants. Miss Brown in charge of Juniors. Headmaster in charge of top standards.*
> *School assembled in the playground as weather fine, and then marched into Prayers.*
> *Text today: 'Be obedient to those set over you.'*

And a very timely text too, thought Alan Lester, for the first day of a new school!

He turned the pages, and soon found a lengthy account of the official opening, which took place on 20 September in the presence of a goodly gathering. As well as dignitaries from the County Education Committee and a fair sprinkling of local worthies, the rector of Thrush Green, the Reverend Octavius Fennel, was much in evidence. He opened the proceedings with a prayer, and also gave a short address, his text being:

'Suffer the little children to come unto me, and forbid them not; for of such is the Kingdom of God.'

A somewhat kindlier text, thought Alan, than the head-master's original one.

Those present at this occasion were carefully listed, and one or two familiar names appeared, such as Lovelock and Harmer. Having found what he needed, Alan Lester returned the weighty volume to its resting place, and pondered on the most suitable festivities to promote on 20 September, 1992.

Meanwhile, Harold Shoosmith and Charles Henstock had been similarly engaged upon their researches, and were beginning to wonder about the best way to celebrate that other official opening, so far away under sunnier skies, at much the same time in 1892.

Both men had found Octavius's diary fascinating. The entries were brief, and one of the earliest was for 7 December, 1892. It read:

Received with joy letter from N. All well.

The diary was not kept daily, but very few weeks went by without some entry. Charles read it with particular sympathy. As he turned the pages, it became clear that his predecessor had been a man of outstanding kindliness and with a wide range of interests.

He obviously shared with so many Victorians the fascination of scientific discoveries. He mentioned meetings of the Lulling Scientific Society ('Lantern slides by courtesy of Oliver Love-lock, Esq.'). The Astronomer Royal had honoured them with a visit on his way to Somerset. He himself had felt obliged to speak out against some of the theories of Charles Darwin.

What came through most strongly was his steadfast belief in God and the teachings of the Anglican Church. Those theories of Charles Darwin's, about which he disapproved, were evidently contrary to his own religious beliefs and, no doubt, he looked upon them as heresy.

But the diary gave evidence not only of an upright man of God, but also of an endearing fellow who loved his neighbours, was compassionate and generous to the poor and sick, and was passionately fond of flowers, animals and the natural world about him.

Picked a dozen pyramid orchids by Lulling Woods. Took them with butter and eggs to poor old Biddy Bolton at Drovers' Arms. Lower limbs much afflicted with dropsy.

Entries mentioning Nathaniel came two or three times a year, each ending with 'see accounts'. It was plain that Octavius had financed this venture of Nathaniel's entirely from his own pocket.

By piecing together the material relating to Nathaniel in the diary, it was quite apparent to Charles and Harold that they now had a very good idea of the story.

Oliver Lovelock's useful article in 'Local Benefactors' on the subject of the Reverend Octavius Fennel was also very enlightening. Oliver obviously had great affection and respect for his clergyman friend, and also threw light on the relationship between Octavius and his protégé Nathaniel.

It appeared that the young missionary had been in his twenties when he embarked on his great adventure. There had been some preliminary correspondence with the Dr Maurice, already in Africa, mentioned in Nathaniel's first letter, and who was obviously about to welcome the young man on his arrival.

Oliver Lovelock's account gave something of Octavius's background. His wealth came from the Lancashire cotton industry. The fact that earlier generations in his family had thrived at the expense of slave labour in the cotton fields of America seemed to weigh heavily upon the clergyman's conscience. Was this one of the reasons, wondered Charles and Harold, which prompted his compassion and generosity to his contemporaries?

As a young man he had travelled extensively, mainly in Europe, visiting various capitals rather in the manner of earlier travellers undertaking the Grand Tour. Russia in the days of the Tsar had much impressed the young man, and he evidently gave a lecture on the subject later in Lulling, according to Oliver Lovelock's biography.

After being ordained he spent some time in the poorer parts of London, taking great interest in the children, and in his early thirties he was given the living of Thrush Green, where he was to spend the rest of his life.

Charles Henstock's comment was typical. As a home-loving man himself, he told Harold that Octavius must have felt as if he had found a safe haven after so many trips abroad.

But Harold wondered if such a lively mind as Octavius's ever looked back upon his adventures with nostalgia. Would he ever have secret regrets for the life he had given up? On the other hand, Harold reminded himself, he, too, had travelled widely but had not regretted, for one instant, his decision to settle in the little world of Thrush Green.

No doubt Charles was right and Octavius was content with his lot. Certainly his diary gave proof of that.

There was a photocopying machine at the stationer's in Lulling High Street, and Harold used it to make copies of the relevant pages of 'Local Benefactors'.

On his way back, he called at the Lovelocks' house to return the leaflet and the torch to the ladies.

He was invited into the drawing-room, and sat among the clutter of occasional tables, armchairs, china cabinets, book cases and even a what-not, and told the three sisters how much he had appreciated their father's account of Octavius and his good works.

'My father had a great regard for him,' said Bertha. 'Of course, we hardly knew him, as we were in the nursery then. In fact, I doubt if Violet was born. If I remember rightly, Octavius died just before the 1914–18 war.'

'Quite right,' said Harold.

'He brought Father a charming little paperknife from St Petersburg. It is still on the desk in his study.'

'And he gave us a Russian egg,' recalled Ada. 'I wonder what happened to it?'

'I think I saw it in the loft,' Harold told them, 'with other toys.'

'One day,' said Bertha, 'we must get someone to clear out that loft for us, and dispose of the contents.'

She gazed speculatively at Harold. He saw again, in his mind's eye, the stack of iron bedsteads, the heavy trunks crammed with the detritus of years, the decrepit chairs, the hip baths, the towel rails and the floor sprinkled with mouse droppings.

'I really must be off,' he said rising. 'Thank you again for your help. Your father's notes have been invaluable.'

Violet escorted him to the front door.

'What a nice man!' she remarked to her sisters when she returned. 'And he has put a new battery in the torch, too.'

'We may as well keep it downstairs,' said Ada. 'There's no point in having a new battery in a torch which is going to be kept in the loft.'

'It would be a wicked waste,' agreed Bertha. 'Put it in the hall, Violet dear; it will save us switching on the electric light.'

The diary was probably of greater interest to Charles than to Harold, for the good rector was intrigued with the view of Thrush Green and Lulling seen through the eyes of a man doing the same work a century earlier in much the same surroundings.

He was as much impressed as Harold with the portrait of the man which emerged. He took a lively interest in his natural surroundings, his parishioners, and also in wider issues such as the conditions of the workers in industry, the might of the British Empire and the uneasy state of Europe.

Charles was interested to see his predecessor's comments on new scientific discoveries, but noted, too, how steadfastly he set his face against anything which, in his opinion, threatened the teachings of the Church. He spoke scathingly of spiritualism, and deplored the use of such toys as ouija boards, and the gatherings of people at seances, in attempts to get into touch with other worlds.

Across the years he spoke to Charles as a friendly, highly intelligent and thoughtful man. He possessed an intellect, Charles recognized humbly, far in advance of his own. But one thing they shared in common. They did indeed love their God.

It was Nathaniel's letters which gave Harold the most acute joy. Just to touch those frail pieces of paper, and to know that Nathaniel's hand had rested where his now lay, gave him a feeling of kinship and exquisite pleasure.

The diary had given only the briefest hint, now and again, of the strong bond between the two men: a father-and-son relationship as well as true friendship, for Octavius was some twenty years older than Nathaniel, and was also in a position to help the younger man, not only with his wisdom and advice, but also with regular and generous donations, as the accounts showed.

Occasionally, there had been a wistful and fatherly comment in the diary.

Only God can understand my grief at N.'s determination not to take Holy Orders. But N. is a fine young man, and God guides him as He does me. We are in His hands.

Nathaniel's letters threw more light on this vexed question. To Harold's disappointment, he soon discovered that a great many of the letters were missing. There were references to earlier matters, and it was clear, from the carefully dated relics, that only about a third of the letters were remaining.

From these, however, it was plain that Nathaniel grieved as sorely as his benefactor about his inability to enter the Anglican Church.

Your unfailing goodness to me [he wrote in 1895] *is my constant support and inspiration. It makes my seeming opposition to your wishes, in the matter of taking Holy Orders, doubly painful to me, and I should be a happier man if my conscience would allow me to follow your dictates. As it is, I know that you understand my feelings, and will not allow this basic difference to injure the friendship we share under God's blessing.*

There was no mention of Nathaniel's marriage, either, in the remaining letter nor, strangely enough, in Octavius's diary, but later letters mentioned his dead wife, and the little daughter whom he proposed to send to friends in England for her education.

As a murky January drew to its close, Harold and Charles realized that there would be very little more to be discovered about the long-dead friends.

All that remained now, they agreed, was to choose a fitting tribute to honour two fine men of Thrush Green.

6. Hard Weather

February came in with the same dismal clammy weather which had held sway throughout January. But after the first week, the weathervanes spun round to the north-east, and a vicious wind tossed the bare branches of the chestnut trees on Thrush Green.

It was during this bleak spell that Winnie Bailey was admitted to hospital, for the various tests had shown that it was, as suspected, gall bladder trouble, and surgery would, after all, be needed.

Speculation on the outcome of the operation was rife at the Two Pheasants.

Albert Piggott told Percy Hodge that, in his opinion, no one was ever the same again.

'My old uncle what was gamekeeper up Nidden was on slops for the rest of his life. Rice pudden, mashed potato, drop of broth – that was all he could take.'

Percy was unimpressed. 'My Gladys,' he replied, naming his present wife, 'says it don't make a mite of difference having your gall bladder out. Some bits of us are real useless. Look at my appendix, for instance.'

But nobody appeared to be interested in Percy's appendix,

which perhaps was just as well because it had been removed years earlier.

Mr Jones, who rather fancied himself as a medical man, a sort of hedge-doctor, told the assembled company that you could blast gallstones into dust with a few shots of laser rays, but you had to be careful that they didn't damage the red corpuscles.

Blinded with such sophisticated knowledge the company dropped the subject of gall bladders and their treatment, but all agreed that Mrs Bailey 'would have to watch it' when she came out of hospital.

'If she ever does,' said Albert lugubriously. He liked to have the last word.

News of Winnie had reached, via Isobel Shoosmith, the two retired schoolteachers at Barton-on-Sea.

Loving messages had been despatched to St Richard's, and Interflora had been directed to send a flower arrangement to their old friend.

'I told them to send a *small* one,' Dorothy told Agnes. 'The right size for a bedside locker but smelling particularly sweet. Freesias, say, or carnations. I must say that the girl who replied seemed to understand what was wanted.'

'I'm sure she knows all about flowers for hospitals,' Agnes assured her.

'Well, I don't know about that! When I did my leg I had great towering bouquets of irises and gladioli, I remember, and the nurses were quite cross. They would keep falling over. The vases, I mean, not the nurses.'

Later that day Dorothy had a bright idea. 'Do you think Winnie would like a week or so here when she is convalescent? We could easily put her up, and the air here is so particularly good. It might be just the thing to pull her round.'

Agnes was delighted with the idea, and the evening was

spent in happy anticipation of entertaining an invalid in the good air of Barton-on-Sea whenever she felt ready to accept their invitation.

But just as Agnes's euphoria was at its height, a chance remark of Dorothy's as they made their way to bed caused it to plummet.

'By the way, I wrote a little note to Alan Lester yesterday, to see if I could be of any help in those centenary celebrations Isobel mentioned.'

Agnes said nothing, but once in bed her fears flocked round her like a plague of bats.

What might come of this? Why must dear Dorothy, for the best of reasons, of course, feel obliged to *meddle*!

Ella Bembridge struggled against an icy wind to pay a brief visit to Dotty Harmer's cottage.

The sky above Lulling Woods was ominous, the clouds low and a menacing grey. If that doesn't mean snow, Ella told herself, I'm a Dutchman.

She found Dotty, as before, at her kitchen table surrounded by papers.

'My word,' said Ella, 'you look as though you're halfway through that book of yours.'

'I don't know about that,' replied Dotty, thrusting her pen through her scanty hair. 'I'm getting rather tired of literary work.'

'Why? What's put you off?'

'I showed my manuscript to Harold, and he said that it wouldn't make one chapter, let alone a whole book, and he couldn't see any publisher taking it on. I said to him: "What about all those reviews talking about 'this slim volume' and 'a charming monograph of a much-loved father' and all that sort of thing?" But he still says it's not long enough.'

'So what will you do? Scrap it?'

'*Scrap it?*' squeaked Dotty indignantly. 'After all my hard work? Of course I shan't scrap it!'

'Well, it seems a bit pointless to carry on,' said Ella. 'Can't you pad it out somehow?'

'I do not propose to lower my standards for the sake of *length*,' said Dotty loftily, 'but I have had another idea. I have asked a number of old boys of the grammar school to write down their memories of my father, and I intend to incorporate them.'

'A splendid notion,' said Ella.

Dotty shuffled the papers before her with a claw-like hand. She looked perplexed.

'The only thing is that they all seem to dwell on Father's disciplinary side, and it makes him appear in rather a harsh light. I hoped they would discuss his fine mind, his interest in astronomy and photography. After all, he founded several scientific clubs at the school, and was most generous with gifts to the science side. I remember him handing over his own microscope and an auxanometer.'

'And what's that?'

'Well, dear, I rather forget, but I've an idea it measures the

growth of plants. Father was a great botanist as well as everything else. I must say, I am rather disgusted with these old
boys' narrow views.'

'Then I shouldn't use them,' said Ella stoutly. 'Just finish
your notes and publish them privately.'

Dotty looked more cheerful at this gleam of hope for her
cherished work. 'I am sure you are right, Ella. And now let me
make you a drink. Some of my lime-flower tisane, or a cup of
Nescafé?'

'I think Nescafé,' said Ella, who had tried Dotty's concoc-
tions too often for comfort.

A quarter of an hour later she left Dotty sorting out her
papers, and stepped out into the bleak world.

A few flakes of snow were fluttering down, and by the time she
emerged from the field path on to Thrush Green, a whirling mass
of snowflakes gave promise of a white world before morning.

From her hospital bed Winnie watched the snowstorm spreading a carpet of white and shaking the trees in the grounds.

It made a strange contrast with the over-heated room, heavy
with the mingled scent of flowers, floor polish and disinfectant.

On her locker stood the bouquet from Dorothy and Agnes,
and another from Jenny. More flowers lined the windowsills

and a side table, and Winnie thought how lucky she was to have so many loving friends.

Among other things on the locker top stood a glass screw-top jar containing a number of dark objects ranging in size from walnuts to peppercorns. Winnie had screened this from her own gaze by propping up a large 'get-well' card in front of it, for it was a gruesome reminder of Mr Philip Paterson's (St Thomas's) successful surgery a few days earlier, and Winnie felt she could not face its presence much longer.

Winnie's first impulse had been to beg her nurse to throw the lot in the hospital dustbin, but when several colleagues burst in to look at the jar with awe and delight, she felt unequal to the effort. When the surgeon visited her that evening she hoped that he would remove the revolting jar, but he was even more delighted than the nurses at the result of his skills.

'Do you think,' said Winnie faintly, 'that they could be thrown away now that I've seen them?'

Mr Paterson clutched the jar to him, as a mother might clutch her baby. 'But surely you want to take them home?'

The very thought sent a wave of nausea through poor Winnie, but as a doctor's wife she did her duty. 'I think you did a wonderful job,' she said, 'and I shall always be grateful. But I cannot have those ghastly things here any longer.'

Mr Paterson appeared astounded. 'Well,' he said, looking deeply hurt, 'I'll leave them where they were on the locker, in case you change your mind, and you can have a look later. After supper, say. I believe you are having a little fish soup tonight.'

He gave his usual comforting smile and departed.

Really a charming fellow, thought Winnie, and so conscientious with his night and morning visits.

Nevertheless, she resolved to get one of the nurses to dispose of the jar, and if she and the other girls complained of such ruthlessness it was just too bad.

As for Philip Paterson, he would have to endure the loss of his handiwork with all the fortitude of a true St Thomas's man.

The snowstorm raged for over twenty-four hours, leaving the Cotswolds in a white shroud.

The dry-stone walls surrounding the fields had disappeared beneath drifts, leaving vast expanses of unbroken snow, reminiscent of the steppes of Russia or the awesome wastes of Antarctica. The steep roofs were covered, and all the stone house walls which faced north and east were plastered with frozen snow. When the sun appeared, low on the horizon for about three hours of the day, it did little to mitigate the intensity of the cold.

In Lulling the main road was soon cleared, and those leading south to the coast and north to the Midlands had first attention. But Thrush Green and the lanes leading from it remained snow-covered for almost a week, and people were obliged to stay indoors until the thaw arrived.

This was no hardship for Winnie Bailey, now in her own home and relishing the comfort of her own bed and the ministrations of Jenny and John Lovell. She was making a steady recovery from surgery, and could potter about the house and help Jenny with a little cooking and cleaning, but she was surprised, and secretly ashamed, at the weakness which engulfed her every now and again, and realized that even if the weather had been kindly she could not have gone very far outdoors.

It was at times like these, she thought, that the telephone really came into its own. Friends rang to enquire about her progress; and among the enquiries was a welcome call from Dorothy Watson inviting her to stay at Barton when the weather allowed, and she felt strong enough to face the journey.

Gazing at her snow-filled garden through the window, at

the sagging branches of the bare plum tree and the ancient cypress which Donald had planted, she felt a wild longing to see and smell the sea again.

'There is nothing I should enjoy more,' she told Dorothy. 'The very thought of it is wonderfully cheering. I shall look forward to it eagerly.'

'Then I shall get in touch again,' promised Dorothy, 'as soon as it's possible to travel.'

After a little more exchange of news Dorothy put down the telephone.

'She would like to come,' she told Agnes, who had just emerged from the bathroom with her newly washed hair tied up in a towelling turban.

'Perfect!' said Agnes.

And when Jenny brought Winnie's supper to her that evening she stood and surveyed her with considerable satisfaction.

'You look a lot stronger,' she told her. 'Turned the corner, as they say. What's done it, do you think?'

'The thought of seeing the sea again,' replied Winnie. 'And, of course, good friends.'

The number of children at Thrush Green school was almost halved during the worst of the snowy weather.

For two days the school bus was closeted in its garage, and the pupils from outlying parts were joyful prisoners in their homes. There were quite a few children who lived closer to the green, but were equally imprisoned by high drifts between their homes and the school.

Added to this was a spate of winter coughs and colds which kept children indoors, and John Lovell busy on his rounds. His usual car was sealed in the garage for three days before he and helpers could dig it out, but his brother-in-law, the architect Edward Young, lent him his Land-Rover during the worst of the weather, so that the patients who needed attention urgently could be visited.

As soon as it was possible to get about again, Charles Henstock paid a visit to Harold Shoosmith.

'It was about fixing a date for our celebration,' began Charles. 'Alan Lester tells me that his school was opened formally in August a hundred years ago.'

'That's rather early for us to think of combining our festivities, if that's what you had in mind.'

'I agree,' said the rector, 'but the *official* opening of the school, he has discovered, was on 20 September of that year, and that makes things seem easier.'

'Is he agreeable to sharing festivities?'

'Indeed he is! And so am I, but how do you feel? I know you want to give full honours to Nathaniel and Octavius. Would you mind if we combined?'

'Not at all,' said Harold sturdily. 'In many ways it will make everything better. After all, we are all part of Thrush Green, young and old, alive and dead. I'm all in favour of one great day we can share.'

'Well, I must admit that I am relieved,' confessed Charles. 'You've worked so hard at your researches into the history of our two friends that I didn't want your efforts to be overshadowed by the school's celebration.'

'I'll have a word with Lester if you like,' said Harold. 'What would be best, do you think?'

'Late September seems the obvious choice, doesn't it? The new term will have begun, and the weather should be fine for outdoor affairs.'

And so it was left.

The next day Isobel invited Alan and his wife to have a drink and discuss the matter, but their two little girls were among Thrush Green's juvenile patients, and the invitation was reversed, so that the invalids need not be left alone.

Margaret Lester greeted them affectionately. The little girls had left their beds and, clad in nightgowns, called their greetings over the landing handrail.

'Now get back quickly,' ordered their mother, 'or those coughs will start again, and you don't want any more of Dr Lovell's cough mixture, do you?'

'Is it as bad as that?' queried Harold, as the two children vanished.

'I believe so. Ruth Lovell told me that John never dreams of taking his own cough mixture. But to give him his due, the stuff does seem to work.'

It was very snug in the schoolhouse sitting-room. The log fire crackled, the red-shaded lamps gave a warm glow, and the drinks gave an inner one.

The matter of a date for a joint celebration was soon under discussion, both men being very careful to respect the other's wishes.

'The only rough plan I've made so far,' said Alan, 'is to have the minimum of activities outside. I've had too many occasions washed out during my teaching days, and now I settle for something indoors.'

'Very wise,' said Harold. 'I'm sure our own ideas will match that. In any case, I think a celebratory memorial service in the church is in the rector's mind, and I'm sure that will be the chief part. After all, both men were churchmen first and foremost.'

'Miss Robinson had the bright idea of a day in the school as it might have been a hundred years ago. We've a pretty good idea of the timetable, and the children will enjoy dressing up. We could even have the cane in evidence!'

'I wonder if it was used much,' mused Isobel.

'According to the first log book,' Alan told her, 'it was kept pretty busy on one or two of the older boys who would far rather have been out in the fields.'

'No doubt the farmers could do with them,' commented

Harold. 'And a few extra coppers would be welcome in any farm labourer's home, from all I can gather. Octavius's diary gives a glimpse of rural hard times. Some of those fellows must literally have been worked to an early death, as one or two records show.'

Alan began to turn over the leaves of a calendar. 'Now, I think you said that the mission station was opened on 1 October. That's a Thursday. It would fit in with school affairs very well.'

Harold felt greatly pleased. He had secretly hoped that the exact date of Nathaniel's mission-opening would be kept, but having agreed to cooperate with the school's centenary he had been quite prepared to give way.

'It would give me great pleasure,' he told Alan, and despite the formality of the words, it was apparent to all present that he felt enormously grateful.

'We'll be present at the service, of course, as a school, I mean,' went on Alan, 'and I shall make a point of telling the children all I can about the lives of the two men. I just wonder, though, if we could have a real Thrush Green beano at that time, on the green itself.'

'We'll think about it,' said Harold. 'As you say, the chief part of the celebrations will be under cover, but we ought to be able to risk at least an hour or two for a general jollification outside.'

The date having been provisionally fixed, the talk grew more general.

'I must say there seems to be a lot of interest in these affairs,' said Alan. 'Our Parent-Teacher Association wants to take part. They'll be very useful in the dressing-up side of my project.'

'And someone said that they thought we ought to try to raise some money to buy something – a tree, perhaps,' said Margaret.

'No doubt Charles will put a note about it in the parish magazine and get ideas from people,' said Isobel.

'By the way,' said Alan, 'I had a letter from Dorothy Watson offering to help with any school festivities.'

'Oh!' said Isobel and Harold at the same time, and with an identical tone of apprehension.

'Very kind,' said Alan firmly, 'but I shall turn down the offer as politely as I can.'

Relief was apparent on his guests' faces, but no further comment was made, and before long the party broke up.

Some days later Dorothy Watson read out a letter to Agnes as they sat at breakfast in Barton-on-Sea.

'Just listen to this. From Alan Lester!'

Agnes felt a little shiver of fear. Was he cross? She put down her egg spoon and listened obediently.

Dorothy cleared her throat, just as she used to before addressing Thrush Green school at morning assembly.

Dear Miss Watson,

Your kind offer of help in connection with our proposed activities is very much appreciated.

As you may imagine, at this early stage we are still weighing up various possibilities, but I am quite positive about keeping things as simple as we can.

I look forward to letting you know our plans as soon as they are made, and of course you and Miss Fogerty will be among our most honoured guests.

Dorothy beamed across the table at her friend. Agnes felt relief flooding her.

'A very nice letter,' she ventured.

'And so sensible to keep things simple,' agreed Dorothy. 'I always felt that we had left the school in safe hands.'

Agnes took up her egg spoon again. She could not help but recall the doubts her friend had expressed vigorously about the headmaster who had been appointed in her place. Was he *competent*? Was he *understanding*? Was it *wise* of him to live at a distance, as he certainly did when he first took up the post? And above all, would he carry on the methods of his predecessor which had been so much valued by pupils, staff and parents alike?

Agnes had done her best to counter her headmistress's fears during those last hectic weeks of their teaching days, and had endured many private sufferings.

But now, sitting at the breakfast table, with Alan Lester's letter lying between them, was not the moment to remind her friend of those earlier misgivings.

Dorothy had gradually come to accept the fact that her school was safe in Alan Lester's hands. What was more, she began to feel considerable respect for the way he was coping.

And now he had written most kindly, appreciating her offer of advice and help, and promising to keep them informed. Better still was the thought of visiting Thrush Green school again, 'as honoured guests', and taking part in its festivities.

'I always liked that man,' said Dorothy, reaching for the toast.

'Me too,' echoed Agnes. 'He always struck me as *wise*.'

7. Comings and Goings

As so often happens when a perfectly simple project is planned, complications and difficulties arose.

The rector had put a short message in the parish magazine announcing the proposed date and the fact that it seemed appropriate for the two celebrations to combine.

The poor man at once received a number of notes and telephone calls pointing out that they – the writers and ringers – would be:

a) away from home
b) attending a much more important function in London or the county town
c) expecting confinements, visits from bedridden relatives, or proposing to enter hospital at the time stated.

Harold Shoosmith told him to 'let them get on with it'. But he, too, had his critics, and none more vociferous than Mrs Gibbons who lived far too near him for comfort.

The Gibbons were newcomers to Thrush Green and had embraced village life with a fervour unknown to the local population. They were soon enrolled as chairmen, secretaries, treasurers, and so on, of almost all the village activities, much to the relief and amusement of their lazier neighbours.

As Mr Gibbons was still working in some unspecified but highly important business in London, it was Mrs Gibbons who was more in evidence, although she was always keen to stress the support she had from her husband who, she hinted darkly, wielded power over a great many influential people in government circles.

Harold Shoosmith had secretly dubbed him 'Gauleiter Gibbons'; certainly when he did take charge of any village meeting he was as dictatorial as his spouse, and Harold always had the feeling that a banner should be waving behind him, and that the assembled company should rise, chanting, to its feet when the leader appeared.

Harold was unfortunate enough to encounter Mrs Gibbons one morning, as he was coming back from the postbox.

'Ah! Just the man I wanted to see!' she carolled.

Harold's heart sank.

'I believe you started this ballyhoo about the great Nathaniel,' she continued, with dreadful facetiousness.

Harold's heart ascended again. No one, and certainly not Mrs Gibbons, was going to denigrate Nathaniel in his presence.

'Of course, any jollifications should be put in charge of the Thrush Green entertainments committee, of which I am chairman.'

'I know,' said Harold.

'And as for the school's celebration, that of course should be a matter for discussion between the headmaster and the Parent-Teacher Association, of which again, I am the chairman.'

'I know,' repeated Harold.

'I've a mind to call on Alan Lester now, while I'm here,' said the lady sharply.

'He's just gone off to Cornwall,' Harold told her, with considerable satisfaction. 'School ended last week.'

'I'm quite aware of that,' snapped Mrs Gibbons.

'In any case,' Harold pointed out, 'things have hardly begun to move yet. All that has happened is plainly laid out in this month's parish magazine. So far, we've simply planned a date convenient to everyone –'

'How do you know it's convenient to *everyone*?' cried Mrs Gibbons, flushing pink.

'And announced the Sunday chosen for the combined service,' continued Harold equably. 'Now if you will excuse me, I must hurry home. I am expecting a telephone call.'

No doubt the Gauleiter would hear all about this encounter when he arrived home from running the nation, thought Harold. Poor devil!

The ladies of Thrush Green had decked St Andrew's church for Easter, and its Victorian plainness was adorned with daffodils and narcissi on every windowsill, little bunches of violets and primroses arranged by the children at the foot of the font, and some magnificent hot-house lilies on the altar.

The Reverend Charles Henstock and the choir made their

entry by the west door that morning, and proceeded down the aisle to the cheerful strains of 'Christ is Risen', sung with great gusto by all present.

Winnie Bailey, standing in her usual place, thought what a joyful celebration Easter was. There were some lovely hymns, the spring flowers were doubly beautiful after the darkness of winter, and the time of the year was full of hope.

The sun, streaming through the east and south windows, threw shafts of coloured light upon the altar and the chancel floor. No one could truthfully say that the stained glass of St Andrew's had much to commend it, but in the general rejoicing of Easter it added to the church's ambience.

Charles would be busy today, thought Winnie, settling back to listen to the first lesson. This morning's service had been arranged for ten o'clock, enabling Charles to hurry back to St John's for Matins at eleven fifteen, in Lulling. Cold lunch for most of us today, she thought, rising for the next hymn.

The movement brought a wave of dizziness, and she was obliged to hold on to the pew until it passed. Please don't let me fall down in front of everyone, she prayed fervently! A twinge of the old pain made her grit her teeth, but within a minute or two she felt better again.

She started to sing with the rest of the congregation. Words by S. Baring-Gould, she noticed. Donald had had a great regard for the Reverend S. Baring-Gould.

> *On the Resurrection morning*
> *Soul and body meet again;*
> *No more sorrow, no more weeping,*
> *No more pain.*

Perhaps that's a good omen, Winnie told herself. I must cross my fingers!

But wasn't that rather inappropriate – pagan, even; omens

and crossed fingers in the middle of a Church of England festival?

Amused at her thoughts, the pain gone, Winnie raised her voice in praise.

Not long after this, when Thrush Green school was open again, a meeting for all interested was held to go through the suggestions put forward for the two celebrations.

The rector took the chair, and there were more people present than he had expected. Mrs Gibbons was in the front row, seated on one of the children's chairs, for the meeting was being held in the school.

One good thing about the venue, Harold Shoosmith thought to himself, was the fact that the school chairs were so ill-suited to the adult form that the business under discussion got done pretty smartly.

He himself had taken up a strategic and more comfortable position on one of the desk tops, which gave him more room for his long legs. Alan Lester, he noticed, had done the same, having relinquished his headmaster's wooden armchair to the rector on this occasion.

The first proposal to be put was that of combining the two celebrations – the centenary of the school in which they sat, and the centenary of the opening of Nathaniel's mission.

There was surprisingly little discussion on this point. Even Mrs Gibbons, who usually argued at public meetings as a matter of course, seemed to think that a joint celebration had much to commend it.

'Although,' she remarked in her ringing voice, 'with all due respect to our chairman, one wonders if these celebrations may not turn out to be rather too *Anglican*. We must keep in mind that there are a great many people who belong to other denominations. We don't want them to feel excluded.'

'I can assure you,' replied Charles Henstock patiently, 'that all will be invited. Certainly, I myself have approached the other church ministers in the area, and they are enthusiastic in coming to the church service here at St Andrew's, as well as the general celebrations.'

'Anyway,' boomed Ella Bembridge from the back of the room, 'it's a Church of England school, and dear old Nathaniel was an out-and-out Church of England chap, even if he didn't actually take Holy Orders, so what's wrong with bearing that in mind?'

There were general noises of agreement. The proposal to combine was put and carried overwhelmingly.

The rector gave plans and date for the church celebration, and Alan Lester outlined his idea for a Victorian day at the school. There was great enthusiasm for the latter, and several people offered articles of apparel, books and bric-à-brac which had belonged to Victorian forebears.

Alan Lester was plainly delighted at this response and, striking while the iron was hot, said that he would be looking for volunteers nearer the time to help with the dressing of the children and general assistance.

There was a buzz of offers and conversation became general. The rector, quite accustomed to this sort of thing at village meetings, waited indulgently for the gossip to die down before coming to the chief problem.

'Now we are all agreed on the general form of our festivities,' he began, 'which as I'm sure you have noticed will take place under cover. But it has been suggested that we might risk just one outside event.'

'In October?' said one.

'Best be a Saturday then,' said another.

'That's right. It'll be dark around six.'

'Weather's tricky then.'

Thus spoke the more pessimistic of those present, but there were several more optimistic voices raised.

'What about a tea party? Trestle tables and all that, like after the war?'

'Might be warm enough. Have to wear a coat, though, in October.'

'I reckon a tug-of-war would fit the bill.'

'They had a dance up Nidden one year, out in the open, with fairy lights and that in the trees.'

'But the wind got up, remember? Couldn't hear the band. That was one autumn, as I recollect.'

The rector, who had been noting down suggestions, waited, pen poised, for the tumult to subside.

When at last it did, there was a scuffling at the back and Gladys Hodge, the wife of Percy the local farmer, spoke up. She was much respected in the community, and the general opinion was that Percy, who had lost two wives and been turned down by various other ladies, suitable and unsuitable, had done very well for himself in this recent marriage.

Gladys had raised one hand to command the chairman's attention, and was nudging a pink-faced Percy with the other.

'My husband,' said Gladys, 'has a suggestion.'

Percy, much flustered, was pushed to his feet.

'Well,' he began, 'I know all about it being October and maybe cold or windy or too dark too soon, and all that caper, but what about 5 November?'

'What about it?' said one.

'That's Guy Fawkes, soppy,' said another.

'We're talking about 1 October, Perce.'

'I know, I know!' cried Percy doggedly, 'but what I'm saying is, we know everyone comes to Bonfire Night and we all has a rattling good time, even if it is dark, and the fire keeps us warm if it's cold, and the kids love it as much as us old 'uns, and I'll be pleased to give the potatoes to bake in the ashes, for this occasion, just like I always do for Guy Fawkes.'

At this he sat down abruptly on to his uncomfortable chair, and there was a murmur of general approval.

Mrs Gibbons was heard to say that *two* Bonfire Nights were surely too much.

'Can't have *too much* of a good thing,' said Ella loudly, 'and I think it's a grand idea.'

It certainly seemed to please those present, and the rector put Percy's proposal to the meeting. All hands, it seemed, were raised, and the rector thanked Percy for his inspired suggestion, and for the generous offer of baked potatoes which, as was customary, would be cooked by the boy scouts, if that would be all right with the scoutmaster.

He, unfortunately, was not present to clinch the matter.

'Gone to his auntie's funeral.'

'Fell off a ladder and bust his collarbone.'

'Goes to Morris dancing every Wednesday.'

These were a few of the explanations given for the scout-master's absence. As a matter of fact, he had completely forgot-ten about the meeting, and was lime-washing his henhouse ready for the summer.

The rector promised to get in touch with him, thanked everyone present, and the meeting drew to a close.

'Come and have a drink,' said Harold to Charles as the gathering broke up.

'I should like that,' said Charles. 'I find meetings rather tiring, I must say.'

'You're a first-class chairman,' Harold told him as they walked next door to the Shoosmiths' house.

'Oh, no, indeed!' protested Charles. 'I fear I let people talk too much.'

'That's why I say you are a first-class chairman,' repeated Harold. 'And just right for Thrush Green. Everyone goes home happy. In your place I should have got through the business in half the time, and made a host of enemies.'

He pushed open the front door, and Isobel was there to welcome them.

In the same week it was Isobel who drove Winnie Bailey down to Barton-on-Sea to spend a few days with her old friends Dorothy and Agnes.

Dorothy had offered to fetch Winnie in her Metro, but Isobel pointed out that it would be simpler if she could bring their visitor, as she, too, would like to have a few breaths of sea air.

Privately, she felt that Winnie would have a more comfortable and peaceful journey in her Audi, for she herself seldom spoke when she was at the wheel, and she knew that Dorothy kept up a loud monologue, accompanied by waving hands, which could tire and alarm a nervous passenger.

Agnes had prepared a delicious lunch of chicken and ham with pineapple, in a creamy sauce, which was followed by sherry trifle. Replete, the ladies sat in the sunny sitting-room with their coffee, and exchanged news.

Tim, the cat, sat purring on Winnie's knee, and Isobel remembered the trouble his advent had caused between the two old friends. Dorothy had set her face against Agnes's adoption of the stray at first, but Agnes had been so seriously upset that the animal had been accepted into the household, and now, as is the way with cats, quite obviously ruled the roost.

Observing the two friends, looking so relaxed and happy, Isobel recalled another crisis in their lives when Dorothy had become greatly attached to a Barton neighbour. Agnes had confided in Isobel that she was afraid that Dorothy was pursuing this attractive widower with the hope of matrimony. It had been an unhappy time for poor Agnes, envisaging her own search for a new abode should her friend's hopes materialize and the bungalow they shared become a love-nest for the mature pair.

Fortunately, Teddy had fallen for the charms of another local lady, and it was apparent, from the cheerful way Dorothy spoke about them, that her romantic notions had vanished. Dear me, thought Isobel, what a nuisance love can be!

The news from Thrush Green was eagerly welcomed, and the plans for the school's Victorian day much praised.

'As a matter of fact,' asserted Dorothy, 'I had much the same idea in mind when I offered any help I could give to Alan Lester. We had a charming letter from him,' she added.

'Well, I hope you will stay with us for the celebrations,' said Isobel. 'And we'll make sure that you see all your old friends. It's going to be a great event.'

They all took a turn by the sea in the afternoon, relishing the blue skies and blue sea, and the promise of summer ahead.

Isobel set off after tea so that she could make her journey back in the light.

The three friends waved her off, and Isobel felt sure that Winnie was in safe hands.

It was a beautiful drive back: first through the New Forest, hazy with the new green leaves of spring, then through the rolling Hampshire countryside as she went north.

The crops were beginning to spring, clothing the fields with tender green. Celandines starred the banks in the sunshine of late afternoon, and small birds darted across the road, trailing dried grass or the odd feather, as they busied themselves with their nests. The hawthorn hedges were showing their first red shoots, and soon the copses on either side of the road would be misty with bluebells.

April, thought Isobel, had its charms, and also its hazards. The clear sky above her might well presage a frost tonight. Her favourite month was May, when blackthorn blossom made snowy drifts in the hedgerows, and wild cherry blossom lit the woods.

She looked forward to the garden blossom too: the white cherry hanging its snowy fringe along the branches, the plum trees scattering their pale confetti, and later the rosy knots of apple buds on the trees planted in their garden by some long-dead owner.

As she drove, the look of the countryside changed gradually. The flint and brick cottages with their thatched or tiled roofs began to give way to the stone-built buildings of the Cotswolds, their steep gables silhouetted against the now-darkening sky.

The lights were beginning to glow from windows at Thrush Green when Isobel ended her journey.

She shivered as she stepped from the car. The Cotswold air was sharper than that at Barton-on-Sea, and frost might well touch them here tonight. She noticed a plume of smoke rising from the chimney of her home, and felt a surge of pleasure at the thought of an evening by the fire.

Perhaps, after all, April was a perfect month. It combined the outdoor joys of spring and the equally enjoyable pleasure of the domestic fireside. Her favourite month was still May, she told herself, but meanwhile she would be very content to take all that April offered.

Later that evening, stretched out by the welcome fire, their feet on footstools, Harold and Isobel exchanged the news of the day.

'And to see the sea again was a bonus,' added Isobel when she had described the old friends' welcome, and Winnie's pleasure at seeing them again. 'I wish we were nearer. Nothing can beat a walk on the sands, or on a cliff top.'

'My walk,' said Harold, 'was much less exciting. Just along Lulling High Street to get some half-inch screws. Still, I did bump into the Lovelock sisters.'

'And what were they doing?'

'Going into the Fuchsia Bush for their lunch, I gather. We

had quite a gossip. They were very good about lending me that pamphlet of their father's.'

He began to look rather uneasy, and cleared his throat before speaking again.

'I thought – er – I wondered if it might be nice to invite them up for tea one day.'

'Nice for whom?'

'Oh, come on, darling! Don't be awkward. I just felt we should do something about them as they helped me with that essay about Octavius.'

Isobel smiled forgivingly. 'They can come, but you know how I feel about those dreadful old harpies. We shall have to hide all the bits of silver from their beady eyes.'

'Oh, and I saw Charles. He and Dimity are going to a concert at the Barbican.'

'Good heavens! How dashing of them!'

'Robert Wilberforce has invited them. Evidently he's down in London for a day or two on business.'

'I hope Charles isn't thinking of driving. Parking's bad enough in Lulling, let alone London.'

'No. They're going up by train, he said, and Robert is meeting them at Paddington. I'm so glad for them. They get away so seldom. They seem really excited.'

'Well,' said Isobel, yawning. 'I think it's bedtime. It's been a long day, and I've a lot to do tomorrow.'

'Don't forget to ring the Lovelocks,' Harold reminded her.

'I'm not likely to forget that,' Isobel told him tartly.

8. Plans Go Ahead

As the summer term progressed, preparations for Thrush Green school's centenary celebrations started to take shape.

Few preparations were necessary for the school's part in the church service, or in the general joint celebrations, in which it would participate with even greater fervour, one suspected, but the Victorian day at the school needed more particular care.

Alan Lester called upon the Parent-Teacher Association to co-ordinate the plans. It was as well, he thought, to get the formidable Mrs Gibbons on his side without more ado, and in any case it was only right and proper that they should take an active part.

Many of the parents were old pupils. Some grandparents were, too, and although of course, there was no one alive who could remember the school as it was in 1892, there were a number who had heard their own parents and grandparents talking of their schooldays. This sense of continuity in a small community touched Alan Lester deeply.

He was delighted at the general enthusiasm for the idea of a Victorian schoolday when he spoke to the assembled company one evening.

Mrs Gibbons, in the chair, occasionally raised a query, but
he felt it was more as a way of reminding them all that she
was in charge, rather than from a genuine desire to alter the
arrangements.

'The daily timetable for that period,' Alan told the gathering,
'is clearly set out in the first log book, and I have left it open
on the desk, in front of Mrs Gibbons, so that you can have a
look at it later.'

Mrs Gibbons tapped the stout volume in a proprietorial
manner. 'Only *three* at a time,' she said. 'Otherwise it will be
difficult to study it. And *after* these proceedings, of course.'

'Of course,' agreed Alan, giving her the smile which disarmed
even such dragons as the present chairman.

'The biggest problem,' he went on, 'is finding the right
furniture of the time. There were long desks for six pupils
then, and of course most of them vanished long ago. I have
discovered a couple at Nidden school which closed some time
ago, and I think we can borrow them.'

'There's one in my dad's garage,' said one mother. 'He
bought it off of the chap as was at the sale years ago.'

'And the chapel's got a couple in the back kitchen,' called
another. 'They keeps the tea urns and china and that on 'em.'

'They did have one up the cricket pavilion,' said a third, 'but
some kids got in and scandalized it one night. Daubed paint
on it. Might be all right if you could get the paint off of it.'

'This is marvellous news,' exclaimed Alan, turning the smile
on Mrs Gibbons, who had begun to tap her pencil vigorously
on his desk to draw attention to the fact that questions were
not being addressed to the chair.

One would have imagined, thought Alan, still smiling, that
any chairman in Thrush Green, or any other village community
for that matter, would be quite resigned to the general conversation which took over proceedings every now and again.

'I must say, *through the chair*,' he said, 'how grateful I am for these suggestions. I shall follow them up, and if anyone has any news of other contemporary school fittings I should be delighted to hear about them. If not, we might get some made.'

Mrs Gibbons smiled graciously and the pencil stopped tapping. 'Now, about clothes,' she said briskly. 'Mr Lester has pictures of the sort of thing the children would have worn then. The Misses Lovelock have kindly lent some old family photos. They are on the wall there. You might like to study them when you come, *three at a time*, to see the log book.'

'The urn's bubbling,' said someone. 'Shall I make the coffee?'

A look of exasperation passed over the chairman's face, but she spoke patiently. 'Very well. Better perhaps to have our refreshments now, and we can clear everything away before looking at the display material.'

Within five minutes there was a cheerful racket of gossip and coffee cups, and Mrs Gibbons turned to Alan Lester, who was now sharing the desk with her.

'All going very well, I think,' she commented.

'Very well indeed,' Alan agreed sincerely.

Although the Henstocks' trip to London had been generally noted and approved by the residents of Lulling and Thrush Green, it was some time before Harold and Isobel heard the details of that memorable evening.

They were sitting in the Shoosmiths' garden one balmy evening of early summer enjoying the scent of pinks in the border and the sharp fragrance from the Albertine rose on the wall.

'Beautiful music,' enthused Charles. '*Real* music, you know, Haydn and Vivaldi, or one of those thumpy bits from Handel that you ought to know and never do.'

'It was Bach, dear,' said Dimity. 'And Robert took us to a very good Italian restaurant just off the Strand. So welcoming the owners were. A family concern, with Papa and Mama, and

I should think Grandpapa in that basket chair, wouldn't you, Charles?'

'Definitely,' agreed Charles, 'and such delicious food. It really was a great treat for us.'

'And so nice to see Dulcie Mulloy again,' added Dimity.

'So she was there,' commented Isobel, refilling glasses.

'Yes, she works in the City and met us at the restaurant.'

'By the way, Robert had more news of the Fennel family. You know that our Octavius's money came from the Lancashire cotton trade originally?'

'Yes, I remember. We wondered if he might feel guilty about it.'

'He was looking up a name in his local directory in the Fs, and came across some Fennels. He was talking to his doctor a day or so later and he told him that quite a few wealthy Fennels retired to the Lake District. One of the survivors was one of his patients, who lived in a hideous Victorian mock-castle built by one of his rich forebears near Windermere.'

'How extraordinary!' exclaimed Harold. 'And are they related to our Octavius? It's an unusual name.'

'Robert went to see him. Yes, he is vaguely related, I gather. He's in his nineties, a bachelor, very frail, and living in part of the old house. He was most interested in all Robert had to tell him.'

'Had he ever met Octavius?'

'No. But his father had visited Octavius several times and thought a great deal of him.'

'And what about the other Lake District Fennels?'

'Distantly connected evidently, but no contact. Different generations, and not in touch with the old man Robert met. He wants to be kept informed about our celebrations. I wonder if we should invite him?'

'Would he come? He sounds rather past travelling,' said Harold.

Charles nodded thoughtfully. 'Nevertheless, I think I will send him an invitation when I get round to sending them out. Incidentally, I have sent a copy of the parish magazine to Nathaniel's African mission station, to show them that we are celebrating their opening.'

'Good!' said Harold. 'It all sounds very exciting, and your evening was a fruitful one. What was the journey like?'

'Very simple, thanks to Robert. He met us at Paddington and took us back there after the concert. I fear we must have taken him out of his way.'

'You see,' explained Dimity, 'he insisted on taking Dulcie home to her flat in north London, after dropping us off. She said she could easily go back on the Tube, as she does every day, but Robert didn't like the idea. He was quite firm, wasn't he, Charles?'

'Indeed he was! He said he thought that women should be escorted home safely, particularly after dark. He was rather anxious about Dulcie on our first meeting at the vicarage, you may recall, because she had to set off rather late.'

'I well remember,' replied Isobel.

It was agreed that the invitations should go out early.

'It's amazing,' said Charles, 'how quickly one's diary gets filled, and after all 1 October will soon come round.'

There were not many personal invitations, for everyone in Thrush Green and Lulling had been apprised of the date and of the welcome awaiting them at the celebrations.

But Robert Wilberforce, as the person who had discovered the letters and the diary, headed the list, and Dulcie Mulloy, as a direct descendant, came next, and the aged and unseen Mr Fennel in the Lake District was also invited, and a few others.

Harold himself wrote to the head of the mission station and hoped that he or anyone else interested might be able to make the journey to join them, and offered hospitality in his own home. But somehow he doubted if anyone from so far away would undertake the trip.

The question of raising money for a modest memorial to the two men had been discussed. Charles, from the first, had felt that the offerings on the Sunday nearest 1 October should be used for such a scheme, and it had been decided to plant two trees, one for Nathaniel and the other for Octavius, as part of the celebrations.

It was a chance remark of Alan Lester's, some time after the Parent-Teacher meeting, which made Charles and Harold wonder if more could not be done, and when letters arrived from the African mission station, the three men met at the Shoosmiths' to make some plans.

'I suppose I set the ball rolling,' confessed Alan. 'I let the children send a card to the children at the mission school, telling them briefly about our festivities here. I had a long letter back from the head there, and he asked us to write regularly.'

He put a packet of leaflets about the project and the letter on the coffee table in front of them.

'I've had these, too,' said Charles, handling the leaflets, 'but my letter came later separately.'

Harold had also received a letter from the mission's head. 'They don't feel that they can send anyone on the day in question, as they will be holding their own celebration, of course, but when the head gets leave later he will come and see us, he says.'

'What's quite apparent,' said Alan, 'is their own centenary project of adding a room to the present school so that they can admit younger children. Can we afford to send them something towards that?'

'It's a nice idea,' commented Harold. 'Let's have a really rousing fundraising effort.' He looked at Charles.

'It is indeed,' said the rector thoughtfully, 'but I felt from the start that we shouldn't look upon this affair as a money-making project. That's why I sincerely hope that the church offerings on that Sunday will cover the cost of the two trees, and in any case we can supplement the sum from the Free-Will offering fund, if need be.'

'I think everyone appreciates that,' agreed Harold, 'but nevertheless I have had one or two people offering a contribution if we are collecting funds. Robert Wilberforce for one. He says that he has had such pleasure in being involved with this fresh slant on the lives of Nathaniel and Octavius. There will be others.'

'Mrs Gibbons,' added Alan, 'I suppose I should say the Parent-Teacher Association, wants to give something to the school to celebrate the centenary, and we proposed to have a bird bath in the playground. But there might possibly be some money over.'

'I think the best thing to do,' said Charles slowly, 'would be to leave it to individuals to do as they please. No pressurizing. Perhaps a note in the parish magazine, and a box in the church and elsewhere for any donations? Let's see what sort of response we get, and we can decide then about any help towards the new schoolroom.'

'I think that's wise,' agreed Harold. 'But there's just one thing. I feel that any cash given to our own school should remain for the school's needs. If parents like to give to the boxes or at the church service, well and good, but we must not lose sight of our own centenary.'

And on this note the informal meeting broke up.

Thrush Green looked at its best in the summer, thought Winnie, looking from her front garden across the expanse of green to the Two Pheasants.

Mr Jones had six hanging baskets full of geraniums, lobelias and fuchsias adorning the front of the public house. In the great tub by the front door a blaze of petunias showed up against the background of creamy Cotswold stone. Winnie recalled the Christmas tree with its twinkling lights which had stood there in December, and remembered, too, how wretched she had felt with her internal troubles.

Now she felt as bonny as Mr Jones's flowers, she told herself. The sun was warm on her back as she leant over the gate. To her right the Youngs' house glowed in the dazzling light. Sunshine brought out the warm glow of the local stone; winter weather seemed to turn the buildings to a duller shade, and skies were overcast for far too much of the year for Winnie's comfort. Sometimes she looked back to the fresh charms of the holiday at Barton, and wondered if she would like to settle by the sea one day. But she knew, in her heart, that she would never leave Thrush Green.

A scarecrow figure came into view across the green, preceded by a King Charles's spaniel on a long lead. Obviously, Flossie and her mistress, Dotty Harmer, were taking a little exercise.

Winnie walked across to meet them.

A toddler was sitting on the grass beside a young girl. Winnie recognized them as part of the large Cooke family, noted in the district for fecundity and a distaste for orthodox matrimony.

But the pair were charming, Winnie thought, greeting them. They were busy making a long daisy chain. The little boy stumbled towards the blossoms starring the grass, collapsing unsteadily beside his protector (sister, mother?) while she threaded them industriously together.

They were both fair-headed, chubby-cheeked and exuded robust health. Donald had always admired the toughness of the Cooke tribe, Winnie remembered, giving as its reason 'a fine mixture of blood'.

They smiled at Winnie as she spoke to them, displaying splendid teeth which Winnie envied.

Flossie now bounded forward, at the extreme end of her long leash, and began to lick the child's face.

'Ah! Dear pussy!' cooed the boy. 'Nice pussy!'

He attempted to feed the excited dog with a fistful of daisies.

'It's a *dog*, dear,' said Dotty approaching. 'Not a *cat*.'

The child smiled disarmingly. 'Pussy!' he repeated.

'No, dear,' persisted Dotty, who disliked inaccuracy. 'You can tell by the coat. A cat has *fur*! This dog has *hair*.'

'He don't know no different,' explained his sister (mother?). 'He calls all of 'em "Pussy", even our tortoise, and Perce Hodge's cows.'

'Ah well!' said Dotty indulgently, 'he is young yet.'

The two old friends entered Winnie's garden and sat down to enjoy a rest and the scent of summer flowers. Bumble bees fumbled at the velvet lips of the snapdragons, and a blackbird foraged busily for fodder in the border.

'Tell me,' said Winnie, 'how is the book getting on?'

Dotty sighed. 'I am finding it very heavy going. Ever since Harold Shoosmith said that it was too short I have felt rather low about it, and as I told you, the accounts about my father from former pupils at the grammar school are really rather disappointing. At times I found them *scurrilous*. I mean, we all know that he saw no harm in correcting a boy, but I am quite sure that some of the writers *exaggerated* the physical discipline he imposed. I really *cannot* include some of their accounts, and I fear there may be jealousy if I use some and not others.'

Winnie doubted this, but simply offered sympathy with Dotty's problems. 'I should give up the idea of getting a publisher to take it,' she advised her. 'Much better to write the whole thing yourself, no matter how short it seems, then get it printed privately. Better still, turn it into a decent-length article for a local paper. It would reach the readers who knew him and would be interested.'

Dotty nodded. 'I must confess,' she admitted, 'that I was so looking forward to a bound copy of my work, but I suppose I must give up the idea. Life is full of disappointments I find, particularly as I get older.'

'Cheer up,' said Winnie. 'Come and choose a lettuce. We've so many that half of them have bolted.'

'Could I have them for my hens?' cried Dotty, literary disappointments forgotten. 'The dear girls love lettuce, and I could easily have a few of the good leaves for my lunch, and not rob you of a perfectly good lettuce. I was brought up to be *frugal*, you know.'

'You are to have the very best lettuce I can find for your lunch,' said Winnie firmly, leading the way to the vegetable garden. 'Let the hens practise frugality with the bolted ones.'

The fine weather continued, and one hot day succeeded another.

On one of these sunny evenings Harold Shoosmith had a telephone call from Robert Wilberforce. He sounded excited.

'I called on my friend Frederick Fennel today,' he said. 'He is delighted to be invited to the festivities, but is afraid he is not up to the journey. He has written to Charles, I gather. But that's not all.'

'How d'you mean?'

'He was a boy when Octavius died in 1912, but his father was evidently in Thrush Green, staying with Octavius a year or two before that, and he attended the interment of Nathaniel. Octavius took the service. This must have been in 1910 or 1911.'

'I'm amazed. Was it Octavius who had the body shipped back from Africa?'

'It was indeed, according to Frederick's memories of his father's account. Octavius got in touch with Dr Maurice at the mission station, and the body was treated with aromatic drugs and spices – embalmed evidently, and with great skill by the Africans – then shipped home to Bristol. It was winter when it arrived, and Frederick's father stayed longer than he expected at Thrush Green rectory, because there was heavy snow. In fact, there was snow still on the ground when Octavius took the funeral.'

'I find this very touching,' said Harold, looking across the sunlit green to the churchyard, and envisaging the black and white winter scene so many years ago.

'I thought you would be interested,' said Robert. 'It has been wonderful to talk to the old boy, and the celebrations have really given him as great an interest as they have us. I wish he could make the journey, but frankly it is out of the question. Still, as you can see, his mind is as clear as ever, even if he is frail of body.'

They talked a little longer, then Harold returned to Isobel in the garden, and told her all about this further evidence of Octavius's affection for his younger friend.

'It's a sad story,' said Isobel. 'Poor Octavius, standing in the snow by the grave of a friend.'

'It reminded me of the burial of Mozart in a snowstorm,' replied Harold. 'All the mourners turned back, they say.'

'Well, Nathaniel had some mourners,' comforted Isobel, 'and a private grave, not the common pit that Mozart was thrown into. When you think about it – the shipment home, the decent burial, the sincere grief and the respect that came to both men – it makes a heartening story, not a tragic one.'

And Harold, seeing the wisdom of this, agreed.

At Thrush Green school preparations for the Victorian day were going ahead with all the excitement and set-backs that usually accompany a school project.

Some of the ancient desks had been tracked down and were to be delivered to the school in good time for 1 October. Only the chapel people were slightly less obliging as Bright Hour took place on the Tuesday preceding the great day, and the desks would be needed to support the chapel china and tea urn as usual. However, Mrs Jones, wife of the landlord of the Two Pheasants, said that she would see that the two desks were brought up after Bright Hour, and woe betide any person who stood in her way.

Alan Lester had no doubt that Mrs Jones would be a reliable assistant in his endeavours, and concentrated on the many other aspects of the celebration.

As might be expected, the question of costume was the biggest headache. The girls were quite excited and co-operative about their attire, bringing various garments for approval and comparing notes on length of skirts, the necessity for aprons, shawls and so on. It was the boys who were awkward and self-conscious.

'We shan't half look clowns,' Alan heard one say.

'Soppy idea,' agreed his companion. 'I reckon I'll stay home that day.'

It was Bill Hooper who saved the day. The biggest boy in the school, and acknowledged king of the playground, he had also been included in a local junior football team when a player had fallen ill at the last minute. Consequently, Bill was something of a hero, and due deference was paid to him by his companions.

When the question of the boys' costumes cropped up, he casually mentioned that his grandfather, a tailor in Lulling, was making him a Norfolk suit for the occasion.

An unusual hush fell upon the classroom, much to Alan Lester's amusement.

'It's a bit of tweed I chose myself,' went on Bill, amidst stunned silence. 'The gamekeepers over Nidden way used to have suits of it in the old days. That was before the place was sold. My grandpa always helped to make their suits.'

'I should like to see it,' said Alan. 'It should look very well on you.'

'If you like,' went on Bill, flattered by the attention, 'I'll wear it to school one day, before October, I mean.'

'Splendid!' said Alan. 'And that's enough about our costumes. Take out your atlases.'

From then on there was little complaint from the male members of the school. In fact, there seemed to be mild enthusiasm as spotted neckerchieves and Eton collars were discussed, and the chance of getting someone's hobnail boots was debated.

All in all, Alan thought, the school was getting truly involved with this portrayal of school life as experienced by their grandparents and great-grandparents in this self-same building, and when Miss Robinson and the young probationer were heard to say that they proposed to wear stockings *with garters* instead of their usual tights, he felt assured of the complete success of the great day ahead.

9. Getting Ready

Summer that year was long and very hot, interspersed with violent thunderstorms which flattened much of the corn. Nevertheless, the farmers had an early harvest in a dry spell, and were hard put to find anything much to grumble about.

As she dressed one August morning, Winnie Bailey looked across the green to the distant fields towards Lulling Woods. In some the golden stubble still gleamed, but already the ploughs had been at work in neighbouring fields, although the corn had only been collected, it seemed, a day or two earlier.

There were plenty of young pheasants about but, looking at the distant stubble fields, Winnie remembered how plentiful the native partridge had been when she had come as a young bride to live in this same house. Now that the fields had been cleared, sometimes fired, and so quickly ploughed or drilled ready for the next crop, the number of partridge had dwindled. Such a pity, thought Winnie, who had always had a soft spot for these squat plump little birds. She had been told that they mated for life, and that they were exemplary parents. Winnie approved of both constancy and family commitment, and regretted the demise of such charming birds.

She leant from her window to survey the green. It was the

time of day which she most enjoyed, particularly at this stage of the year, when dew was heavy and spangled spiders' webs shimmered on the hedges. Soon there would be mushrooms and blackberries about, and the sharp blue-bloomed sloes which Donald had enjoyed picking for the sloe gin he made every autumn. Soon, too, the conkers would be falling from the horse chestnut trees near by, and already a pale carpet made of the lime flowers and bracts lay under the trees by the church. Albert would not approve, thought Winnie.

As if on cue, the old man emerged from his cottage door, and stood in his shirt sleeves looking up at the sky, as if daring it to rain. Even at this stage of the day he wore his old greasy cap on the back of his head. Winnie wondered if he wore it at the breakfast table. Even in bed, perhaps?

She heard Jenny moving about in the kitchen and, idle conjectures shelved, went downstairs to join her.

With the school holidays in full swing, there was little that Alan Lester could do in the way of preparing for the school's part in the celebrations.

The timetable for the Victorian day had been devised and rehearsed for timing and effect. A number of relics had been collected, including several of the original desks and some splendid old photographs of classes of the 1890s which people had lent, and which Alan proposed to hang round the walls. It was interesting to see how many of the boys, and the girls, too, had close-cropped heads. Fashion, wondered Alan? Or, more practically, prevention of head lice? Possibly the aftermath of ringworm?

The girls all appeared to have worn white pinafores, black stockings and laced or buttoned boots. The boys' costumes were more varied: Norfolk jackets, jerseys with collars, coats and trousers obviously handed down from larger brothers, and here and there an Eton collar gleaming among the subfusc ensemble.

There were one or two ragged children to be seen, but on the whole, Alan thought, studying those long-dead faces through a magnifying glass, they appeared to have been a sturdy lot, toughened by plenty of exercise tramping to school and field work for the bigger boys whenever the local farmer was in need of extra hands.

Perhaps country children had always had a slightly easier life than their town contemporaries. Alan remembered his father telling him about barefoot boys, fighting over half a loaf, whom he had seen in the dockyard area of the city where he had lived as a child. In those bleak streets there were no apples to scrump, no blackberries on hedges, no young turnips to pull secretly from a field's edge, and too many sharp eyes looking to catch a wrongdoer.

Looking across the green from his study window, he could see his two daughters playing with their school friends by the swings near the church. All the children were laughing, their hair streaming in the wind, their teeth and eyes gleaming, their limbs straight and strong. They might have been a different race altogether from the crop-headed few who gazed from the old photographs.

Indeed, thought Alan, there were many reasons for celebration.

Down at Barton-on-Sea Dorothy and Agnes were also looking forward to the Thrush Green celebrations.

They were busy with jam-making, for their two plum trees, thriving in the hot summer, had produced a bumper crop, and although Agnes was not over-fond of plum jam, Dorothy had insisted on making as much as they could.

'It's so *useful* for bazaars and things,' said Dorothy, bustling about with jam jars and little waxed discs which fluttered to the kitchen floor in profusion. 'You know how pleased the vicar was with that redcurrant jelly I made. "Ruby red", he called it. "Ruby red, and a real jewel." I thought it most apt.'

Agnes, standing over a hot stove, doing her best to fish out plum stones with a spoon, to be deposited on an old enamel plate steaming near by, thought it was a jolly sight easier making jelly than trying to catch elusive plum stones, the present task, which Dorothy had allotted her. She did her best to put this unworthy thought aside, and Dorothy's next words helped a little.

'I always start thinking of the new school year at about this time,' said Dorothy, rescuing some jam-pot covers from the floor.

'So do I,' agreed Agnes.

'And I must say, I really relish the thought of not having to go back,' added Dorothy.

'I'd rather like to,' confessed Agnes, pursuing a particularly slippery stone. 'The new babies were so sweet.'

'You were always so patient with the newcomers,' said Dorothy. 'I must admit that I really could not have coped with the reception class – all those tears and trips to the lavatories. No, I like them rather more *mental* and a little less *physical*. What on earth is that cat doing?'

The two ladies suspended their operations to gaze down at Tim, who was under the kitchen table. To their horror they saw that the cat had his paw firmly on a small and terrified mouse.

'Timmy,' said Dorothy, in her headmistress voice. 'Take that thing outside.'

The cat growled.

Dorothy snatched up the washing-up mop, and bent down. 'Timmy, be *reasonable*!' she adjured the animal. 'We simply can't have a mouse in here, it's unsanitary.'

'*Insanitary*,' corrected Agnes automatically, 'and in any case Tim might get splashed with hot jam. And the mouse too, for that matter.'

Dorothy, red-faced, straightened up. 'This is no time for humanitarian nonsense,' she puffed. 'Let's just shoo both of them outside.'

She opened the door into the garden and Agnes, abandoning her jam, bent down to persuade Tim to relinquish his captive.

In true cat fashion, he strolled casually away to the open door, and the mouse fled to take refuge under the refrigerator.

'*Really!*' said Dorothy, much exasperated. 'How typical! Now we shall have the impossible task of getting that mouse out.'

Agnes took charge. 'I'm turning the heat down, and making us coffee. Leave the door open, dear, and it's bound to run out eventually. It's time we had a rest in the sitting-room.'

There was a thump at the front door, and Dorothy went to collect the letters.

By the time they were ensconced in the peace of the sitting-room, with their coffee and post, the friends were calm again.

'Look,' said Dorothy, holding up a card. 'It's a proper invitation to the school on 1 October.'

'I've one, too,' said Agnes. 'How nice of Alan Lester to send separate ones!'

'Very extravagant,' said Dorothy, taking a biscuit, but she sounded pleased, and they began to discuss their plans for the journey, and the all-important problem of *what to wear*.

Out in the kitchen a quaking mouse emerged from its hide-out and made a dash for the fresh air.

From his perch on the sunny rooftop of the garden shed,

Tim ceased to wash his paws and watched the mouse with a languid eye.

Really rather a bore, this mousing, on a hot morning.

The new school term at Thrush Green began in the usual back-to-school weather of cloudless skies and warm sunshine, causing much irritation to those who had spent a great deal of money taking a holiday on the rainswept coasts of this island or, even worse, at the far more expensive and even more weatherbeaten resorts overseas.

The first priority was, of course, the final preparations for the great day.

Alan Lester, as an experienced head teacher, had no doubt that all would go well on the day. He also knew that there would be untold hazards to overcome before the dawn of 1 October.

Bill Hooper, true to his word, appeared a week or two before celebration day resplendent in his tweed Norfolk suit. His schoolfellows were duly impressed, and he strode round the classroom amidst awe and admiration.

There was no doubt about it: Bill's unseen grandfather still knew how to cut and sew, and Alan blessed him for smoothing his path on this occasion, for although no other boy could aspire to such sartorial perfection, at least they all looked forward to parading in garments which they would have scorned before Bill's and his grandfather's initiative.

The girls had been enthusiastic about their dressing-up from the first. Alan and Miss Robinson had planned the general look of the rooms, and had been almost overwhelmed by the amount of bric-à-brac sent in by parents and well-wishers.

But a hindrance to progress had been Mrs Gibbons.

From the first, Alan had realized that her position on the Parent-Teacher committee would give her every excuse for interfering, and he was prepared.

It was unfortunate that the lady took to entering the school-room unbidden to make her suggestions and criticisms. Alan Lester knew, as well as she did, that any confrontation before the children put her at an advantage, and he was quick to point out that it was not convenient to discuss plans during school hours.

'I simply wanted to have a look at the *setting*,' protested Mrs Gibbons, waving a hand. 'I had an idea which I think could improve the early part of the proceedings. It concerns the piano, and the children marching to their places.'

'That is already arranged,' Alan told her, with one eye on two giggling girls at the back of the class. 'Miss Robinson and I have been into it thoroughly.'

'But have you chosen the hymns? I have been looking through *Hymns Ancient and Modern* and *Songs of Praise* –'

Here Alan led her firmly to the door.

'I really cannot discuss it now. I will telephone you after school and perhaps we can talk about things then.'

'We certainly will,' replied Mrs Gibbons emphatically, and went, seething, into the lobby.

There had been one or two other visitations, but on the whole she kept her attacks until after school hours. They ranged from strong disapproval of the sort of food the children would bring to school for their Victorian snack, to the fact that the whole school would go to the church service on the morning of 1 October.

'I feel quite sure,' she told Alan, 'that the chapel children would *never* have entered St Andrew's. It is quite wrong that they should go on this occasion.'

Alan explained, as patiently as he could, that this particular act of worship had nothing to do with the Victorian day celebrations, but was a contribution by the school – a Church of England school, he emphasized – to the general honouring of Nathaniel Patten and Octavius Fennel.

The lady, though still antagonistic, gave way grudgingly.

'It will be rather a relief,' said Alan to his wife, as he replaced the telephone, 'to get back to the humdrum of daily teaching when these celebrations are over.'

One morning towards the end of September Charles Henstock received a letter which gave him surprise and delight.

It was beautifully typed on crisp white writing paper and the address was embossed, something which the rector rarely saw these days.

It read:

Dear Mr Henstock,

I wish that I could accept your very kind invitation to the festivities at Thrush Green on 1 October, but ill-health prevents me from travelling.

My young friend Robert Wilberforce has kept me informed of the plans to honour Mr Nathaniel Patten and my kinsman the Reverend Octavius Fennel. I have followed the proposals with great interest, as you may imagine.

I understand that it is hoped to send a donation toward the building of an extra room at the African mission school, and should

like to contribute. Robert Wilberforce is attending your celebrations,
he tells me, and I shall entrust him with my donation then.
    I shall be with you in spirit on 1 October and feel sure that all
your endeavours will be successful.
                              Yours sincerely,
                                   Frederick Fennel

Half an hour later, Charles rang Harold to tell him about the
proposed donation.

'That's most kind of him,' said Harold, 'and will be very
welcome. I must admit, Charles, that contributions are not
coming in as I had hoped, despite your note in the parish
magazine.'

'I felt that might be the case,' said Charles. 'There are so
many claims on people's purses, and charity begins at home,
of course.'

'Naturally, and I believe that our school fund is receiving
more support than Nathaniel's, which, I suppose, is only to be
expected. I feel rather a fool, though, looking back at all the
high hopes I had of raising a goodly sum for Nathaniel.'

'Don't worry,' Charles said. 'There's still time.' But was there?

'By the way,' added Harold, 'a warning! Mrs Gibbons has a
new idea for adding to the glory of the great day, and may be
coming to tell you about it.'

'Oh dear!'

'Oh dear, it certainly is. She thinks it might be nice to have
large photographs of Nathaniel and Octavius propped up on
their graves in Thrush Green churchyard during the celebrations. The Gauleiter would be glad to make the enlargements
from the photographs we have.'

'The Gauleiter?'

'Sorry. I mean Mr Gibbons. Just my facetious name for him.'

'But I don't like the idea at all,' cried Charles pathetically.

'Neither would anyone else,' Harold assured him. 'I told her that she was trying to turn an English country churchyard into an Italian cemetery.'

'Oh dear,' repeated Charles. 'Was she offended?'

'*Very!*' said Harold, with intense satisfaction.

'Well, thank you for warning me. Now I am going to write to Frederick Fennel.'

'It's wonderful news,' said Harold, 'and I wish he were well enough to join us.'

Towards the end of September the wind turned from the quarter which had given the sunny clear spell, to the south-west.

Grey clouds lowered over Thrush Green, and although the rain that fell from them was welcomed by everyone, and particularly by the gardeners, it did not bode well for the day of celebration to come.

It grew chilly, too, in the evenings and Winnie began to look ahead.

'I'm getting my overseas Christmas parcels ready in good time this year,' she told Jenny. 'And we ought to think about having our flu inoculations, and checking the state of the coal cellar.'

'Well, I've done that,' Jenny told her. 'Summer prices for the coal. I don't know as I'm all that keen on a flu jab this year.'

'Now, Jenny,' began Winnie, in her doctor's-wife voice, 'I'm sure these jabs really help.'

'Nothing more than faith healing, I reckon.'

Winnie pondered on the comment. 'Faith healing or not,' she pronounced. 'I've never had flu really badly since I started them.'

It so happened that the next morning she saw John Lovell arrive, in driving rain, and hurry into the surgery. She slipped on a coat and hurried across the drive to catch him before his patients arrived.

It always gave her a feeling of comfort to enter Donald's old place of work. She approved of the familiar central table with magazines neatly set out in rows, the vase of garden flowers on the mantelpiece, and on the wall the photograph of Donald himself which John had placed there.

'Am I a nuisance?' said Winnie when John opened the door from the waiting-room to his surgery. 'It's just about making a date for a flu jab.'

'Never a nuisance,' John told her, turning over the leaves of a diary on his desk. 'What about a Wednesday towards the end of October?'

'I'd better let Jenny make her own arrangements,' said Winnie, watching him fill in an appointment for herself. 'She's a bit anti-jab at the moment, but I think she'll come round to the idea.'

'And how are you feeling? No after-affects of Paterson's work?'

'I had a twinge or two soon after the operation,' Winnie confessed, 'but they have been few and far between, and the last one was weeks ago.'

'It's probably just the internal scar healing,' said John, 'but would you like me to have a look? Better still, I could send you back to Philip Paterson if you're worried.'

'I honestly don't think it's necessary, but if I get any pain at all I promise to tell you.'

There were sounds of footsteps and voices, and Winnie moved towards the door.

'I mustn't keep you any longer.' She looked at Donald's photograph. 'I always liked that photo of Donald. He looks thoroughly pleased with life, doesn't he?'

'I think he was,' replied John seriously. 'He had a worthwhile job, lots of friends and a splendid wife.'

Winnie smiled at the compliment.

'It's good to have him there,' went on John. 'The old people like to remember him. As I do, too. He was always an example to me of what a good doctor should be.'

The outer door opened and a blast of damp air blew in.

'Dratted rain!' said a country voice, and Winnie hurried past the first of John's patients to regain her home.

Dorothy and Agnes set off for Thrush Green on the last day of September. They had been invited to stay at the Shoosmiths for a week, but Dorothy had decided that they should go back on the day after the celebrations.

'We both thought we should have time on our hands when we retired,' she explained to Isobel on the telephone. 'But as it is we seem to be always busy. We are giving a coffee morning in aid of the RSPCA on the Saturday, and I'm on the flower rota at church for that weekend, and Agnes has an appointment with the chiropodist, and that's how it goes!'

Isobel was sympathetic, and Harold, when he heard the news, was secretly relieved. Much as he respected their old neighbours, he found Dorothy's setting of the world to rights somewhat tiring, but he kept these thoughts to himself.

In truth, he had other worries. The rector's note about donations in the parish magazine had had little response. The amount for the annexe to Nathaniel's school was less than a hundred pounds, and although Harold proposed to add his own contribution, there was no doubt in his mind that the final sum would be insignificant.

He understood the position. Thrush Green school had prior claim, and Alan Lester would certainly have more than enough for the bird bath envisaged.

He realized now that he had been absurdly optimistic. In his enthusiasm for anything connected with Nathaniel, he had been over-ambitious. As a proud man he was now suffering secret humiliation, and it hurt.

However, he comforted himself, Charles was right. Charity begins at home, and that was as it should be.

*

The rain fell relentlessly, and Dorothy drove with the windscreen wipers working full time. In places there were floods across the road, and the rivers of Hampshire, Berkshire and Oxfordshire, which had dwindled dramatically throughout the long summer, were now being rapidly replenished and flowing with their usual speed and volume.

They stopped on the outskirts of Lulling, and Dorothy braved the rain to enter a florist's near the Fuchsia Bush in order to buy a magnificent hibiscus plant for Isobel.

Agnes held it carefully on her knees as they passed the familiar sights then climbed the steep hill to their old home.

'Stop the car for a minute,' cried Agnes. 'I must just have a look at dear old Thrush Green.'

Dorothy obliged, and turned off the engine. In the sudden silence of the car they became conscious of the outside noises.

Rain pattered on the roof above them. Drops dripped from Mr Jones's brave flower baskets, and little rivulets gurgled their way towards the hill which dipped to the town. The grass of the green looked soggy and the chestnut trees drooped with the weight of wet leaves.

'Dear, oh dear!' said Dorothy at last, breaking the silence. 'It's a sad sight. What will it be like tomorrow?'

'It will be absolutely splendid,' Agnes told her, undaunted. 'Rain or shine, we shall *celebrate*, and I don't care if it *snows*, Dorothy, as long as we're at Thrush Green.'

Smiling at such enthusiasm Dorothy started the car again and they splashed the few yards to their destination.

10. Celebration

Little Agnes Fogerty awoke during the night. By the clock in the Shoosmiths' spare bedroom she saw that it said ten to three and, as always at that time, thought of Rupert Brooke and honey, before making her way to the window.

Thrush Green glittered under a full moon which was hidden every now and again by ragged clouds which rushed across from the west. Puddles gleamed in the fitful light, and the trees tossed their branches, sending raindrops sparkling to the sodden grass. The windowpane was spangled with silver drops, but the rain itself had stopped.

Perhaps, thought Agnes, returning to her bed, this wind will dry things. In any case the bonfire should burn splendidly.

And with this comforting thought, she fell asleep again.

She was not the only person in Thrush Green to take particular note of the weather during the hours of darkness, and by morning there were very few who were not peering through windows, or standing in their gardens, assessing the chances of a dry day for the celebrations.

To be sure, things did not look very hopeful. The wind still roared in the trees, the puddles shivered under its onslaught, and Willie Marchant, the postman, was tacking back and forth uphill from Lulling against a powerful cross-wind.

But in the east the sky seemed lighter, and by nine o'clock a watery sun occasionally cast a gleam between the scudding clouds.

At the school the children were in a state of great excitement. Any departure from routine, as all teachers know, is welcomed by pupils and staff alike, and although the dress rehearsal had taken place on the Tuesday, amidst much general ribaldry about appearances of costume and demeanour, the actual day brought even more noise and disruption to the metamorphosed classrooms.

Alan Lester's command of his troops, however, ensured suitable decorum from all as they prepared to walk in twos across to the church at ten o'clock.

Charles and Dimity drove down together in good time, but Dimity's attention was divided between the ceremony to come and the lunch preparations she had left behind.

Dulcie Mulloy and Robert Wilberforce were driving down together from London for the service, and had been invited to lunch at the vicarage.

Harold and Isobel had also been invited, and as soon as Dimity heard that Dorothy Watson and Agnes Fogerty would be staying, they too were included in the invitation.

Had she forgotten to put sugar in the plum crumble? wondered Dimity, agreeing with Ella Bembridge that the wind had dropped a little. Should she have done a dish of potatoes? Men ate rather a lot, and Robert Wilberforce looked as though he ate heartily.

She took her place halfway down the church, and there was the sound of children being marshalled on the gravel outside the west door.

While they awaited the entry of the school children, Dimity cast an appraising eye round the congregation. St Andrew's was rarely as full as this. There was Winnie across the aisle, sharing a pew with Dotty Harmer and her niece Connie, and Connie's husband Kit.

Percy Hodge and his wife Gladys sat behind, and Dimity appreciated the fact that such a staunch chapel-goer as Gladys had come to this church to give thanks for the lives of Nathaniel and Octavius. What's more, thought Dimity, she has persuaded Percy to come, too, although she suspected correctly that Percy would be quite agreeable to go to any religious establishment if Gladys told him to, for Percy really had no religious convictions of any kind, as she well knew. Nevertheless, it was good to see him and many others of the same sort, coming to do honour to the long-dead, and on a Thursday morning, too.

In the front left-hand pew she saw Robert Wilberforce and Dulcie Mulloy. They had been ushered into this prominent position by Albert Piggott (now hovering by the west door to make sure that the children wiped their shoes), on the command of the rector of Thrush Green who had pointed out to Albert the importance of these two visitors to the celebrations.

At this point the school entered, looking both uncommonly devout and demure in its Victorian garb. There was a rustle of movement as people turned to watch them file to the pews at the right-hand front of the church, and Alan Lester, bringing up the rear, felt a glow of pride at his pupils' appearance and behaviour.

They had hardly settled when the organ crashed into a joyous noise, and the choir and vicar processed from the west door down the aisle, leading the congregation in the hearty singing of 'Christ whose glory fills the skies'.

How right, thought Dimity, to choose a hymn whose words were by Charles Wesley! It was well known that John Wesley had preached on the green outside this church, and commonly believed that Charles, too, had occasionally accompanied his more famous brother here.

The service continued, and Charles Henstock gave a moving address about the occasion. He spoke of the mission school so far away, and yet so close to their hearts. He reminded them of Christ's words quoted by Octavius Fennel: 'Suffer the little children to come unto me', and also the exhortation from Ecclesiasticus: 'Let us now praise famous men', which they were obeying today.

He also said how grateful they all were to Robert Wilberforce, whose public-spirited action in bringing Nathaniel's letters and Octavius's diary to light had made these celebrations possible, and had, moreover, been instrumental in bringing Nathaniel's great-granddaughter to Thrush Green to join in their rejoicing.

After the address all rose to sing:

> *Let us all praise famous men*
> *They of little showing*
> *For their work continueth*
> *And their work continueth,*
> *Broad and deep continueth*
> *Greater than their knowing.*

As they sang, the sun sent a few half-hearted rays through the windows on the south side of St Andrew's, and cheered all the congregation.

After the final blessing, the school children walked out first and took their places in the churchyard as rehearsed. The adults followed them, then came Dulcie Mulloy and Robert Wilberforce, each bearing a magnificent wreath which had been standing in the porch.

The gathering moved to one end of the churchyard where stood the graves of the two friends.

Some years earlier, the bulk of the tombstones had been moved to the sides of the graveyard, allowing easier use of the mower by young Cooke, and easier maintenance, such as it was, by Albert Piggott. But at one end of the churchyard grew several lime trees which drooped their branches over the line of graves by that wall, and it had been decided to leave those tombs undisturbed. Among them were those of Nathaniel and Octavius, and after a short prayer, Dulcie, as direct descendant, advanced to put her wreath on Nathaniel's grave.

Robert Wilberforce performed the same honour for Octavius Fennel, and the service ended.

The children were ushered back to school by the three teachers, ready for the next part of their anniversary celebrations, and their elders lingered by the church gate to discuss the service, the improving weather and, of course, the immediate news of Thrush Green.

Dotty Harmer, wearing a hat which could only have come from a jumble sale or charity shop, and might have been new in the 1930s, put a restraining hand on Winnie's arm.

'What a celebration! And I have a private one of my own.'

Winnie had a twinge of apprehension. What now? Had Dotty discovered yet another allegedly edible autumn fungus which she was turning into some fearsome comestible ready for distribution to her friends? She was already concocting a white lie about the delicate state of her digestion since the gall bladder operation, when she was relieved to hear that Dotty was talking about the biography she was writing about the formidable Mr Harmer, late of Lulling Grammar School.

'It's going to be *published*, my dear,' cried Dotty. 'Isn't that wonderful?'

'Wonderful!' echoed Winnie. 'Who has taken it?'

'The county magazine. You know, that thing that comes out monthly. It was Harold who suggested it. They are running a series called "Local Men of Influence", and the editor rang me himself.'

'But isn't it rather long for an article in a magazine?' queried Winnie.

'Yes, it is,' admitted Dotty, 'but he is going to suggest some cuts, and there will be a photograph of Father, and one of me at the top. The photographer came last week and spent *hours* snapping away at me in the garden. So exciting!' Dotty beamed like a child at the pantomime.

'Well, I'm absolutely delighted, Dotty. You've worked so hard, it deserves to be printed.'

'Such a nice young man, the photographer,' continued Dotty as they walked away from the church. 'No tie, of course, but he had one gold earring. I suppose he had lost the other, but when I expressed concern he only laughed. I gave him a pot of my strawberry preserve.'

'Oh, that couldn't hurt him,' said Winnie, and then thought that that involuntary cry of relief might seem a little tactless in the circumstances. However, she decided, as she walked alone towards her home, Dotty's present state of euphoria would protect her from taking umbrage.

At the school everything was ready for the influx of parents and friends. It was an Open Day from now on, and a number of local people came straight over from St Andrew's to enjoy the spectacle of a Victorian school.

The staff and children had achieved a wonderful transformation, largely by removing the colourful friezes and the other bright objects of modern education.

A blackboard propped on an easel bore the precepts, written in Alan Lester's best copperplate hand-writing:

> *Cleanliness is next to godliness.*
> *Do the work which is to hand.*
> *Obedience is a child's first duty.*
> *God watcheth over all.*

The bigger children were copying this work into lined exercise books using wooden pen holders with steel nibs. The younger ones were squeaking slate pencils on slate boards, or using sticks of chalk on individual blackboards about a foot square. These relics of the past had been lent by local museums and interested elderly friends who had dug them out of attics or dusty toy boxes, but one slate board, it was claimed by its owner, was still in regular use, propped in her porch, as a means of communicating with the tradesmen when she was not at home.

At twelve o'clock work stopped and the children took out the lunches they had brought from home. These they ate in the playground to save crumbs in the classroom, for only in very severe weather were the Victorian pupils allowed into the lobby during dinner hour. A pail of drinking water and an enamel mug by it stood on the lobby floor to supply drinks, for there was no piped water at Thrush Green at that time.

During the afternoon, friends of the school watched the infants creating a long chain of bright chrysanthemum flowers intended to hang around the neck of Nathaniel Patten's bronze statue outside on the green.

This was being created amidst great excitement (and some

frustration by those rebelling against their constricting Victorian clothes), like a giant daisy-chain, and was the children's own idea of paying tribute to the man who had loved children both in Thrush Green and Africa. Many a local garden had been raided for this garland, and the effect was stunning.

On a side table were displayed some of the toys which Harold Shoosmith had seen in the Lovelocks' loft. Some were Edwardian, such as the Russian egg brought back by Octavius, but there were two beautiful Victorian dolls which the sisters had inherited, a clockwork mouse and a child's wooden wheelbarrow. The Lovelocks' own dolls' house had also been sent up, for although it was not Victorian, it was in the fine tradition of 'baby houses' and a joy for the children and their parents to behold.

It was Harold who had mentioned the many trunks in the loft to Alan Lester. Would they hold untold treasures of Victorian clothes? A young and nimble friend of the sisters had been sent up to investigate for the school children, but there was nothing among the mouldering remains fit to wear, except a black straw bonnet, trimmed with jet, which none of the Thrush Green school girls could be persuaded to wear.

Along one wall were pinned the letters of the alphabet in capitals and small type, painstakingly executed by Miss Robinson over many an evening. This sight was greeted with much enthusiasm by the onlookers, which surprised the teacher, until she heard one mother remark to another:

'My schooldays coincided with a complete ban on teaching the alphabet, and I have a terrible time finding anything in the telephone directory.'

'I reckon the Victorians could teach us a thing or two about the three Rs,' agreed her friend.

While the school children ate their bread and cheese, or bread and cold bacon at Thrush Green school (supplemented, luckily, by a real school dinner soon after), there was a much more festive occasion being enjoyed at Lulling vicarage.

The same people who had been at the first meeting earlier, when Dulcie and Robert had been introduced to the Shoosmiths and Henstocks, had been invited to lunch after the service at St Andrew's. In addition, Dorothy and Agnes would be at this Sunday lunch.

The sun had emerged but the air was chilly with a hint of autumn on the way.

'But you must have a look at the garden,' Charles had said when drinks were over, and Dimity had departed to the kitchen to see about the dishing-up of lunch.

Obediently, the guests followed Charles into the garden, and indeed the flower borders were in fine form with dahlias, Japanese anemones, late marigolds, hardy fuchsias and Michaelmas daisies making a riot of mixed colours and attracting plenty of butterflies into the bargain.

'Now look, Agnes,' commanded Dorothy, stopping by a low rose bush, 'this is exactly what we need under the front windows.'

The company stopped to admire the plant, and various suggestions were exchanged about its name.

'Charles!' called Harold, but the vicar had hurried ahead with Dulcie and Robert to the greenhouse at the end of the garden. Speculation continued among the group left behind.

'My geraniums have been quite outstanding this year,' said Charles to his guests, when they were in the welcome shelter of the greenhouse. 'I came across a wonderful pelargonium called Aztec, and I've taken lots of cuttings, and I have put aside half a dozen for you.'

'How nice of you,' said Dulcie.

'You will need to keep them under cover through the winter,' said Charles, busy with pots. 'I know the Lake District can be very cold.'

'I have a small conservatory,' said Robert.

'And have you?' asked Charles of Dulcie.

'Well, no, but I shall cherish them on my windowsill.'

'In fact,' said Robert firmly, 'Dulcie will keep them in *my* conservatory.'

'Indeed?' said Charles, puzzled, as he looked from face to face, a flower pot in each hand.

'We are getting married in December,' said Robert, taking Dulcie's hand.

'Oh, my dears!' cried Charles, his chubby face growing pink. 'What news! What wonderful news!'

His hands were trembling with excitement, and Dulcie removed the flower pots from him and replaced them on the slatted bench. It was the same competent manner in which he remembered her dealing with a cabbage she was cutting up, as a child long ago, in her mother's kitchen in Wales.

'We became engaged last week,' Dulcie said, 'and first of all we thought of telephoning you, but it seemed so much nicer to tell you ourselves.'

'We owe so much to you,' said Robert. 'We met here first, you remember.'

'And we wondered,' went on Dulcie, 'if you would be willing to take part in the marriage service. It will be in my parish church, but our vicar is most enthusiastic about your taking part.'

'I should count it a great honour,' Charles told them. 'In December, you say?'

'I wish it could be next week,' Robert told him, 'but Dulcie has to go with her boss to a business conference in Boston, Massachusetts, at the end of November. Also she will be training her junior to take over her duties at the office, so I've simply got to be patient.'

'How I wish I could marry you here at my church in Lulling,' cried Charles.

'It would have been lovely,' agreed Dulcie, 'but you see Tom Evans, our vicar, has been so kind to me, and was marvellous with my mother all though her last illness and of course it is right that I should go to my own parish church –'

'Of course, of course,' Charles hastened to agree. 'And I shall look forward very much to taking part in the ceremony.'

At this point, his other guests arrived, agog with enquiries about the name of the rose which Dorothy admired. At the same time, there was the sound of a hand bell being energetically swung by Dimity who was awaiting her visitors.

'May I tell them?' whispered Charles to Robert and Dulcie, as they all trooped back to the house.

'Of course,' smiled Dulcie.

Dimity had prepared a lunch which needed little last-minute attention. She had made a chicken and asparagus quiche for the main course, with a side dish of sliced home-cooked gammon and hard-boiled eggs, and a vast salad. Late raspberries and cream were to follow, and she had also made a plum crumble which had cooked alongside the quiche.

The evening before, when the cold rain lashed Lulling and Thrush Green, Dimity had become concerned about her proposed meal. Wasn't it a little *bleak*?

She departed to the kitchen, leaving Charles to watch a television programme about inter-planetary warfare which might have appealed to prep-school boys, Dimity supposed, but which she deplored. Charles seemed to be entirely engrossed, and she left him while she made enough chicken soup for a dozen, let alone the eight guests expected, and later went to bed content with the knowledge that tomorrow's first course could stand up to any Cotswold cold which the day might bring.

It was while she was dispensing this nourishment that the vicar said:

'Before you take up your spoons, I must tell you of another cause we have today for celebration.'

The Shoosmiths and their guests looked at him hopefully. Dimity, too, looked expectant. Dulcie and Robert studied their steaming soup.

'You've remembered the name of that rose,' guessed Dorothy.

'You've had another wonderful donation for the mission school,' guessed Dimity.

'Better than that,' smiled Charles. 'Our dear friends here are to be married.'

A hubbub of congratulations broke out, and Dimity was beginning to wonder if the soup should be returned to the stove when Robert took charge and said:

'Thank you on behalf of us both. You can guess how much it means to us to meet again here and to give you the news.'

'Do you want to make a speech?' asked Dimity anxiously. 'I can easily reheat the soup.'

'He can make one when we toast them in my best claret during the next course,' Charles told her. 'I suppose we should really have champagne, but we don't have such a thing here.'

'I'm so glad,' said Agnes. 'The only time I had champagne it went straight to my forehead in an icy lump. I had to have a cup of tea to thaw it.'

But Agnes's sole experience of champagne created little interest in the face of this stupendous news of the coming wedding, and the rest of the meal passed in happy conversation about the couple's future plans.

Later, Charles took Robert aside to show him the letter which he had received from Frederick Fennel.

'Oh, this is Miss Fothergill's good work,' he said, studying the immaculate typing.

'Miss Fothergill? His secretary?' guessed Charles.

'Secretary, housekeeper and nurse, all rolled into one,' Robert told him. 'She's looked after him for years. I think he has left her everything in his will, and quite right, too.'

He gave a sudden start, and dropped the letter. His face was pink as he fumbled in his breast pocket and drew out an envelope which he handed to Charles.

'I almost forgot among all our excitement. Frederick asked me to deliver this personally.'

He bent to retrieve the dropped letter from the floor while the rector opened the envelope. There was silence while Charles studied the enclosure.

He looked up at last, and spoke huskily. 'He has sent a donation. An overwhelmingly generous one. For five thousand pounds. I can scarcely believe it. It will be such a relief to Harold. I know he has been grieving about the small sum we have been able to collect here.'

'Wonderful!' said Robert. 'But it doesn't really surprise me. He took such a great interest in hearing about the mission school and our celebrations. Miss Fothergill told me that he was so cheered by all that was happening.'

The rector looked suddenly diffident. 'I hope this won't make any difference to Miss Fothergill's future?'

Robert laughed. 'No difference at all. Frederick Fennel is an exceptionally rich man, and whatever he leaves Miss Fothergill will support her in the greatest comfort for the rest of her life.'

'I am relieved to hear it. Sometimes old people do odd things with their possessions.'

'Not Frederick,' Robert assured him. 'He has more sense in money matters than all the Bank of England directors rolled into one.'

'I am greatly relieved. Miss Fothergill seems an admirable person.'

'Miss Fothergill is worth her weight – and that's considerable, let me say – in gold. And when you come to visit us I will take you and Dimity to see Frederick and Miss Fothergill.'

'We shall look forward to it,' the rector told him. 'I shall write at once to Mr Fennel to thank him for this wonderful gift. I notice you talk of Frederick, and not Mr Fennel, so what is Miss Fothergill's Christian name?'

'I've no idea,' confessed Robert, 'and even if I knew, I should never dare to use it. Miss Fothergill is certainly a saint, but she's a dragon as well.'

Laughing, the two men went to join the others.

Later Charles drew Harold into his study and showed him the cheque. He had never seen his friend so moved. Harold's hands trembled as he held the cheque, and he spoke with emotion.

'It's unbelievable! What a relief this is, Charles! I've worried so much about it in these last few weeks, and now this means that we can really send something worthwhile to the mission. God bless Frederick Fennel, and I mean that sincerely.'

There was another shower of rain during the afternoon, and the people of Thrush Green began to look out mackintoshes and umbrellas for the evening's festivities.

'How sensible of Alan Lester to have an indoor event,'

remarked Winnie to Jenny, as they sipped their tea by the drawing-room fire.

'And Mr Henstock too,' said Jenny. 'That's one good thing about religious affairs – they're under cover.'

Winnie could not help feeling that this was a somewhat diminishing view of church festivals, but let it pass.

As it grew dark, activity increased on the green. Percy Hodge arrived in his Land-Rover with the sack of potatoes. The scoutmaster appeared with his troop who were to cook and distribute Percy's largesse, and Albert Piggott was seen tottering across from his house carrying a paraffin can in case the bonfire was sulky because of the night's downpour.

Luckily, the rain had stopped by the time the celebrations were due to begin, and although the wind was boisterous it was not as savage as it had been during the night.

Charles Henstock drove his party up the hill from Lulling, and met Harold, Isobel, Dorothy and Agnes walking from their house.

A great crowd was gathering, and even the three Miss Lovelocks appeared, having been transported by the local taxi.

'Cor!' said Albert to Percy. 'That must have hurt them old ducks, paying out for Bert Nobbs' old banger!'

'Shows how much they wanted to take part,' replied Percy with approval.

It had been agreed that the youngest scout should have the honour of igniting the bonfire. A diminutive figure, brandishing a flaming torch made from a fire-lighter tied to a long dry stick, leapt to his task and, to everyone's relief, the bonfire began to crackle and blaze.

By the light of the flames Nathaniel Patten's statue showed clearly. The children's garland encircled his neck adding a raffish touch to his Victorian garb. Alan Lester thought his pupils had made a very good job of this, their own idea, and felt a pang of pride.

He was there with his wife Margaret and their two daughters, among many other parents now in charge of their own excited offspring.

Suddenly the first rocket went up. It was Harold Shoosmith's suggestion that fireworks should add to the general rejoicing, and certainly there was something wonderfully exhilarating about the bangs and crackles, the whooshing and waving, the sparkle and whirling of innumerable lights against the blackness of the autumn sky.

There was constant movement, too, among the company as friends met and mingled, the scouts scurried about their cooking duties and the excited children scampered about enjoying the last few hours of this never-to-be-forgotten celebration.

It was ten o'clock before the fire began to die down, and the last Catherine wheel had slowed its whizzing to a stop. The potatoes had been eaten, the scouts congratulated, and the crowd began to straggle away as soon as the final 'Hip, hip, hooray!' had been raised by the rector.

The Lovelock sisters departed early, taken back to their home by Harold. Robert Wilberforce and his betrothed also set off before the last cheers, and there was much speculation about the pair as they walked across the green to their car, Robert's arm protectively around his companion.

Soon only the scoutmaster and his valiant troop remained. It was the scouts' duty to see that the fire was safe to leave, and very zealously they discharged their responsibilities. The fact that an occasional baked potato turned up was an added bonus.

Now that the flames had gone and only a dim glow came from the hot ashes, it was possible to see the stars shining above Thrush Green. The wind had dropped to a light breeze, hardly enough to rustle the leaves of the chestnut trees, or to stir the trailing geraniums in Mr Jones's hanging baskets against the stone walls of the Two Pheasants.

At midnight Harold Shoosmith was alone downstairs. His spirits were buoyant. How wonderfully well everything had turned out, after his worries! Isobel and their two guests had retired an hour earlier, tired by the excitements of the day. Tomorrow Agnes and Dorothy would return to Barton-on-Sea, and the household would be as usual again. Frankly, Harold would be glad of it.

But as well as relief, Harold realized that there would be a sense of anti-climax after the activity of the last months. The excitement of the search was over. The outcome had been deeply satisfying, but what lay ahead?

He opened the front door and walked down the path to the open stretch of grass where Nathaniel Patten stood beneath the night sky.

The air was cool. How often, thought Harold, must Nathaniel have longed for this cool freshness, as he himself had done, under the burning African sky?

These immediate surroundings had changed little since the time when Nathaniel had set out, as a young man, for Bristol, accompanied by his older friend, mentor and benefactor, the good rector of Thrush Green.

How many lives those two had touched! His own, for one. He had chosen to come to Thrush Green on his retirement because he revered the memory of Nathaniel whose work he had admired in Africa.

Here he had met Isobel and made her his wife. Here he had revived the memory of Nathaniel Patten and caused this statue to be raised. Pride in their most famous son had been rekindled in present-day Thrush Green, and the work of his mission in Africa honoured.

It was through Nathaniel's letters that the true greatness of Octavius Fennel, one-time rector of this parish, had been discovered. It was those letters and the rector's own diary which had inspired so many people to carry on the good work begun so long ago.

And Robert Wilberforce and Dulcie Mulloy would not have met but for Nathaniel Patten. It was a happy thought.

What was more, Nathaniel's mission could continue, thanks to good friends and, in particular, the generous and unseen Frederick Fennel. Celebrations at Thrush Green had been justified.

Harold looked with affection at his old friend. The garland around his bronze neck was fast withering, but his memory would stay fresh with all at Thrush Green.

The words which the congregation had sung that morning came back to Harold.

And their work continueth,
Broad and deep continueth
Greater than their knowing.

Far away and close at hand, thought Harold, that was true.

He returned home, closed the door, and went, greatly content, to bed.

THE YEAR AT THRUSH GREEN

To Beryl and Ray
with love

January

Snow had fallen, snow on snow,
Snow on snow.

Christina Rossetti

The snow came on Twelfth Night.
Dusk was thickening over Thrush Green, and the lights in the nearby High Street at Lulling were already flickering into action.

The first flakes fluttered down so sparsely that Winnie Bailey, the doctor's widow, thought that the last pale leaf was floating by from the wisteria by the front door, as she drew the curtains against the bitter cold which had gripped Thrush Green for days.

Near by, at the most beautiful house in this Cotswold hamlet, Winnie's neighbour, Joan Young, hurrying in from the garden, caught sight of a pale fragment descending slowly. A feather, she wondered, or a particle of ash from a recent bonfire? Somehow she, in common with other Thrush Green residents, gave no thought to snow at that time.

Only Albert Piggott, the gloomy sexton at St Andrew's church on the green, realized what was falling, as he shuffled back to his cottage close by.

'It's begun,' he told his cat, as he unwound the muffler from his skinny neck. 'There'll be a foot of the dratted stuff before long.'

*

Albert Piggott had been expecting snow for weeks. So, for that matter, had the rest of the community, but they had waited so long for its arrival that when at last it came, on that bleak January evening, it was barely noticed.

The gripping cold had taken hold early in December, and the general talk had been about a white Christmas. The children everywhere were full of hope. Old sledges had been dug out from lofts, garden sheds and garages, dusted and oiled and put by to await a white world which failed to materialize during the whole of the Christmas holidays.

The school at Thrush Green had opened for the spring term the day before those first tentative flakes had floated down.

Alan Lester, the headmaster, heard the children's bitter comments with mixed feelings of sympathy and amusement.

'It's not *fair*!' cried one six-year-old. 'I was going to make a snowman.'

'So was I. My dad give me an old pipe for it. And a cap.'

'I'd got my sledge oiled up lovely, to go down the slope to Lulling Woods,' grumbled a third.

'Well,' said Alan reasonably, 'you can play with all those things after school. Or on Saturday, for that matter.'

'It's not the *same*!' wailed another child. 'You need *all day* to play in the snow!'

Clearly, there was going to be no comforting of the younger generation in the face of such injustice.

Alan Lester ushered them from the playground back to the warmth of the classroom.

His charges did not appear grateful.

It had snowed intermittently throughout Twelfth Night, but only an inch covered the iron-cold earth by morning.

But the sky was covered with dark grey clouds, and there was an ominous stillness everywhere as though the world awaited something menacing.

Joan Young, well muffled against the cold from woolly hat to wellington boots, crossed the corner of the green to take some magazines to Winnie Bailey, who welcomed her.

'No,' said Joan, 'I won't come in, but I'm going down to Lulling and I thought I'd bring back anything you needed. Don't go out, Winnie, it's so slippery.'

'Well, you are kind! I remember Donald always said that if the wind came from Oxford or Woodstock it was time to get in the potatoes and an extra bag of flour.'

'The wind's certainly going to be there soon,' agreed Joan. 'Shall I get those potatoes and the flour?'

Winnie laughed. 'It might be as well. Then we can withstand the siege if need be.'

She watched her neighbour returning to her house, leaving black footprints in the new snow. Shivering, she returned to the warm kitchen, where Jenny, her maid and friend, was chopping onions.

'Onions keep the cold out,' said Jenny.

'We shall need a good supply then,' Winnie forecast.

Equally prudent residents of Thrush Green and Lulling were also stocking their larders.

Across the green, opposite Winnie Bailey's house, Harold Shoosmith and his wife Isobel were making a shopping list while coffee cups steamed near by.

The Shoosmiths were relative newcomers to Thrush Green. Harold had arrived first, some years earlier, a single middle-aged man of handsome appearance, recently retired from a post abroad.

He was a lifelong admirer of a former Thrush Green resident, one Nathaniel Patten, a missionary in Africa who had formed a school there and been greatly loved by all who met him. Nathaniel had long been dead when Harold came across his good works, but his influence still flourished in the African settlement, and when Harold discovered that a house in

Nathaniel's birthplace was on the market, when he was house-hunting, he quickly put in his bid, and soon found himself living happily at Thrush Green.

Next door to his house was the village school, and the headmistress at that time was a competent woman, Dorothy Watson, who lived in the schoolhouse with her friend and fellow-teacher Agnes Fogerty.

All three were good friends and neighbours, and it was through Agnes that Harold eventually met his wife Isobel. She had been at college with Agnes, and the two had kept in touch throughout the years.

When she came to stay at Thrush Green with her old friend, Isobel was recently widowed. The friendship which sprang up between Harold and Isobel flourished, grew warmer, and led to an exceedingly happy marriage, to the delight of their friends at Thrush Green.

It was Harold who had instigated the setting-up of a fine statue of Nathaniel Patten on the green. He had been shocked to find that so little was known about the Victorian missionary who had done so much good overseas, and he set about educating his neighbours.

Harold's enthusiasm had been infectious, and now the memory of one of Thrush Green's most famous sons was a source of pride in the community, and his statue and memory greatly revered.

This morning a sprinkling of snow spattered Nathaniel's head and shoulders, and a noisy family of starlings squabbled on the white ground around him. Near by, the children's voices, as noisy as the starlings', had suddenly ceased.

'Alan's getting the children in,' commented Harold, looking at the kitchen clock. 'I'll get down to Lulling before things get too busy.'

He went to wrap up well before crunching his way to the garage through the bitter cold.

*

An hour later, his shopping done, Harold pushed open the door of the Fuchsia Bush, Lulling's most notable restaurant in the High Street.

Harold was not a frequent visitor to this establishment, but he was so cold that he felt that a cup of coffee would thaw him before he visited the bank and the local building society, the last duties to perform before driving home.

The Fuchsia Bush was warm and welcoming. Coffee was provided promptly, and soon the ample form of Nelly Piggott appeared from the kitchen bearing a tray of scones hot from the oven.

She greeted Harold with affection. 'Nice to see you, Mr Shoosmith. Parky today, isn't it?'

'That's putting it mildly,' said Harold. 'May I have one of those delicious scones? I can't resist your cooking.'

Nelly beamed at the compliment, and Harold wondered, yet again, how such an attractive woman as this buxom one before him could ever have taken miserable Albert Piggott for a husband.

It had always been a mystery to Thrush Green, this marriage of two such opposites. Even Charles Henstock, the much-loved rector of Thrush Green, had doubted if the marriage would last.

In fact, it was the Fuchsia Bush which had rescued that marriage from the rocks some years earlier. Nelly had always been a first-class cook, and had very little chance to use her skill when catering for Albert. He suffered from peptic ulcers, and Nelly's use of cream, butter, plenty of sugar, honey and golden syrup did nothing to help his digestion. It was a happy day for her when the owner of the Fuchsia Bush appeared on Nelly's doorstep to ask if she could help at the restaurant while the cook was ill.

This had led eventually to a thriving partnership between Nelly and Mrs Peters and to the Fuchsia Bush gaining a name in the neighbourhood for delicious food.

To Nelly it was her whole life. She set off for work every day in the highest of spirits. The kitchen at the Fuchsia Bush was her kingdom, the compliments from customers balm to her spirit. Nelly was probably the happiest worker in Lulling, and even Albert's gloomy company could not quell her new-found ebullience.

'And how's Mrs Shoosmith?' asked Nelly, putting a plate before him. 'Had her flu jabs, I hope. They say this new flu's a real killer.'

'Months ago,' Harold assured her, spreading butter.

'Good,' said Nelly. 'Well, I must get back to the oven. I've got some brandysnaps in at the moment, and you know how quickly they catch.'

Harold did not, but watched her bustle away to her duties.

As he put the car away in the garage, he saw his friend and neighbour Edward Young emerging from his house.

'I was just coming to see you,' called Edward.

'Come indoors,' said Harold, but Edward, who always seemed to be in a hurry, refused the invitation.

'It's about the fête,' said Edward, banging his gloved hands together to keep warm.

'But that's not till July,' protested Harold.

'I know, I know! But the fact is that we are trying to plan a holiday while young Paul's home from school, and I don't want to be tied down this year with fête arrangements. Could you possibly have the administration side at your house?'

'No bother at all,' replied Harold. 'You go ahead and leave the fête to me this time.'

Edward clapped his friend rather painfully on his shoulder. 'That's a great relief. Terribly grateful, old boy. Must dash now. I've got some urgent posting to do, and I want to get back by the fire pretty soon.'

'Don't we all,' agreed Harold, turning home.

By midday a vicious little wind had sprung up. It threw a spattering of dead leaves against the window of the Youngs' house where Joan was watering a bowl of early hyacinths.

She looked across the garden, and saw the branches of a lime tree tossing in the wind, and its last few leaves being swept away.

She heard the slamming of the back door, and her husband's voice, and went to greet him in the kitchen.

He was standing with his back to the Aga, rubbing his cold hands together. Molly Curdle, once Molly Piggott, daughter of Albert, was rolling out pastry at the kitchen table. She and her husband Ben Curdle lived in a cottage which the Youngs had converted from their stables for Joan's parents, now both dead.

Molly had started working for Edward and Joan when their son Paul was a little boy. She had taken him for walks, played with him, bathed him and put him to bed. The bond between them had strengthened over the years, and although Paul was now away at boarding school, it was Molly he rushed to greet first on coming home.

'Wind's getting up,' commented Edward. 'And due north-east too.'

The sky grew darker. Black clouds gathered ominously, swept along by a bitter and relentless wind. Dead leaves, twigs and a couple of paper bags eddied across Thrush Green, now airborne, now dashed spasmodically along the ground.

There was a howling in the trees in the garden, and an even more intense roaring in the avenue of horse chestnut trees outside the Youngs' house.

By three o'clock the snow was whirling across the scene, blotting out the view of St Andrew's church and the wind-tossed trees surrounding it. It was a wild and fearsome land-scape, suddenly devoid of human figures. Joan Young, watching from her windows, thought of arctic wastes, of the cruelty of nature and of man's sudden diminution in the face of weather extremes.

But, as she watched the fury of the blizzard sweeping across Thrush Green, she saw signs of humanity.

From the school on her right a few small figures emerged, as two cars drew up at the gate. The children were bundled up in coats with upturned collars and hats pulled down over their ears, and some had long scarves round their necks, tied crosswise round their swaddled bodies to form a bustle at the back. They clambered into the cars, and drove away through the whirling maelstrom, out of Joan's sight.

Soon, she knew, others would be collected, and for the few

who lived along the lane to Nod and Nidden, no doubt, kind and conscientious Alan Lester would act as taxi-man in his own car. The numbers at Thrush Green school did not warrant a school bus.

Shivering in the draught from the window, Joan crossed the room to add logs to the fire. She reviewed the food situation as she went about her duties. Had she forgotten anything vital should the snow keep them penned indoors?

Bread, flour, potatoes, root vegetables and all those things which her old friend Donald Bailey had advised his neighbours to get in, once the wind had taken up its unwelcome quarter in the north-east, she thought she had remembered. But it was other vital things which invariably escaped the memory. Salt, sugar, the special Frank Cooper's marmalade which Edward so much relished – all these, in the past, had been casualties of the demands of emergencies, and no doubt would be again sometime.

The wind howled in the chimney, and every now and again there would be a sharp hiss from the logs on the fire as a snowflake descended to a fiery death. A particularly violent gust sent a puff of smoke into the room, and Joan went across to pull the curtains against the bitter world outside.

It was almost dark, and one or two lights were showing in the houses round the empty green. The children had gone, though the lights showed in the schoolroom. Normally, Betty Bell from Lulling Woods arrived to clean up at about this time, but Joan doubted if she would be able to make the journey in such conditions.

She drew the heavy velvet curtains together, grieving for any living thing that had to endure that world behind the windows, and thankful that she had warmth and shelter and, she hoped, adequate provisions under her own roof.

The violent wind continued to batter all in its path until the early hours of the morning.

Then it died down, but still the snow fell, thickly and silently, for the rest of the night. It was still coming down when the first grey light appeared.

Harold Shoosmith woke to see the strange light upon his bedroom ceiling, and knew at once what caused it. He slipped from his bed and went to look upon the white world of Thrush Green through the snow-spattered window. Behind him his wife Isobel still lay in sleep.

The view was awe-inspiring in its strange beauty. Snow had drifted in the fierce winds into fantastic shapes of varying depths. The statue of Nathaniel Patten close by wore a deep skirt of snow, covering the base and extending halfway up the plinth. Nathaniel's shoulders wore a cape of snow and his head a round white cap.

The railings of St Andrew's church were engulfed and the oak tubs, which stood each side of the doorway into the Two Pheasants hard by, were also hidden beneath a snowy blanket. Swirls and hillocks, gullies and valleys, banks and little cliffs stretched in every direction. It was an arctic landscape which Harold viewed with mixed wonder and fear. What damage, he mused, would the Cotswold world discover when the short hours of daylight finally arrived?

He looked down upon his own front garden, now a smooth white sheet of snow covering path, flower beds and lawn. Only the tops of the gateposts broke that surface, and brought home to the watcher the necessity of getting downstairs and finding a spade for a good deal of hard work.

At that moment, Isobel sat up and stretched her arms.

'Well, what's it like?'

'Siberia! But superb,' said her husband.

Later that morning there was plenty of activity on Thrush Green, as Harold and his neighbours set out to clear their paths to the road.

It was a Saturday, so the school was empty, but Alan Lester was hard at work, digging with the rest to clear the access to the schoolhouse which was next door to Harold's home.

Occasionally they stopped to rest on their spades, their breath blowing out in small clouds in the frosty air.

'I've asked the Cooke boys to give me a hand with the playground,' said Alan surveying the vast waste behind them. 'I only hope we don't get more tonight.'

'How did you get in touch? Are the phones still working?'

'Luckily, yes. But Albert Piggott says they're sagging dangerously across to Lulling Woods.'

'Well, you know Albert!' commented Harold, looking farther along the road to where the bent figure of the sexton of St Andrew's was plying a stiff broom.

'Always looking on the bright side,' agreed Alan, with a smile.

They returned to their labours.

Turning over this brief exchange as he made his arduous way towards the gateposts, Harold thought of his old friend Dotty Harmer who lived at Lulling Woods. Would she be engulfed? The house was in a lonely spot, and years before, he remembered, in just such weather, he had collected a rescue party to fetch the old lady on a sledge.

That, of course, was when she lived there alone. Things were better now, for her niece Connie and her husband lived with her, and would look after her.

Nevertheless, Harold promised himself that he would telephone Dotty as soon as he went back to the house.

'Coffee!' called his wife from the window.

And thankfully Harold set aside the spade.

At the Youngs' house there was equal activity. Ben Curdle and Edward Young had cleared a pathway between their houses, and Molly was already in the kitchen of the big house. With her, clutching a doll, was her youngest child Anne. George, her first-born, now eight years old, was busy with his father and Edward Young dealing with the snow.

'I had a Christmas card this morning,' said Molly, tying her apron round her.

'Rather late in the day,' commented Joan.

'It had a funny stamp on it,' contributed Anne, now settled comfortably at the kitchen table undressing the doll.

'It had been around a bit,' said Molly. 'In fact, it was sent down from the Drovers' Arms, and it's years since I worked there, as you know.'

'How strange!'

'Very. And from someone I don't really know. He says he's a vague relation, an American.'

'Can you place him? Did any of your relations go to America?'

'Not as far as I know. Old Grandma Curdle had only the one boy George, and he was killed in the war, leaving only one son, my Ben. It's a mystery.'

'Any address?'

'No. So I can't do much about it. Ah well! I'm not a great hand at writing anyway, so I shall just forget about it.'

'Except that George wants the stamp,' Anne reminded her mother, tugging a petticoat from the doll.

At midday Molly had finished her time at the Youngs' house, and returned with Anne to her own, on paths newly cleared.

Although she had told Joan that she was not going to think about the late Christmas card, she found herself speculating about the identity of the sender.

Molly had met her husband Ben when the annual fair arrived at Thrush Green on May Day. Old Mrs Curdle, head of her tribe, a real gypsy queen, of awe-inspiring dignity, ruled her business with an iron hand.

The travelling fair stayed only a few days at the most in each place, but Ben had fallen in love with Molly at first sight. He had to wait another year before he could seek her out again.

Albert Piggott had not approved. He did not want to part with a daughter who was also housekeeper, cook and occasionally, when he had drunk too much, nurse.

Mrs Curdle was more sympathetic. Ben, her only grandchild, son of George who had been killed in battle, had been brought up by the old lady, and was the apple of her eye. If Molly could make him happy, and was willing to throw in her lot with her travelling band, then she would be welcomed.

Thrush Green was Mrs Curdle's favourite stopping place on her travels. She had been befriended by the local doctor Donald Bailey, and never forgot the kindness he and his wife had shown her. Each year, at the beginning of May, she called at the Baileys' house bearing a large bouquet of artificial flowers which she had made from finely pared wood dyed in brilliant colours.

The Baileys greatly loved the old lady, but her bouquets, being indestructible, were a source of some embarrassment as the years passed and storage places grew fewer for Mrs Curdle's bounty.

When Mrs Curdle died she left instructions for her body to be put to rest in St Andrew's churchyard, where Molly and Ben faithfully tended the grave.

Ben had been left the fair by his grandmother, but parted with it a few years after her death. Their first child was expected, Molly's father was ailing, and it seemed best to settle at Thrush Green.

Before long, the Youngs invited them to take over the converted stable. Ben carried on his work as a motor mechanic in Lulling, and Molly was glad to help in the house she knew so well.

When the second child arrived, they called her Anne after

her redoubtable great-grandmother, and everyone hoped that the child would grow up as fine a character as her forebear.

For two days the skies were clear, and the countryside was transformed into a white glistening wonderland.

It was freezing all day long so that the winter sunshine melted nothing, and the trees spread tracery like white lace against the clear blue of the sky.

The icicles fringing the roof of the Two Pheasants shone like glass fingers, and an icy shape reared from the upthrust lid of Mr Jones' water-butt where the water had frozen solid and pushed outward to find release.

All sound was muffled. Cars, inching their way through the piles of snow at each side of the road, made little noise. Those on foot walked as quietly as if they trod upon fleecy white blankets.

Shapes too were softened by the snow. Roof ridges were veiled by a snowy sheet. Gateposts, steps and porches wore cushions of white. In the forks of the chestnut trees were soft beds of snow.

The light was dazzling. As far as the eye could see the whiteness stretched away, across the fields towards Lulling Woods, a dark blue smudge on the skyline against the paler blue.

The snow ploughs came out, chugging along the main road from Lulling, and clearing a way for the sparse traffic. The side roads, such as the one which joined Thrush Green from Nidden and Nod further west, remained piled with snow. Only the tractor from Percy Hodge's farm had drawn dark lines across the snowy wastes from his gate as far as the Two Pheasants where custom took him daily.

There was general relief at the opening of the road to Lulling, for the Christmas bounty was running out, and householders were looking forward to replenishing stocks of fresh food and vegetables.

At the Fuchsia Bush the customers became more plentiful, not only those who were doing everyday shopping, but also the bargain-hunters who had braved the elements to attend the High Street sales, which were having an extended season because of the weather.

Mrs Peters, the proprietor of the Fuchsia Bush, came to the

assistance of her young waitresses one morning at coffee-time. Delicious smells of baking scones drifted from the kitchen where Nelly Piggott was hard at work. The three aged Lovelock sisters had arrived and were unexpectedly treating themselves to morning coffee.

They had been born, and lived all their long lives, in the beautiful Georgian house next door to Mrs Peters' premises. As neighbours they had presented difficulties. They complained about cooking smells, the sight of tea towels blowing in the yard at the rear of the restaurant and, chiefly, about the charges for anything purchased there.

The Misses Lovelock were renowned for their parsimony, and when Miss Bertha took to shoplifting, which included the occasional scone or shortbread finger from the Fuchsia Bush itself, no one was really surprised.

Mrs Peters, who was a magnanimous woman and had borne with her trying neighbours with exemplary patience and forbearance, had felt compelled to point out the matter to Miss Violet, who was really the only one approaching normality.

Violet had done her best to curb her sister's deplorable lapses, but Mrs Peters still kept a sharp eye on easily removed objects when Bertha was around.

She greeted the old ladies warmly, and summoned Gloria to take the order, as she proffered the menu.

Gloria, reluctant to be called away from the shop window which gave an absorbing view of Lulling High Street, ambled over to the table.

'I don't think we really need the menu,' said Violet. 'Just coffee for the three of us, don't you agree?'

She looked at her two sisters, who were busy uncoiling loops of scarves from their skinny necks and gloves from their claw-like hands. Mrs Peters could not help wishing that they would attend to their noses, all three of which sported a glistening drop of moisture.

'Perhaps a biscuit,' murmured Bertha, 'or just *half* a scone.'

'We'll have one each,' pronounced Ada with unusual firmness. 'We have been to the sale at the new draper's, and it really is quite exhausting in this cold weather.'

Gloria licked her pencil and wrote laboriously before making slow progress to the kitchen.

'Well,' said Mrs Peters brightly, 'and did you have any success with your shopping?'

'I was somewhat surprised,' said Bertha, 'to find that *hat elastic* was not included in the "Everything half-price" notice.'

'Hat elastic?' echoed Mrs Peters. She looked bewildered.

Violet sent a sharp glance around the shop before lowering her voice to answer. 'Latterly, I believe, it was called "knicker elastic", but that is *not* the sort of thing we like to ask for in public.'

'Quite,' agreed Mrs Peters, still wondering if it was possible to buy knickers which had elastic threaded at the waist. Surely such garments had vanished thirty or forty years ago?

'Ada looked at a very nice dress which was much reduced in price,' said Violet, speaking in her normal voice now that knickers had been dismissed from the conversation. 'Unfortunately it had a white collar.'

'We've given up things with touches of white at the neck,' explained Ada. 'In the old days our maid used to remove little collars, and cuffs too, of course, and wash them out and starch and iron them, and sew them back after use. We find that rather tiring, don't we?'

The other two nodded in agreement, and Mrs Peters noted, yet again, the number of brooches which the three were wearing pinned to their headgear. At least two of Bertha's were embellished with diamonds, she guessed, which flashed fire as she moved.

Ada had a splendid gold arrow among the half dozen which decorated her fur hat. Violet, more restrained in her decorations, simply sported a silver-mounted monkey's paw pinned across her velvet tam-o'-shanter.

'A pity in some ways,' continued Ada. 'I always liked a touch of white, but one has to forgo these little pleasures when one has no staff.'

At that moment, Gloria appeared with the tray, and Mrs Peters made her escape to take up a strategic position behind the counter, which offered a great many temptations to klepto-maniacs.

She felt a pang of pity for the three venerable figures intent on their refreshment. How their world had changed! No *hat* elastic, not even *knicker* elastic, and no maid to remove, wash, starch, iron and replace those little touches of white last thing at night!

She looked indulgently upon her neighbours. Poor dears, she thought.

Mrs Peters was a thoroughly nice woman.

While the Misses Lovelock were enjoying their coffee, Albert Piggott was making slow progress from his cottage along the snowy lane which led to Lulling Woods. He was bent upon calling to see Dotty Harmer.

These two odd characters shared strong bonds. They both liked animals. They did not care a fig about other people's opinions of them. Sturdy independent individuals, they found a strange comfort in each other's company.

He made his way to the end of the house where Dotty had her quarters. The larger part of the home was now occupied by Dotty's niece Connie and her husband Kit, but Dotty relished her independence and muddled along in what she refused to call 'her granny flat'. She was lucky in that Connie and Kit respected the old lady's feelings whilst still keeping a loving eye on their sprightly relative.

Dotty welcomed Albert and invited him into her cluttered kitchen.

'I'll take off me boots,' said Albert, hopping about in the porch, before sitting down at the kitchen table. It was strewn with a variety of objects ranging from an onion cut in half, a saucer of peanuts, various tins and a collection of papers at one end upon which Dotty appeared to be working.

She pushed them to one side, almost capsizing a glass jar containing a cloudy liquid in which floated some yellow objects which Albert could not identify.

'Fungi,' Dotty said, following his gaze. 'A very nutritious type of bracket fungus which grows on those wild plum trees at the southern end of Lulling Woods. Delicious with cold meat. I'll give you a jar.'

'Thank you,' said Albert, realizing that this offering would join many others in the hedge as he went home. 'Dotty's Collywobbles' was a common local complaint, familiar to Dr Lovell and his partners, and the inhabitants of Thrush Green and Lulling had soon learnt that it was wiser not to broach any of Dotty's sinister brews. No one had actually died, but many had hoped to, when suffering from sampling Dotty's offerings.

'Kettle's on,' said Dotty briskly. 'I shan't offer you coffee. It's bad for that ulcer of yours, but I'll give you some of my hot blackcurrant.'

Albert's heart sank, but obviously there was no obliging hedge to hand, and he resolved to take evasive action as best he could.

The kettle gave an ear-splitting scream and Dotty switched it off whilst she bent to rummage in a low cupboard. Several sinister-looking bottles emerged, and from one of them Dotty poured an inky fluid into two mugs.

'There,' said Dotty triumphantly, putting two steaming mugs on the table. 'Just try that! That'll tone up your innards, Albert.'

He took an exploratory sip, repressed a shudder, and watched his hostess attack her own mug.

'You been busy?' enquired Albert, eyeing the profusion of papers.

'Trying to sort out my funeral arrangements,' said Dotty.

'You don't want to start thinkin' about such things,' said Albert. 'It's morbid, that is.'

'Rubbish!' replied Dotty. 'I think one should leave matters as tidy as possible. I'm not so much concerned with the actual *funeral* arrangements. Connie has very good taste in music and choice of hymns, although I have made sure that we don't have "Ur-bide with me", which I detest.'

'I like it meself,' said Albert.

'It reminds me of the *Titanic* disaster,' reminisced Dotty. 'Those poor people singing that hymn – unless it was "Nearer my God to thee", equally lugubrious – as they slid into that awful Atlantic. I find it terribly upsetting.'

Albert was dismayed to see that his old friend's eyes were brimming with tears.

Before he could decide how best to cope with this strange behaviour, Dotty had recovered herself and was rattling on again about her demise.

'It's the disposal of the *body* which is the difficulty, as murderers always find. I should *really* like to be buried in the vegetable garden. All that good humus and those minerals being released slowly into the soil would do so much for the plant growth. However, there seems to be a great reluctance to let me have my way about this, and I suppose it must be cremation after all.'

'They do it very nice,' said Albert comfortingly.

'Well, I hope so,' said Dotty doubtfully. She picked up her mug and drank deeply.

'I suppose the ashes would contribute a certain amount of nourishment,' she continued more cheerfully. 'I shall tell Connie to put most of it by the rhubarb.'

Albert felt it was time to change the subject. 'I really come along to see if I could do any little job outside for you. How's the goats? And how's the hens?'

'Most kind of you, Albert! Kit has cleared the snow from the pens, I know, but I should appreciate it if you would check that they all have plenty of dry bedding. And I've got some cabbage leaves here which they'll all enjoy.'

She made her way into the larder, and Albert was about to nip to the sink with his unwanted drink when Dotty returned with a large basket.

'I'll do it right away,' promised Albert, taking the basket and making for the door.

Dotty watched him stumping towards the chicken run, and then turned back to the table.

'There!' she exclaimed, seeing Albert's mug. 'He forgot his delicious blackcurrant!'

For the rest of January the fields around Thrush Green lay white and unblemished, stretching their glistening purity as far as the eye could see.

But at Thrush Green and Lulling the scene was different.

Here the snow was pock-marked with drips from the trees, and stained by the traffic which had thrown slush upon it.

Each day it shrank a little in the hour or two of comparative warmth at midday. The piles of besmirched snow at the road-sides dwindled slowly. The crisp crunchiness had vanished, and boots now squelched rather than squeaked as their wearers went their way.

It was still bitterly cold at night when frost came with the dark-ness. The first excitement about the snow had long vanished, giving way to a feeling of endurance and a longing for spring.

On the last evening of the month Harold Shoosmith went upstairs to draw the curtains in the bedroom. A new moon, a silver crescent, was rising above the houses across Thrush Green. He opened a window and looked out.

Everything was still. The lights from the Two Pheasants shone upon a black-and-white world. Nathaniel Patten's statue threw a black stain across the snow around him.

Harold's face grew cold. His breath blew a little cloud into the silence about him.

Suddenly, from the bare branches of a lilac tree the stillness was broken by the sweet sad song of a robin.

Gently, Harold shut the window.

February

And in green underwood and cover
Blossom by blossom the spring begins.

A. C. Swinburne

O n the second day of the new month the wind changed
course and turned from north-east to south-west, much
to the relief of everyone.

Now the snow shrank faster, revealing the brown ploughed
fields around Thrush Green, and the gardens which had been
hidden for so long.

With the thaw came floods. The River Pleshy which bisected
Lulling overflowed its banks and spread sheets of water across
the meadows beside it. At the lowest point in the town, near
the ancient bridge which spanned the Pleshy, the water was
two feet deep at one time, and the cellars of the adjacent houses
were full of muddy water in which floated such things as deck
chairs, garden tables, demoted chests of drawers and other
household flotsam, together with beer barrels and smaller kegs.

At Thrush Green the last of the snow slid from the roofs
with soft plops, and little rivers gurgled along the gutters
and down the hill to join the floods in Lulling High Street.
Wellington boots were the only sensible footwear as people
slid and squelched their way around.

But it was warm again. The sun shone, lighting the dripping
trees into chandeliers of shining droplets. The snowdrops were

out, and the stubby green noses of later bulbs pushed above the glistening earth. Nature was on the move again, and everyone rejoiced.

Molly Curdle, making her way across the green from her house to her father's, breathed in the fresh air with rapture. It seemed a very long time since she had been outside and able to enjoy a world beyond that of her own kitchen and that of Joan Young's. The return of colour to the view was particularly welcome. The harsh light from the unrelenting snow every-where had had a depressing effect, and to see green grass, brown earth, and one or two brave early flowers such as snowdrops and the yellow fronds of witchhazel raised the spirits of all who had been housebound for so long.

Albert Piggott was not in, but Molly had a key and let herself into her old home. It was warm and quiet. Tired after struggling through the mud of the green, Molly sat down to rest for a moment before seeking her father in the church which she could see through the cottage window.

She looked appreciatively at the room which she knew so well. Everything was in apple-pie order, and shone from Nelly's ministrations.

She had not approved of Nelly when they first met. Her own mother had died when Molly was in her teens, and she had automatically taken over as housekeeper to her curmudgeonly father.

They had not been happy years for Molly, and the fact that she could escape into the welcoming Youngs' household every afternoon was her salvation. Later, after meeting Ben Curdle at one May Day fair on the green, life really took on some meaning, and the happy marriage which followed had trans-formed her outlook.

Her dislike of her stepmother Nelly began to change to appreciation. It was true that she still regarded Nelly as over-boisterous and vulgar. She suspected that Nelly was the one who brought Albert to the altar, and not the other way round. In this she was right, and her own natural modesty and feeling for what was correct could never come to terms with this knowledge.

Nevertheless, as time passed, Molly began to realize that Nelly's sterling qualities had been a blessing to all. For one thing, she had released Molly from bondage. She had, within limits, done much to improve Albert's lot. His home was clean and warm, his meals superb, even if too rich and abundant for Albert's ailing digestion, and her income was the only money which really contributed to the household funds.

There was no doubt about it, reflected Molly, noting the shining pans on the hob, the thriving cyclamen on the window-sill – her own Christmas present to Nelly – and the spotless walls and floor, Nelly was a first-class manager and deserved the wages and appreciation which her work at the Fuchsia Bush gave her.

She rose to cross the road to the church to find Albert, but at that moment the door opened, and her father appeared.

His welcome was typical. 'Ain't you got the kettle on? I'm fair shrammed with the cold.'

Molly shifted the kettle to the centre of the stove. It began to hum immediately, and she went to the wall cupboard.

'Tea or coffee, Dad?'

'Coffee.'

He sat down with a sigh, and began to blow his nose into a red-and-white spotted handkerchief.

Molly made the coffee and put his mug on the table.

'And what brings you over?' asked Albert. 'Want something, I suppose?'

Molly ignored the churlishness, as she had done so often, and put a Christmas card in front of him.

'I've been meaning to ask you for weeks about this man,' said Molly, 'and kept forgetting.'

Albert studied the card, turning it back and forth.

'What's so special about it?'

'I just wondered if you knew anything about this fellow. He's an American. Anyway, it had an American stamp.'

'Don't mean nothin' to me,' announced Albert, pushing the card across the table. 'What does Ben say? I take it that this was addressed to you two Curdles.'

'That's right.'

'Well, I've done me best to keep away from gypos,' said Albert nastily. 'One of the blighters stole my daughter. In marriage, in case you've forgot!'

Silently, Molly put the card back in her bag, and drank her coffee. It was clear that her father was in one of his more spiteful and truculent moods.

Once again, she decided that the small mystery of the Christmas card should be ignored.

As soon as she had finished her coffee, she made her departure, wishing Albert goodbye at the door.

By this time he was immersed in the local newspaper, and

made no reply. Molly relieved her feelings by slamming the door shut as noisily as she could, and set off again across the slippery green.

For once, sympathy for her stepmother was her dominant feeling, but Albert's remark about 'gypos' still rankled.

He had never forgiven her for marrying into the Curdle family. It was plain he never would.

Well, thought Molly robustly, he'd just have to lump it! If it ever came to a choice between her father and her husband, it would be Albert who would go to the wall.

As the flood water subsided and the ground began to dry out, the people of Thrush Green and Lulling started to venture forth from their homes and to meet their friends again.

The news, naturally, was of the weather and all its attendant horrors. Tales of leaking roofs, ruined carpets, power cuts, and the prevalent wave of coughs and colds resulting from such conditions, were exchanged with the greatest animation and exaggeration.

Shopkeepers rejoiced in the return of customers, farmers went out into their fields again, and the Reverend Charles Henstock, vicar of Lulling and rector of Thrush Green, set out with joy to visit those who had been kept from his care by snow and water.

He decided to walk the mile from his home at St John's vicarage through Lulling High Street to Thrush Green. He did not hurry. Everyone stopped to speak to him. He was hailed by the shopkeepers, the dustmen, the window cleaner and his friends at the garage near the river's bridge.

Charles Henstock had no enemies. There was an innocence, a modesty, and a genuine love of his fellow men which protected him from malice of any sort.

He had lived at Thrush Green for many years in a hideous Victorian house which had caused his neighbours, and

particularly Edward Young, the architect, considerable pain
and loathing.

Charles was not upset by the ugliness nor the discomfort of
his home. He had met his second wife, Dimity, at Thrush
Green, and they had lived in their uncomfortable quarters in
the greatest harmony, until the house burnt down, to the relief
of Edward Young, and Charles was given the living of Lulling,
Thrush Green and two other adjoining parishes.

Some of his closest friends lived at Thrush Green. Harold

Shoosmith was a tower of strength when financial affairs had to be tackled. Dr Lovell and Winnie Bailey were two more, and Ella Bembridge was yet another.

His wife Dimity had lived with Ella for several years, and they were near neighbours and friends during Charles's widowerhood. All three remained close friends.

On this particular morning, he called at Ella's first. She opened her door, inviting him in, but Charles was a little dismayed to see that she was dressed ready to go out.

'No, no!' he protested. 'You are just off somewhere, I can see.'

'Come in for half a minute,' said Ella, in her gruff voice. 'I've got a letter for Dim. From Australia. Came just after Christmas, and I keep forgetting to send it on.'

She made her way to the kitchen, and Charles followed her. Whilst she rummaged through a dresser drawer which appeared to hold dusters, string, jam-pot covers and a collapsible lacy affair which Charles could not place, he looked happily about him.

In this very room he had proposed marriage to his dear Dimity. For him it would always be a hallowed place.

'There we are!' cried Ella triumphantly. She began to shovel the clutter back into the drawer.

Charles put the letter in his pocket.

'And what is that?' he asked, as Ella was about to thrust the white lacy bundle into the drawer.

Ella snapped it open. 'It's a cover to keep off the flies,' she explained. 'Very useful when we have tea in the garden, or leave meat out for second helpings.'

'Most intriguing,' murmered Charles, his eyes wide with wonder behind his spectacles.

Ella laughed indulgently at Charle's naivety. Who else would be so impressed by such a simple contrivance?

They went together through the front door. Ella turned left

to Lulling, leaving Charles gazing happily about him, wondering whom to visit next.

Before him stood the attractive collection of old people's homes, built on the site of his own burnt-out house. Here were several of his friends and parishioners, under the care of Jane and Bill Cartwright who were joint wardens.

Should he call now, or leave that visit to the afternoon? He consulted his watch, and was dismayed to find that it was almost noon.

That decided it. He would call on the Shoosmiths first.

He set off across the green, passed his church where Albert appeared to be in a state of meditation as he leant on a broom by the porch, and made his way in high spirits.

It was good to be home again.

From her bedroom window Joan Young had seen Charles Henstock making his brisk way to the Shoosmiths.

She and Molly were sorting out garments for the next jumble sale. It had seemed, at the outset, to be a simple straightforward task, but it was proving to be uncommonly difficult.

Joan had been the more ruthless of the pair, holding up jumpers and cardigans and ready to put them on a mounting pile on the bed. But Molly, brought up to be more prudent, acted as a brake upon such hasty progress.

'That's too good to give away. You always looked nice in that pink. I'd keep it for a bit.'

Reluctantly, Joan removed it from what she thought of as 'the slush pile' and put it on a chair.

A heap of Paul's outgrown clothes had to be tackled, and here Joan was firmer in her approach. The better items of school uniform were destined for the school's second-hand shop, but such things as shabby pants, vests and holiday wear were being sorted quickly.

'My George could use those,' said Molly as some things were being held up.

'Then do take them,' said Joan. 'In fact, anything you can make use of, Molly, just put on one side. Most of these are going to end up as dusters.'

It was at this stage that she caught sight of the rector crossing the green, and left her labours to gaze upon the scene she loved.

Thrush Green had changed little since she came to live there as a married woman. She and her sister Ruth had known the place from childhood and she hoped that she would never have to leave it.

The old rectory had gone of course, but few had mourned that architectural monstrosity. Now Rectory Cottages, the homes designed by her husband, stood in its place, and Joan looked upon the buildings with affection. Edward had done a good job, and Jane and Bill Cartwright were equally successful in their care of the old people who lived there.

She had known Jane as a child and followed her career as a nurse with admiration. She was indeed 'a chip off the old block', for her mother Mrs Jennings had been the local nurse and midwife for many years. Old Dr Bailey had relied on her skills hundreds of times, and his successor John Lovell also knew her worth. It had been a great satisfaction to Dr Lovell, as a trustee of Rectory Cottages, when Jane Cartwright and her Yorkshire-born husband had been appointed as wardens.

'Mr Henstock's around,' said Joan.

'Going to see the old folk?'

'Not at the moment. I think he's calling on Harold Shoosmith.'

'Well, he'll be welcome wherever he goes,' said Molly, joining Joan at the window.

'Could my Ben have this cotton T-shirt for cleaning the car windows? Nothing like a bit of real cotton, Ben always says.'

'It's his,' said Joan, turning back to her task, refreshed as always by a glimpse of Thrush Green.

Charles Henstock found Isobel Shoosmith setting the table for lunch, and began his apologies.

'Join us,' said Isobel. 'It's not quite time yet, but do stay.'

'Well –' began Charles diffidently.

'Or is Dimity expecting you back?'

'Well –' said Charles again.

'What's wrong?'

'I don't like to intrude.'

'Charles! Really!'

'But the truth is,' said honest Charles Henstock, 'Dimity's gone shopping in Oxford, and she's having lunch there with an old schoolfriend.'

'Then you can stop,' said Isobel firmly. 'That's settled.'

'She left me something cold,' went on the rector, looking worried.

'Have it this evening,' said Isobel briskly. 'Now, if you want Harold, he's in the garden.'

He found his friend tending a bonfire which seemed reluctant to burn. His sleeves were rolled up, his grey hair on end, and his face decorated with a few black streaks, but he seemed very content.

'Nice to see you. I'm not making much headway with this – everything's so wet after the snow. But what brings you here?'

'The pleasure of seeing Thrush Green again,' said Charles, 'and one or two little parish matters.'

'Come in and have a drink,' said Harold, abandoning his work and leading the way to the house.

'It's about this summer's fête,' said Charles, when they were settled with their glasses.

'You're the second person to mention the fête,' commented Harold. 'Heavens, man, it's not till July! Edward Young wants me to do his usual job, by the way, as he's hoping to go away during Paul's summer holidays.'

'Well, we shall have to bring it up at the committee meeting,' said Charles, 'but I just wondered if you had any strong feelings about where the proceeds should go this year.'

'I hadn't thought about it. It's usually the church roof or the organ that's in need. What's in your mind?'

'Rectory Cottages.'

'But surely they are in good nick? We're both trustees. There's no doubt there, is there?'

'Well, no. But Jane Cartwright has been wondering if the communal room is really big enough. You see, it's not just the residents of the seven cottages that use it, but their visitors sometimes. And, of course, if they have a party of any sort, it does get rather crowded.'

'But Edward Young went into all that very carefully when he designed it. And also when the conservatory was added.'

The rector began to look unhappy. 'I know. and I should not like to hurt his feelings by suggesting that it is too small, but as a matter of fact, Mrs Thurgood rang me about the matter the other day.'

'Oh!' said Harold, with feeling. 'I begin to see.'

Mrs Thurgood was also one of the trustees. She was an elderly woman who spoke her mind, irrespective of the feelings of others, and was a power to be reckoned with. Mrs Thurgood usually got her way.

The rector had crossed swords with her before over the matter of kneelers at St John's church at Lulling, where she and her daughter were regular worshippers. It had been a doughty battle which the rector had won, for despite his gentle manner, which some took for weakness, when it came to sticking to his guns Charles Henstock was as ferocious as the next.

Nevertheless, his heart sank when Mrs Thurgood approached. It usually meant that there was trouble ahead.

'I thought I'd have a word with Jane,' he told Harold, 'when I call there this afternoon. It is best to find out at root level if there is any need for an enlargement. It would cost a great deal, and mean quite an upheaval while the building was going on.'

'Too true. And then there is Edward.'

Charles sighed. 'Yes indeed. There is Edward.'

They sat surveying their glasses for a moment.

'He'd probably understand,' said Harold at last.

'He's very sensitive,' responded Charles. 'I suppose it is because he is *creative*.'

'Well, aren't we all? I'm creative when I'm gardening, Isobel is creative when she's cooking, but we don't throw tantrums about it.'

Charles laughed. 'You're quite right of course. Nevertheless, I don't like upsetting Edward. He's a good man, but just a little – what shall I say?'

'Touchy?' suggested Harold. 'He was a real pain in the neck when John Lovell said his steps at the Cottages weren't safe. He just can't bear criticism.'

'I know.'

The rector looked sad, and Harold adopted a rallying tone.

'Cheer up! It may never happen. Cross that bridge when you come to it, and all that.'

The rector nodded, and put down his empty glass.

'In any case,' went on Harold, 'I'd sooner face Edward than Mrs Thurgood.'

Isobel put her head round the door. 'Ready for lunch?'

'Always,' smiled Charles.

The mild weather continued, and heart-lifting signs of spring were everywhere.

Yellow tassels of the hazel catkins fluttered from the hedge. Yellow aconites, with ruffs of green, appeared with the snowdrops. Yellow early dwarf irises and early crocuses were about to burst into bloom, and over all spread the kindly yellow sunlight.

Soon yellow primroses would star the woods, and the daffodils would blow their trumpets in the gardens of Thrush Green. Yellow, gold and green, spring's particular colours, would bring hope again after the bleak black and white of winter.

On one of these hopeful mornings, Winnie Bailey and Jenny were discussing the possibility of a lunch party for a few of their old friends.

'We can't seat more than ten,' said Winnie, 'and as far as I can see it will really be a hen party.'

'And what's wrong with that?' asked Jenny.

'Nothing, I suppose. I mean I must ask the three Lovelocks, and Ella and Joan Young. They've been so good, fetching and carrying for me through the bad weather. I think Dimity would come too, but that means two men as well. What do you think?'

'I'd let the men fend for themselves that day,' said Jenny. 'Besides they wouldn't want to be swamped by all of us women.'

'Fair enough. Well, that's eight counting us. What about Dotty and Connie?'

'Ideal,' responded Jenny. 'Now, it's just the food to think about.'

'I'll ring them today and arrange a date,' said Winnie, 'and then we can work out some menus. Something *soft*, I think.'

'*Soft?*'

'Jenny, dear,' explained Winnie patiently. 'Half of us have lost a great many teeth, and the other half have unreliable dentures.'

'I never thought of that,' confessed Jenny.

'You don't when you've got plenty of your own,' said Winnie sadly.

'We might have tapioca,' suggested Jenny.

Winnie snorted. 'I'm not sinking to *tapioca*, teeth or no teeth,' she declared.

It was that same night which hid some very mysterious goings-on in the peaceful confines of Thrush Green.

Later, no one could recall anything unusual during the hours of darkness. Joan Young had stirred at about three in the morning, being obliged to visit the bathroom, much to her annoyance. Harold Shoosmith had padded downstairs at much the same time to switch off the porch light which had been forgotten. Nelly Piggott, asleep in the back bedroom of her home, was dead to the world from twelve until six in the morning, and Albert, in the only other upstairs room, facing the green, was equally oblivious to what was happening across the road.

For something certainly had happened, and it was Albert who made the discovery.

It was nearly half past six when he awoke to the sound of Nelly moving about below. He heard the kettle being filled, the stove being riddled, and the cat mewing for its breakfast.

He also became conscious of the squeaking and banging of the church gate. Someone had left it open, he thought morosely. One of them Cooke lot as like as not.

It was beginning to get light as he crossed the road to shut the gate. Behind him the appetizing smell of rashers frying wafted from the kitchen, and he looked forward to his breakfast.

The gate was damp. There might have been a shower in the night, but the air was mild and it was going to be another pleasant spring day.

Albert sniffed the morning freshness with relish, and was about to return to his cottage when he noticed a strange object in the church porch.

At first sight he thought it might be a large basket or trug left by the flower ladies. So often, heady with the floral displays they had just created, the church floral arrangers left their impedimenta behind, and Albert was quite used to retrieving secateurs, unwanted twigs, lengths of wire and, as in this case, baskets of varying size and shape.

Grumbling to himself, Albert reopened the gate and made his way to the church porch. The sight which met his eyes stopped him dead in his tracks.

The object certainly was a basket. It was a large one with a kind of hood covering half the base, and it was lined with a tartan blanket. Fast asleep in this shelter lay a curled-up dog, no more than a puppy.

It wore a collar from which a long piece of rope led to the iron ring of the church door handle. Albert bent to look more closely, fumbling with the dog's collar to see if there were any signs of identification. There was none.

Albert stood up and reviewed the situation. It was a nice little dog, a white Highland terrier, obviously well cared for, and in an expensive basket. What worried Albert was its complete inertia. It had scarcely stirred when he had moved its collar round. It had not so much as blinked an eye. Could it be ill?

Deciding that there was nothing to be done immediately, Albert began to shuffle back to his breakfast. The dog was in a safe sheltered place, deeply asleep, and Albert needed time to come to terms with this extraordinary situation. Perhaps Nelly could help?

Nelly put Albert's breakfast on the hob to keep warm and returned with him to the church porch.

'The little love!' she exclaimed on seeing the sleeping puppy.

'But what's to be done?' asked Albert. 'The police?'

Nelly was on her knees stroking the white head. 'Poor little soul! It don't seem to be very lively.' She looked up at Albert.

'Why don't you see Dotty? She's the best one for a job like this. She'll know what to do.'

'I'll go down straightaway,' said Albert.

Nelly struggled to her feet.

'Not till you've had your breakfast you won't,' she said firmly. 'For one thing, Dotty won't be up, and more important, there's a good plate of food waiting for you.'

Even in a crisis Nelly's first thoughts were of her cooking.

The lunch party which Winnie planned took longer to arrange than was first envisaged.

One would have imagined that collecting eight women guests, all apparently free from regular outside employment or the demands of young children or invalids at home, would be a simple affair.

Winnie spent the best part of two days trying to find a time which was convenient to all.

Bertha Lovelock had a doctor's appointment. The dentist was doing something which demanded Violet's attendance and co-operation. Ella Bembridge had an embroidery class. Joan Young, as a magistrate, had to go to her duties on the bench.

Only Dotty and Connie, it seemed, were delightfully free to come whenever it could be arranged.

At last the date was fixed for 1 March, which, as they all reminded each other over the telephone, was not far off, and wasn't it incredible how time flew? Here we were almost at the end of February! Almost into March! Quite astounding.

Much relieved to have the date settled, Jenny and Winnie got down to the serious business of catering for a lunch party for ten elderly ladies with, possibly, dental troubles.

'I suppose a nice round of beef is out?' said Jenny wistfully. 'Can't beat a nice roast, with Yorkshire pudding and horseradish sauce.'

'I know, but I think something in a casserole, or some minced dish would fit the bill. What about a really luscious fish pie? With shrimps in it?'

'I know for a fact Miss Harmer's averse to fish. Percy Hodge took her down a lovely trout last summer, and she never gave him so much as a thank-you.'

'Oh dear! Shepherd's pie? A dish of minced beef?'

'Not very *festive*, is it? *Mince*, I mean. Sounds like school dinners.'

Winnie was obliged to agree, and silence fell.

'Tell you what,' said Jenny at last. 'What about those tube things you like? Pasta things stuffed with mince? We shouldn't need potatoes with those, but have lots of interesting vegetables.'

'Cannelloni?' cried Winnie. 'Why, I think that's a very good idea, Jenny.'

'And the cauliflowers are lovely just now,' continued Jenny, 'and we've lots of our own spinach in the freezer and runner beans.'

'And a starter? Something simple, I think.'

'Grapefruit?'

'Too acid for Ella. Let's have half an avocado pear apiece. Always looks rather luxurious, and should suit everyone.'

'Particularly the Lovelocks,' agreed Jenny. 'They'd never pay out for an avocado pear, even if they split it three ways!'

Much cheered they began to draft the menu.

Nelly Piggott had to depart for her work at the Fuchsia Bush, but Albert made his way to Dotty's cottage as St Andrew's clock chimed half past eight.

He guessed that Dotty would be about, and he was right. He found her clearing away her breakfast things, and twirling a spoon which she had just removed from a jar of honey.

'Want to lick it?' asked Dotty hospitably.

Albert shuddered, and Dotty put the spoon into her own mouth with evident relish.

'So good for one,' said Dotty when she had removed the spoon and flung it into the sink. 'Now, Albert, what brings you here so early?'

Albert told her. Dotty listened attentively until he finished his account.

'And it is still asleep?'

'Well, it was when I had a look just afore I come down, but I think it had moved round in its basket. Looked more lively-like.'

'Very odd,' mused Dotty. 'I shall get Kit to bring me up as soon as he's ready, and we will bring the poor thing here. Leave it with me, Albert. I will get in touch with the police, and the vet too, if need be.'

'But what about old Flossie?' he asked, nodding to Dotty's ancient King Charles spaniel, a former derelict who had lived happily with Dotty for many years.

'Flossie won't make any trouble,' said her mistress. 'She's got quite enough to worry her with her arthritis, poor love, and in any case, her sight is not what it was.'

'You don't want fightin' and all that,' pointed out Albert.

'There will be no hostility in this house,' Dotty told him firmly. It might have been her redoubtable old schoolmaster father speaking, thought Albert, as he went on his way.

Within an hour Kit, Connie and Dotty had met Albert in the church porch, and stood surveying the puppy. It was now attempting to get out of its basket, but was very wobbly on its legs. It was also whining in a very pathetic manner.

'I think,' said Dotty, 'the poor thing has been sedated.'

'Been what?' asked Albert bewildered.

'Drugged. He's now coming round.'

'He?' echoed Albert, peering short-sightedly.

'Indeed it is. A fine young dog,' insisted Dotty, 'and I think the best thing to do is to take him to my kitchen and give the poor chap some hot milk.'

All four set about transferring the animal and his basket to the waiting estate car, and within minutes Albert was watching it make its way home.

'Be all right with Dotty,' he murmured to himself as he shut the church gate firmly.

Dotty was at her most energetic in her kitchen. The newcomer had been given a light meal, a long drink of water, and been introduced to Flossie.

She had behaved admirably after the initial sniffing had been done. She wagged her plumed tail and then repaired to her basket and fell asleep. Flossie was accustomed to stray animals in the kitchen, from orphaned lambs, goat kids and ailing kittens, to injured birds and small reptiles. She took the new-comer's presence philosophically.

Dotty settled down to her telephoning and rang her old friend, the local vet. She explained the position and requested an early visit.

'I'm going to Percy Hodge about midday. He's got a cow off colour. I'll pop in and see you between twelve and one.'

'Oh good,' exclaimed Dotty, 'you could have some lunch with me.'

'Very kind of you,' replied the vet hastily, 'but I really can't spare the time.'

He had once suffered from 'Dotty's Collywobbles' after drinking one of Dotty's brews, and had learnt to be prudent.

Her next telephone call was to Lulling police station, a charming building near the great parish church of St John's.

The local police had a reputation as good gardeners as well, of course, as of being exemplary officers, and the police station was adorned with climbing roses and wisteria, and tubs of fine fuchsias each side of the front door, as well as hanging baskets dripping with lobelias, geraniums and petunias in the summer.

In February there was not quite the same pressure on the force's horticultural pursuits, so Dotty was attended to by the sergeant on duty within seconds.

He listened to Dotty's account, and put a few questions.

'In good health, you say, madam?'

'Splendid, apart from some drowsiness still after sedation.'

'And you would like us to take it into custody? I mean, into care?'

Dotty became agitated. 'No, no, no! I am quite capable of caring for him here, as you know. *All* my animals thrive. It is simply that I want you to have the facts so that the owners can be found.'

'We'll do our best, madam,' replied the sergeant, holding the telephone some distance from his ear.

'I can't think why the poor little thing has been abandoned,' went on Dotty, in full blast now. 'He has obviously been looked after very well, coat in excellent condition, nose just the right degree of dampness, and the most expensive basket and rug. It is a complete mystery, officer. A complete mystery!'

The sergeant acknowledged a mug of coffee being put before him by one of his younger colleagues, rolling his eyes heavenward at the same time to show how much he was enduring.

'Leave it with me, Miss Harmer,' he said at last. 'I'd better send someone along to make a few notes later today. For our records, you know.'

'Of course, of course. I shall be at your disposal for the rest of the day. If you are here about four I can offer you a cup of fresh herbal tea. I know you must not take alcohol on duty.'

'Thank you, madam, but no doubt one of us will call before four.'

He put down the telephone with a sigh. 'John,' he said to

the younger policeman. 'There's a job for you up at Lulling Woods early afternoon. A Miss Dotty Harmer. And whatever you do don't eat or drink anything while you're there.'

'Why not?'

His superior officer told him.

March

... daffodils
That come before the swallow dares, and take
The winds of March with beauty.

William Shakespeare

M arch came to Thrush Green like a lamb rather than a lion.
The mild weather of February continued during the
first few days of the new month. The sun shone, the birds
began a flurry of mating and nest-building, and the flowers of
spring began to appear in woods, meadows and cottage gardens.

At Winnie Bailey's house the new month was greeted with
more than usual activity, for this was the day on which her old
friends were coming to lunch.

After much cogitation and rearranging, the menu had been
settled. Avocado pears would be followed by cannelloni served
with spinach and runner beans from the freezer and cauliflower
from the Women's Institute stall.

The dessert course had proved more difficult. Jenny was
loud in her praises of 'a good crumble-top', and cited the
home-grown gooseberries and plums bottled last summer.

'Rather *searching* perhaps?' mused Winnie, still anxious about
the digestive efficiency of her aged guests. 'I think a well-
sweetened apple meringue would be better, and perhaps a fruit
jelly as well. And we must remember to order plenty of cream
from Percy Hodge.'

'Cream might be too rich,' commented Jenny, slightly piqued at being denied the pleasure of making a large crumble-top, and the undoubted compliments she would have received on bringing it to the table.

'We might have yoghurt,' said Winnie doubtfully. 'What do you think?'

'Things are quite fancy enough with avocado pears and cannelloni,' said Jenny firmly. 'Yoghurt as well would put some of the old ladies into a proper tizz-wazz. They'll like a nice English dish like your apple meringue and cream.'

And no doubt, she thought rebelliously, they would have preferred a nice gooseberry crumble-top if they'd been given it.

By twelve o'clock on the great day the table was spread with a fine pink cloth and matching napkins. The silver was dazzling after Jenny's ministrations, pink candles added to the ensemble, and a low pot of dwarf pink tulips stood in the centre. The sun shone upon all this splendour, the cannelloni was ready for the oven, and Winnie and Jenny hovered by the windows awaiting their guests.

Ella and Dimity were the first to arrive, each bearing a pot of recently made marmalade, and were greeted affectionately, and while they were being helped with their coats, Joan Young's car drew up and the three Misses Lovelock were assisted from it.

'I'll fetch them,' Joan had said when she had heard about the invitation. 'The thought of having to hire a taxi would spoil the whole day for them.'

This was probably true, Winnie realized, but only someone as forthright as Joan would have said so. And no one as generous, thought Winnie, would so readily have offered to fetch the ancient sisters.

Soon they were all ensconced in the sitting-room sipping sherry, or mineral water, or orange juice, while Jenny shuttled between the kitchen and the visitors, keeping an eye on the cooking.

Dotty and Connie were the last to arrive, and the conversation turned naturally to the extraordinary affair of the abandoned dog.

'Doing very nicely,' Dotty assured them. 'Very friendly, eats well, gets on with Flossie, though of course she finds him rather boisterous.'

'But whose was he?' queried Bertha Lovelock.

'Still a mystery,' Dotty told her. She dipped a finger in her orange juice and sucked it.

'Do you think I might have a knob of sugar, or preferably a little honey in this?' she enquired. 'It seems a little sharp.'

Without a word Jenny went from the room and reappeared bearing a pot of honey on a saucer flanked by a teaspoon.

Oblivious of all eyes upon her, Dotty scooped out a spoonful and stirred it briskly into her glass. The spoon she sucked with relish before replacing it on the saucer.

Amidst a stunned silence Dotty took a sip.

'Delicious!' she announced, and took up her tale again.

'So far we've had no reply to all the questions we've asked. As you probably saw, the local paper had a paragraph about the dear thing, asking for help in tracing the owners.'

'And a charming photograph,' said Winnie. There was a polite murmur of assent, though in truth the photograph had been rather fuzzy, and as the photographer had posed them with the dog held close to Dotty's face, it was quite difficult to distinguish the rough white hair of one from the other. Luckily, Dotty's spectacles came out clearly, which helped a little.

'Could it have been stolen, and then dumped because the thieves were scared off?' asked Dimity.

Ella pointed out that thieves would hardly take the trouble to bring a basket and rug for their captive, and to make sure it was humanely secure in the church porch, and comment was brisk and wildly conjectural until Jenny announced that lunch was ready, and with much fluttering and cries of appreciation the ladies took their places.

The mystery of Dotty's dog was left, as other local topics were discussed over the avocado pears.

'Was it true,' asked Violet Lovelock of Joan Young, 'that there might be an addition to Rectory Cottages?'

She had heard, she said, that the original common room, or drawing-room, or whatever it was called, was turning out to be too small, even with the added extension.

Joan, fiercely protective of her husband's reputation as an architect, parried the question.

'It's the first I've heard of it,' she replied. 'That room has always seemed adequate to me, and I know Edward went into the dimensions most carefully when the building was designed.'

'Oh, I'm quite sure of that!' agreed Violet, helping herself to a spoonful of spinach. She was conscious that she had made a gaffe, which was particularly unfortunate as Joan had been kind enough to collect her and her sisters, and would be needed very soon to return them to Lulling.

'If they do want more room,' said Dotty brightly, 'those glasshouses you stick on the end of one room might be just the thing.'

'But that's been done,' said Joan.

'The new fellow near the Drovers' Arms,' continued Dotty, 'has just had one put outside their dining-room, and I had coffee there the other morning. Very good, wasn't it, Connie?'

'Very warm and light,' agreed Connie.

'I meant the coffee,' began Dotty, quite ready to embark on coffee, tea, herbal beverages of all sorts, not to mention the recipes for making them, but was forestalled by Jenny who helped her to runner beans and stopped the flow.

Conversation grew more general, much to Joan Young's

relief, though she still worried about the possibility of the enlargement of the room Edward had originally designed. She was sure that he had not heard any of these rumours, and she hoped that he never would.

Joan was devoted to Edward, but knew only too well that criticism infuriated him, and that peace would vanish from their household if he felt that his work was being denigrated.

'And how is Paul?' asked Winnie, sensing tension.

'Ah, Paul!' smiled Joan. 'We had a marvellous time when he was home at half-term.'

And to Winnie's relief, she was told about a visit to an animal sanctuary which had been a day in paradise for a twelve-year-old schoolboy.

Less controversial topics than the possibility of an enlargement of Rectory Cottages were being discussed around the table. Connie enlarged on the beauty and intelligence of the new dog. Ada Lovelock told Jenny about a wonderful new cure for arthritis which Jenny might be glad to know about as time passed so quickly when you reached seventy. As Jenny was still in her forties, she might have resented this aspersion on her age, but being a good-hearted woman and quite used to the eccentricities of the Lovelock sisters, she listened with every appearance of interest.

Ella told her neighbour about the tapestry she was making for an altar kneeler, and Dimity told Bertha Lovelock that milk was supposed to be good for cleaning patent leather shoes, and Violet Lovelock told everyone within earshot about the brisk business being done at the Fuchsia Bush these days, and Jenny and Winnie exchanged contented glances at the success of the party which had been their main concern for so long.

By half past three the last of their visitors had gone. Dotty had returned for her handbag, but otherwise all had departed flushed and happy with their modest outing, and Winnie and Jenny subsided into armchairs.

'I'll stack the dishwasher,' said Jenny, attempting to get up.

'You won't yet,' said Winnie. 'And before we do that we'll have a cup of tea. But first all, Jenny, do you think there's any truth in these rumours about the old people's home? I hope it's not true. Edward would be so upset.'

'Well, let's hope it's only a rumour,' comforted Jenny.

There were other people who could have told Winnie more about the rumour.

On that February day when Charles Henstock had enjoyed lunching with Harold and Isobel, he had gone afterwards to see his old friends and parishioners at Rectory Cottages.

Jane Cartwright, one of the wardens, had welcomed him, and without preamble, the rector mentioned the matter of enlarging the room. Was it necessary, he asked?

Jane looked a little taken aback, but answered readily. 'I'm not sure how this cropped up, and in ordinary circumstances the room is quite big enough now that we have that glass annexe. If we have a party of visitors then I must say it is a bit of a squash.'

'The thing is,' said Charles, 'finding the money. We've raised an amazing amount over the last few years for Nathaniel Patten's settlement in Africa, and the Roof Fund and the Organ Repair Fund, and one or two items for the school and so on, and I really don't think we can face another large fund-raising effort if it is not needed.'

'Quite,' said Jane. 'Besides, it might upset Edward Young.'

'That is so,' agreed Charles, looking unhappy.

'Though that's his chicken,' said Jane robustly. She had no time for imagined rebuffs, and was used to coping with the day-to-day misunderstandings among her elderly charges which she privately dismissed as 'senile tantrums'.

'I must sound out one or two other people,' went on the rector, 'and you might make a few enquiries here to see if people feel the need for a larger room. Perhaps we could enlarge the conservatory? What do you think, Jane?'

Jane said that if it came to it, then adding to the conservatory would be lovely. What had put this idea into his mind?

Charles was hard put to it to tell her. Something to do with the church fête in July. Not that anything like the amount from the receipts would cover the cost of this extra glass affair, which was why he was anxious not to start another large fund-raising project so soon after the others.

Leaving matters at this unsatisfactory stage, the rector bade Jane farewell and went to visit her charges.

Molly Curdle was the innocent cause of the rumour coming to the ears of Edward Young.

In Joan's kitchen one morning, she asked Joan if Mr Young would be asked to add to Rectory Cottages if the need arose.

Edward Young, who was searching in a dresser drawer for a particular old kitchen knife in constant demand by all the household, turned to confront Molly. Joan's heart sank.

'What's all this about?' he demanded.

Poor Molly recognized at once that she had made a serious gaffe. She knew the signs of wrath well enough, and had been familiar with the raised voice, red face and blazing eyes for many years.

'It was just something I heard,' she faltered.

'Who from?'

'It may have been my dad.'

Joan came to the rescue. 'Calm down, Edward. You know what John told you.'

John Lovell was Edward's brother-in-law, the local doctor, and knew Edward could be the victim of his own worries.

Edward turned away muttering to himself. 'Well, if there's any truth in these rumours, I shall find out who is spreading them.'

He strode out of the kitchen, and the two women exchanged looks.

'Oh lor'!' whispered Molly. 'That's torn it. I shan't mention *that* again.'

Nelly Piggott, bustling about in her kitchen at the Fuchsia Bush, had also heard about the possibility of the annexe to Rectory Cottages, but had given the matter scant attention.

She was quite used to hearing stray bits of gossip from Albert which he had picked up at the Two Pheasants. Half the time nothing came of these rumours, and Nelly had quite enough to do without wasting time and energy on such conjectures.

At the moment she was concerned with a certain small poster which had been pasted on the door of the Fuchsia Bush ever since the discovery of the abandoned dog in St Andrew's church porch. On that exciting morning she and Mrs Peters had decided to assist in finding the owner, and had put up the notice in the hope of finding someone who might know more about the mystery.

But now, it seemed, the dog was happily settled with Dotty, the police were no nearer solving the problem, and the notice was looking decidedly shabby. To Nelly's discriminating eye, it was detracting from the spruce appearance of their establishment. Some naughty person had written a very rude word at the foot of the poster, and Nelly felt that the time had come to remove the whole thing.

She glanced at the clock. It said half past eight. Mrs Peters was probably in the office already, she thought, for they were always early at the premises, making a start before the staff arrived.

But the office was empty, and Nelly was about to return to her duties when the telephone rang.

It was Mrs Peters, sounding weak and distraught.

'Nelly, I don't know what's hit me, but I can't come in at the moment. I'll try and make it later this morning.'

'Something you've eaten?' queried Nelly, her first thoughts, as always, on cooking.

'I just don't know. I feel so sick. Anyway, there's nothing specially urgent today, is there?'

Nelly mentioned the poster on the door.

'Yes, yes! By all means take it down, Nelly. See you before long, I sincerely hope,' she apologized.

Nelly replaced the receiver. She was full of sympathy for her suffering colleague, but quite confident about running their business on her own for a short time, for this had happened before.

She went to the door and tore off the notice. Nothing had come of it, she thought sadly, but they had done their bit.

On returning to the kitchen Nelly was annoyed to see that the new young kitchenmaid Irena had not arrived. She was just out of school, not very bright, but was engaged to do the vegetables and wash up the cooking utensils.

'Drat the girl!' said Nelly crossly. 'Now I'll have to get Gloria to help me.' This would be extremely unpopular, for Gloria was employed as a waitress and considered herself much above helping in the kitchen.

Two minutes later the back door opened, and Irena appeared. Her right thumb was heavily bandaged, and Nelly's heart sank.

'And what, pray, have you been and done?'

The girl flushed. 'It was the bread knife. I was just testing the blade like, and my little brother 'it me on the back. It's bled awful.'

Nelly examined the clumsy bandage. It appeared to have started life as a piece of shirting, and was grubby and blood-stained.

'Well, I'm not having that in my kitchen,' said Nelly vigorously. 'Germs fair oozing out of it, and the customers flocking along to the hospital in droves by the end of the week.'

The girl drooped her head and began to fiddle with a wooden spoon on Nelly's well-scrubbed table.

'Don't you touch nothing now,' shouted Nelly. 'You'd best go straight home and tell your mum to take you to the doctor. You might need a shot of whatever-it-is to kill them germs. You can't handle food like that, my girl. We'd all end up in court, and that's the truth.'

The girl began to sniff and looked so forlorn that Nelly's heart was touched.

'There, don't take on! It'll be all right in a day or two, I don't doubt, but you stay home till it's healed.'

She rummaged in a dresser drawer, found a bar of chocolate and handed it to the tearful Irena.

'Off you go now, and let me know what the doctor says.'

She hustled the girl to the back door, and watched her cross the yard. In the outside store room stood a sack of potatoes, two dozen fresh cauliflowers and a great basket of carrots.

Gloria will have to see to that, thought Nelly, and there will be plenty of black looks flying about this morning.

What next, she wondered? It was not long before she found out.

While Nelly Piggott was busy in her kitchen, and the forlorn Irena and her mother were making their way to the surgery of one of Lulling's doctors, Dotty Harmer was busy preparing breakfast for Flossie and her new dog, which she had christened Bruce.

'Being Scotch, you know,' she told Connie. 'If it had been a bitch I should have called it Bonnie for "Bonny Scotland", you see.'

She patted the white head of the Highland terrier, and was

rewarded with a loud barking and much tail-wagging. Bruce was now thoroughly at home, and Dotty hoped that his former owners would never appear to claim him.

'It's so strange that no one has come forward,' commented Connie. 'It's obviously from a distance. I mean, anyone within six miles of Lulling and Thrush Green would recognize the dog from its description in the *Gazette*. And it was so well-cared for. I can't think why it was simply abandoned like that. After all, if some tragedy had happened surely the RSPCA would have taken care of it?'

'Maybe the owners didn't like the idea. Maybe they were religious people and thought that one of the saints would look after it if it were left on church premises. St Francis, for instance,' said Dotty brightly.

'But he's been dead for centuries,' pointed out Connie, 'and anyway he lived in Italy.'

Dotty surveyed her niece with severity. 'At times, Connie, you are far too apt to take things *literally*. I was trying to point out that some people would look upon the church as a *sanctuary*, and where anyone in need would find help. I can't help feeling that Bruce's owners might have had that in mind when they left him there. Of course, I don't think St Francis would have personal intervention in the matter.'

Connie could see that the old lady was quite prepared to launch into an interesting discussion on the intervention of saints into contemporary life at Thrush Green, with particular reference to St Francis of Assisi who, Connie had heard her say, 'must have been a charming man'.

But Connie had lunch to prepare, and four telephone calls to make, so she gave her aunt a quick kiss, and left her with her pets.

At the Fuchsia Bush things were not going easily for Nelly Piggott. Gloria was late arriving, and decidedly sulky about having to do Irena's vegetables' preparations.

'I'm not paid for this sort of work,' she told Nelly. 'It's

Irena's job. She gets above herself, that one. It's having that stuck-up name. She's always getting out of doing things.'

'Irena's granny was from Russia or Prussia, I forget which, and she was named after her. And as for shirking her jobs, I see she doesn't do that!'

Gloria flounced to the sink, muttering darkly, and Nelly hurried into the shop when she heard Willie Marchant, the local postman, shouting to inform her that he'd propped the post by the basket of rolls.

He was banging the door behind him as Nelly took the letters to the kitchen. Almost all were for Mrs Peters, and these she put in the office, but one was addressed to Mrs Nelly Piggott, and this she took to the kitchen.

Gloria's back registered umbrage and Nelly had a pang of pity.

'I'll give you a hand in half a minute,' she promised, and sat down to read her letter. She rarely received a letter, and she took her time in studying the postmark on the envelope and then the address at the head of the flimsy lined paper inside. The letter came from someone in Leicester who signed herself as Mrs Jean Butler.

It read:

Dear Mrs Piggott,

Charlie asked me to write when he was took ill. I am sorry to say he died in hospital last week. He was a lodger here since last summer working on the roads.

We are burying him next Friday, and if you want to know more the lady I work for don't mind you phoning of a morning.

Yours truly,

Mrs Jean Butler

There was a telephone number at the foot of the page, but Nelly was too stunned by the news to notice it.

Charlie dead! Charlie so full of life and fun, cracking jokes, teasing everyone, the life and soul of every party! He couldn't be dead.

She dropped the letter on the kitchen table, staring ahead as tears began to fill her eyes.

She had loved that man. For him she had left Albert and Thrush Green and gone to share Charlie's life for over a year. For most of that time they had been riotously happy, laughing with friends at pubs, going to dances and bingo, enjoying their shared bed and board.

But towards the end Charlie had shown himself as a liar and a deceiver, sharing his affection with a woman whom Nelly had considered a friend.

There had been a violent row. Hard words had flown across the kitchen, and harder saucepans had accompanied them. Nelly had stormed out, and returned to Thrush Green, dreading Albert's wrath and possible rejection.

The wrath had certainly been in evidence, but Albert was so relieved to see her back to cook his meals and keep house that she was allowed to stay. Albert was glad to have this secret weapon of retaliation in his armoury when warfare broke out in the home, and Nelly, ebullient as ever, soon became her cheerful self, and forgot Charlie.

Only once had she seen him, and that was when he called into the Fuchsia Bush some two years before the arrival of the sad letter before her.

He had been a beaten shabby figure making his way to see an old friend in Birmingham with hopes of a job there.

Nelly had given him a meal and money, and sent him on his way saying that that was to be their last meeting.

And it was, thought Nelly.

'You going to give me a hand?' called Gloria, 'I can't do this lot alone.'

Nelly mopped her eyes and went to do her duty.

'What's up?' asked Gloria, suddenly solicitous on observing Nelly's ravaged face. 'Bad news?'

'An old friend. He's dead.'

Gloria put a wet hand on Nelly's ample back, and patted her kindly. This was as good as the telly really, and poor old Nelly wasn't such a bad old soul, although she was a bit of a slave driver.

'Local?' enquired Gloria.

'No. Though he did come here once.'

Light dawned. Gloria, and her fellow waitress Rosa, had been greatly intrigued by that traveller who had called one snowy morning and made Nelly's heart flutter.

'That nice chap,' said Gloria diplomatically, 'who was after a job?'

Nelly nodded and attacked a carrot. She was afraid to trust her voice, and the lump in her throat was painful. They worked together in silence, until Irena appeared at the back door holding up a neatly bandaged hand.

'Two stitches, and some tablets for something called Auntie Bi-something, and I can't come to work for a week.'

She sounded proud and happy, and quite oblivious of the air of tragedy hanging over the kitchen.

'See you next week then,' said Nelly dismissively, and Irena vanished.

Mrs Peters did not arrive, but luckily the Fuchsia Bush was not too busy that morning, and there were no outside commitments.

Since Nelly had been made a partner in the business, outside catering had increased and had proved rewarding. The Fuchsia Bush had built up a reliable reputation and catered for functions such as weddings, christenings and other family occasions.

It was Nelly too who had instigated the making of a daily batch of rolls filled with ham, tongue, cheese or other delights for the local office staffs to purchase for their lunches. This venture had proved very successful and greatly added to the profits.

Her heart was heavy as she supervised the depleted staff, but the fact that she needed to be extra busy kept her from brooding over the death of dear Charlie. Later, she told herself, she would ring that Leicester number and find out more, but she had no intention of attending the funeral. Should she send flowers? She thought not. It would be best to keep all this from Albert. He had had quite enough of Charlie in the past.

During the afternoon when Nelly was helping to set the tables for tea, the telephone rang again. A neighbour of Mrs Peters told Nelly that the doctor had sent her to hospital as her stomach pains were so severe.

Mrs Peters had asked Nelly to carry on. Perhaps Mrs Jefferson could lend a hand, or knew of someone? Mrs Jefferson had worked for many years at the Fuchsia Bush and was now enjoying retirement. Mrs Peters would be in touch as soon as possible.

Nelly put down the receiver, and went to tell Gloria and Rosa.

'Never rains but it pours,' said Rosa.

'What do we do now?' asked Gloria.

'We carry on,' said Nelly, rolling up her sleeves.

A little further south in Lulling the rector was also answering the telephone.

Mrs Thurgood, a parishioner and fellow trustee of Rectory Cottages, was enquiring – one might say *demanding* – if Charles Henstock had done anything about enlarging the premises.

Trust Mrs Thurgood to push matters along with unnecessary velocity, thought poor Charles, holding the receiver some distance from his ear. Mrs Thurgood had a powerful voice.

'I have had a word with Jane Cartwright who seems to think that the present room is quite adequate for general purposes.'

'That's not how I heard things were.'

'And I've spoken to Harold Shoosmith –'

There was a snort at the other end. Mrs Thurgood did not approve of Harold. Too often he had been the victor in their clashes. Charles, she thought, was made of tenderer stuff, and it was he whom she approached first when beginning a campaign.

'And he feels as I do,' continued Charles undaunted, 'that there is no real necessity to consider the matter further.'

'Oh really?' said Mrs Thurgood, heavily sarcastic. 'And what about the old people's needs? I have their welfare very much at heart. They should be considered.'

Charles decided that he must be firm. 'It is the first thing we all think of, as I'm sure you know. But there is the matter of finance to consider as well. We have raised a great deal of money recently for Nathaniel Patten's African settlement, and helped Thrush Green school at its centenary, and there are a great many repairs due to be done on the churches of the parish. I think the enlargement of the room can wait.'

'I shall bring the matter up at the next meeting of the trustees,' said Mrs Thurgood.

'Please do,' said Charles in his gentlest voice, and put down the receiver.

Sometimes, he thought sadly, it was very hard to love one's neighbour as oneself. He escaped into the garden which always lifted his heart.

A blackbird piped from the lilac tree, and at the further end of the lawn a thrush was poised, head on one side, listening for the sound of a worm underground.

The daffodils were in bud. Some early narcissi were already flowering, filling the air around them with heady scent. The polyanthus plants turned their velvety faces to the morning sunshine, bright yellow, orange, red and a deep mauvish-blue which Charles particularly admired.

The almond tree was beginning to scatter the pink blooms which had cheered the February days, but the nearby cherry tree was in bud and soon would be in flower.

Charles remembered the words of A. E. Housman, who wrote of the wild cherry tree in Shropshire:

> *Stands about the rural ride*
> *Wearing white for Easter-tide.*

Easter-tide, thought the rector with mingled joy and alarm! Very soon now, and much to prepare for that lovely festival. Perhaps he should return to his desk?

He looked up at the blue and white sky above the nearby spire of St John's. '*From whence,*' thought Charles, '*cometh my help.*'

And went, serenity re-established, to face his tasks.

Nelly Piggott did not ring the Leicester number that morning. She did not trust her voice, for one thing, and added to that was the more pressing situation at the Fuchsia Bush.

As soon as the bustle of lunch was over, Nelly sat down in Mrs Peters' office and rang Mrs Jefferson. Could she help?

The answer was enthusiastic. Obviously the old lady was thrilled to be asked, and keen to come, but there were certain reservations. She was still under doctor's orders, and she had better ring him about the invitation. She would do so at once, she promised Nelly, and ring back.

Nelly then telephoned the hospital and was informed by a crisp voice that Mrs Peters was at that moment being examined by Mr Pedder-Bennett himself.

If she had said that the archangel Gabriel was at Mrs Peters' bedside she could not have sounded more reverential, thought Nelly crossly.

'If,' said the voice, 'you ring this evening, we shall know more.'

Within half an hour Mrs Jefferon rang again to say that Dr
Lovell said that as long as she only did four hours a day, that
was fine by him. Could she come from ten until two? Thankfully, Nelly agreed. Mrs Jefferson, well-versed in the ways
of the Fuchsia Bush, knew just when help would be most
welcome.

Nelly sat for a moment in the quiet office. She was unutter-
ably tired, and for two pins would have put her heavy head on
the desk and gone to sleep.

But there was much to be done, and she roused herself.
Later she would ring the hospital at the callbox on Thrush
Green. That was essential. Another telephone call must be
made, for tonight was bingo night, and she could not face that
at the moment. She would ring Mrs Jenner who lived along the
lane from Thrush Green to Nidden, and explain matters, telling
her not to bother to call on her way, as was her usual custom.

And then tomorrow morning she would ring the writer of
the letter which lay crumpled in her apron pocket. She would
make the call here in the privacy of the office, away from Albert
and with time to compose herself before facing the world again.

Nelly had resolutely put all thoughts of Charlie from her
mind since their last meeting, but the news of his death had
made her realize, with sharp poignancy, just how much that
damned dear deceiver had meant to her.

April

It is very well to hear the cuckoo for the first
time on Easter Sunday morning. I loitered up
the lane again gathering primroses.

Francis Kilvert

No one at Thrush Green heard the cuckoo on Easter Sunday,
for the festival came early in the month. The Cotswolds
too can be colder in spring than the Welsh valleys which the
Reverend Francis Kilvert so loved over a hundred years ago.

But the primroses were out, and bunches of them decorated
the font at St Andrew's, and in the churchyard the daffodils
swayed in the wind.

The little church of St Andrew's had been lovingly dressed
with spring flowers and leaves by the local ladies, and very fine
it looked. The larger and more venerable church at Lulling
would no doubt be more lavishly decorated, thought Winnie
Bailey, as she rose with the rest of the congregation when
Charles Henstock and the choir processed down the aisle from
the west door.

St John's at Lulling, standing dignified and serene behind its
large expanse of Church Green spread before it, had a devoted
band of worshippers, many of them with far more money than
those at Thrush Green, and they made sure that their noble
church was splendidly decked at all times, and particularly at
the great festivals of the Church.

Hothouse flowers from nearby glasshouses were willingly given. Arum lilies, fuchsias, geraniums, and even orchids delighted the eyes of St John's congregation at such times, but nevertheless, thought Winnie surveying their more modest efforts, St Andrew's could hold its own on a bright Easter Sunday.

The church was fuller than usual, even though the service had been put forward by one hour to allow Charles to fit in as many attendances as possible in his four parishes.

Winnie was among many friends. She supposed she knew everyone there, she thought, sitting down to listen to Harold Shoosmith reading the first lesson behind the shining eagle which spread out its wings obligingly as a lectern.

She glanced across the aisle, recognizing with pleasure Mrs

Jenner's summer straw hat which proved that winter was really over. This year it was refurbished with a navy-blue ribbon with short streamers at the back. Last year it had been encircled with imitation wild roses. Winnie felt that the ribbon this year was more dignified.

With a slight shock she realized that someone unknown to her was sitting immediately in front of Mrs Jenner.

A man with very thick blond hair was listening attentively to the lesson. He was wearing a grey suit with a chalk stripe, and it reminded Winnie of the suits, termed 'demob suits, which had been issued to returning warriors after the Second World War. But this one was better cut and seemed to be made of very good cloth. She wished she could see his tie and shirt, for Winnie had an eye for clothes and had always taken an interest in Donald's wardrobe.

Unfortunately, she could see only the stranger's broad shoulders, but when Percy Hodge came round with the collection bag the man turned to put in his contribution and Winnie was pleased to see that his shirt was a blue-and-white striped one, and his tie was dark blue. He was certainly a very handsome fellow, and Winnie was not the only one in the congregation to speculate about the stranger in their midst that Easter morning.

After the service Charles Henstock waited in the church porch to greet his parishioners, as was his wont. The tall stranger was among the throng as they came out, but seemed to be anxious not to obtrude upon the vicar and his friends. Many eyes were turned upon him, but nothing was said.

When the last of the church members had straggled away, the rector was about to hurry to his car for the service at St John's when the man approached him.

'Could I have a word, sir?'

The accent was American, the manner almost timid, contrasting strangely with the size of the man.

Charles gave him the warm smile which had melted so many female hearts, and held out his hand. 'Of course. How can I help?'

'I'm over from the States to look up some relatives. Name of Curdle.'

'Ah! We are very proud of the Curdles in these parts,' Charles told him. 'In fact, the most famous one is buried only a few yards away.'

'I found her grave yesterday,' replied the man. 'She's the one I wanted to visit first. Now I want to find some living Curdles. Can you tell me where to go?'

'I can indeed.' The rector looked at his watch.

'I could take you over to meet them myself, but there are two things against it. I am due at my next service in a few minutes, and I know that the Curdles are away this weekend. But let me show you where they live.'

He took the stranger by the arm in a companionable way, and they stepped round the church path to the north side where Charles stopped and pointed out the fine old house belonging to the Youngs.

'My!' said the man. 'They've gone up in the world if that's their place!'

Charles explained that Ben and Molly had a more modest abode in the garden.

'But come and see me at the vicarage,' urged Charles. 'How long are you staying?'

'I want to look up friends in Edinburgh, and I have some business which may detain me there. I reckon I'll have to go there on Tuesday, or whenever it fits in with their schedule. My name by the way is Andersen, with an E, and my forename is Carl.'

'How do you do?' said Charles, shaking hands again. 'And I am Charles Henstock. Do come to the vicarage at Lulling if you can spare the time. Anyone will direct you. I am so sorry that I have to hurry away now. Perhaps I can give you a lift?'

'Thank you, sir, but I'll look around for a bit. Perhaps when I get back from Scotland?'

'That would be ideal. I shall look forward to it, Mr Andersen,' said Charles, turning back to the church.

'Mr Andersen with an E, and "skedule" not "schedule",' said Charles to himself, as he drove back to St John's. 'And what a nice fellow! I hope he comes again, and I can be of help.'

Across the road from St Andrew's church, Nelly Piggott noticed the stranger wandering about the churchyard. He stopped every now and again, and seemed to be copying the inscriptions on some of the tombstones into a little notebook.

Nelly, who had always had an eye for male beauty, was impressed by the blond good looks of this ambling giant, but had other matters on her mind which took precedence that morning.

For one thing, she was cooking a small turkey with all its accompaniments. For another, she had a great deal to think about the job at the Fuchsia Bush. And lastly, but by no means least, she thought about the pathetic news of Charlie's departure from this life.

She had said nothing to Albert about this matter, but had rung the Leicester number and spoken to Jean Butler. As far as Nelly could make out, that good woman had virtually looked after Charlie for the best part of a year, and though she talked of him as 'a lodger', she had evidently received no payment from him.

It was typical, thought Nelly, as the tale unfolded, that Charlie should land on his feet. Obviously, the old charm was still there. Jean Butler had been in tears, and spoke of her late lodger with true affection.

Nelly told her that it would be impossible for her to leave her job to attend the funeral, and expressed her sympathy. She almost added that they were in the same boat, but managed to resist the temptation. She was also careful not to give her address or to express the hope that they might meet one day. She rang off, glad that she had ended the affair with such discretion, but shocked by the description of Charlie's sufferings.

He had, Jean Butler told her, 'just wasted away'. He had cut his foot which had turned septic. Gangrene had set in. It had not responded to treatment, and his foot had been amputated. All through this time Jean Butler had seen him daily. According to her, he had remained brave and cheerful to the last, and had promised to take her to a dance as soon as his new foot was fitted.

It was this last flash of Charlie's spirit which particularly upset Nelly, and the poignancy of it haunted her thoughts.

It was perhaps as well that the day-to-day running of the Fuchsia Bush was now entirely in her hands, for Mrs Peters remained in hospital. Mrs Jefferson, Rosa, Gloria and the now-healed Irena backed up the establishment and two temporary girls had been taken on to help with the running of the place. There was little time for tears, and for this Nelly was grateful.

She had also found some comfort in confiding in Mrs Jenner, one of her weekly bingo companions. Mrs Jenner was much respected in the neighbourhood. For years she had been the local midwife, and was the mother of Jane Cartwright who ran Rectory Cottages with her husband Bill.

Mrs Jenner had lived all her life in the old farmhouse along the road to Nidden. Percy Hodge, her brother, still farmed there, but lived next door with his new wife Gladys. When Charles and Dimity Henstock had become homeless overnight following the fire at Thrush Green rectory, it was Mrs Jenner who had come to the rescue, and given them lodgings at the farmhouse.

As soon as Nelly had rung on that sad evening, to say that she would not be at bingo, Mrs Jenner guessed that something serious had happened.

'Come up here one evening soon,' she said to Nelly. 'Just you and me for a nice chat.'

'I'd like that,' said Nelly. 'Can we make it on Friday?'

Albert was ensconced in the Two Pheasants when Nelly walked through the dusk of evening to visit her friend.

As the tale unfolded, Mrs Jenner listened with growing sympathy. Like most Thrush Green residents, her first impressions of Nelly had been censorious. It was generally agreed that she was noisy, pushy and 'a bit common', that damning phrase which had blighted so many villagers' characters.

Her affair with Charlie, the oilman, whose van visited the area once a week, was soon being discussed with much head-shaking.

Not that Albert, as the injured husband, merited much sympathy, and when Nelly scandalized the community by going to live with Charlie, some people said openly who could blame her with that old misery Albert for a husband?

But latterly things had changed. Nelly's success at the Fuchsia Bush, her unfailing cheerfulness, and her exemplary cleanliness had made her neighbours willing to admit that there was a lot to commend Nelly Piggott.

Mrs Jenner had been one of the first to offer friendship, and her example had prompted others to welcome Nelly into Thrush Green society.

On that April evening the bond between the two women grew stronger than ever. Although Mrs Jenner deprecated Nelly's passion for the flibbertigibbet Charlie, she was wise enough to recognize that love can strike in the most uncomfortable and unpredictable ways, and that really Nelly was perhaps more sinned against than sinning.

Certainly, as Nelly poured out her tale, with her tears, sitting in Mrs Jenner's wicker armchair, her hostess was almost as moved as her sorrowful guest.

She fell back on the common panacea in times of stress. 'I shall make us a nice pot of tea, dear,' she told Nelly.

And she did.

It was about this time that Edward Young came across Jane Cartwright, as they had both gone to post letters in the box by the wall of the Youngs' house.

'Ah!' greeted Edward. 'Just the person I wanted to see.'

Jane smiled happily. She had no inkling of what was in

Edward's mind, but she had always looked upon him as a good friend.

She put her two letters in first, and Edward thrust a fat bundle of mail in after hers.

'It's about that room of yours. I hear it's considered inadequate.'

Jane's heart sank. From his tone she realized that he was annoyed, and knowing his reputation for 'touchiness' she felt dismayed.

However, she was a brave woman, and answered straightforwardly. 'It's perfectly adequate for its purpose,' she said. 'I don't know who started these rumours. I've heard them myself, so I know they may have worried you. If we have a party, of course, which doesn't happen very often, I suppose we could do with more space.'

Edward grunted. 'So there's nothing to complain about?'

'Indeed not. We love the building and the added conservatory.'

Edward looked slightly mollified. 'Anyone else spoken to you about this affair?'

'Well, the rector asked me what I thought. I told him exactly what I have told you. He seemed relieved. He said we couldn't really afford to make any enlargements.'

'That's quite true. And I'm glad he was relieved. I am too. I did my level best to make those buildings absolutely right at the time.'

Jane was glad to see that he seemed calmer. 'You did a first-class job there,' she told him, 'and we all appreciate it.'

They parted company with relief on both sides.

During April the trustees of Rectory Cottages met in the Henstocks' dining-room at Lulling.

The meeting was at eight o'clock and Dimity had provided coffee and drinks for the assembled company. Having supplied her guests she retired to the vicarage sitting-room and watched a gardening programme on television. She found it very peaceful.

In the dining-room next door, the even tenor of the Usual Business had also gone its peaceful way, until Charles, as chairman, had enquired if there were any other business, and Mrs Thurgood raised her voice.

'I am greatly perturbed to hear that the communal room is too small,' she stated.

All eyes turned towards her. Charles, who had expected this matter to be raised, found that his attention was caught by Mrs Thurgood's hat.

Usually that lady's hats were high-crowned affairs with wisps of veiling or silk swathed around them, reminiscent of Queen Mary's toques of Charles's youth. But this evening she was wearing a round straw hat with an upturned brim and two streamers of ribbon hanging at the back. It seemed rather a youthful style for such a formidable figure, and Charles felt that it was vaguely familiar.

'Any comments?' he asked the assembled company, still secretly puzzling about the hat.

'I don't think,' said Harold Shoosmith, 'that the room is really too small. I had a word with Jane Cartwright and one or two of the people at Rectory Cottages, and everyone seemed quite happy with the present arrangements.'

Mrs Thurgood bridled, and the two streamers quivered. Light dawned on Charles. Of course, the hat was exactly like those worn by Edwardian children at the seaside! A sort of summer sailor's hat! He smiled with relief.

Mrs Thurgood shot him a disapproving glance. For two pins, Charles thought, she would tell him that it was 'no laughing matter'. But the lady's attention was directed to Harold.

'That is not what I heard,' she said firmly. 'It was Captain Jermyn himself who mentioned it to me.'

There was a visible relaxation of tension. Captain Jermyn, a crusty old veteran of two world wars, was known to be an inveterate troublemaker.

Charles rallied to Harold's support, making a mental note to consult Dimity about the hat when the meeting ended.

'I too have spoken to several people, and all seemed to find the room adequate.'

John Lovell also added his mite, saying mildly that he knew his brother-in-law, Edward Young, who had designed the building and the annexe, had taken infinite trouble over the dimensions of the sitting-room. He himself had always thought it pleasantly spacious. 'What's more,' he added, 'it would be horribly expensive to enlarge.'

'We've raised money before,' snapped Mrs Thurgood. 'Jumble sales, fêtes, coffee mornings, whist drives – I've helped with all of them *myself*! And I've had another idea recently. Janet, my daughter, would be quite willing to have an exhibition of her abstract paintings, and I'm sure people would flock to see it.'

From the expressions of dismay which were apparent on the committee members' faces, this hopeful vision of queues jostling to see Miss Thurgood's incomprehensible daubs seemed unlikely.

'But where could it be held?' asked someone, playing for time.

'I thought the town hall,' said Mrs Thurgood. 'Of course, the rental of the place would have to come from our funds, but the profits should easily cover that. I propose a fund-raising effort.'

Charles took charge. 'I think we should put Mrs Thurgood's proposal to the vote. Can I have a seconder?'

There was a stony silence, whilst looks were exchanged.

'Well,' said Charles, 'it looks as though we must let the matter rest.'

'*You* may,' said Mrs Thurgood forcefully, 'but I shall not!'

And five minutes later the meeting ended.

In bed that night, Charles asked Dimity if she had noticed Mrs Thurgood's hat.

'It reminded me of the sort of thing my father wore as a boy at Walton-on-Naze, according to family photographs.'

'It's a Breton straw,' Dimity told him.

'A Breton straw?' echoed Charles mystified.

'Sailors wear them in Brittany,' yawned Dimity. 'I had one just after the war. They seemed to be in fashion after D-Day.'

'But surely there wouldn't be any sailors in Brittany wearing hats like that on D-Day,' replied Charles. 'I mean the beaches were swarming with troops, and any Breton sailors would be in uniform. Don't you think that style really goes back to earlier times?'

But Charles received no answer. Dimity had fallen asleep, and Charles shelved these sartorial problems and followed suit.

Edward Young, who was also one of the trustees, had been unable to attend the meeting, which was just as well, for he would have become extremely heated in the light of Mrs Thurgood's assertion that the sitting-room he had so carefully designed was too small. John Lovell, as Edward's doctor, felt particularly relieved that his irascible brother-in-law was absent. Such an atmosphere might well have brought on Edward's shingles again.

Nevertheless, Edward, who still found the rumour rankling, asked several local friends for their opinion. All did their best to reassure him. Most of those asked were genuinely of the opinion that the room was quite all right as it was.

One or two, including Molly Curdle who knew Edward's quick temper, kept any doubts about the adequacy of the room to themselves. Anyway, all agreed that it would cost a great deal of money.

Edward calmed down, and general relief was felt in the Youngs' household.

Edward was gazing from his drawing-room window one fine April morning, and feeling pleasantly relaxed as he surveyed Thrush Green and Rectory Cottages looking particularly fine in the spring sunshine. He admired the tubs of velvety polyanthus and wallflowers which stood each side of the Two Pheasants' doorway. Nearer at hand he saw that the lilac bushes near his own gate would soon be in fragrant bloom. There was no doubt about it. Spring took a lot of beating at Thrush Green!

As he gloried in the view before him, he noticed a small car pulling up near his gateway. A large fair-haired man got out, consulted his wrist-watch, and then went rather hesitantly across the road to stroll on the dewy grass of Thrush Green.

Edward watched him with curiosity. One did not often see strangers on Thrush Green.

Near by, Winnie Bailey and Jenny, busy changing sheets in the front bedroom, also noticed the stranger.

'Now who can that be?' wondered Winnie aloud, stuffing a pillow into a fresh pillowslip.

'Can't see properly,' said Jenny, approaching the window.

'I do hope it's not one of those *travellers*,' said Winnie. 'I believe they send out a sort of scout to find out the lie of the land. Thrush Green is just the sort of place for dozens of broken-down vehicles to park, isn't it?'

Jenny was reassuring. 'He looks too respectable to me. Might be one of those reps just stretching his legs before he goes down to Lulling to sell something to the shops there.'

'I do hope you're right. Connie was telling me a fearful tale about a friend of hers in Dorset who was absolutely surrounded by caravans and buses and tents for weeks. She couldn't get her car out of the garage.'

'She should have rung the police.'

'She did, but there's some stupid business about letting
people stay for a certain length of time before action can be
taken. At least, that's what Connie told me. Her friend was
virtually a prisoner in her own home.'

The two women peered out of the window. The stranger
was approaching the Two Pheasants, and Mr Jones emerged
and engaged the man in conversation. There was a good deal
of nodding and smiling, and Mr Jones pointed towards the
Youngs' house.

'Well,' said Winnie after a few minutes, 'he seems to be
going to see Edward and Joan.'

'Then he *must* be respectable,' said Jenny. 'Nothing to worry
about.'

The two returned to their bed-making.

Edward Young opened the door.

'I'm looking for Mr and Mrs Curdle,' said the stranger. 'Have
I come to the wrong house?'

'Actually, their house is over there,' replied Edward, pointing
to the old stables, across the garden.

'I'm sorry to have troubled you,' said the stranger, retreating,
but Edward called him back.

'There's no one there at the moment. Molly has gone across
to see her father who lives over there near the pub, and Ben's
at work in Lulling. Why don't you come in and wait for Molly?
She'll only be a few minutes.'

'That's sure kind of you,' said the man, following Edward
into the hall.

Edward was curious about his visitor. Obviously he was an
American, but why did he want to see the Curdles? At least he
sounded as though he had a genuine reason for being in Thrush
Green. For one awful moment he had wondered, as Winnie
and Jenny had, if the fellow were spying out the land for an
invasion of unwanted self-styled *travellers*. The trouble with

such people, Edward had thought, was that they seemed to be *settlers*, rather than *travellers*, and Thrush Green could do without them.

He saw now that his guest was well-scrubbed and his blond hair recently washed. He was dressed in very good clothes of an informal type, a silk shirt and a cardigan which looked suspiciously like cashmere, and Edward looked at his shining shoes with envy.

At that moment, Joan came in and Edward turned to the stranger who had leapt politely to his feet.

'Oh, I didn't realize you had someone here,' said Joan.

'My wife, Joan, and I am Edward Young,' said Edward.

'And I am Carl Andersen,' said the stranger, 'with an E.'

'How do you do?' said Joan. 'With an E? Like Hans Andersen? Is he a relative, by any chance?'

'No such luck, ma'am, but my folk came from his country, Denmark, way back.'

'From "*Wonderful, wonderful Copenhagen*"?' laughed Joan, quoting from the musical.

'Nearer Odense, I'm told, where Hans Andersen was born. I was brought up on his stories.'

'Me too,' said Joan, 'and now I'll get some coffee.'

'I've been admiring the houses here,' said Carl Andersen. 'Those new ones have fitted in real well.'

Edward smiled. 'I designed them,' he said with some pride.

'Is that so? I'm in the building line myself. I take it you are an architect?'

'That's right. And you?'

'More in the way of construction. Large stuff like bridges and dams.'

Edward looked at him with greater interest. 'You're not Benn, Andersen and Webbly, by any chance?'

'That's right. At least, it was my pa that was the first Andersen. I just fell into his shoes, as it were.'

'A most prestigious firm,' said Edward reverently. 'They've done outstanding work all over the world. I've followed all they undertake with the greatest interest.'

'Well, I'm sure proud to be with them,' replied Carl. 'I've just been up to Scotland to discuss a big project up there. All pretty exciting.'

Joan appeared with the coffee, and the conversation became more general, until Edward, full of curiosity, asked directly what brought their visitor to Thrush Green.

'It's something my mother asked me to do. She's an old lady now, and an invalid, but she was born and raised at Woodstock near here, and old Mrs Curdle was her godmother.'

'Well,' cried Joan, 'this is absolutely amazing! Ben is her grandson, you know. She brought him up, but I've never heard about her godchild.'

'I expect you know that Mrs Curdle's fair used to go on to Woodstock after it had performed here. Old Mrs Curdle and my mother's mother were old friends, and Mrs Curdle took a great interest in her god-daughter. My mother has never forgotten her. She wanted me to look up her relatives in these parts.'

'Well, Ben is her grandson, as we said. Whether he remembers your mother from so long ago, I just don't know.'

'But how did your mother go to America?' Edward wanted to know. Joan, not for the first time, deplored her husband's uninhibited questioning, but said nothing.

'My pa was stationed at RAF Upper Heyford near Woodstock, during the war, and he met my ma at a dance.'

'But this is really romantic,' cried Joan. 'So he took her back with him when the war ended?'

'Not quite. This is where Mrs Curdle comes into it. My ma wrote regularly to my pa when he returned to the States, but she got no mail from him for months, and began to think he'd dropped her. Maybe even had a wife over there all the time. You know how it is.'

'So what happened?'

'She was beginning to wonder if she'd think about getting tied up with a guy from Eynsham who was pretty persistent. She told her godmother all about it, and Mrs Curdle told her to be patient because she said my pa would surely be writing soon. She told my ma she had something called "second sight", and all would turn out fine and dandy. And it did. My pa came over, whipped her up and took her back home.'

'But why hadn't the letters got through?'

'As soon as my pa got back he took up his old job with Benn and Webbly, as it was then. He was working full steam for them, and had rooms in Chicago near the firm. The daughter of the house was sweet on him, and kept any mail from Woodstock out of sight. Burnt it, no doubt. And for weeks my pa left his mail on the hall table to be sent off, and that young good-for-nothing burnt them too, I guess. Anyway, they each thought the other had stopped feeling the way they did, until my pa came to his senses, guessed what was happening and sent a cable.'

'Amazing!' said Joan. 'So dear old Mrs Curdle was right.'

The visitor looked at his wrist-watch and stood up. 'I've taken up too much of your time,' he said. 'Thank you for the coffee. I'll go and see if Molly Curdle's in now.'

They said goodbye to him at the kitchen door, and watched him approach Molly who was pegging clothes on a line near by.

'Well, I must say,' said Edward, 'I enjoyed all that. Not many of our visitors are so entertaining. I hope he comes again.'

Later that morning the Youngs saw Carl Andersen driving towards Lulling, and a few minutes later Molly Curdle came into the kitchen where Joan was making a cake.

'Isn't it exciting?' said Molly, sitting down at the table.

'And isn't he handsome? Could be a film star. I've always liked fair men.'

'I'm surprised you picked Ben then,' commented Joan, sprinkling sugar into the mixture in the bowl. 'He's a real dark beauty.'

'Oh well,' said Molly indulgently, 'that's different. Ben was always special.'

'Where is Mr Andersen staying?'

'At the Bear in Woodstock. His mother used to work there when she was a girl. She was there when she met his dad. He wants to meet Ben, and he's gone down to the garage to fix a time for a chat. I hope he'll come to supper tonight.'

'I'm sure he'd enjoy that.'

Molly looked doubtful. 'I don't know about that. It wouldn't be half as grand as dinner at the Bear, but he seems keen to come.'

'Of course he does! And Ben will be able to tell him more about Mrs Curdle than anyone else I know.'

'Dad must remember some things,' said Molly thoughtfully. 'He always said a lot on Fair Day.'

'Complimentary?' asked Joan with a smile.

Molly laughed. 'It was usually a good old moan about the noise and the mess to be cleared up next day! I don't think I'll send this nice Mr Andersen to see my dad!'

The reason for nice Mr Andersen's presence at Thrush Green was soon known and widely discussed.

Mr Jones at the Two Pheasants regretted that the handsome stranger should think the Bear at Woodstock could offer better accommodation than his own.

'Ah, but his mum used to work there,' said Albert Piggott, who had learnt a lot from Molly.

'I wonder if she was that girl young Steve Smith was so keen on just after the war,' speculated Percy Hodge. 'He used to cycle over from Eynsham every evening. Good old pull that was, on a windy night.'

'Love'll drive you anywhere,' said another customer, in a maudlin tone. There was a heavy silence while the old men contemplated their distant romantic pasts.

'Before my time,' said Mr Jones briskly. 'I was in hospital getting over working for the Japs on the Burma railway.'

Across the green Winnie Bailey and Jenny enthused about the wonderful good looks of the stranger, and tried to remember if they had ever come across his mother in days gone by.

Rosa and Gloria at the Fuchsia Bush had been intrigued by Nelly's news of this blonde giant who had excited so much interest in Thrush Green. He had not yet visited their establishment, but they had seen him walk by, and agreed that he was almost as handsome as Paul Newman and Robert Redford, though Gloria admitted to preferring dark men, preferably with a moustache and a pigtail.

But Nelly soon cut into their romantic conjectures by telling them sharply to lay up for lunch and to give the front window a bit of elbow grease.

For Nelly had enough to think about. Mrs Peters was still in hospital, and the nurses were remarkably unforthcoming about her coming out in the near future.

And if she did, Nelly told herself, it would be a long time before the poor soul would be strong enough to take up her duties again.

What would the future hold for the Fuchsia Bush?

May

But winter ling'ring chills the lap of May.

Oliver Goldsmith

The last few days of April had been bright but cold, but on the morning of May Day the skies were dark and the wind boisterous.

It was as well, thought Joan Young, gazing from her bedroom window as she dressed, that Mrs Curdle's May fair was not obliged to perform in such inhospitable surroundings.

The horse-chestnut trees, in bright young leaf, tossed their tormented branches, and the puddles below shivered in the wind. The spring flowers, jonquil, daffodil and tulip, were thrown this way and that by the wind. Some had succumbed altogether and were lying broken and besmirched on the ground.

How unlike the firsts of May that she remembered! Somehow Mrs Curdle's fair had always seemed to take place in sunny weather. Was this the result of old age, wondered Joan? Was she looking back through rose-coloured spectacles at those distant days when she and her sister Ruth had swung on the swing-boats and looked down upon the roofs of the Two Pheasants and Piggott's cottage and their own house, with such heady rapture?

Nearer in time she recalled the excitement of her young son Paul on May Day. It was the high spot of Thrush Green's year for him, just as it had been for herself and Ruth and countless other children.

She turned away from the streaming window and the lashing wind, and found comfort in times past.

Near by, Winnie Bailey was also remembering those days when Mrs Curdle's fair enlivened Thrush Green. It was many years now since that formidable figure, dressed in black, had advanced up the garden path with the enormous bunch of artificial flowers which she had made for her annual tribute to Dr Bailey and his wife.

These bouquets were received with due ceremony and greatly admired for their handiwork. Mrs Curdle carefully bound split wood with fine wire to make great mop-heads of an exotic type of chrysanthemum. The blooms were dyed in gorgeous colours, so vivid that nature had no chance here to emulate art.

Mrs Curdle herself was an honoured visitor, and sat upright

and regal in the Baileys' drawing-room, graciously accepting a glass of sherry and exchanging the year's news.

No, thought Winnie, watching the rain beating down her forget-me-nots, the first of May was not what it was. How she missed dear old Mrs Curdle!

There were others who remembered her on that wild and wet morning. Dotty Harmer, turning the calendar page from April to May in her untidy kitchen, thought sadly of times past when she had hurried up the lane to see the excitement of Mrs Curdle's fair, with Flossie tugging at the lead.

Today she was worried about Flossie. The old dog wanted only to lie in her basket. Any movement seemed to pain her, and an occasional yelp and whine gave voice to Flossie's growing arthritis.

All Dotty's home-produced herbal cures seemed to be useless. Soon she must call in the vet for some professional advice, loath though she was to do so, but she was not going to let dear Flossie suffer unnecessarily.

Meanwhile, she diverted young Bruce with a ball rolled along the floor, to keep him from annoying the invalid. He was a dear little dog, thought Dotty indulgently, but like all young things, *over-active*. She would like to have let him run free in the garden, but the lashing rain deterred her, and he was still at the adventurous stage when he would rush off and get lost if he were on his own.

Perhaps the only Thrush Green resident who did not hark back to the days of Mrs Curdle was Nelly Piggott, who had braved the elements to arrive early at the Fuchsia Bush.

To be sure, Albert had made some comment about May Day in a gloomy way, but Nelly had been too busy washing up the breakfast things, and flying about the place with a duster, to take much notice. She had hardly known Mrs Curdle, and was too preoccupied with affairs at the restaurant to take much notice of Albert's meanderings.

For things at the Fuchsia Bush were worrying. Mrs Peters was still in hospital, and although the day-to-day running of the business did not daunt Nelly, and the catering was as efficient as ever, the financial side posed a serious problem.

It was Mrs Peters who kept the books in apple-pie order; she who dealt with wholesalers and discounts, with invoices and deliveries, auditors and accountants. Nelly was completely out of her depth with the office work, and she and Mrs Peters had agreed that someone must be responsible for this side of the business until the invalid was judged fit enough to return.

To Nelly's relief, one of the women from the accountant's office had been charged with the task of taking over Mrs Peters' duties. She was an elderly spinster who had been with the firm ever since leaving school. She was soon to retire, was polite, efficient and wholly respectable.

Nelly loathed her. She thought her stuck-up, bossy and condescending. Nevertheless, she realized that Miss Spooner was doing a good job which she was quite unable to tackle herself, and with her usual good sense she came to terms with this unwanted stranger in their midst. In any case, Miss Spooner only came in twice a week, which caused Nelly some relief.

She was fierce if she heard the girls criticizing the newcomer, and was careful to hide her true feelings. To staff and customers Nelly displayed complete loyalty to Miss Spooner, declaring that she 'was doing a wonderful job at the Fuchsia Bush'.

But how she prayed for Mrs Peters' early return!

Farther afield in Woodstock, Carl Andersen watched the rain through the windows of the Bear. It drummed on the flagstones of the courtyard at the rear of the hotel, and the raindrops spun like silver coins as they hit the hard surface.

It was ten thirty in the morning. In three days' time he would be flying back home. It had been a rewarding trip, he told himself, both from the firm's point of view, and his own personal search for Mrs Curdle's descendants.

Ben had been extremely helpful, supplying memories of his redoubtable grandmother and some photographs which Carl had had copied to take back with him to give to his mother.

He decided that he would like a last look at the church records, and wondered if Charles Henstock would be at home.

On impulse he rang the number at St John's vicarage and Charles answered. He invited Carl to come as soon as he liked.

'We have coffee about eleven,' he said hospitably, and Carl said he would set off at once.

He found Lulling High Street awash, and very few pedestrians about. One or two brave folk were struggling along, heads bent against the onslaught, clutching umbrellas which threatened to blow inside out at any moment.

It was good to gain the peaceful atmosphere of the vicarage sitting-room. He apologized for troubling Charles again, for he had called to see him soon after Easter and in the rector's absence he had studied the church records which Charles had left out for him.

A slip of paper with Charles' neat writing on it lay on the table by Carl's coffee cup. It was simply a confirmation of the note which Carl himself had made earlier. It gave Mrs Curdle's name and dates, and the date of her interment in Thrush Green churchyard and the name of the officiating clergyman.

'You see there is so little more to tell you,' said Charles apologetically. 'She had no permanent address. She was a true itinerant, and the caravan was her home. I am so glad to know that you met Ben, and have been in touch with people who remember your mother in Woodstock.'

Carl agreed that he had found a great deal which would interest and comfort his mother.

'I fear she's not long for this world, sir,' he told Charles. 'And she'd always planned to come back and see Mrs Curdle and thank her for all she did for her when things looked black. She used to tell me that I wouldn't be here at all but for Mrs Curdle, and would never have been a true American with the finest pa in all the world, if it hadn't been for Mrs Curdle.'

'She spoke the truth.'

'I might well have been an Oxfordshire boy,' went on Carl, 'perhaps living in Eynsham.'

'Well, you could have done a lot worse,' Charles told him, with a smile. 'You would probably be just as proud of your background, though if I may say so, perhaps not as handsome.'

Carl had the grace to flush. 'I'm sure you're right. As for looks, I simply take after my old man who was a real good-looker, streets ahead of me.'

'Then I can quite understand why your mother was content to wait for him,' replied Charles.

'I spent quite a time with the old folks at Rectory Cottages,' said Carl. 'Jane Cartwright gave me a lot of help, and an old lady who used to live near here, I believe, remembered Mrs Curdle, and so did Jane's mother Mrs Jenner. I've got a real bundle of notes to take back home.'

'And you've made a lot of friends too,' Charles told him, as Carl made for the door.

'I guess I have,' agreed the other. 'I'll be coming back to see them sometime.'

'We shall all look forward to it,' Charles assured him.

By nightfall the rain had ceased and the wind had dropped, much to everyone's relief.

Nelly Piggott, sitting at the kitchen table with a mug of coffee in front of her, relished the peace of the house, for Albert was next door at the Two Pheasants and all was quiet.

It had been a tiring day and a visit to Lulling Cottage Hospital to see Mrs Peters had been particularly upsetting. She had been moved from the large hospital in the county town, and as soon as she was strong enough to be discharged, she would move to her home.

Meanwhile, arrangements were being made for help in the house, home nursing and all the other matters which were necessary for the return home of the invalid.

'You let me know what I can do,' said Nelly, privately shocked by the pale face and evident weakness of her old friend.

'You're doing more than enough now,' Mrs Peters told her. 'If it weren't for you the Fuchsia Bush would have packed up long ago.'

'Rubbish!' said Nelly stoutly. 'Anyway, you'll soon be back.'

Mrs Peters remained silent, but her thin hands began to pleat the edge of the sheet. To Nelly's horror she saw a tear fall upon her work.

'I'm sorry,' sniffed the invalid.

'There, there! Don't take on. It's only weakness, my love. You'll soon pick up.'

She pulled her chair closer to the bedside, and patted one of the frail hands. The invalid raised her head and looked through her tears at Nelly.

'I don't think so, Nelly. They won't tell me anything, but I don't believe I'll ever get over this one. I'm done, Nelly. This time I'm done.'

For once, Nelly could say nothing, and after a few minutes she left the hospital and made her way home.

With infinite sadness, she perceived that her friend had spoken the truth.

It was Ben Curdle who drove Carl Andersen to Heathrow in the hired car which Ben would return to the Lulling garage.

The two men spoke little on the journey, but there was a companionable feeling between them as Ben coped with the heavy traffic and Carl considered the results of his visit.

'You're coming back soon, I hope,' said Ben as they swung into the approach to the airport.

'Sure. Later this year. And Ben, think about that trip to see us over there. You and Molly and the kids, of course.'

'We'll think about it. Of course we will.'

'It would make my old ma so happy. Don't leave it too late now.'

They drew up, and Carl got out. He seemed to have a mountain of luggage, but refused to let Ben help.

The two shook hands warmly.

'I'll write,' promised Carl. 'It's been great to find some of the family.'

'Family?' queried Ben.

'Well, I suppose we're sort of cousins in a way. What you might call god-cousins!'

Ben laughed. 'If you're sure you can manage I'll get back then,' he said, gazing at the string of cars which had formed behind him. 'Seems that folk here prefer my room to my company.'

And he turned the car in the direction of Lulling.

While Ben was driving homeward on the motorway, Dotty Harmer was watching the vet carrying out routine tests on poor Flossie.

The spaniel was submitting to all these attentions with very little reaction. She had wagged her plumy tail feebly when the vet had arrived, but been to weak to emerge from her basket.

Dotty had greeted him warmly and indicated a large bundle of pink rhubarb, swathed in two of its own great leaves, which lay on the kitchen table among various jars and bottles.

'I hope you like rhubarb.'

'Very much. Most kind,' said the vet, kneeling by the basket.

'So many people dislike it. My old father called it "a noxious weed", but he ate it all the same.'

The vet rolled back one of Flossie's eyelids and studied his handiwork.

'Healthy?' queried Dotty.

He grunted noncommittally, and pressed Flossie's chest. Dotty fell silent, and watched.

After some minutes he rose to his feet. 'She's pretty groggy.'

'You don't have to tell me that,' said Dotty tartly. 'That's why you're here.'

'I'd like to have her at the surgery for a day or two. Under observation, you know. I've some new tablets that I'd like to try. They've been very successful in cases like this.'

Dotty looked at him steadily. Her eyes were very bright behind her spectacles. 'Can't I give her the tablets here?'

He shifted uncomfortably under that sharp gaze. 'It would be quieter for her, and I could give her more attention,' he countered. 'I really should feel happier if I had her with me.'

There was silence as the two looked down upon the invalid.

'Very well,' said Dotty at last. 'I will give you an extra rug that she particularly likes.'

She rummaged in an untidy cupboard, and emerged with a piece of blue blanket. The vet had picked up the basket, with the unprotesting Flossie, and Dotty tucked the blanket over her.

She accompanied the vet and his load to the car, and saw the invalid comfortably settled.

The vet strapped himself in, and gave a reassuring smile. 'Don't worry. I'll take great care of her at the surgery.'

'I know you will. And I shall want the body back here for burial,' said Dotty with frightening gravity.

The car drove off. There was no pulling the wool over those sharp eyes, thought the driver, feeling unusually shaken. His father, he suddenly remembered, had been taught by Dotty's martinet of a father at the local grammar school.

It seemed that his daughter was made of the same stern stuff.

Of course, news of Flossie's removal to the vet's care was soon common knowledge at Thrush Green. The general feeling was that poor old Dotty had seen the last of Flossie, and that the vet had been humane enough to see to the spaniel's last hours away from her doting mistress.

It was Betty Bell who brought the news to Harold and Isobel Shoosmith when she blew in to set about her domestic chores. Betty also spent one morning a week at Dotty's though, as she said, it was 'love's labour lost', as the muddle which she cleared up reappeared as soon as her back was turned.

Nevertheless, she was fond of the old lady, and grieved with her over Flossie's expected demise.

'Ever such a sweet nature that dog had,' said Betty to Harold, as she bustled about his study, snatching up books, ornaments and any bric-à-brac that stood in the way of her flying duster.

'Well, luckily she has the new puppy to comfort her,' said Harold watching his pipe-rack swinging on the wall after one of Betty's onslaughts.

'Not the same,' said she, taking a swipe at a distant curtain rail. 'He'll be all right when he's calmed down a bit, but to my mind he's too boisterous for an old lady like Dotty to manage.'

'If she can cope with those devilish goats of hers,' said Harold, who had twice been knocked to the ground by Dulcie and her progeny, 'she can manage a puppy. But maybe Flossie will get over this. While there's life, you know.'

Betty stopped whirling for a moment, and shook her head sadly. 'No, I don't think that's possible. The vet's a good chap, but I reckon he took poor Flossie off to do her in compassionate-like, to save Dotty's feelings.'

'Maybe,' said Harold, eyeing the clock. 'Have you finished in here, Betty? I've got a mound of letters to write.'

'Just done,' cried Betty, having a final flick at Harold's desk. 'Got you straight, and now I'll tackle the stairs.'

She went singing from the room, and Harold straightened his papers and tried to straighten his wits. Betty, he felt, was like a strong wind. It cleared all in its path but was dreadfully exhausting.

It seemed impossible, everyone agreed, that Flossie could return, and the general feeling was that the vet had acted in the kindest possible manner, and that Bruce, the new puppy, would be some comfort to Dotty in her sad loss.

It was a great surprise, therefore, when the invalid returned to Dotty's kitchen, amidst general rejoicing. Whether the vet's new pills had done the trick, or the temporary respite from Bruce's boisterous attentions, or whether just a change of scene had brought about Flossie's recovery, no one could say, but everyone was delighted to hear about the reunion. Congratulations poured in and the vet's stock, always high in Thrush Green and Lulling, grew higher still.

Albert Piggott, who had secretly been surveying Dotty's garden for the best plot in which to inter her spaniel, now set aside his spade, comforting himself with the thought that his labours had been only postponed. The preparation of final resting places had always given Albert gloomy satisfaction.

Meanwhile, the invalid enjoyed her cosseting and the loving attention of Dotty and Bruce.

On sunny days, her basket was put in a sheltered spot and she dozed or simply gazed about her old haunts, at the apple blossom above her, and the daisies starring the grass by her bed.

Sometimes she took a gentle walk down the path, and pottered about in the meadow beyond, sniffing the old familiar scents and returning, splendidly gilded, from the yellow buttercups which had engulfed her.

Flossie had returned to life, and found it sweet.

*

By the middle of May, 'that loveliest month' was living up to its name. The cold winds and heavy rain which had marred its advent had given way to sunshine and all the heady promise of early summer in the Cotswolds.

The gardens of Thrush Green were bright with tulips, forget-me-nots and wallflowers. The roses were showing plump buds, and the wisteria on the southern walls drooped massive tassels against the Cotswold stone. The hawthorn hedges along the road to Nidden were spattered with white flowers, and here and there a briar rose added its pink frailty.

Winnie Bailey had decided to take a morning walk along her favourite lane, cow parsley frothing each side as far as the eye could see, and was delighted to come across Ella Bembridge, her friend and neighbour, resting her elbows on a farm gate and gazing across the little valley to Lulling Woods.

'Well met!' called Winnie. 'Are you playing truant like me?'

'I'm testing my vision,' replied Ella.

'Testing your vision?' echoed Winnie, joining her at the gate. 'Do you think you need glasses?'

'I have them already for close work, but it's my long sight I'm worried about. I saw the eye chap at Oxford yesterday.'

'And what did he say?'

'I've got something which goes under the pretty name of Senile Macular Degeneration.'

'My word! That sounds rather depressing. Does it hurt?'

'Not a bit, but the retina is not doing its stuff. The worst bit for me is that I can't see colours as keenly as I did. Maddening with my embroidery work.'

'It must be,' agreed Winnie sympathetically. 'So what can be done?'

'Not much. Extra bright light, large-print books, that sort of thing.'

They resumed their walk together, passing Percy Hodge's farm, and patting his collie dog which bounded out to greet them.

'The worst of getting old,' said Winnie, 'is the time one has to spend in patching oneself up. I have to go to the chiropodist tomorrow and the dentist on Thursday.'

'I notice you say "kyropodist",' said Ella. 'I do too, but so many people say "shiropodist". I don't know which is right.'

'I say "kyro" because I imagine it comes from the Greek, but I'm open to correction.'

'I've been meaning to look it up,' said Ella, 'but as soon as I go to find the dictionary, the telephone rings or something boils over on the stove.'

Winnie nodded her agreement at this cussed aspect of life,

and the two paced along together enjoying the May morning and each other's company.

They paused by a small copse of beech and hazel on the left of the lane. A mist of bluebells covered its floor, giving off an unforgettable scent, the very essence, thought Winnie, of a sunny May morning.

Above the bluebells arched long tentacles of bramble, just putting out young leaves and stretching prickly arms to catch at the hazel boughs above. The two women gazed in silence at this timeless scene until, with sighs of content, they turned to make their way back to their duties.

They stopped at Winnie's gate to admire the splendid copper beech tree in the Youngs' garden. The young leaves were now auburn, and thick enough to hide the noble frame of the tree which had been displayed throughout its naked winter form.

'You know it was quite pink a fortnight ago,' said Ella. 'Just a pink haze with all the branches and the trunk showing through. A marvellous sight.'

'I'm glad your sight was up to it,' said Winnie. 'And don't forget, if you want needles threaded or wool or silk matched bring the things to me and I'll help.'

'Thanks a lot, Win,' said Ella gruffly. 'Always does me good to see you. Let's have another potter together before long.'

'Willingly,' agreed Winnie.

Mrs Peters was now at home in her house near Church Green at the farther end of Lulling from Thrush Green. She was glad to be back, and the return to her own surroundings seemed to give her renewed strength and will to live.

A widowed cousin had offered to come and help. She was no nurse, she explained from the outset, but she could run a house, and shop and cook, and be alert for any needs that her patient might require.

The local nurse came in daily, and many friends called for short visits so that the day passed as pleasantly as was possible for one so ill.

Despite her weakness, she was avid for news of her beloved Fuchsia Bush and Nelly was a regular visitor. She was glad to be able to report that all was running smoothly, as indeed it was, despite the absence of the senior partner.

One evening in May, when Nelly was at the patient's bedside, she was surprised to be asked to get in touch with Mrs Peters' solicitor.

'I particularly want to see him about my will,' she said. 'Ask him to come here one morning, whenever he can manage it. And with my will, please.'

'But can't you ring him?'

'I could, but there always seems to be someone about, and if you make the appointment from the office I'd feel happier. He can ring me to confirm his time for calling. Young Mr Venables is always so obliging.'

'Young Mr Venables', as opposed to 'Old Mr Venables', who had been dead for fifty years, was himself in his seventies and officially had retired from the family business some years before.

However, Justin Venables was a man of habit and life did not seem quite right without regular attendances at his Victorian furnished office in Lulling High Street, so twice a week he called in to do a little business with carefully selected and honoured clients. This, incidentally, was a great relief to Mrs Justin Venables who found his presence in the house, after eight-thirty in the morning, the time at which he had departed for years to his office, a great encumbrance to her own domestic timetable.

Nelly walked back to Thrush Green that evening much perturbed. She did not like this talk of wills. To her it sounded ominous. Had poor Mrs Peters been told something by the doctor? Was she in a weaker state than she appeared to be? Did she know, as a fact, that recovery was impossible?

It was all very upsetting, and Nelly was too worried to notice the lilacs and syringas which scented the evening air, or to hear the rooks clattering about the trees by St Andrew's church as they fed their clamorous young.

The house was empty, and Nelly was thankful to sit in its silence recovering from the walk up the steep hill from the town, and trying to come to terms with her worries.

At least one thing was plain. She had promised to ring young Mr Venables, and that she would do as soon as she went into the Fuchsia Bush next morning.

The visit of Carl Andersen which had occasioned so much interest in Thrush Green was soon forgotten by most of the residents. Other excitements had arisen. There was talk of an invasion by the nomadic 'travellers' planned for the last weekend of May. There was an Open Day, later that term, at Thrush Green school, and Miss Watson and Miss Fogerty, who had taught there for many years, were going to attend, leaving their retirement home at Barton-on-Sea for an extended visit.

Two new babies were expected in the Cooke family at Nidden. One was supposed to be Mrs Cooke's, but as she was in her mid-forties there was some argument about this. Most of the Thrush Green gossips thought it unlikely. The more cynical pointed out that the fecundity of the Cooke females was exceptional, and that Mrs Cooke might well be capable of producing healthy infants for years to come.

Nevertheless, the Youngs and the Curdles often spoke of their American friend, and when Willie Marchant, the postman, delivered a fat packet of photographs covered in exciting stamps, they gathered round the kitchen table to pore over them.

They were all splendid specimens. Carl Andersen was

obviously an expert photographer, and the usual sloping land-scapes, tilting churches and the like, so common among a batch of amateur snaps, were nowhere to be seen.

His portraits of the Youngs and the Curdles were particularly attractive, and even Edward, who was usually highly critical of any work of art, agreed that they were a splendid record of Carl's visit.

Edward had troubles of his own at this time. He was a compulsive worrier. The doubt put into his mind about the size of the existing common room at Rectory Cottages still niggled him. Reason told him that it was perfectly adequate as it was. Reason also pointed out that there was no money available anyway for an enlargement of the premises. Reason also told him that he had the assurance of a great many sensible people, such as Jane Cartwright and Charles Henstock, that his original plan together with the glass annexe added later suited everyone perfectly.

But reason did not entirely comfort Edward Young. Just as a nervous woman will fidget with her necklace, or a fretful child will pick relentlessly at a scab on its hand, so Edward worried about the possibility of having made a mistake in his designs.

The subject had been brought painfully to his mind a week or two earlier, when he had attended the funeral of one of the elderly residents, and had returned with other mourners for a cup of tea in the communal sitting room at the home.

The man whose funeral he had attended had helped Edward in the garden for many years. It was Edward who had helped to find him a place at Rectory Cottages when his wife had died and it was apparent that he was unable to cope alone.

Edward would miss him. He took his tea cup to the window and gazed across at the churchyard where one of the Cooke boys, helped occasionally by Albert Piggott, was patting turves into place, and arranging the funeral flowers upon them.

Nearer at hand, immediately beyond the window at which

he stood, his architect's eye noted the level expanse of flag stones on which one or two seats were arranged with some tubs of late hyacinths. There would certainly be room for an extension of the conservatory should it ever be needed.

He turned back to the room, and felt slight panic. It *was* overcrowded. It *was* stuffy. It *was* short of seating.

Jane Cartwright came up to him, offering tomato sandwiches.

'No, thank you, Jane. Rather a crush in here.'

Jane intuitively knew what was worrying him. 'Well, there are nearly thirty people here today. Usually there are a dozen or so at the most.'

She spoke comfortingly, but Edward was not comforted.

'Maybe I should have allowed more space when I drew up the plans. It is so difficult to envisage numbers in a space.'

Jane laughed.

'Numbers vary, as you know. One can only plan for the average number of bodies, and they vary in size too, as you can see if you look around you.'

'You're right, of course,' agreed Edward. But he was not happy, and he took his doubts with him when he crossed the green later to his own home. He should have made that annexe larger, he told himself.

On the day when Carl Andersen's photographs and letter arrived at the Youngs, and Edward was still tormenting himself about Rectory Cottages, Charles Henstock was listening most unwillingly to Mrs Thurgood on the telephone.

His heart had sunk as soon as she had announced herself in the booming voice which so many had learnt to dread.

His dismay grew as he listened to the matter she was explaining, and he sat down on the hall chair in preparation for a long monologue on her side, and a fighting response on his own.

'I have been thinking about that extension at Rectory Cottages,' she began.

'That was settled at the meeting,' replied Charles.

'And it seems to me,' went on Mrs Thurgood, ignoring the interruption, 'that something must be done at some time, and why not now?'

'We can't afford it,' said Charles firmly.

'And what really brought it to my mind again was a lucky meeting with an old friend of ours, a charming fellow who was at school with my late husband. He was having lunch at the Randolph when I was there last week. I always lunch there after visiting the dentist in Beaumont Street. As it happens, he is the director of a well-known firm which specializes in garden-room-conservatories. He could easily extend for us.'

'We abandoned the idea,' broke in Charles.

'I mentioned our little problem,' she continued remorselessly, 'and he said he was sure that they could give us very favourable terms, under the circumstances. He was kind enough to say how much he appreciated our friendship of so many years, and he would be delighted to help when the time came.'

A providential huskiness came into the lady's delivery, and Charles took advantage of it.

'The time will *not* be coming,' said Charles loudly. 'As you are aware, the trustees voted to put the matter aside. There is *no money* available, and the room is considered quite adequate for its needs.

There was the sound of indrawn breath at the other end of the line, but whether it meant that the lady was recovering her full vocal powers or simply preparing for another onslaught, no one could say.

'You are turning down this wonderful offer?'

'Yes, I am.'

'You realize that you may be giving offence to a valued friend of my family?'

'I am sorry.'

'My daughter's offer to exhibit her pictures at the Town Hall to raise funds is also open. No one has had the courtesy to let her know about the arrangements.'

A lesser man than Charles could have been forgiven if he had broken into frustrated screams and banged his head on the vicarage hall wall, but Charles, despite his gentle demeanour, had an inner steel when it was required, and it was certainly needed now.

'Mrs Thurgood,' he said flatly, 'you know as well as I do that it was agreed to let the matter rest. If you have led your daughter and your old friend into thinking that we have plans for a further extension, then it is up to you to disabuse them of the idea which you yourself have encouraged. I refuse to discuss it further.'

'Well,' began an outraged voice.

But Charles put down the receiver, just as the front door opened and Harold Shoosmith arrived.

'Hallo, Charles! You look a bit tired.'

'I've just had Mrs Thurgood on the phone. She's still pressing me about the extension.'

'Leave her to me,' said Harold ominously.

June

Busy in making alterations in my Kitchen
Garden cutting down an Old Hedge by my
Fir Plantation.

James Woodforde

The gardeners of Thrush Green were equally busy. The
hedges and grass were under daily onslaught from clippers
and mowers, as the sun grew stronger and the days longer.

Harold Shoosmith, attacking his privet hedge, was glad to
break off his labours when Betty Bell summoned him indoors
for mid-morning coffee.

'It's a pity we didn't grub out all the privet when we came
here, and plant yew instead.'

'Gloomy old stuff, yew,' commented Betty. 'Churchyards
and that. Gives you the creeps.'

'Why yew?' queried Isobel.

'Only needs one clip a year,' said the labourer. 'This dam'
privet wants three to keep it tidy.'

'Heard about Dotty's – I mean Miss Harmer's – Bruce?'

'Don't say he's ill,' exclaimed Isobel in alarm.

'No, no. I called in on my way here and he's full of beans.
He'd just broken a jar full of rhubarb juice Dotty'd put on the
floor to cool. All over everywhere.'

'On the floor?' echoed Harold. 'What was it doing on the
floor?'

'No room on the table. She was going to make some medicine. She stirs it up with ginger, and then bottles it.'

'It sounds pretty grim.'

'It is. Very *opening*.'

Isobel hastened to change the subject. 'Well, tell us about Bruce.'

'They've found his owners.'

'Good heavens! Where?'

'South America. They done a moonlight flit when they left Bruce in the church porch.'

Harold and Isobel exchanged glances.

'Are you sure about this?'

'Young Darwin the policeman was telling them down the pub yesterday.'

'Young Darwin,' said Harold sternly, 'has no business to be chattering about police matters at the pub.'

'Well, you asked me, so I told you,' retorted Betty. 'They're all that chuffed at the police station. Been working at it for months now. It's going to be in the paper this week.'

She put her empty mug aside, and rose to continue her duties.

'This won't buy the baby a new frock,' she announced. 'I'll go and give that bath a good doing over.'

'I wonder if there's anything in this story,' said Harold to Isobel.

'We shall have to wait and see what the local paper tells us,' replied Isobel. 'I must say it sounds rather sensational.'

'And it still doesn't explain why the dog was dumped here,' agreed Harold. 'Ah well! Back to the privet.'

Of course, Betty Bell was not the only one to have heard the news. Tongues wagged freely at the Two Pheasants, and the mystery of the dog being left in St Andrew's porch was the chief aspect of local conjecture.

'I heard,' said Percy Hodge the farmer, 'as this couple was fond of making trips up this way. Didn't they come in here for a pub lunch now and then?'

Mr Jones the landlord fidgeted uneasily with his beer mugs. 'Blowed if I know. I get all sorts in here in the summer stopping off for ploughman's lunch and that, before going on to Minster Lovell or Oxford. Can't say I've any particular memory of this pair. They hadn't got a dog or I might have remembered.'

'Well, they wouldn't have,' pointed out Albert. 'That Bruce was only a pup when we found him. Bet they hadn't had him more'n a few weeks.'

'What they doing in America then?'

'Done a bunk. With a pile of money evidently. Been up to a bit of no good somewhere. Fiddling the books, they say.'

'You can't fiddle books these days,' said some wiseacre. 'It's all on the computer.'

'And that can go wrong,' pointed out Percy Hodge. 'You only need to get a power cut and – fizz – it's all up.'

Heads were shaken in agreement, and the gossip about the felons, now allegedly in South America, changed to the unreliability of modern inventions and the superiority of earlier equipment.

While her father was enjoying the company of his cronies at the Two Pheasants, Molly Curdle was writing a letter of thanks to Carl Andersen for the set of photographs.

She also enclosed a separate letter for his mother and some more photographs which had turned up after Carl had departed. They were sepia in colour and rather faded, but a long-dead hand had clicked the camera and caught three or four splendid shots of Mrs Curdle near her caravan, with St Andrew's church in the background.

Ben took the bulky letter into Lulling to post and was appalled when he found how expensive it was to post anything by air mail. However, he did not grudge the money, as his father-in-law certainly would have done, for he knew that Molly and Carl's mother would get enormous pleasure from the transaction.

He had become very fond of Carl, his 'god-cousin', during the few weeks that he had been in Thrush Green, and he looked forward eagerly to seeing him again before long. There was an easy friendliness about the American, a warm freshness of outlook which touched Ben deeply. He had always been shy. The fact that his life had been always on the move with Mrs Curdle's fair had meant that his schooling was sketchy. It was Molly who had taught him to become proficient in reading and writing, and after acquiring those elementary skills he had become more confident.

But the early experience of being a 'gypsy boy', and mocked by some of the crueller children he had met in his youth, had left Ben very vulnerable and still inclined to think of himself as less competent than most men.

His mechanical skills were outstanding, and his honesty and his gentle nature were appreciated by all who knew him, but innate modesty made Ben deprecate his own qualities.

In Carl he had found a warm-hearted companion with whom he was instantly at ease. He had been touched by the enthusiastic invitation to visit him in the States, but did not think that he and Molly would be able to accept it. It would be too expensive. The children's schooling might be disrupted. His employer would not relish parting with his labours for any length of time.

No, all in all, it would be more sensible to wait for Carl's next visit. He hoped that it might be soon, and that he would not have to hurry away.

Who knows? Perhaps next year, thought Ben, things might favour a visit to Carl's home. Somehow, he felt sure, the bond between the two families would grow stronger with the years.

*

Thrush Green was at its best in early June. To be sure, the horse chestnuts' pyramids of flowers were almost over, and their pink and white confetti spattered the grass. In the garden too, the still-green daffodil leaves lolled, annoying tidy gardeners who were anxious to put out their bedding plants. The rapture with which the golden flowers had been greeted earlier had now changed to exasperation. All very well for the poet to say, '*Fair daffodils we weep to see thee haste away so soon,*' thought Winnie Bailey, surveying her overcrowded border, but the trouble was that they did not haste away quickly enough. One was forced to wait until the leaves had sent down their nourishment to the bulbs below, and very frustrating it was.

Nevertheless, there was comfort to be found in the shaggy scented pinks, the bobbing columbines and the great blowsy crimson peonies which came year after year with unfailing cheerfulness.

The wisteria cascaded in mauve profusion down the front of the house, and by the gate two laburnums dangled their golden chains. Winnie loved all these faithful old friends which appeared regularly every year, and demanded little attention. She was no great gardener. New strains of plants did not excite her. She was not interested in such things as topiary, old-fashioned roses, water plants, or exotic lilies or orchids, as many of her friends were.

But she relished her own modest patch which she and Donald had largely created when they first moved into the house they shared for many years.

She looked across Thrush Green to the dusky beauty of the Youngs' copper beech tree, and thought of her promise to Ella about another shared walk. She must get in touch with her before this spell of sunny weather deserted the Cotswolds, she told herself.

*

It so happened that Ella was at Dotty Harmer's while Winnie was enjoying her garden stroll.

She found Dotty by the chicken run, flinging armfuls of fresh greenery to the hens.

'So nutritious!' she shouted to Ella, as she hurled leaves of all descriptions to the squawking fowl. Ella bent to collect a mound of chicken salad to assist the operation.

'Not *too* much cow parsley, dear,' puffed Dotty, 'but any amount of dandelions, shepherd's purse and chickweed. They all clear the blood, you know.'

Ella obediently plucked at some fine clumps of dandelion leaves, and remembered ruefully that they stained hands pretty fiercely. Would it come off on the white cushion cover she was in the throes of embroidering? Too late to worry now, she told herself philosophically.

After a few minutes Dotty called a halt and invited her friend into the kitchen. Bruce, who had been shut in there, went wild with excitement, leaping upon Ella's lap and licking her face rapturously.

'He's a fine fellow,' said Ella. 'Does you credit, Dotty.'

She was wondering if Dotty had heard the rumour about Bruce's former owners, and turning over in her mind the wisdom of broaching such a delicate subject.

She need not have worried.

'Betty Bell tells me that the wretches who abandoned him have been found. I only hope they are brought to justice,' said Dotty.

'I gather that they left the country owing a great deal of money,' replied Ella. 'The police will want them for that.'

'To my mind,' said Dotty sternly, 'the money is of secondary importance. Cruelly abandoning a young dog is *far worse!*'

She began to fill the kettle.

'Lime tea or peppermint?' she enquired. 'Both homemade.'

Ella hesitated. Like the rest of Dotty's friends, anything

homemade by Dotty could have a devastating effect on even the most robust alimentary canal.

'Well,' began Ella.

'You can have instant coffee, dear, if you prefer it. I have a private fear that it can give some people peptic ulcers, though Dr Lovell assures me that I am quite mistaken.'

Ella clutched at this straw. 'Coffee then, please, Dotty. And I'm sure John Lovell would know about such things.'

'He didn't know about the healing properties of woundwort,' Dotty replied. 'I lent him my *Gerard's Herbal* to put him right.'

She brought two steaming mugs to the table, and returned to the subject of Bruce's owners.

'One thing I'm sure of,' she announced. 'I shall *refuse*, absolutely *refuse*, to return Bruce to such callous people. They are not fit to have animals in their charge.'

'Oh, come now, Dotty! He was obviously well cared for, and in a splendid basket, with food and drink. They were just desperate to get away, but they did leave him in a sheltered place – one might almost say a sanctuary – where he'd soon be found.'

Dotty brushed this aside. 'How did they know he would be found? And they doped him to keep him quiet. Quite unforgivable! My father would have horsewhipped them on the spot! And quite right too!'

Two red spots glowed on Dotty's wrinkled cheeks, and Ella hastened to calm her.

'Well, no doubt they'll get their just deserts when they are picked up,' said Ella. 'And I'm sure no one will expect you to part with Bruce.'

'I should hope not. Where are they, anyway?'

'South America, I heard.'

'America?' cried Dotty, spilling her peppermint drink as she thumped the mug on the table. 'And *South* America too? Why, that's even worse than *North* America, and you know how badly *they* behaved, rebelling in the naughtiest way, and wasting all that good tea in Boston Harbor! I doubt if we shall ever see those miscreants if they have hidden themselves in *South America.*'

'We'll have to wait and see,' said Ella, rising. 'Many thanks for the coffee, Dotty, and can I have the goats' milk while I'm here?'

'Of course, of course,' said Dotty, bustling to the larder, 'and I've put up a bottle of rhubarb and ginger cordial for you. It's wonderfully effective.'

Ella thanked her civilly and put the bottle in her basket.

Walking home she wondered whether it would be a good thing to pour it down the sink. Would it block the pipes, she wondered? On the other hand, it might clear out the drain effectively. It would make an interesting experiment.

Edward Young was restless.

Joan Young was used to these periodic upsets. They often coincided, as in the present case, with some hold-up in his work, and she did her best to calm him, although she knew, from experience, that only the resumption of the job in hand would cure his frustration.

Work on a splendid Regency house in Cheltenham had kept him engaged for some time, but the builders had been held up by a shortage of vital material and work had stopped for almost a week.

In his present state of impatience, Edward had turned again to the unresolved problem of Rectory Cottages' communal room. His doubts remained, and it was particularly unfortunate that it was at this time that he came across Mrs Thurgood in Lulling High Street.

She seized him by the arm so violently that he spun in his tracks.

'Just the man I wanted to see,' she trumpeted. Edward's

heart sank at these ominous words. 'I should like a word in your ear about Rectory Cottages.'

'I'm afraid I can't stop now,' began Edward, but was ignored, just as poor Charles Henstock's protests had been.

'I shan't keep you a minute,' replied Mrs Thurgood, hemming him into a corner between the steps leading up to the Lovelock sisters' front door and the Fuchsia Bush. She pushed her tartan-covered shopping trolley across Edward's line of escape, and started to hold forth to her captive.

'It seems,' she began, 'that the sitting-room is proving rather small, and as you designed it I wondered if you felt it should be enlarged. I gather that is the general opinion.'

Taken aback as he was, and literally hemmed in on all sides, Edward did his best to fight back.

'I stand by my original work,' he began, but was interrupted by his persecutor, who had now raised her voice to a remarkable pitch to overcome the din of a large and slow vehicle which was sweeping the gutters at enormous expense to the Lulling rate-payers.

'Times change!' she shouted. 'It may have seemed adequate at the time, but it now appears to be too small.'

'No one else thinks so,' retorted Edward. 'As I understand it, the matter was discussed at a meeting of the trustees, which unfortunately I had to miss, and it was found perfectly adequate.'

'That's not what I hear,' bawled Mrs Thurgood. The driver of the giant sweeper had now paused to greet a friend near by and their voices added to the bedlam.

'In any case,' responded Edward fortissimo, 'there is *no money*!'

Half a dozen people now appeared and began to push their way towards the Fuchsia Bush, chattering noisily. One person shoved Mrs Thurgood's trolley aside and Edward escaped.

Mrs Thurgood, greatly disgruntled, continued on her way.

Inside the Lovelocks' house, Miss Ada said to Miss Violet: 'I don't know what the High Street is coming to. There was a dreadful brawl going on right outside our front door.'

'Oh, it was only Mrs Thurgood,' said Violet. 'She was talking to someone I couldn't see who was pinned against our wall.'

'Humph!' snorted Ada, 'that Mrs Thurgood gets more vulgar every week. Short of deporting her, I cannot think what can be done about her.'

'Just ignore her,' said Violet.

'I do that already,' said Ada tartly.

Edward Young was profoundly disturbed by this encounter. Reason told him that he should ignore the whole incident, that

Mrs Thurgood was nothing but a troublemaker and that this wretched business of the communal room should be set aside.

Reason, however, was being overwhelmed by agitation for poor Edward as he mounted the steep hill to Thrush Green in time for lunch.

The schoolchildren were already at play. Their midday dinner had been demolished, and now, replete with shepherd's pie and rhubarb crumble, they were cowboys, aeroplanes, spacemen or, in the case of the infants, simply mothers and fathers in the quietest corner of the playground.

Alan Lester was talking to his neighbour Harold Shoosmith just outside the school gate. Edward went to join them.

'The sun has brought us all out,' said Alan, waving to the children. 'Hope it's like this on Open Day.'

'When's that?'

'Early July. That's if we're ready. I live in hope.'

'It's often perfect then,' said Harold, 'but in any case you won't have everything outside, will you?'

'In this climate?' replied Alan. 'Not likely! We've a couple of things planned for outdoors but only if the weather's fine.'

'At least you have the school to shelter in if it pours,' observed Edward. 'When it has teemed down on fête days we've had to invite everyone into the house. This year we shall be away, so Harold here had better be warned. He's nobly taken over my duties, as you probably know.'

'We'll keep our fingers crossed,' promised Alan.

Betty Bell appeared wheeling her bicycle. She was making her way home after her morning's work.

'There's a steak and kidney pie just being dished up,' she informed Harold. 'Smells a dream!'

'Then I'd better go and see about it,' agreed Harold, and the three friends parted.

*

It was in this week that Ella and Winnie took their promised walk. They were both early risers, and agreed that the country was at its best in the first hours of daylight.

They set off, sticks in hand, soon after nine o'clock, two sturdy middle-aged ladies in coats and stout shoes, for although it was June the morning was fresh despite the sunshine.

The lane to Nidden was as peaceful as ever. People who worked in Lulling or Woodstock or Oxford had already gone. The schoolchildren were safely at assembly, and Winnie and Ella had the quiet road to themselves.

One of Percy Hodge's black-and-white Friesian cows put her head over the hedge and gazed speculatively at them.

Her eyelashes were fringed with mist. She chewed the cud slowly, ropes of saliva dripping from the great pink tongue. She looked infinitely content.

'It's funny how soothing cows are,' observed Ella. 'All that milk, I suppose, comes to mind.'

'I think it's the smell of their breath,' said Winnie. 'So soporific. Very calming. And so completely the opposite of bulls which frighten the life out of me.'

The mist of early morning had now cleared, and the view to Lulling Woods lay spread before them, a gentle rolling patchwork of varying greens, here and there enlivened by a vivid yellow field of rape. The two friends propped their arms on a convenient field gate, and gazed their fill in companionable silence.

A blackbird flew past, its yellow bill stuffed with squirming insects. It vanished into the hawthorn hedge beside them, and the air was instantly aquiver with the cries of young birds greeting their meal.

The brambles and goosegrass at the base of the hedge glistened with dew in the shadow, but already the shiny hawthorn leaves and may blossom in the sun were lightly steaming in the growing warmth.

'It's going to be a scorcher,' said Winnie, stirring at last.

'And about time too,' said Ella. 'I like summer to *be* summer.'

The cow parsley was now over. The froth of white flowers had turned to green seed heads, but among the luxuriant leaves the crane's-bill was appearing, its startling blue flowers giving colour to the verge. Pink campion, starry marguerites and the rusty spires of dock added their portion, and low on the ground, among the dusty edges of the road, spread the grey leaves of silverweed.

They strode past the cottages where the Cootes lived. Even here, among the derelict cars, mowers and wheelbarrows and building materials, there were signs of summer. An elder tree leant from the hedge, showing its great creamy blossoms to the sun, and some exuberant crimson peonies had found their way through the detritus to flaunt their beauty.

The two friends walked on, past the copse where the blue-bells had so stirred them on their earlier walk, and on towards the scatter of cottages which comprised Nidden. A tabby cat sat on a stone gatepost, and responded to Ella's stroking by opening a pink triangle of mouth and giving little purrs of appreciation. A toddler stumbled down the path to the gate, and gazed, thumb in mouth, at the two strangers, but refused to speak.

Ella looked at her watch. 'I'm supposed to be back for the laundry man,' she said. 'Do you mind turning back now?'

'Not a bit. I'm mightily refreshed in body and spirit.'

They waved goodbye to the unresponsive child and the friendly cat, and turned for home.

At Thrush Green school preparations were well ahead for Open Day towards the end of term.

Alan Lester had already sent out invitations to parents, governors and other friends of the school, including one to his predecessors Miss Watson and Miss Fogerty, now enjoying retirement at Barton-on-Sea.

'Really,' commented Miss Watson at the breakfast table, 'it is most gratifying to be kept in touch with school affairs. But it seems a pity to me to see that the children have not written the invitations in their own handwriting. I suppose they have a copier now. It no doubt cost a fortune.'

Little Miss Fogerty, at the other side of the table, rallied to Alan Lester's defence. She knew how much dear Dorothy missed her position as a respected headmistress, but she saw no reason why she should find fault with her excellent successor.

'You must admit, Dorothy, that the invitations are easier to read. And I believe that the parents raised the money for the copier. I think it is a good idea.'

'Would you pass the marmalade?' enquired Dorothy somewhat coldly.

There was silence for a few minutes, broken only by the crunching of toast.

'You're quite right, dear,' said Miss Watson at last. 'I must say I am looking forward so much to our visit. Isobel asked if I would be willing to judge the children's fancy dress competition at the fête. Alan Lester had broached the subject.'

Miss Fogerty recognized this speech as an overture of reconciliation and forbore to tell her friend that Isobel had already mentioned the matter to her in a recent telephone conversation. The two had been friends since college days, and the fact that they had been neighbours at Thrush Green had strengthened the tie.

'I do hope you will do it,' said Miss Fogerty. 'You are quite the right person to appreciate the work and ingenuity that goes into these affairs.'

'I don't know about that,' replied Dorothy, with unusual modesty, 'but I shall do my best, and hope that Thrush Green will forgive any shortcomings.'

'I'm just going to have a look at some cuttings in the cold frame,' said Agnes Fogerty folding her napkin. 'I promised

Isobel some slips from our shrubs, and I must say they are looking very perky.'

'You have green fingers, Agnes,' said Dorothy kindly, propping up the invitation on the mantelpiece. 'And a much more generous nature than I have.'

But the second comment, though strongly felt, she kept to herself.

Willie Marchant, the postman, dropped three letters through Albert Piggott's door one sunny morning and, as usual, it was Nelly who bent to pick them up.

Two were addressed to Albert, and looked like run-of-the-mill circulars, but the third was addressed to Nelly, in a hand she did not recognize immediately.

It was quite heavy and bulky, and Nelly saw that the postmark bore the stamp of Leicester. She slipped it into her apron pocket, out of sight of Albert, and handed him the two which were addressed to him. He gave them scant attention.

'More rubbish!' was his only comment.

Nelly did not open her letter until she was safely in the office at the Fuchsia Bush. To her surprise, a cellophane bag containing a gold chain was enclosed with a letter from Mrs Butler, Charlie's landlady.

The letter read:

Dear Mrs Piggott,
  Charlie asked me to send you this as a little keepsake. It belonged to his mother, and it is real gold. He hoped you would like it to remind you of happy times past.

The letter was signed with Mrs Butler's shaky scrawl, and Nelly undid the present with mixed emotions.

The long necklace slid out of its wrapping. Nelly knew gold when she saw it, and this was certainly the real thing. It was of Victorian design, quite heavy, and well over two feet in length.

Her first feeling was that it was too valuable for her to accept. Her second was that it was typical of Charlie's generosity, and that she was overwhelmed by it.

Remembering her last glimpse of Charlie, shabby and almost destitute, she wondered that he had not sold such a valuable object. But it was also typical of him to have kept something of his mother's which he prized on her account.

Nelly sat alone in the quiet office, remembering those days with Charlie. They had ended in Brighton with the deepest humiliation and hurt that she had ever suffered. Even now, the remembrance made her shudder and feel sick.

When he had thrown her over for another woman, and Nelly had no alternative but to return to Thrush Green and the recriminations, and probably the rejection by Albert, she would never forget that long miserable journey home, shaken by Charlie's treachery and fearful for what lay ahead. Although Albert was remarkably forbearing, contenting himself with a few wounding words now and again, the general disapproval of her neighbours was harder to bear. Nelly knew that in such a close-knit community her shame would never be completely forgotten. But her natural exuberance and hard work gradually overcame the censure of her neighbours, and as the years had passed, Nelly's backslidings, if not quite forgotten, were almost quite forgiven.

Nelly picked up the beautiful chain. Dear Charlie, she thought fondly! She still had a soft spot in her heart for the scamp, and she would treasure this generous gesture from her dead lover.

She slipped it over her head, tucking it under her blouse so that it was hidden. It slid down between her ample breasts, cold but strangely comforting.

*

News of the apprehension of the owners of the dog Bruce was annoyingly short. The local paper, which all had expected to give exciting accounts of the miscreants, had let down its avid public badly.

Normally, any mention of Lulling or its surrounding villages and their inhabitants merited a paragraph or two. In fact, one of its endearing qualities was the ability to find some local connection, however remote.

Harold Shoosmith always enjoyed this aspect of the local paper. Having read the obituary of a bishop one morning in *The Times*, he was delighted to find half a column in the local paper claiming that the bishop's younger brother had once been mayor of Lulling.

On another occasion a famous but fickle actress, whose latest peccadilloes were making headlines in the national press, was given prominence and a photograph in the local paper because she had opened a church bazaar in Lulling some three years earlier.

So it was even more galling to its faithful readers to find that there was next to nothing about those dreadful people who had pinched masses of money, done a bunk to Bolivia or Peru or one of those fancy places where criminals went and, worse still, had left a poor starving dog tied up in their church porch.

Instead of a half-page of juicy reading, there was a meagre paragraph stating that the police were investigating certain allegations about the appropriation of missing funds from a number of companies in the area.

'Never a word about Bruce and Miss Dotty,' cried Betty Bell indignantly. 'I've half a mind to give up having it, except you have to look down the deaths every week to keep upsides with things. My mum never got over meeting an old school friend in Lulling one market day and asking her, jolly-like, if her Fred still liked his pint, and the woman burst into tears and said he'd died the week before. She didn't tell my mum at the time, but he'd choked on a mouthful of rum. Since then I've always had a quick quiz at the deaths. No point in upsetting people.'

'Quite,' agreed Harold, moving three letters he was trying to answer from the path of Betty's duster flailing round his desk.

'Tell you what, though,' said Betty, suddenly still, 'I'm going over to my sister's at the weekend, and she has that Hampshire paper. Maybe it's got something in it as those bounders lived that way, didn't they? Time they was caught and strung up, leaving that poor animal like that.'

Harold was then left in peace as Betty continued her duties in the hall. It seemed, he thought with some amusement, that the fugitives were already condemned before trial, and that by far the greatest of the charges they might have to face in the future was the abandonment of the dog Bruce, which was of paramount importance in the eyes of Thrush Green.

He returned to his letter-writing, putting Betty's indignation against unsatisfactory local papers and callous dog owners out of his mind until she arrived some days later waving another local paper triumphantly.

'Here you are! A lovely bit in it, page three, and a photo too. You can keep it, as I've had a good read of it. For two pins I'd show it to our lot so they could see how a proper paper should be.'

Harold thanked her and put it aside to read later. Certainly some enterprising editor had sent his reporter to the place where the missing couple had lived, and the result had been most satisfactory from the readers' point of view.

A garrulous old lady, of formidable appearance according to the accompanying photograph, had kept the key of the missing pair's house and generally looked after affairs in their absence.

'Mrs Ivy Potts, 74' began the account, causing Harold to wonder, yet again, why newspaper editors imagined that the ages of those mentioned in their columns were of the slightest interest to readers.

Carrying on, after this momentary mental pause, Harold

discovered that the aged Mrs Potts had been struck dumb
when she found the place deserted. A note had been left on
the kitchen table with a week's wages, and she had been told
to carry on as usual until further notice.

After a week with no word ('not even on the telephone') she
became worried. For one thing, the milk was getting too much
for reasonable consumption and it seemed a wicked waste to
pour it down the sink with all those starving people in Africa
you saw on the telly, and there was a stack of papers, the sort
you couldn't really read, especially that pink one which was all
figures, which her employers seemed to read most of all.

But she was worried most about the dog, she told the
reporter. (Thrush Green would like Mrs Potts, thought Harold,
reading avidly.) Of course, they might have taken it with them.
On the other hand, it might have run off and got killed. She
felt she ought to tell the police, and they said she had been
quite right when she went to the police station. From now on
it was up to them, concluded Mrs Ivy Potts, 74.

Harold agreed, as he folded the newspaper with satisfaction.

Albert Piggott was normally the most unobservant of men
when it came to the appearance of womenfolk. He did, however, notice the gold chain which Nelly had hung over her best
blouse before going out with Mrs Jenner and Mrs Hodge,
formerly Mrs Lilly, to spend an evening at bingo.

'Where'd you get that thing?' enquired Albert suspiciously.

'What, this?' exclaimed Nelly, with assumed casualness.
'Why, it was sent with that mail order as come last week. Free
gift, you know.'

'Trumpery stuff!' grunted Albert. 'A sprat to catch a mack-
erel. Just hopin' you'd spend good money buying more fal-
de-lals.'

'Well, I don't ask you to pay for 'em,' said Nelly tartly. 'So
I'll wear what I like!'

There was a knock at the door, and her two friends were outside, waiting for her to join them.

Halfway through the evening there was a break for refreshments, and Mrs Jenner admired Nelly's chain as they drank coffee.

Nelly repeated the tale she had told Albert, but was beginning to wonder if she should ever display Charlie's last gift in public. Until this evening she had kept it hidden under her clothes, relishing its secret comfort. Tonight she had felt a desire to wear it openly before her friends, proud of its beauty. But Albert's questioning, and now Mrs Jenner's interest, made her uneasy, and she resolved that this would be the last time she would display it.

'They make things really marvellously these days,' commented Mrs Jenner. 'That necklace could pass for real gold anywhere, I do declare. And how,' she went on, leaving the subject, 'is poor Mrs Peters?'

'A sad sight,' said Nelly. 'I dread what I might find every time I go in.'

'Would she like me to pay her a visit?' asked Mrs Jenner. 'Not professionally, of course. I wouldn't want to be in the way of her proper nurse, but just a short friendly visit, say.'

Nelly said that she was sure the invalid would enjoy a visit. They were called back to their tables, and hopes of fortune to come put the matter of Nelly's new necklace to one side.

But later that night, after Mrs Jenner and Mrs Hodge had seen Nelly into her home and were continuing along the dark Nidden road to their own abodes, the subject of Nelly's chain cropped up again.

'I've never had a free gift like that,' said Gladys Hodge. 'Most I've ever had was those things you find stuck on the cover of your women's magazines like a phial of scent or a nail file.'

'It certainly looked very nice on Nelly,' said Mrs Jenner

diplomatically. She was almost sure that the chain was made of gold, for she had one very like it, of Victorian design, which she had inherited from her mother.

'Yes,' agreed Gladys, still sounding puzzled. 'It looked so real, didn't it? But where would Nelly get a valuable necklace like that if it was real?'

Mrs Jenner, who had learnt to be discreet during her years as the local midwife, was not prepared to pursue the matter further. Her own conjectures she intended to keep to herself. However Nelly acquired the chain was her own affair, and that was that. She had no intention of starting a rumour which might upset her friend Nelly.

The two stopped at the Hodges' gate.

'Care to come in for a drink?' invited Gladys.

But Mrs Jenner declined, pleading tiredness and a longing for her bed.

'I've just thought,' said Gladys excitedly, as she was about to open her gate. 'That necklace of Nelly's might have come from Mrs Peters. They tell me she's been giving away one or two keepsakes to friends and relations, poor soul. Knows she hasn't got much longer, I hear. She'd want Nelly to have something, wouldn't she?'

'It's a possibility,' agreed Mrs Jenner, glad that her friend had found some answer to her queries.

'Well, goodnight then,' cried Gladys. 'See you soon.'

She vanished up the path to the back door of the farmhouse, and Mrs Jenner, keeping her own counsel, went thankfully to her bed.

July

We were greatly amused by a Country Dancing
School. They kickit and jumpit with mettle
extraordinary, and whiskit and friskit, and toed
it and go'd it, tattooing the floor like mad.

John Keats

Alan Lester, the headmaster of Thrush Green primary
school, was a fair-minded man and believed in letting his
staff have as much freedom as was compatible with the good
running of the school.

But during the preparations for the school's Open Day his
toleration was being sorely tried by the noise from the infants'
room.

Miss Robinson, who had begun her teaching career under
Miss Watson's tutelage, was an enthusiastic dancer, and encouraged her young charges to excel in bending and stretching,
pointing toes, waving arms and legs, and generally pursuing all
those exercises which would add grace and beauty to youthful
deportment.

She soon realized that she would have to modify her aims.
Young children, particularly sturdy country ones, are apt to fall
over when asked to stand on one leg with the other stretched
gracefully behind. Ballet-like arm movements, in a confined
space, can lead to clashes with neighbouring bodies followed
by recriminations.

Very sensibly Miss Robinson accepted that her pupils' dancing ability was limited, but she turned her attention to the type of dancing which they enjoyed and which, she hoped, would lead them to more artistic heights.

The simpler rhythm and movement of country dancing suited her aims perfectly. The clapping, the stamping, the twirling and the whirling were greatly enjoyed by her class, and she had spent the last few weeks of the summer term rehearsing three particularly noisy and energetic examples of such dancing.

These dances had originated in middle Europe, and poor harassed Alan Lester in a neighbouring classroom began to wonder if perennial troubles in the Balkans and the surrounding areas might not have their roots in the aggressive expression of the inhabitants' infant years. There was a ruthless militarism about the sounds which caused the classrooms' flimsy partitions to shudder under the onslaught, and Alan did his best to encourage Miss Robinson to rehearse her charges in the playground, at the end farthest from the school, whenever the weather allowed.

The whole school looked forward to showing parents and friends the results of its yearly labours, and Alan was secretly very proud of its achievements. He knew the school was doing well under his guidance, and hoped that Miss Watson and Miss Fogerty, in the company of parents and old pupils, would approve of their school in its present form.

This inner confidence gave Alan the ability to suffer the infants' zealous endeavours with mitigated pain.

In any case, he told himself, it would soon be the end of term, and he and his wife and family could relax in Wales.

Two postmen delivered letters and packets to Thrush Green and both were called Willie. It was Willie Marchant who liked to test his own and his bicycle's strength on the steep hill from Lulling to Thrush Green. Willie Bond preferred to dismount and push his bicycle up the hill, as did most of his fellows.

Willie Marchant liked to tack from one side to the other, puffing heavily, and causing great alarm to any traffic on the road. The screeching of brakes, the horrified faces looking through car windows, perturbed Willie Marchant not at all.

'I bin doing it all me time,' he was wont to say. 'They knows my ways, and it's up to folks to look out for me. I ain't gettin' off for nobody. I got enough right to be on the highway as the next.'

It was Willie Marchant who delivered an air-mail letter to Ben and Molly Curdle one bright summer morning, and they settled down to read it in their kitchen. They knew it was from Carl, and both hoped that it would give news of his arrival in time for the fête, which he hoped to attend.

But the news was sad.

Dear Molly and Ben,

I am sorry to have to tell you that my mother died last week. She had a severe heart attack and was rushed to hospital, but died that night. I am badly shaken, and don't mind admitting it.

She was delighted with your letter and photos, Molly dear. So glad she was well enough to enjoy them.

My visit to Thrush Green must be postponed as I have a mass of my mother's affairs to attend to, but I will keep you informed about plans, and you can guess how much I look forward to seeing you both again.

As ever,
Carl.

'Poor old lady,' sighed Molly, putting down the letter.

'Poor old Carl,' commented Ben. He remembered his own devastation when his grandmother, old Mrs Curdle, had died. He sympathized deeply with Carl's grief at such a time, and wished that he and Molly could be with him.

'Well, there it is,' said Ben, rising to prepare for work. 'We must just hope things are simpler to clear up than he seems to think.'

'He won't be at the fête, though, will he?' said Molly sadly. 'He would have liked that.'

Ben patted her shoulder.

'Well, anyway, she enjoyed your letter and the snaps. Good thing you wrote when you did.'

He left Molly looking slightly comforted.

Although Carl was scarcely known in the neighbourhood, and his mother had left Woodstock some fifty years earlier, nevertheless the news of her death was soon common knowledge in the little world of Thrush Green and Lulling.

Much sympathy was felt for Carl, and those who knew him comparatively well, such as the Youngs and Charles Henstock, wrote immediately to their new friend.

Charles Henstock even wondered if there were relatives still in Woodstock who should be informed, and mentioned this to Dimity, as she sat topping and tailing gooseberries in the kitchen.

She, knowing Charles's soft heart and his selfless concern for those in trouble, could see that he was quite capable of scouring the streets of Woodstock, whatever the weather, if he felt that he could be of any use to any of Carl's mother's bereaved relations.

'It is really a matter for Woodstock's vicar,' she pointed out. 'He would know if there are any relations who should be told. But I doubt if anyone would really be interested in the death of someone who left the parish so long ago.'

Charles's brow cleared. 'You are quite right, of course. I'm glad you mentioned it. I should have been sorry to meddle in a matter which is a neighbouring vicar's concern. As it is, I don't think Carl had any close relations here in Lulling, so we must let the matter rest.'

He stood for a moment or two watching Dimity's scissors snipping busily at the gooseberries.

'That seems a very tedious job,' he observed. 'Is it necessary to take the ends off?'

'Quite necessary, dear. And I quite enjoy it. I think of how much you will relish a gooseberry pie when I cook these in the winter. It's a labour of love.'

'I am a very lucky man,' replied Charles, and went back to his study in a happy mood.

Down at Barton-on-Sea Miss Watson and Miss Fogerty were busy with their preparations for their visit to Thrush Green.

As always, Dorothy Watson's first worry was about her wardrobe. She was fond of her clothes and critical of her appearance. Agnes, who had always put decency and economy before sartorial grandeur, could do little to calm her friend's agitation. Shortage of money had always limited Agnes's scope, and as the years passed she found it rather restful to have so few clothes to choose from.

Dorothy called from her bedroom one morning, just as Agnes was wondering about that day's pudding. Should it be the raspberries left from yesterday? (Hardly enough to cover the bottom of a fruit dish.) Or open a tin of apricots? (Surely rather extravagant with fresh fruit in abundance in July.)

She hastened to obey Dorothy's summons, and found her surveying a pile of clothes spread out on the bed.

'It's so difficult to decide,' cried Dorothy. 'If it were *winter* I should definitely take my black for evenings, but one likes to look more festive in *summer*. On the other hand, the evenings may be chilly and I really don't want to drag any old cardigan over my summer dresses.'

Agnes, who relied heavily on 'any old cardigan' to supply extra warmth whatever the occasion, pointed out that a silk dress with long sleeves might be the best answer to the problem.

'This green always looks well,' she ventured, lifting up the garment in question.

'Thrush Green must be sick and tired of that old thing,' responded Dorothy. 'I bought it for a party at Ella and Dimity's years ago.'

'Well, what about the blue?'

'Waist's too high. Right under the bust. Most uncomfortable.'

'I always liked you in this pink one.'

'Too youthful. Mutton dressed as lamb, and no shoes to go with it.'

A less patient woman than Agnes might have suggested that it had been a mistake to buy these things in the first place, and that a jumble sale was the best place to dispose of such problems, but Agnes held her peace.

'I still think the green would be best,' she said diplomatically. 'You can wear black or brown shoes with that, and different silk scarves if the weather is chilly. It has a most becoming neckline.'

Dorothy's agitation was subsiding, she saw with relief.

'You are such a help,' said Dorothy. 'I might pack that light

stole I bought in Prouts' sale one year. It goes with everything,
and dear Anthony Bull once said I looked distinguished in it.'

With the blessing of the Reverend Anthony Bull, Charles
Henstock's predecessor at Lulling, it was quite apparent to
Agnes that most of Dorothy's worries were over.

She returned thankfully to eking out the raspberries with
some chopped banana.

Barton-on-Sea, with the rest of southern England, was enjoying
a long hot spell of summer weather.

Holidaymakers rejoiced. Weddings, carnivals, cricket
matches and meals out of doors all thrived in the glorious
sunshine. Even the farmers were comparatively happy, for the
winter barley had ripened early, and harvesting could begin. Of
course, they complained that the lack of rain meant that the
ears of corn were not as heavy as they should be, and that the
pests which attacked their crops were particularly virulent in
hot dry weather, but no one took much notice of their grumbles.
The majority basked and felt thankful.

The roses were at their best, and the delphiniums, penste-
mons and lilies made a glory in the cottage gardens. The scent
of pinks and honeysuckle sweetened every breeze, and in the
warm dusk of evening the tobacco plants sent out waves of
heady fragrance.

The lime trees round St Andrew's church at Thrush Green
and the avenue of limes leading to the splendour of St John's
at Lulling were massed with pale scented flowers, above the
clover-spattered grass. Wherever one looked there were
flowers, below, above and all around. Summer had come in
true splendour this year, after the dark months of winter and
spring.

In the cottage gardens, black, red and white currants were
ripe under their protective coverings of old lace curtains or, in
more sophisticated places, secure in large fruit cages.

Cherries were being eyed appreciatively by the birds, and the apple trees displayed green marbles of embryo fruit.

Amidst the glory of summer these signs of autumn were manifest, and none was so obvious as the waving rosebay willowherb which rioted in the verges of the lanes, tossing pink heads in the breeze above the dried grass below.

But the prolonged spell of sunshine had its darker side. Good gardeners were having to water night and morning to keep their flowers and vegetables alive. Lawns were scorched, bird baths were dry, and many trees were beginning to shed their leaves far too early.

But these were minor worries. On the whole, life was sweet in such a summer, and Alan Foster looked forward with growing confidence to fine weather when the school had its Open Day, and Joan and Edward Young, getting ready for their holiday, told each other that Harold Shoosmith looked like having fair weather for the fête for which he had nobly undertaken Edward's responsibilities.

'Fingers crossed,' said Joan. 'There's plenty of time for it to change.'

'Well, if it does decide to rain on the great day,' responded Edward, 'to quote the Duke of Norfolk about the Coronation, "We get wet", and that's happened before. But somehow, this year, I think we're going to be lucky.'

And Joan, thankful to see him in a cheerful mood, hoped that he was right.

Near by, Harold and Isobel Shoosmith were getting ready to welcome Dorothy Watson and Agnes Fogerty. Dorothy would be driving, for she had become an intrepid driver since her retirement.

Ben Curdle had been her instructor when she had bought her first car in her last few years at Thrush Green, and she could not have had a more competent and reassuring tutor.

As usual, it was Agnes who was ready first. Always an early riser, and with only half the amount of packing to do, compared with her friend's luggage, Agnes was ready to go by nine o'clock, but Dorothy was still fussing with last-minute affairs.

At twenty past nine Dorothy staggered to the car with two suitcases which she put into the boot.

'Don't shut it, dear,' she called to Agnes who was sitting patiently on the hall chair, handbag on lap. 'I've one or two little odds and ends to put in, and I'm just popping down to see Teddy and Eileen. I promised them some magazines.'

'Can't they wait until we come back?' protested Agnes.

'No, no! It won't take me a jiffy,' shouted Dorothy, vanishing through the back door.

Agnes put down her handbag and paced up and down the hall with growing irritation. Teddy again! That everlasting Teddy!

Some years earlier, when the two ladies had settled at Barton, they found that one of their neighbours had recently lost his wife. As the poor man was also blind, good friends did what they could to help, and Dorothy practically took charge and caused Agnes acute embarrassment.

To be frank, Dorothy had fallen in love with the man. He was charming, intelligent and bore his afflictions bravely, Agnes was the first to concede, but Dorothy's ruthless pursuit of their neighbour was not only absurd, in Agnes's opinion, but also dangerously disruptive to the life which she had set out to share with her friend and former headmistress.

She had confided her fears to Isobel Shoosmith, who found the news equally dismaying. However, she cautioned patience and hoped that time would bring Dorothy to her senses.

It was a great relief to Agnes and Isobel when another friend of Teddy's, named Eileen, had married the man, and all seemed set for a trouble-free future. Even Dorothy had accepted the situation cheerfully at the time, but lately, it seemed to Agnes, her attentions to Teddy were growing again.

It was all so frustrating and pointless, thought Agnes, looking at the hall clock, which said twenty-five to ten. And Eileen must notice, and probably feel very hurt.

'Never come between husband and wife,' Agnes's mother had often said to her, and although little Miss Fogerty, with her mouse-like looks and timid ways, was not likely to become a *femme fatale* she had remembered her mother's words, together with such dicta as: 'Let your underclothes be as neat and clean as those that are seen,' and 'Look after the pence and the pounds will look after themselves.'

The situation was quite dangerous, thought Agnes with some agitation. Dorothy should have more sense than to meddle in this way.

At a quarter to ten Dorothy bustled back, looking very happy, and apologized to Agnes for keeping her waiting.

'You get in, dear, while I lock up. I'll bring my raincoat and walking shoes, and then everything's done.'

Five minutes later they were leaving Barton-on-Sea and heading through Hampshire to Thrush Green.

'Isn't this lovely?' cried Dorothy. 'It will do us good to get away for a bit.'

Agnes fervently agreed. Pehaps Teddy would be forgotten, she thought, surveying the countryside as it flashed past.

But her hopes were dashed a few minutes later when Dorothy spoke.

'You'll hardly credit this, Agnes, but Eileen is going away for a few days.'

'So are we.'

'But leaving Teddy! In his condition! Alone in the house!'

'He lived alone long before he married Eileen,' Agnes pointed out.

'He could stumble over something, and hurt himself dreadfully,' went on Dorothy, ignoring the interruption.

'So could anybody.'

'I think it is quite heartless of Eileen. She, of all people, must know how helpless he is.'

Agnes felt that the time had come for a little plain speaking.

'Teddy is well able to look after himself. He managed perfectly when he lived alone, and I'm sure he realizes that Eileen needs a change now and again.'

'I daresay. Teddy is always thinking of others. I only know that I couldn't leave him, if I were in Eileen's shoes.'

'I think,' said Agnes slowly, 'that you sometimes let your kind heart overrule your head. It is not really your place to worry about Teddy. He probably finds it embarrassing, and Eileen must see how things are.'

Dorothy swerved to avoid a child who was see-sawing along the side of the road on a bicycle much too big for him.

'How do you mean?' demanded Dorothy, 'when you say that Eileen must see how things are?'

'You show your feelings too readily.'

Agnes noticed that her friend's neck and face were becoming red, a sure sign of danger ahead. Nevertheless, she stuck to her guns.

'Of course I do,' replied Dorothy shortly. 'I'm fond of Teddy.'

'So am I,' said Agnes. 'And so are all his friends. But he is a married man, and one has to be careful not to upset his wife, and through her, to hurt him.'

She was also wondering if she could quote her mother's warning verbatim about 'coming between husband and wife', but held her tongue. Already she felt she might have gone too far.

Silence fell for a few minutes, and then Agnes saw a welcome sign.

'Oh look, Dorothy! We're just coming to a Little Chef café and it's coffee-time. How fortunate! And their toasted tea cakes are so good. Shall we call in? My treat this time.'

'What a good idea,' said Dorothy cheerfully.

Agnes was relieved to see that Dorothy's flush was fading.

Two days after their arrival at Thrush Green, the long-awaited Open Day dawned.

To everyone's relief it was calm and sunny. The children were unnaturally spruce and tidy, Alan Lester was in his new summer suit, and Miss Robinson in an ankle-length cotton frock of drab colouring which was fashionable at the time, and which made her look like a refugee. As this was exactly what she wanted, she was blissfully happy.

The school too was unnaturally spruce, and the walls were adorned with children's paintings, maps and charts and samples of needlework and handiwork. On every desk was displayed the work in progress, the exercise books lying open at the neatest page.

The children welcomed their parents and friends with a summer song, chosen and accompanied by Miss Robinson.

> *Summer is icumen in*
> *Lhude sing cuccu!*
> *Groweth sed, and bloweth med,*
> *And springth the wude nu –*
> *Sing cuccu!*

Although the words were largely incomprehensible to the listeners, the applause was hearty, for the children looked so angelic, and coped with the thirteenth-century vocabulary so well, that the audience was enchanted.

Then Alan Lester gave a short address of welcome, taking care to mention the two distinguished guests Miss Watson and Miss Fogerty in the front row, and to thank everyone who had contributed to the occasion in one way or another.

The programme went ahead smoothly. The infants clapped

and stamped – almost together – through their much-rehearsed folk dance, and Alan Lester led the applause, privately thinking that this would be the last time he would have to endure such noise.

Work was inspected and much admired in the school itself, and tea was set out under the lime trees in the playground which gave parents, friends and staff a chance to mingle over the tea cups.

Margaret Lester, Alan's wife, was in charge here, looking prettier than ever, and Dorothy Watson observed quietly to Agnes, 'When you *think*, dear,' and needed to say no more, for nearly all those present remembered that Margaret Lester had arrived at Thrush Green with a serious drink problem that had threatened their family happiness. She had overcome it bravely, and Thrush Green had rejoiced.

Alan Lester was buttonholed by an earnest parent who told him all about her child's dyslexia, with which he was already acquainted, and how the doctor had told her that it was often the sign of a particularly brilliant mind. With commendable courtesy, Alan nodded agreement but kept his thoughts to himself.

Miss Robinson was less lucky. Mrs Cooke, mother and grandmother to many of her pupils over the years, sat firmly beside her and described, in appalling detail, the facts of her sister's hysterectomy.

Poor Miss Robinson found herself now violently opposed to the state of matrimony, and quite unequal to eating the jam tart in her hand. She hastily shrouded its red stickiness in a paper napkin, excused herself by saying her class needed her, and fled.

It was almost six o'clock by the time the school and playground had emptied. Parents and children had trickled away. Margaret Lester and her helpers were busy with the last of the washing up, and Alan said goodbye to young Miss Robinson.

'It went splendidly,' he said. 'I thought your class danced very well indeed.'

Her face lit up. 'Miss Watson said the same. She thought it would be a good idea to repeat it at the Christmas concert.'

'That's quite a thought,' said Alan Lester.

Nothing had been said about Teddy, between the two ladies, since the conversation on their journey to Thrush Green.

Agnes secretly wondered if she should have spoken at all, and hoped that she had not hurt Dorothy. Although she had not been affected by love in her sheltered and limited life, she realized how important a part it played in the affairs of most people.

The fact that Dorothy was now in her sixties, and might have been considered able to withstand Cupid's darts, had nothing to do with the case, Agnes realized. She had known several mature people, of both sexes, who had formed attachments, some disastrously, with as much passion as those half their age. It was an unaccountable phenomenon which Agnes could not understand, but it undoubtedly existed.

She felt extremely sorry for Dorothy, and decided to say no more on the subject. She would do her best to make Dorothy's stay at Thrush Green as pleasant as she could.

With this laudable aim in mind, little Miss Fogerty had no difficulty in enjoying her day and sleeping peacefully at night in the dear familiar surroundings of Thrush Green.

But for Dorothy in an adjoining bed in Isobel's spare bedroom, matters were not as easily dismissed. Agnes had given her much to ponder.

In many ways she was superior to Agnes, better educated, stronger in health, more travelled and well read. It was no surprise that she had become a respected headmistress while little Miss Fogerty remained an assistant, and in the same school, for many years.

She was a well-balanced and energetic woman, willing to play her part in local affairs and zealous in keeping up with modern ideas, particularly in education. She also had the ability to reject any trends which she shrewdly recognized as silly and short-sighted, and to support others which, although new and debatable, had a sound basis of practicality for teaching.

In her younger days she had enjoyed many friendships with young men, and had been engaged to be married twice. One man had been killed in the last days of the war. The other, Dorothy soon discovered, was bombastic, a bully and mean with money. If he was like that in his twenties, Dorothy thought, what on earth would he be like in his sixties? She dismissed him, much to his surprise, and never regretted it.

She had enjoyed her teaching career. She had found retirement a little disconcerting with so much time to organize. Perhaps it was this, combined with pity for Teddy's plight, which had sparked this attachment to him? Perhaps he took the place of all the children she had cared for over the years? Perhaps some latent and unsuspected maternal instinct had manifested itself? Who knew?

Dorothy had been surprised by the strength of her feelings for Teddy, but gave them full rein. It had never occurred to her, until Agnes spoke, that there was an element of silliness and possible embarrassment in this relationship.

Looking at it soberly Dorothy began to see that Agnes was right. She could be causing Eileen pain. She could be embarrassing Teddy. She could be a laughing-stock to their friends in Barton-on-Sea. It was something she had never considered before, and she lay awake, listening to Agnes's small genteel snores, and studied the position carefully.

Agnes was so often right. Her life might have been more confined and narrow than her own, but those very limitations had made Agnes know the difference between right and wrong, with no blurring of lines which a more sophisticated mind might allow.

She must mend her ways, she decided. She would say nothing to Agnes, for 'Least said, soonest mended' was a motto which she favoured. She would not be able to feel any less warmly towards dear Teddy, he meant too much to her, but she would cut down her visits, remember that he was Eileen's husband, and generally behave with more decorum, as befitted a retired headmistress of mature years.

What really hurt, she was honest enough to admit, was the fact that she was making a fool of herself before her friends.

Somewhere, years earlier, she remembered reading a great truth which had stayed with her. Was it written by that discerning literary man Bonamy Dobrée? It was to the effect that no one minded being thought *wicked*, but one hated to appear *ridiculous*.

Perhaps she had been both, thought Dorothy? Well, there was always tomorrow and, thanks to dear Agnes, she would do her best to reform.

Joan and Edward Young, with their son Paul, departed the next day for their holiday. Ben Curdle drove them to Heathrow in their car, and would drive it home, and lock it safely in the garage for a fortnight.

Harold Shoosmith had been left with a sheaf of notes about the arrangements for the fête, for Edward was a conscientious man and felt slightly guilty at leaving his usual post on fête day.

It was to take place on the Saturday after the school's Open Day, and everyone hoped that the weather would hold.

The programme proudly displayed on the door of the Two Pheasants, on trees in Thrush Green and Lulling, and in various shop windows, announced such excitements as a Bouncy Castle for the very young, a visit from the morris dancers, pony rides, innumerable stalls and competitions and a fancy-dress display.

The last, of course, was the one which particularly affected Dorothy Watson as judge. She had no fears about her competence to be discriminating and fair, but *what to wear herself* was her main concern.

Luckily, the day dawned as fine and warm as those which had preceded it, and Agnes and Isobel were soon able to assure Dorothy that the pink frock, which she thought too youthful, was exactly right for the occasion, and most becoming to her.

Dorothy allowed herself to be persuaded, and on remembering that Thrush Green had never seen it before, as it had been bought in Barton-on-Sea a year earlier, she donned her pink splendour immediately after the cold buffet lunch provided by her hostess.

The fête was to be opened by Lady Penge, who lived near Lulling and was often called upon to perform such duties. She was noted for her good works in the area, sat on innumerable committees, and was patron to a host of charities and a local magistrate.

But apart from all these qualifications, it was her distinguished appearance which gave the occasions she graced such style. She was six feet in height and as slim as a poplar tree. From her silver hair to her triple-A handmade shoes she oozed fine breeding. Some thought her supercilious, but others maintained that her highly arched eyebrows gave her this air, and it had nothing to do with her innate kindness.

Her clothes were expensive and impeccable, her smile sweet if a trifle vague. She had no memory for faces, and frequently cut dead old friends, and even her own family, in Lulling High Street, but was readily forgiven.

'Well, she's *gentry*,' one would say indulgently to his neighbour.

'Too much inbreeding,' one farmer would comment to another.

'But she do look a real lady,' the women would tell each

other, admiring the picture hats, the silk dresses, or the furs and tweeds, according to the season.

Lady Penge was due at ten minutes to two for the opening at two o'clock, and everyone rested assured that she would be on time. A welcoming committee headed by Harold Shoosmith were to assemble in his drawing-room before making their way to the dais.

But before opening time, activity at Thrush Green was hectic. The firm engaged to install the electrical equipment which was needed for the relay of Lady Penge's speech, not to mention the announcements by Harold and his helpers during the afternoon, and the general racket of so-called music which would provide a background to the afternoon's amusements, was having difficulty with the cables which snaked everywhere about the green.

Flustered women set out their wares on half-a-dozen stalls. Pudding basins, Oxo tins and handleless cups rattled with loose change. Bunches of garden flowers stood in buckets of water in the shade, and inside the tea tent the activity was frantic as wobbly card tables were draped in the very best cloths with edgings crocheted by long-dead hands. Urns were being inspected, teaspoons counted, sandwiches and homemade cakes shrouded in polythene against inquisitive wasps, and all was bustle.

This excitement was echoed in the houses around Thrush Green, and nowhere was the fever more acute than in Molly Curdle's living-room where she and two other young mothers were getting their children ready for the fancy-dress parade which would be one of the first items on the programme.

It was a full-time job. Lunch had been demoted from the usual sit-down meal to a hasty snatching of a sandwich or sausage roll from a large pile in the kitchen, which Molly had prepared beforehand.

Young George Curdle had insisted on being an Egyptian mummy, adequately swaddled, as seen on television, and reclining in a sarcophagus. Molly and Ben had done their best to dissuade him from this project, and had suggested more practical roles such as a highwayman, a pirate or even a pierrot, as Joan Young had offered a costume from her own young days. But George was adamant. Highwaymen and pirates were old-fashioned, and the pierrot costume was just plain sissy. He was going to be an Egyptian mummy or nothing at all!

His little sister Anne was quite content to wear a fairy costume, complete with wobbly wings, a silver crown made of oven foil, and a wand with a star at the top.

The two other mothers, having turned their docile daughters into a gypsy and a teddy bear, were helping Molly in the difficult task of wrapping George's limbs, torso and finally head in yards and yards of toilet paper stuck here and there with inches of Scotch tape. Already they were using the second roll, and no doubt, thought Molly agitatedly, a third would have to be found. George was an anxious victim.

'You sure that box is like a real carsophagus?' he enquired, nodding towards an enormous dress box supplied by Winnie Bailey the day before.

'*Sarcophagus*,' corrected Molly, 'and it's as big as you'll need. And *ftand ftill*,' she added, holding the end of the sticky tape between her teeth.

The job was interminable. The toilet paper kept breaking. George complained that he was hot, that there were gaps in the wrappings and how would he go to the lavatory?

'You don't,' said one of the helpers shortly. 'Egyptian mummies have to wait.'

'I'd better have a sausage roll before you do my face,' he announced, and his sister fetched him a couple as his neck was being swathed.

By a quarter to two the mammoth task was complete, and George was told to lodge himself carefully on a kitchen chair, and to hold his coffin in readiness.

'And what are you?' enquired a neighbour, looking in to borrow tea towels.

'I'm a mummy. And this is my carsophagus,' said George's muffled voice.

'Well, well,' said the woman, mystified. 'Fancy that!'

Everyone agreed that it was wonderful to have fine weather for the fête. It was bound to hold, and that dark cloud to the west was nothing to worry about.

Lady Penge, accompanied by the welcoming dignitaries, emerged from Harold Shoosmith's house and they made their way to the dais set up near the lime trees by St Andrew's church.

Promptly at two o'clock, Harold approached the microphone and introduced Lady Penge to the waiting crowd.

'Does this thing go up and down?' were the first words heard by the attendant populace, as Lady Penge fingered the microphone.

There were some ear-splitting crackles as the instrument was adjusted, and one of the electricians leapt forward to see to it.

'A friend of my dad's was electrocuted with one of them,' remarked an elderly woman to her neighbour. 'The power was off for three hours. Couldn't boil the kettle.'

'Shush! Shush!' said someone on the platform, as Lady Penge's dulcet tones began to reach her audience. Her speech was received with the usual deference and a hearty round of applause, and the youngest and cleanest of the Cooke grandchildren presented a bouquet of what the locals called 'boughten carnations', with a commendable curtsy, and everyone was free to visit the stalls and part with their money.

The cake stall, as always, was the one which was first besieged. Nelly Piggott had supplied a generous amount of sponges, shortbread, gingerbread and the like, and would have loved to have been present. Duty at the Fuchsia Bush on a busy Saturday forbade this, but she had done her part nobly beforehand.

Dorothy and Agnes were in their element, meeting old friends and pupils, and relishing the tit-bits of news which would furnish them with many happy memories when they returned to Barton.

Many people complimented Dorothy on her pink dress, and Agnes, in her grey silk shirtwaister, now four years old, was glad to see how Dorothy glowed with pleasure. If only, she thought, with a sudden spasm of pain, they could stay at Thrush Green far from Teddy's insidious presence!

The microphone came into use again. Above the alarming crackles and explosive noises, Harold announced the fancy-dress competition which was to be judged by 'their old friend Miss Watson'.

'I don't care for "old",' said Dorothy, 'and surely there are others to help me judge?'

Charles Henstock who was near by assured her that everyone would have complete confidence in her choice.

But Dorothy was not to be persuaded. 'You must help,' she said firmly, grasping his arm. 'I might choose all from the same family. You know the dangers. Come to my aid!'

'Of course, of course,' said Charles soothingly, and the two stood side by side as the children assembled.

There was the usual hubbub.

'Mind my wings!'

'My shoe's come off!'

'Where's Miss Muffet's spider?'

And over all, the stentorian if somewhat muffled yells from George Curdle. 'Lay me in my carsophagus!'

At last the three age groups were sorted out by Miss Watson, to whom this sort of chaos was nothing.

'Under fives first!' she announced, and half-a-dozen small rabbits, fairies, a tramp and a crawling green object which represented a dinosaur lined up self-consciously.

'Walk round in a circle,' commanded Dorothy. 'We want to see backs as well as fronts.'

She turned to her fellow judge. 'Well?'

'I think the fairy is the prettiest,' said Charles.

'But we must consider other things,' pointed out Dorothy. 'Has *ingenuity* been used? Is the *workmanship* adequate? On the other hand, is the costume *hired* or something already made for another occasion?'

'Well,' said Charles, somewhat deflated by all the apparent criteria needed for judging fancy-dress competitions, 'I think I must rely on your judgement.'

By this time, the dinosaur's costume was falling to pieces. Wailing came from its wearer.

'I do hope,' said Dorothy to Harold who had appeared, 'that *every* child will be given something for entering.'

'Indeed,' Harold assured her, showing her a pile of tickets. 'This gives them a free ice-cream at the stall.'

Satisfied, Dorothy returned to her task.

'I rather like the tramp,' she said to Charles. 'That tin cup tied with string round his waist, and the beard. A lot of thought has gone into that.'

'I agree,' said Charles, and the tramp was awarded first place, amidst general applause. Rabbits, fairies and dinosaurs seemed content to rush off to the ice-cream stall, and the next group, containing George Curdle and his dress-box, took the stage.

'And what are you, George?' enquired Dorothy.

'I'm an Egyptian mummy, and this is my carsophagus.'

'*Sarcophagus!*' corrected Dorothy, ever the teacher. 'Well, you obviously can't walk round with the others if you're dead, so the rector will help you to lie down.'

George was lowered gingerly into his coffin, and lay looking skyward as his companions circled round the two judges.

A few minutes later they looked down upon his supine body, and retired a few paces.

'Definitely!' said Dorothy.

'Without question!' agreed Charles.

The outcome was announced. George was helped to his feet, his bandages fast disintegrating, ice-cream tickets were handed out amidst general rejoicing, and Dorothy and Charles prepared to judge the last entries.

The winner of the final group was a fourteen-year-old Cooke girl, dressed as a Bright Young Thing of the twenties, complete with a long cigarette holder and knee-length strings of pearls. As she also did an extremely competent Charleston as she paraded round the judges, everyone agreed that she was 'quite something', and Charles was obviously enchanted.

After this, the morris dancers were the centre of attraction, clapping and thumping, twirling and frisking, reminding Alan Lester, who was selling raffle tickets, of his infants' recent efforts, and the unwelcome possibility of suffering, yet again, before the Christmas concert.

By half past five the crowds were thinning, and the black cloud had moved over the sun. The stalls were almost cleared, and the ladies in the tea tent were stowing away plates and cutlery and folding the tablecloths, now far less pristine than when they were first spread.

Lady Penge had departed after her duty round of the stalls, bearing her bouquet, some homegrown beetroots, four pots of jam and a knitted tea cosy. As she had also left a ten-pound note with Harold Shoosmith 'for the funds', everyone agreed that she had performed her duties with honour, as always.

At six o'clock the first drops of rain pattered on to the chestnut trees and began to darken the trestle tables. There was a mad rush to get everything under cover. Mackintoshes were put on, head scarves tied, children exhorted 'to run home', and Thrush Green, scattered with pieces of paper, ice-cream wrappers and all the debris of the day's activity, emptied rapidly.

'We really ought to get this cleared up,' said Charles anxiously to Harold, as they sheltered under the lime trees by the church.

At that moment, a flash of lightning tore the black cloud apart, thunder shook the earth and the heavens opened.

'It'll keep till morning,' shouted Harold above the din. 'Let's make a run for it!'

The two men, clutching the cash boxes which held the proceeds of the day's work inside their jackets, ran with their heads down to the sanctuary of Harold's house.

Isobel threw open the front door. 'Quickly, quickly! I've put on the kettle for a cup of tea.'

'Always welcome,' gasped Charles, mopping his wet face.

August

In working well, if travail you sustain,
Into the wind shall lightly pass the pain.

Nicholas Grimald

Work was everywhere evident in Thrush Green in August. The winter barley had been harvested, and golden bales stood in the fields awaiting collection. Soon the great combines would be chugging round the wheat crops and the farmers were praying for a dry spell over the harvest period.

In the gardens the strawberries had given way to raspberries, and red and white currants dangled from the bushes, much to the delight of the marauding birds. Apples and plums were filling out on the trees, and prudent housewives were tidying their freezers and looking out ancient kilner jars, ready for the winter stores.

Gardeners were busy collecting seeds or taking cuttings. In most homes the gardening catalogues were in evidence, and bulbs were being ordered for the garden and for the adornment of the house during the dark days of winter.

Everywhere, it seemed, crops of some sort were being collected and preparations made for the months ahead. What the poet called 'sustained travail' which was happening in Thrush Green and, for that matter, everywhere else, was going on busily and giving a great deal of satisfaction in the process.

It certainly provided some of Thrush Green's inhabitants

with some comfort amidst their troubles. Nelly Piggott was one who was glad to busy herself with preparations for winter, and particularly for Christmas, as she went about her duties at the Fuchsia Bush.

They kept her from dwelling too painfully upon her partner's rapid decline. Mrs Peters seemed to be more wraith-like at every visit paid by Nelly to her bedside. She greeted Nelly with the same warm smile and little cries of welcome, but day by day her face grew paler and her arms more stick-like. When Nelly put her own fat arms round her friend, she felt as if she were embracing a child, so small and fragile was the little figure.

But the mind within that gaunt head was as clear as ever, and Mrs Peters continued to question Nelly about the state of affairs at her much-loved business. It was, thought Nelly privately, about the only thing which kept that small bright flame fluttering in its frail container.

Edward Young too was glad to have such jobs as mowing, hedge-trimming and fruit-picking to take his mind from other matters. The question of the extension to the communal room at Rectory Cottages still worried him. During the holiday abroad he had been able to dismiss his secret unease. 'Out of sight was out of mind,' to a certain extent, and he had thrown himself into the joys of a strange land and the company of Joan and Paul, and put his cares aside.

But now that he was back in his home, with Rectory Cottages within constant view, his old doubts had come back to torment him. Joan had discovered him standing by his work table, pencil in hand, studying a diagram before him which was plainly a plan of enlargement of the present premises.

Joan had said nothing, but worried secretly. It was one thing to be married to a gifted and conscientious architect, but being married to a dedicated perfectionist who was capable of worrying himself into another attack of shingles or, even worse, a nervous breakdown, was something which Joan found most alarming.

It was she who made sure that he did his share of harvesting and tidying-up in the garden, trusting that, as the poet said so long ago: '*The wind shall lightly pass the pain.*'

At Barton-on-Sea Dorothy and Agnes were equally busy.

They had returned much refreshed from Thrush Green, with a great many pieces of news which would keep them happy for weeks to come.

Agnes wondered if the return to their own surroundings would rekindle the fire for Teddy which, it seemed, had quite died away in the alien air of Thrush Green.

She sat in the little garden shelling peas. Dorothy had gone shopping, and it was very quiet in the sunshine. Agnes let her hands rest for a moment and lay back in the wicker garden chair.

Every now and then some thistledown floated across her line of vision. She thought how pretty it looked, silvery miniature umbrellas drifting in the warm air. Her neighbours, and Dorothy too if she were present, would be adversely critical of these airy seeds, for a neglected garden near by produced a fine crop of weeds, including thistles, and the good gardeners of the neighbourhood were highly censorious. Secretly, Agnes found great pleasure in a rampant white convolvulus which had draped itself along the wire fence, but she was alone in her admiration.

The old lady who had lived there had died some months earlier. Her children lived overseas, and although it was said that the agent had been told to keep the garden tidy, nothing had been done.

Only Eileen, it seemed, had struck a happy note among all the disapproval for she claimed that she had seen goldfinches feeding on the thistledown.

'A *charm* of goldfinches,' murmured Agnes aloud, returning to her task. What a pretty group name, she thought! So much nicer than a *school* of porpoises or a *flock* of sheep.

As the fat green peas rolled into her basin, Agnes wondered about Eileen. Had she noticed that Dorothy was calling less frequently? Was she aware of Dorothy's unfortunate infatuation for Teddy?

Agnes remembered how shocked she had been when she realized that Dorothy used to make a point of visiting Teddy on the afternoons when Eileen was pushing the book trolley round the local hospital. Certainly the book service happened only once a fortnight, but surely Eileen must have noticed?

Or perhaps Teddy did not tell his wife? Was he embarrassed? Or was he just flattered? It seemed to Agnes that males, even those of six years old, with whom she had been familiar for many years, found it necessary to have attention, preferably from doting mothers or older sisters, and later, of course, from their wives.

It was hardly surprising, thought Agnes, removing a piece of thistledown from the shelled peas, that widowers were so much more helpless than widows.

Women were used to coping with a variety of activities – shopping, cooking, cleaning, caring for children and writing letters. When their husbands died, they buckled to and did their best to cope with the jobs which formerly had been their husbands' department. They learnt to mend a fuse, to change a bulb, to understand the bank statements, and if they could not manage one of their husbands' jobs they soon found someone who would do it for them, if suitably reimbursed.

Men seemed to go to pieces without a partner. Teddy, she had to admit, was an exception. He had managed admirably as a widower, but then his innate courage in coping with his lack of sight had no doubt given him extra strength in adversity. But Agnes recalled other bereaved men who had had no idea how to cook the simplest meal, or how to wash and iron clothes. Sad souls indeed, thought Agnes, and no wonder so many married again!

She popped open the last pea pod. What a blessing it was to be single, she mused happily. She was free and as footloose as the thistledown which floated by her in the sunshine.

Very content Agnes carried the peas into the kitchen.

In the kitchen at Lulling Woods Dotty was as busy as her neighbours. She was stringing runner beans at the kitchen table. The door into the garden was open, and outside in the sunshine young Bruce was happily worrying a bone.

'He looks fighting fit,' said Ella, who had called to see her old friend and to collect her goat's milk.

'He's a very healthy little dog,' agreed Dotty, knife poised.

'No news of his owners, I suppose?'

'I am his owner!' said Dotty forcefully. 'They have forfeited all right to him.'

She looked quite fierce with the knife in her grip. Ella hastily changed the subject.

'And Flossie?'

The old dog lay in her basket near by, and wagged her tail when she heard her name.

'Rather pianissimo,' said Dotty. 'I don't think it is worth getting the vet in, but she is rather up and down these days. Still, she eats quite well, and seems happy enough. Like us, Ella, she's getting old.'

Ella nodded her agreement. 'I hear Mrs Peters is in a bad way,' she said. 'I imagine the Fuchsia Bush will be on the market before long. It's sad, I think. She spent years building it up.'

'Piggott tells me that Prouts may buy the premises. Some talk of specializing in expensive blouses and jewellery and stuff, and calling it a *boutique*.' Dotty's tone was scornful.

'Nelly will miss the work. She's an absolute wizard at cooking. She'll soon get a job elsewhere, probably in one of the hotels.'

'She won't stay at home,' agreed Dotty, putting the last shredded bean into the colander. 'Now, what about a nice cup of mint tea before I get your milk?'

'No, no, Dotty,' said Ella hastily. 'I'm off to the dentist very soon, and I'm afraid I can't spare the time.'

'Ah well! I shall look forward to seeing you very soon, and meanwhile you must take a pot of my beetroot preserve. I've put in some rather special herbs for flavouring. You must tell me what you think of it.'

Ella thanked her, making a mental note to concoct a comment which combined truth with civility for a future occasion.

She knew, from experience, that it would not be easy.

*

Before long the dry spell of weather broke with a spectacular thunderstorm one hot August night.

In their beds, gardeners listened happily to the patter of rain on thirsty soil, and farmers listened less happily, wondering if the downpour would flatten the wheat.

Lightning flickered over Thrush Green, thunder roared and rumbled, babies woke and screamed, dogs barked and Nelly Piggott, who had been unable to sleep, rose from her bed and covered the mirror, as her mother had advised years before, and returned to her tousled sheets to go over, yet again, the amazing and upsetting scene in Mrs Peters' bedroom earlier that evening.

She had found her old employer lying listlessly against the pillows. She smiled weakly at Nelly.

'I can't sit up,' she apologized. 'My neck has no strength in it.'

Nelly drew a chair close to the bedside and held the thin hand lying on the counterpane.

'It's about the Fuchsia Bush,' whispered the invalid. 'Young Mr Venables knows about it.' She began to cough.

'Don't worry then,' said Nelly, alarmed. 'I'll find out what you want done from him.'

The coughing eased.

'It's done,' she breathed. 'I'm leaving it to you, Nelly.'

Nelly was stunned. She was also deeply unhappy. She recognized the outstanding generosity of the frail woman before her, but the thought of taking over the responsibility of the business filled her with horror.

'But I'm not up to it! You know I love the place, and I've been pleased to keep it ticking over while you've been laid up. But to own it!'

Mrs Peters smiled. 'Nelly, it's like this. I've no one close to me to leave it to. It's been my whole life. I put into the Fuchsia Bush all my money and youth and energy. I want it to go on. And you're the one who knows how to do it.'

The thin hand gripped Nelly's plump one desperately.

Nelly took a deep breath. 'It's a wonderful thing to hear,' she said shakily, 'and don't think I'm not grateful for what you've arranged, but I've no head for business. I'm just a good cook, no more than that.'

'The business side can be looked after, just as it has been for the last few months, and Justin Venables will advise you about that. I wasn't going to tell you, but lying here I suddenly thought that it wasn't really fair to spring it on you when I'd gone.'

A tear rolled down the pale cheek, and Nelly too found that she was crying, and did not attempt to mop her tears away.

'You see, Nelly, everyone loves you, and the customers and staff will rally round, you'll see. The thought of leaving the Fuchsia Bush is the only thing that I regret. I shan't be sorry to leave this pain and all the other problems. But if I know my life's work is going on under your care, I'll be happy.'

Nelly was unable to speak. Pity for her employer, the overwhelming news and the knowledge that there was no choice for her, but only one course to take, as well as the choking pain in her throat, kept Nelly silent.

'Say you will,' pleaded the invalid. 'Nelly, say you will!'

Nelly swallowed the lump in her throat. 'I'll do my best. That's a promise. I'll keep your Fuchsia Bush going as you'd like it to be, to the best of my ability. And I'll never cease to be thankful for such a wonderful present. You know that!'

She bent forward to kiss the invalid, and realized how exhausted she looked. This interview had been too much for her. It was obvious that she had summoned up all that remained of her strength to tell Nelly her plans.

Nelly herself felt exhausted, and stirred herself to go.

'You must rest now,' she said. 'Is nurse coming in this evening?'

'She's due any minute.'

'Then I'm going to leave you, my dear. Sleep well, and I'll see you tomorrow.'

Mrs Peters nodded, closed her eyes, and Nelly tiptoed away.

It was beginning to get dark when Nelly emerged at last on to Church Green. The noble bulk of St John's church was casting a long shadow, and Nelly sat down on a seat against a drystone Cotswold wall, and did her best to come to terms with the astounding news she had just heard.

There was nothing to be done about the offer. It was the wish of a dying woman, a plea from one she loved, and it was her duty to accept the situation. It was an honour to be asked to carry on the Fuchsia Bush, and the most generous gift that anyone could bestow.

Nevertheless, the outlook struck despair into Nelly's heart. She could rule her kitchen. She could rule the front of the house, the customers, the counter trade and the organization of the mobile van which trundled round Lulling with delectable fare for the office staffs. She was beginning to understand the ordering from wholesalers, the timing of deliveries, those she could trust absolutely and those who needed watching.

But the overall business arrangements were beyond her. The maintenance of the premises, the insurance of the staff and the property, the tax returns, the round of incomprehensible forms, all these things confused her, and she knew that she would never be able to understand them. If any unscrupulous persons wanted to steal from the firm by 'fiddling the books', Nelly knew she would be powerless to thwart them.

She sat there in the gathering twilight, deeply unhappy and oblivious to the growing chill in the air. Across the green, she saw the rotund figure of the rector making his way to the distant post box. She felt an overpowering desire to hurry after him, to pour out her worries and to be comforted.

She knew that such comfort would be freely given. No one

appealed to Charles Henstock in vain, but Nelly remained seated, the tears returning.

This was something she must face alone. Not even Charles Henstock could provide complete satisfaction. Certainly, Albert could not even begin to understand how she felt.

Her fingers strayed to the gold chain which hung round her neck and was hidden under her clothes. If only Charlie were here! He would provide comfort and cheering advice. His first reaction would be a disbelieving whistle at such a stroke of fortune, but that done he would bring a shrewd streetwise mind to the practical difficulties and give Nelly generous support and sympathy. He was a scamp, Nelly was the first to admit. He had hurt her badly, but in a matter like this he would have been able to offer good advice.

She fingered the chain lovingly, remembering the giver, and became conscious of inner comfort. Something would turn up. People would help her. She would go to see young Mr Venables, if need be, and the rector, two good men who would give sound advice.

She began to feel chilly and rose from the seat. As she bent down to retrieve her shopping bag, she heard a man's voice.

'Want a lift home?'

It was Percy Hodge, who farmed along the Nidden road, the husband of her bingo companion.

'Thank you,' said Nelly. 'I'd be glad of a lift.'

He held out his hand for the shopping bag, and peered at her face. 'You all right? You look upset.'

Nelly decided that the plain truth was needed. 'I've just come from Mrs Peters. She's not long for this world, Percy.'

'I'm sorry. No wonder you're upset.'

He led the way to his ancient Land-Rover across the road.

'I had to come down to the police station,' he explained, 'about my gun licence.'

He opened the door, and Nelly heaved herself up to sit beside him.

They drove slowly down Lulling High Street. There were very few people about in the dusk. The street lights were beginning to flicker into life, and some of the shops had lighted windows.

The Fuchsia Bush was shut, and there were no lights there. Nelly could hardly bear to look at it.

'That's real sad about Mrs Peters,' said Percy, slowing down as they met the Oxford road. 'She was a real nice woman. A good worker too.'

Nelly nodded, not trusting her voice.

Percy changed gears and the Land-Rover began to grind noisily up the steep hill to Thrush Green.

'I wonder what'll become of the Fuchsia Bush?' queried Percy when they reached the top.

'I've been wondering about that too,' said Nelly tremulously.

The nurse had called in while Nelly was sitting unhappily on Church Green. She knew at once that her patient was dead, and rang the doctor.

By morning, it seemed, all Lulling knew the sad news. At Thrush Green it was Betty Bell who told the Shoosmiths as they were clearing the breakfast table.

'Mind you,' said Betty, after sincere tributes had been paid to the late owner of the Fuchsia Bush, 'it was a happy release really. Poor thing had no hope of getting better. I wonder who'll be the third?'

She looked speculatively at her employers.

'Third what?' asked Harold.

'Death.'

'Does there have to be a third?'

'Oh yes! Haven't you heard that? Why, deaths always go in threes.'

'But Mrs Peters' death is the first I've heard.'

'There was that nice Mr Andersen's mother,' Betty pointed out. She went to the dresser drawer for a clean duster to start her morning's work.

Harold addressed her back. 'But she was in *America*, for heaven's sake. She wasn't *local*.'

'Don't have to be *local*,' responded Betty, inspecting the duster. 'It's deaths what you hear about. Well, we've heard about Mrs Andersen, and now Mrs Peters, and soon we'll hear about a third.'

'Really, Betty,' broke in Isobel. 'You are positively ghoulish!'

'If that means bilious you're right. I had some of Dotty's – I mean Miss Harmer's – marmalade for breakfast. Don't worry though. I'll work it off!'

She vanished upstairs, and soon they heard her singing.

Later that morning, the news was being spread at the Two Pheasants.

Percy Hodge was in a position of some importance as he had had first-hand news from Nelly the previous evening.

'Your Nelly was proper upset,' he told Albert. 'I could see she'd been crying.'

'Ah!' agreed Albert. 'My Nelly's real soft-hearted. She's been working overtime to keep things up together at the café for Mrs Peters.'

'I suppose it'll be up for sale,' ventured someone.

'It's got a good position in the High Street,' commented another.

'Will Nelly be looking for another job?' queried a third to Albert.

'I don't know nothing about it,' said Albert crossly, slamming his empty beer mug on the counter. 'I don't much like all this talk when that poor woman ain't been dead for less than a day.'

He thrust his way between his cronies and went out of the door, slamming it behind him.

'What's bitten old Albert?' said Percy to Mr Jones, the landlord.

'Well,' he replied, 'I don't think Nelly tells him much, and that rankles. And besides that, I think he's wondering if Nelly will be out of a job.'

'Then he'll just have to do a bit more himself,' said one of the men with malicious satisfaction. 'Won't hurt him!'

His hearers agreed with him.

Mrs Peters' funeral took place on a Friday morning, and St John's church was almost full, for she had been a popular figure in the little town and its environs.

Towards the front of the church sat the three Lovelock sisters, much to the surprise of most of those present, who had only heard about some of the complaints made about the Fuchsia Bush in early days.

Now, they realized, the frail and querulous old ladies knew that they had lost a friend, ever ready to provide practical support, and to forgive any little upsets. Their mourning was sincere for their departed neighbour.

Charles Henstock took the service, and the sincerity and simple grace of his short address summed up the feelings of the congregation.

The Fuchsia Bush was closed for the day, and Nelly and the staff were among the chief mourners.

Nelly was outwardly calm now, but still inwardly in turmoil. In her handbag was a letter from Justin Venables, asking her to call at his office on Tuesday morning next 'in connection with her late employer's Last Will and Testament'.

Somehow, those capital letters had increased her fears. She would be glad to get the interview over, to have some guidance, to be given some support in this alarming situation.

Since Mrs Peters' death Nelly had kept her own counsel. It was useless to confide in Albert, she realized. Most women, she thought, with some bitterness, have a husband, or a son, or a brother to rely on, at such times.

Fingering Charlie's gold chain she thought sadly that her only support came from a fickle lover long dead. What lay before her must be tackled singlehanded. It was going to be a lone furrow to plough, and an uphill one.

Speculation about the future of the Fuchsia Bush was rife. The general opinion was that the property would be sold, perhaps as a going concern, and if so the new owner would surely have the sense to keep Nelly in charge of the kitchen.

Some thought that such a prime site in Lulling High Street might attract one of the supermarket giants, but as there was not much space for loading and unloading it seemed doubtful.

However, this issue made a pleasant source of interest, and with the death of Carl's mother, as well as the possibility of catching the criminals who had absconded with thousands of pounds, and worse still, abandoned Dotty's dog, kept tongues happily wagging during the month of August.

Charles Henstock had his own worries, for Mrs Thurgood had renewed her attack about the '*gross inadequacy*', as she put it, of the common room at Rectory Cottages, and to add to his discomfort he had met Edward Young, whilst walking in the High Street, and was surprised to find him reviewing the possibility of an enlargement to the existing annexe.

'But, Edward,' Charles had protested, 'you were quite satisfied with it before. You know we took a vote on it.'

'I wasn't there,' Edward reminded him. 'Since then I've been in there once or twice, and I must admit it does seem a bit cramped.'

'Well, cramped or not,' said Charles, raising his hat politely to a passing parishioner, 'you know we have no money to take on such work. We must cut our coats according to the cloth. I keep telling Mrs Thurgood so.'

Edward looked alarmed. 'Is she still being a nuisance? I find her absolutely appalling.'

'So do I,' agreed Charles ruefully. It was so unusual to hear Charles uttering anything that was detrimental about his flock that Edward realized that he had suffered much.

'Far be it from me to join forces with that awful woman,' he told Charles, 'but I do just wonder . . .'

He paused to let a perambulator pass him.

'We ought to get Harold to tackle her,' he continued. 'He'll settle her hash!'

'He does,' sighed Charles. 'Frequently. But she bounces back!'

On the following Tuesday Nelly awoke feeling that something unpleasant was about to happen, and remembered that she had to pay the dreaded visit to young Mr Venables' office that morning.

She lay in bed, watching the sunshine wavering across the ceiling, and wondering what would be the appropriate wear for a visit to a solicitor. Something, she decided, between funeral garments and the sort of formal dress one would put on for a business lunch.

Mentally she surveyed her wardrobe and settled on a light-weight grey suit, rather tight to be sure, and a white silk blouse. The ensemble, she hoped, would be suitably ladylike, and yet not too smart to invite speculation from Rosa and Gloria. In any case, a voluminous overall could hide her unusual morning splendour before she left for her appointment.

That settled, Nelly rose, washed and dressed, and went downstairs, where Albert was shaving at the kitchen sink.

He caught sight of her in the mirror. 'You're all dolled up,' he grunted, razor poised. 'Where are you off?'

'I've had this years,' said Nelly truthfully. 'And I'm off to work, where you should be. The weeds round that churchyard of yours would keep a couple of Percy Hodge's cows going for a month.'

Silenced, Albert continued to scrape his face, while Nelly dashed about her duties in her usual early-morning fashion.

By eight thirty she was at the Fuchsia Bush, and at a quarter to eleven she told the staff, and Miss Spooner, the visiting accountant's assistant, that she would be back in about an hour. She had some of Mrs Peters' business to discuss with young Mr Venables, she explained. It was as well, she knew from experience, to give people some little nugget of information, preferably truthful, to chew on, rather than leave them to speculate.

Justin Venables' office was little changed from the time when he had first entered it. To be sure, the black gauze which had shadowed the lower half of the sash window looking out into the High Street had been replaced with a white net curtain, so the room was much lighter, but still screened from public gaze.

Justin did not smoke, and did not encourage his clients to indulge by offering them cigarettes, but a hideous cast-iron ashtray had stood on the desk for almost a century, and still remained there for those who were addicted to tobacco. It bore the legend, 'Long Live Victoria 1837–97' and would no doubt be snapped up, at great expense, by any collector of Victoriana, if given half a chance.

Nelly sat nervously opposite Justin at his enormous desk.

'Would you care for some coffee?' asked Justin.

'Thank you,' said Nelly, and Justin struck a bell sharply on his desk, and Miss Giles, much the same age, it seemed, as her master, appeared at the door.

'Just two cups,' nodded Justin, and in silence Miss Giles vanished, only to return two minutes later with a tray containing two steaming cups, sugar and a plate of digestive biscuits.

She must have had the kettle at the boil, thought Nelly, and felt somehow comforted by this little domestic interlude.

'I wonder if you have any inkling of how Mrs Peters left her affairs?' queried Justin spreading out a document before him.

Nelly put down her cup. The coffee was rather nasty, and she hoped that Justin was not paying the full price for good quality instant coffee when obviously he was getting the cheapest.

She wrenched her mind from this to reply to Justin's question. It seemed right to answer him truthfully.

'Just before she died,' she answered, 'Mrs Peters told me she was leaving the business to me, but I don't know if that's correct.'

'Quite correct. I hope it pleases you. It shows how much she thought of your ability.'

Nelly shook her head. 'I was knocked sideways. I still am. It's too big a job for me to do, Mr Venables. I've no head for the money side.'

Justin nodded understandingly. 'I know exactly how you feel, Mrs Piggott. Now, I propose to read this Last Will and Testament, and then I will explain anything which puzzles you, and try to advise you about steps to take for the future running of the business.'

He cleared his throat and began, while Nelly did her best to follow the incomprehensible legal vocabulary, and failed after five minutes.

Justin still had a musical voice, and while the sonorous phrases droned round the room Nelly let her attention wander to the rows of envelopes bound with pink tape that stood along the shelves, and the black tin boxes stacked higher still bearing white-painted names. The wooden cupboards could have done with a good polish, mused Nelly, and the windows had not been cleaned for weeks. It was a pity too that the Turkish carpet was so dusty. Nelly would have liked half a day in the room to put it to rights.

After a time, Justin put down the will, and bent towards his client.

'Now, to business! I believe Miss Spooner still calls twice a week to attend to the office side.'

Nelly agreed.

'She is excellent, of course, but I should see if you could get someone younger, perhaps trained by her, and able to cope with modern office equipment and make things more manageable for you. Let me suggest one or two other things.'

The large clock on the wall ticked the hour away, while Justin talked and made a few notes for Nelly to consider later.

It was chiming the half hour after midday when Nelly

made her farewells, still bemused but much comforted, as she returned to the bustle of the Fuchsia Bush.

The latter part of August was unusually hot. The verges along the lanes were dusty and crowned with dry grass and dead flowers.

The grass on Thrush Green was crisp and brown, the earth like iron, and all the gardeners were tired of daily watering and asking each other how soon hosepipes would be banned.

Winnie Bailey and Jenny took their mugs of coffee into the garden, and sat under the shade of an ancient plum tree.

'It's as hot as Africa,' commented Jenny. 'Or America, according to the telly. People are dropping down dead with the heat.'

'Really? I missed that.'

'I wonder if that nice Mr Andersen's all right?' continued Jenny. 'Is he coming back soon?'

'He wants to. I believe Molly has heard from him.'

'I expect he'll stay in Woodstock again, if he gets over. My cousin's a chambermaid at the Bear. She seems to think he'll be coming back there.'

'Did he say so?'

'I'm not sure, but he got very friendly with a nice woman who was there for a few months.'

Winnie digested this interesting morsel of gossip. 'What does this woman do? Is she on holiday?'

'No, she works in the big houses. Tells people what curtains to buy and how to change their wallpaper and that. She goes up to London getting great samples of material and wallpaper books. Sometimes she's got three or four houses in the neighbourhood, and then she takes one of the biggest bedrooms at the Bear with a great desk in it, and works there.'

'It must be rather expensive,' commented Winnie.

'I expect the people who employ her pay for that,' said

Jenny, 'and maybe the Bear gives her a special rate as she stays quite a time. Shall I ask my cousin?'

'Good heavens, no!' replied Winnie. 'Her affairs are her own business. Is she nice? She sounds very busy. An interior designer, I suppose we would call her.'

'They all like her there. She tips very generously, and don't give any trouble. She and Mr Andersen sometimes shared a table in the evenings. Both a bit lonely I expect.'

Winnie was intrigued by this news, but forbore to ask further. Could romance be in the air? If so, Winnie knew from experience that the good news would reach Thrush Green before very long. Jenny's cousin, or one of her friends, would see to that.

It was later in the week that she came across Joan Young. They were both shopping in Lulling High Street, and met at the greengrocer's.

'Are you good at melons?' queried Joan. 'I believe you're supposed to smell them to see if they're ripe.'

'I press the top,' replied Winnie, trying her luck on a nicely mottled one. 'I should think this is about right.'

'Edward can't bear them when they're still hard. He says he'd just as soon eat raw marrow.'

'I sympathize,' said Winnie. 'It's nectarines I can't fathom. The reddest ones are often the least ripe. All very tricky.'

They entered the shop to pay for their purchases, and while they were waiting Joan told Winnie that they had heard from Carl Andersen.

'He's coming over in September, and hoping to be here for several weeks. He *telephoned* last night,' she added. 'Think of that! I hope he won't be ruined when his bill comes in.'

'I'm sure he can manage that,' said Winnie. 'I gather that he is a prosperous businessman. Where's he staying?'

'At the Bear again. They made him very comfortable, and although we wanted to put him up, I can understand that he likes to be free. I gather he's following up that business venture in Scotland that he's interested in. It will be lovely to see him again.'

'Indeed it will,' agreed Winnie. She also wondered, as she added a fine cucumber to her purchases, if the gifted interior designer would be pleased too. But of this she said nothing.

After lunch that day, Winnie took her rest in a deckchair in the shadiest part of the garden. Jenny had boarded the two o'clock bus to Oxford to do some shopping for clothes, and it was very peaceful under the trees.

The bees were busy among the lavender flowers, and forcing their way between the velvety lips of the snapdragons. Somewhere nearby a young bird was piping for attention, and high above the swallows swooped and soared. Soon they would be gathering together to chatter about their plans for migration. Then, thought Winnie sadly, it really would begin to feel like autumn.

In the distance, somewhere along the Nidden road, she could hear the throbbing of a combine, bringing ever closer the thought of cleared fields soon to be ploughed for next year's crop. Yes, autumn would soon be here.

She remembered inconsequently an English lesson at her school. The class had been asked to provide adjectives describing autumn, and she had proffered 'wistful' and 'mellow'. The English mistress had said rather brusquely that they had already put 'yellow' on the blackboard, and the young Winnie, somewhat piqued, had pointed out that *her* adjective was 'mellow' and not 'yellow'.

The mistress had looked at her with fresh interest, and enquired if she had learnt any poems by John Keats, who had written 'To Autumn'.

Winnie had replied truthfully that she had never heard of John Keats, and 'mellow' was written below 'wistful', and justice had been done.

She leant back and closed her eyes. How extraordinary one's memory was! She had not thought of that school for years, and yet that memory was vivid. So, suddenly, was the vision of her first paintbox with the fascinating names printed neatly below each bright square of paint. Crimson Lake, Bice Green, Prussian Blue, Viridian Green, Chinese White, Gamboge and a dozen more which she would have in tubes as she grew older and more expert, but that first paintbox was the one she remembered most clearly.

She recalled her attempt to paint a cabbage in an early art class, when an arrangement of vegetables, carrots, young turnips and pea pods – some closed, and others open displaying a row of glistening peas – had been that day's still life subject.

She had found, with a thrill of discovery, that Viridian, Chinese White, and then a touch of Crimson Lake, had produced the most satisfactory soft green wash which had gained her a gold star on the finished picture. Such idle memories, mused Winnie, half asleep.

A yellow leaf fluttered from the plum tree and landed on her lap. Soon, thought Winnie, there would be mushrooms, those magical pearls thrusting up overnight through the dewy grass.

She held the dead leaf between her thumb and finger, enjoying its roughness, and closed her eyes again.

September

Read Boswell in the house in the morning,
and after dinner under the bright yellow
leaves of the orchard. The pear trees a
bright yellow. The apple trees green still.
A sweet lovely afternoon.

Dorothy Wordsworth

The trees of Thrush Green were also beginning to have a golden tinge. The lime trees round St Andrew's church were a paler sunnier green than at the time of the July fête.

The sturdy chestnut trees still boasted dark green foliage, but on the grass beneath there were a number of wrinkled palmate leaves which presaged the coming of autumn.

There was a definite chill in the morning and evening air. Thoughts turned to stocks of coal and logs, of bulbs to be planted for Christmas flowering, and the thud of catalogues about the festive season, still months away, was heard on many a doormat in the area. Sensible people refused to be hustled into panic buying, and preferred to enjoy the mellow sunshine and the last of the summer flowers which made September one of the loveliest months at Thrush Green.

The news of Nelly's inheritance was soon common knowledge, and occasioned much speculation.

Nelly, well versed in the reactions to news in small communities, decided to tell Albert the day after she had visited Justin

Venables' office. She was quite prepared for his usual disgruntled response to her pieces of news, although she felt sure
that the prospect of money might mitigate the gloom.

They had finished their evening meal, and were sitting at the
kitchen table, stirring the cups of tea with which they liked to
finish their repast.

'I had some good news today,' ventured Nelly.

'Oh ah!'

'I went to see young Mr Venables.'

Albert looked up in alarm. 'What you bin up to? You don't
want to get muddled up with them legal blokes.'

'It was about Mrs Peters' will. She left me the Fuchsia Bush.'

Albert dropped his teaspoon with a clatter into the saucer.

'Left you the Fuchsia Bush?' he echoed with astonishment. 'What for?'

Nelly surveyed his unusually animated countenance. 'What for? For me to run, of course.'

There was silence while Albert tried to come to terms with this staggering piece of news. His voice was husky when he at last found words.

'You'd never be able to run the Fuchsia Bush, girl. You ain't got the brain.'

Although this was exactly Nelly's own private opinion, and had been so since that sad evening of Mrs Peters' death, to hear it put into such disparaging words, and by Albert of all people, brought out all Nelly's fighting spirit.

'You don't know nothing about it! Mrs Peters wouldn't have left it to me if she hadn't thought I'd be able to cope.'

'She was wandering, poor soul. Must've bin. Why, you gets in a muddle with the grocer's bill! You ain't no businesswoman.'

'I'll soon learn,' said Nelly shortly, taking the tea cups to the sink. 'And don't go blabbing about it in the Two Pheasants. Time enough when the news gets out later.'

'You'd best by far sell the place,' shouted Albert, above the noise of clashing crockery. 'Bring us in a tidy bit. We could move somewhere bigger.'

Nelly turned off the taps, left the sink, and resumed her place at the table. Albert surveyed her stern face with some trepidation.

'There's no "us" and "we" about this, Albert Piggott! Mrs Peters left it to *me alone*, and I'm the one as will say what happens to the Fuchsia Bush.'

'All right, all right,' muttered Albert. 'Keep your hair on. I was only suggesting –'

'Then you can keep your suggestions to yourself. I'm going to keep the Fuchsia Bush running as Mrs Peters wanted. It was her dying wish.'

'Maybe. But she'd never know if you sold it,' said Albert rallying. 'I wonder as Mr Venables didn't tell you to! Best all round, I'd say.'

'Say what you like,' retorted Nelly. 'I'm the one that has the last word, and the last word is that I'm not selling!'

'You could have one of them new houses up towards Nidden. Fitted kitchen, bathroom and all that. And never need to go out to work. Me neither!'

Nelly looked at him with utter contempt. '*I am not selling!* And work is what I like. You'd be a happier man, Albert Piggott, if you took the same pride in your job.'

Silenced, Albert rose to make his way next door to the public house. He knew when he was beaten.

'And watch your tongue,' shouted Nelly after him. 'No need to broadcast the news to your good-for-nothing pals. It'll get round soon enough, if I know anything about gossip.'

Nelly was right, of course. The news flashed round Thrush Green and Lulling, and the general feeling was that Nelly was lucky to have dropped into a fortune.

'Of course, she'll sell it,' was the comment most frequently heard. 'I just hope whoever buys it will keep it going as it is. The Fuchsia Bush is an important place in Lulling High Street.'

People began to stop Nelly as she went to and fro to her work.

'Aren't you lucky?'

'What a windfall!'

'You've certainly hit the jackpot this time, Nelly.'

These remarks irritated Nelly beyond measure.

In the first place, she resented the envy which prompted these comments. She was the first to recognize her indebtedness to her late partner. She grieved for her daily, missing her companionship and steady good sense.

But she did not consider herself unadulteratedly *lucky*. The responsibility of owning the business quite overshadowed her feelings of pleasure and gratitude. It was a burden she could well do without, and only the fact that Mrs Peters had shown such faith in her gave Nelly some comfort.

She replied civilly to all who commented, telling them that she hoped to continue Mrs Peters' work to the best of her ability, and with advice from Mr Venables. And, she always added with some emphasis, she was definitely *not selling the property*.

That, at least, was greeted everywhere with relief. Violet, Ada and Bertha Lovelock made a point of calling at the Fuchsia Bush for coffee one morning, and expressing their pleasure at the news. It was a changed attitude on the part of the old ladies, thought Nelly, from the days when she had been maid, cook and general dogsbody for a short time at the house next door.

There, she recalled, the doling out of minuscule amounts of the cheapest margarine, a handful of currants, a half teacupful of sugar with the request to make 'a good fruit cake for tea'. She remembered too the dab of metal polish, in an old saucer, which was deemed adequate for polishing the vast amounts of silver knick-knacks covering several tables in the drawing-room.

Then she was treated as 'a skivvy', thought Nelly, receiving her former employers graciously. Now she was being acknowledged as a property owner and a sound businesswoman in her own right.

It was such encounters which began to give Nelly the confidence to tackle the sacred trust which had been thrust so dauntingly upon her.

News of Carl Andersen's return was welcomed by everyone who had met him on his first visit. But it was Edward Young who was particularly pleased at the news.

He had been greatly impressed by Carl Andersen, and even more stirred by the fact that Carl was one of the directors of the world-famous company of Benn, Andersen and Webbly whose work was respected in both hemispheres.

The firm had been much in the news over its bold and inspired work on such projects as dam-building, bridge-making and the laying-out of airports in the vast areas of Africa and Asia. Edward had followed the fortunes of the company in a number of articles in his architectural journals, and marvelled at the massive concept needed to visualize these mighty schemes.

His own architectural skills were confined to domestic work. He had a flair for designing modern houses which would fit well into their settings, and an equally strong feeling for the modernization of the small stone cottages which were scattered within a few miles of his own home. He had built up a reputation for this type of work, and as he had some domestic talents himself he was alert to the difficulties of planning kitchens for families or bathrooms for the disabled.

He relished his work, and was at pains to get every detail correct as well as pleasing to the eye. It was this anxiety for perfection which sometimes made him short-tempered, and which Joan understood and readily forgave.

It was she who shared his pleasure at the thought of Carl's return. Molly and Ben were also delighted, but Joan's feelings went further. Edward would have a companion with whom he could discuss all kinds of architectural matters. He would have a friend whose accomplishments he respected and whose work he found absorbing.

With any luck, thought Joan, he would put this wretched business of enlarging the sitting-room at Rectory Cottages to one side, and find the peace of mind he so needed to do work of his own.

All in all, the coming of Carl Andersen was awaited by everyone in Thrush Green with the greatest pleasure.

Dotty Harmer had heard the news of the American's expected visit, and of Nelly Piggott's inheritance, but had more pressing matters to engage her attention.

Flossie was not well. She had certainly rallied after the vet's attentions earlier, and had pottered about her domain and endured the boisterous attentions of Bruce with commendable tolerance.

But now she was listless. She could not be bothered to eat, and Dotty kept her going with a dribble of evaporated milk now and again which was all, it seemed, that would tempt the patient.

'She can't go on like this,' said Kit, who had come to Dotty's kitchen with Connie to confer with her. 'I should get the vet again.'

Connie, more worried about Dotty than Flossie, heartily

agreed. At this rate, she could see, she would have two invalids to care for.

'I'm sure you're right,' she said at last. 'It's just that I dread him saying that he can do no more for poor Flossie.'

'I'll ring him at once,' said Kit, making for the door. He was as anxious as his wife to get some knowledgeable support in the situation.

Dotty squatted down beside Flossie's basket and fondled her ears.

'In theory, of course, I am entirely in favour of the vet putting Flossie out of her misery, if misery it is,' she said to Connie when Kit had vanished. 'If only doctors would do the same for us!'

'Now come!' protested Connie. 'You know they have to take the Hypocrites Oath –'

'*Hippocratic!*' interrupted Dotty.

'Well, whatever it is. And they have to swear to try and save life, not terminate it.'

'I know that! I know that,' snapped Dotty. 'All I'm saying is that if you are human you are caught all ways. No one will help us out, no matter how bad the pain. As Hamlet very sensibly said,

> *When he himself might his quietus make*
> *With a bare bodkin*

we still have to go on suffering! I shan't let Flossie suffer, and that's flat, but I just hope the vet can give her another few months of happy living.'

Connie was alarmed at Dotty's ferocity, and the pink patches which had flared in the old lady's face. She bent down and helped her to her feet.

'I think you could do with a drink,' she said gently. 'Shall I get you a little brandy?'

'No, no, I should much prefer a cup of lime tea.'

'Very well,' agreed Connie, 'and I will have one too.'

She filled the kettle, thinking that lime tea, at least, was fairly harmless. There was agitation enough in the household at the moment, without adding alimentary complications into the present climate.

While Dotty awaited the vet's visit with some trepidation, Albert Piggott had put aside his broom in the church porch, and crossed the road to the open door of the Two Pheasants.

The news about the Fuchsia Bush had been widely discussed in both bars during the last few days, and Albert was heartily sick of the heavy-handed teasing he had to endure.

But nothing, he told himself sturdily, was going to make him change the habits of a lifetime, and when the doors of the pub opened he intended to enter and refresh himself, as was his wont.

There was only one other customer in the bar, and that was Percy Hodge. He looked up as Albert entered.

'How's the millionaire this morning?' he greeted Albert, grinning at his own wit.

'You shut up!' growled Albert. 'You're asking for a thick ear, and that's flat.'

'Now, now, gentlemen,' cried Mr Jones, who was never free from the possibility of getting a name for 'a disorderly house', as the licensing justices put it. 'My old mother used to say: "Little birds in their nest agree, or else they will fall out."'

Both customers found themselves wholeheartedly disliking Mr Jones' long-dead mother and her platitudes, but had the grace to remain silent.

'Bit parky in the morning now,' continued Mr Jones cheerfully. 'Have to think about getting the coal stocks in.'

'When we had a station at Lulling,' said Percy, accepting the olive branch offered by this change in conversation, 'my old dad used to buy a wagonload and share it out with his neighbours. Much cheaper that way.'

'Not many people nowadays to share in a wagonload,' commented Albert. 'They mostly has gas or electric.'

'Dr Bailey had some,' reminisced Percy, 'and old Mr Harmer, Dotty's father. By the way, I hear her Flossie's in a bad way.'

Albert was alarmed. He was as fond of Flossie as Dotty was. He made up his mind to visit them both later in the day.

'What's up then?'

'Just old age, I should think. Betty Bell told my wife when she was at bingo. Dotty was on about getting the vet. She'd tried all her own homemade remedies.'

'Humph!' said Mr Jones, but said no more. A publican learns to be discreet in a small community.

'I'll pop down later,' said Albert, putting down his glass. 'Same again, please. Perce, d'you want another?'

Surprised at this unusual generosity, Percy pushed his glass forward.

'Don't mind if I do,' he said, and was careful not to make any wisecracks about the *nouveaux riches*.

Later that morning the vet arrived at Dotty's to examine the patient.

He took a long time over the job while Dotty and Connie watched him anxiously. Flossie had waved a languid tail to show that there was no ill-feeling over past indignities she had suffered at his hands, but otherwise had stirred little.

'There's nothing really nasty to worry about,' he assured the watchers. 'It's simply a case of general ageing. Most of the vital organs, lungs, heart and so on are just getting less able to do the job. I could take her back with me, if you agree, and try that new remedy, or I can give her an injection here and now, and leave some pills with you.'

'I'll keep her here,' decided Dotty. They watched the syringe being carefully filled, the injection given and Flossie gently massaged with an experienced hand.

'Looking like autumn,' said the vet, as he washed his hands at the kitchen sink, and gazed through the window. A flurry of yellow leaves had fluttered from Dotty's old plum tree, as a gust of wind stirred the branches.

'Plenty of sloes about,' he went on, as he dried his hands. 'I shall have to get on with my sloe gin.'

'Do you still prick them?' asked Dotty. 'I used to use a silver hatpin of my mother's until Connie told me of a much better way.'

'And what's that?' enquired the vet. 'Never too late to learn, you know.'

'Spread them on a dish and put them in the freezer,' Connie told him, 'then they burst when you take them out, and are all ready for the gin when they've thawed.'

'Now that's worth knowing,' agreed the vet, shrugging himself into his jacket.

'Don't worry about the old lady,' he added. 'She's in no pain, and got plenty of mileage in her yet.'

Connie thought privately, as they watched him make his way to the car, that his comments would be applicable to Dotty as well as her pet.

September was running true to form. It was chilly in the early morning and evening, and summer clothes were being put away, and warm woollens were donned thankfully.

But by mid-morning the early mists had usually cleared, giving way to pellucid blue skies and the particularly mellow sunshine of early autumn.

In the gardens at Thrush Green the dahlias blazed supreme, making the most of their brief flamboyance before the frosts turned their glory to brown death. The summer flowers of such hardy types as penstemon, phlox and geraniums still showed colour, and gardeners were reluctant to cut them down, clinging to these last brave vestiges of summer beauty.

Blackberries, as well as sloes, were in abundance, and in Lulling Woods there were some exotic-looking fungi, some with shiny red-spotted caps reminiscent of the countryman's red-spotted handkerchiefs, which most people, even Dotty Harmer, rejected as fodder.

But there were mushrooms in the field behind Dotty's house, and these were quickly garnered by the knowledgeable inhabitants of Thrush Green, and relished with their breakfast bacon.

At the village school the nature table was crammed with the bounty of the hedges and trees, and strings of shiny conkers accompanied the boys whenever they were in the playground. Early apples, such as Beauty of Bath, or the early purple plums, took the place of biscuits or cake at elevenses time. Soon, Alan Lester knew, the school heating system would need to be stirred, and winter would be upon everyone with preparations for the joyous celebration of Christmas at the end of term.

He recalled the dreadful threat of mid-European dances all over again. He put the thought firmly behind him, and decided to concentrate instead on these last few golden days of a Cotswold summer.

It was during this halcyon spell that Carl Andersen arrived.

Ben Curdle went to Heathrow to meet him. It was a welcoming sort of morning, he thought happily, as he took the car from the garage. Gossamer threads and spiders' cobwebs spangled the garden hedge, and the sun was dispersing the mist and promising a fine day ahead.

As he approached the airport the traffic slowed to a halt. On one side of him loomed an enormous lorry with a radio going full blast in the cab, and a fat young man nodding his head in time to the racket. He seemed to be quite at home in these conditions.

On the other side was another fat man, somewhat older, balder and better dressed. He was obviously in a state of some agitation, drumming his fingers on the steering wheel, looking at his watch, and picking at a scab on the back of his hand.

Ben felt sorry for him. No doubt he had an important appointment to keep. Maybe it involved a lot of money, he speculated. He was thankful that he had no such pressing worries.

If he was late, Carl would know that he had been held up and would be content to wait, just as he himself would be patient if the flight was delayed.

Perhaps he was too submissive to what Fate threw at him, mused Ben, watching his unhappy neighbour getting more and more agitated. But what good did it do to get steamed up like that? You took life as it came in the country. Thrush Green folk were used to waiting, waiting for crops to ripen, for lambs to be born, for pheasants to hatch. It all came right in the end, thought Ben philosophically as he saw that the traffic had begun to inch along again.

As it happened, Carl's flight was delayed by almost an hour, but Ben enjoyed a cup of coffee and surveyed his companions as he waited.

They certainly seemed a jumpy lot on the whole, was his opinion, as he slowly stirred his coffee. He was the first to admit that flying somewhere must be a worrying business, what with tickets and luggage and excitable children and confused elderly relations, but he felt sure that if the proposed visit to America ever took place, he and Molly would be a lot calmer than most of those about him.

In one of his rare periods at school, an irate teacher had called him 'thick, boneheaded and a country bumpkin'. Ben thought he was probably right. He knew that he was also patient and obedient. Rebellion would never occur to him. At times like the present, mused Ben, it was a good thing to be 'a thick, boneheaded country bumpkin'.

As the passengers on Carl's flight gradually emerged, it was easy to spot Carl himself by his great height and the thatch of fair hair which overtopped his neighbours.

Both men beamed with delight as they saw each other, and Ben held out a welcoming hand. But Carl dropped both his bags and enveloped Ben in a muscular bear-hug of joy.

'Good to see you,' he cried. 'Sorry I'm late.'

'No bother,' said Ben, stooping for a bag. 'The car's this way.'

Halfway home Ben uttered the words he felt must be said. 'Molly and I were real upset to hear about your mother.'

'I know, I know,' replied Carl, his voice suddenly husky. 'I can't believe it myself. Still expect to get a phone call or a letter. Somehow I can't believe she's really gone. She sent all sorts of loving messages to you both.'

There was silence as they sped westward, until Ben spoke again. 'Bill and Jane Cartwright were saying that there are a couple of old people in the home who remember your mother. I'm sure they'd like to tell you about her, if you felt like it.'

Carl's face lit up. 'That's good news! I want to find out all I can about her connections with Thrush Green and Mrs Curdle.'

'If only Gran were still alive,' said Ben, 'she'd be able to tell you so much. She had a memory as sharp as a razor. A tongue to match too, at times!'

The men laughed, as Ben raised a hand from the wheel and pointed to a distant church tower.

'In ten minutes' time we'll be home!'

The arrival of Carl Andersen was one item of news at Thrush Green, but a more dramatic one was centred on Dotty Harmer.

Flossie was a trifle stronger after her injection, and although Dotty was still anxious about her, the general feeling was one of relief.

As Betty Bell told Isobel and Harold one morning, 'They're all breathing again at Lulling Woods.'

But three days later there was more sensational news.

It appeared that Connie had made her usual morning visit to Dotty's bedroom and found it empty. It was seven o'clock, just getting light on a misty September morning.

Connie quickly searched Dotty's bathroom, sitting-room and kitchen. All were empty.

Clad only in her nightgown and slippers she ran into the damp garden. Sometimes Dotty wandered down to see her beloved hens and goats, no matter how skimpily clad.

But all was quiet, and the garden deserted. However, the gate to the fields beyond stood open, and Connie went through to survey the scene.

No one was in sight.

She ran back to tell Kit. Dotty could not have gone far, she felt sure. These days she only wandered a few hundred yards from her home, but she had been known to get as far as Lulling Woods that summer, stopping to rest every now and again. That time Connie had been with her, and very worried too about their distance from home. Dotty, however, had been adamant that she could easily get back, and was so violent in her reaction to Connie's anxiety that Connie had fallen silent, and simply supported her strong-willed aunt on the return journey whenever the old lady seemed to flag.

On her return to Dotty's kitchen, Connie noticed that Flossie was comfortably ensconced in her basket, but Bruce was nowhere to be seen. Could Dotty have taken him for a run? Could he have escaped and Dotty had gone to look for him?

Kit was shaving when Connie returned with her troubles.

'I'll ring the Shoosmiths first,' he said. 'They would spot her if she has wandered towards the green. Then we'll try to get Betty Bell on the phone. She'll keep a look-out in the Lulling Woods area. I'll be with you in a tick.'

Within a few minutes the calls had been made, and the two had dressed and were out on their mission.

At Betty Bell's house, hard by Lulling Woods, no sooner had she replaced the receiver when she heard joyous barking at her kitchen door, and was almost floored by the exuberance of an excited Bruce who was delighted to come across a dear friend.

Betty shut him in her scullery, with a handful of biscuits, and rang Connie's number but, as she feared, they were already out. Shrugging on an old coat, she went to seach for Bruce's mistress.

Harold and Isobel were greatly perturbed at the news, and both dressed quickly and set out, one towards Nidden and the other towards the hill which led to the town. It was Harold who decided, as he set off, to call at the Piggotts', for their cottage had a good view of the field path from Lulling Woods which Dotty used when making her way to Thrush Green.

The couple were at breakfast, and the delicious smell of fried bacon and tomatoes made Harold realize how hungry he was.

Albert pushed aside his half-finished repast and got to his feet with surprising speed.

'I'll have a look now,' he said, and Harold suddenly realized that beneath Albert's crusty exterior there was a genuinely soft spot for Dotty.

Albert set off along the lane towards Lulling Woods, while Harold descended the short hill, made sure that Dotty was not wandering in the road at the bottom, returned to Thrush Green and made a systematic tour all round it.

Early morning traffic was beginning to stir. A school bus was waiting for older children at a corner of the green. There were a few lights in upstairs windows where people were only just stirring, for the morning was chilly and overcast.

There were lights downstairs at the Two Pheasants, for Mr

Jones was an early riser, and was clearing up the night's debris from the bar, ready for the day's business.

A few dogs were straying around the green, let out for their early morning run, but Harold noticed that Bruce was not among them. Kit had warned him that Dotty's dog was missing as well as his mistress.

Harold met his wife not far from the Youngs' house near the turning to Nidden.

'Not a sign,' said Isobel.

'No luck with me, either,' said Harold. 'I'll try Kit on the phone. It looks as though the police will have to be called.'

'Dotty will be *furious*!' said Isobel.

'Better furious than run over,' responded Harold, as they made their way back to the warmth of their home.

Kit and Connie had just returned when Harold rang to report from his end. All were now in a state of extreme anxiety, and Kit was particularly alarmed at his wife's distress. Connie, usually sturdily calm in any situation, was in tears and beside herself with worry.

'Definitely time to get the police,' agreed Kit, speaking to Harold, as he watched Connie mopping her eyes. 'I'll be in touch immediately, if she turns up, but meanwhile I'm getting on to the police station.'

By this time, Betty Bell had made her way into Lulling Woods. It was murky and rather frighteningly silent. In the open fields leading to the wood things were stirring. A rabbit had lolloped away at her approach. A lark was singing above, and small birds were twittering in the hedges.

But there was something sinister about Lulling Woods in its early morning stillness, and Betty was filled with foreboding. She had set off so hurriedly that she was still in her bedroom slippers, and their shiny soles skidded on the carpet of pine needles.

As a child, she remembered, she had always been frightened if she was alone in this wood, and had always hurried along the main path. When she was with her friends she was happy to play in the little side paths or the bracken, but occasionally her mother had sent her with a message to the Drovers' Arms which was situated at the further end of the woods, and then young Betty had fairly scampered between the tall trees which bordered the main path in order to get to open country again, and the haven of the remote public house.

Today, worried as she was, the wood seemed doubly menacing. Trees dripped, brittle sticks broke beneath her tread making frightening cracks of sound among the silence. There was no sign of movement anywhere, no birds, no beasts and, above all, no comforting human presence.

She stopped for a moment to get her breath. Her heart seemed to be the only thing in motion, and then she heard a distant sound. It was a high-pitched voice. It might have been a child crying, but with a flood of relief Betty realized that it was Dotty calling for the truant Bruce.

Almost in tears, she began to run through the wet bracken, calling as she went.

She found Dotty on her hands and knees at the entrance to what was probably a fox's hide-out. She was scrabbling with her hands at the opening, and peering shortsightedly into the aperture.

Betty knelt to help her up, but the old lady pushed her aside.

'There may be a trap there, you see. Bruce has run off and I'm so afraid he may have been caught in a trap.'

'He's with me,' Betty cried, 'he's quite safe. He's in my scullery.'

She was appalled at the state Dotty was in. Her dressing-gown and the nightgown protruding at its hem were soaking wet and covered in mud. One slipper had vanished, and blood was oozing from a scratch on her ankle. Her hands too were bleeding where she had been trying to scrape away the loose earth. She was trembling with cold and exhaustion, but made no effort to cease her labours.

'Those wretched Cooke boys set traps,' she told Betty. 'They go down at night. I've seen them myself, and spoken to them too pretty sharply, but they take no notice. I wish my father were alive, he would –'

She broke off, and turned to Betty. Suddenly, she looked as if she had returned to this hostile frightening world from one of her own. Pathetically, like a hurt child, she began to cry, and put her muddied arms round Betty's neck.

'I wish he were alive,' she whimpered. 'I do wish my father were alive.'

'There, there,' cooed Betty, patting the trembling back. 'You come home with me, and see old Bruce. You'd like to see Bruce, wouldn't you?'

Dotty nodded, tears still coursing down her cheeks. Slowly Betty led her back to the path, and even more slowly to the warmth of her kitchen, and Bruce's rapturous welcome.

Some half an hour later, Kit made a second call to the police station, telling the sergeant on duty that all was well, and that the missing, both human and animal, were now safely at home.

'That's good news, sir,' said the police officer heartily. 'We can't have anything happening to Miss Harmer, she's a bit special.'

'She certainly is to us,' agreed Kit.

Carl Andersen's tall figure was soon a familiar sight in Thrush Green and Lulling. He seemed very happy to be back, and greeted his friends warmly.

One morning he called at Rectory Cottages to see Bill and Jane Cartwright. As it happened, they were both outside the conservatory, attending to the geraniums which flourished in the sunshine.

They welcomed him enthusiastically and all three sat on a garden seat near by to catch up with the news from each side of the Atlantic.

Jane said how sorry they had been to hear about his mother's death, and added, 'A very nice couple have come to make their home here. They knew your mother when they were working near by, and I'm sure they would love to tell you about the old days, if you've time.'

Carl assured them that he would look forward to meeting them.

'No time like the present,' said Jane, consulting her watch. 'Let's see if they're around now.'

The three went inside, and Jane tapped at a door which was immediately opened.

Introductions were made, and Bill and Jane returned to their duties, leaving Carl to talk to the Millers.

He was thin and tall, and she was short and plump. Both, it appeared, had been in service at Nidden Hall, a large estate between Thrush Green and Woodstock, when they were young, and that was when they had been acquainted with Carl's mother.

'She was a lovely girl,' enthused Mrs Miller. 'She could have had anyone. There was a young fellow at Eynsham who was very keen, wasn't he, Dad?'

'I've heard about him,' said Carl, with a smile. 'I gather that if Mrs Curdle hadn't persuaded my mother to wait for a letter from my father, I might have been a local boy.'

'So you know about Mrs Curdle?' cried her husband. 'Now she was a character, and no mistake.'

Carl explained that she had been godmother to his mother, and that he owed his existence and his American citizenship to her wise counselling long ago.

'We lost touch, of course, when your mother left Woodstock, and then when we retired we came to live at the foot of the hill here, in one of the old cottages. They had to be pulled down, and though we were offered a council flat, we didn't really fancy it, and the rector suggested we might like to come here. He's a good man.'

'I heartily agree. I hope to call on him soon.'

'Come and have a cup of tea one afternoon, and I'll look out any old photos I can find. I believe there are one or two groups with your mother in them, and we'll see what we can remember between us.'

And so it was left, Carl making his way a little later to the Youngs' house, where he had been invited to lunch.

One or two children were straggling across the grass from Thrush Green school, and among them were George and Anne Curdle.

Shrieking with excitement they rushed to the tall figure and threw their arms around his legs.

'And what are you two up to? Playing hookey?'

'No, going home to dinner. Mum likes us home midday as we live so close. Most of the others stay to school dinner.'

'It's not half as good as Mum's!' pronounced Anne.

'And you get more,' asserted George. 'You coming to see her?'

'Later on. The Youngs are giving me lunch.'

'That'll be good too,' George assured him. 'Mrs Young makes smashing jam tarts.'

They parted at the gate, and within minutes Carl was ensconced in the Youngs' sitting-room with a glass of sherry.

'I've just been meeting some old folks who remembered my mother,' he volunteered.

Edward was instantly alert. 'Did you go into the sitting-room?'

Carl looked a little surprised. 'No. Jane and Bill were in the garden, so we sat there. Come to think of it, it was just outside that communal room.'

'I'd like your opinion of it sometime,' said Edward. 'Some of us are wondering if it is too small.'

'Sure. Any time,' agreed Carl.

Joan, veering away from controversial matters, asked about his flight, and soon the conversation became more general.

'I've invited Winnie Bailey to join us,' said Joan, 'and Harold and Isobel. They are just arriving, I see.'

During lunch Carl found himself answering a good many questions from Winnie who sat beside him. Was he well looked after at the Bear? Was the food good?

He was able to assure her that he was thoroughly spoilt, and much enjoying his stay.

'Is it busy at the moment?'

'Not as busy as the manager would like, I gather,' responded Carl. 'A party came in last night, but they haven't a great many regulars just now.'

'What a pity,' said Winnie, still hoping for news of that mysterious interior designer who sometimes shared a table with this handsome American.

'So there's no one there whom you met last time?' persisted Winnie.

'Not at the moment,' agreed Carl. Winnie thought that he looked faintly amused, and wondered if he had guessed what was behind her enquiries. The man was no fool, and no doubt knew as well as she did how quickly rumours fly about.

'I believe you knew Mrs Curdle as well as anybody here,' said Carl, carrying the conversation into her own territory. 'Do tell me, was she as formidable as photos make her look? My mother adored her, but was also very respectful, and Ben tells me that it didn't do to cross her in any way.'

'That's right,' said Winnie warmly. 'She was a woman in a thousand, and we were lucky to be counted among her friends.

If you've got time later, I will show you the bouquets she made for us every year, and find some photographs too.'

'And I believe Dotty Harmer's father wrote a piece about her for the local paper,' Harold added. 'I came across it when I was looking up some facts about Nathaniel Patten some time ago.'

The mention of Dotty at once changed the topic of conversation to the recent worry about the old lady, and her lucky rescue by Betty Bell.

'It seems to me,' observed Carl, 'that life in Thrush Green is pretty exciting.'

'We find it so,' said Edward, smiling at his wife.

October

Busy most part of the Afternoon in making
some Mead Wine, to fourteen Pounds of Honey,
I put four Gallons of Water, boiled it more
than an hour with Ginger and two handfulls
of dried Elder-Flower in it, and skimmed it
well.

James Woodforde

Dotty Harmer took some time to recover from her ordeal, but once she began to feel stronger she chafed at the delay in getting on with her usual autumn collections of fruit and herbs for the winter ahead.

'I'm missing the sloes and those nice crab-apples on the way to Nidden, and I intended to make a really large amount of rose-hip syrup this autumn. It really is most frustrating.'

Connie promised to gather all that she needed for the store cupboard, and did her best to support the doctor's ruling that the patient must have a few days in bed.

At first, Dotty had been too exhausted to argue, and lay back on her pillows dozing or reading. Flossie was glad to be allowed at the foot of the bed, and the two old ladies rested together.

As the days passed, Flossie was the more amenable invalid, while Dotty grew more vociferous about all she had to do, and more anxious about the welfare of the hens and goats at the end of the garden.

'We're managing quite well,' Connie assured her, 'and Albert comes down regularly night and morning, so you've nothing to worry about.'

But the climax came when Winnie Bailey arrived one misty afternoon, bearing a freshly made pot of bramble jelly for the invalid.

'It's a wonderful year for blackberries,' Winnie told her.

'And I'm going to go out and pick some for myself,' said Dotty firmly. 'No matter what John Lovell says. *I'm all right!*'

She looked so fierce as she said this that Winnie felt some alarm. She said so to Connie when she was making her farewells out of Dotty's hearing.

'If she says she's going out then she will,' said Connie resignedly. 'We've been lucky to keep her in bed for these few days. You know Aunt Dotty.'

'Indeed I do,' responded Winnie.

Betty Bell, quite rightly, was acclaimed as a heroine for her double rescue effort, and the finest azalea to be had in Lulling was given to her by Kit and Connie.

She was modest about her achievement. 'Well, if it hadn't been me then someone else would have found her, I've no doubt. Willie Marchant would have been along pretty soon, on his way to the Drovers' Arms.'

At the bingo session that week in Lulling, Nelly, her friend Mrs Jenner and Gladys Hodge all agreed that Dotty might well have succumbed to exposure if she had remained any longer in the chilly wood clad in little more than her nightgown.

'Hypothermia,' Mrs Jenner told them, 'is the biggest enemy of the aged. Jane is always alert to it at the home.'

As Mrs Jenner herself was a retired nurse, and Jane Cartwright, her daughter, was the equally well-qualified and competent warden at Rectory Cottages, her words were accepted with respect.

'I'm a great believer in long-legged knickers myself,' said Gladys.

'And a nice woolly jumper that pulls down well over the kidneys,' agreed Nelly.

'It's a great pity, I think,' put in Mrs Jenner, 'that shawls have gone out. My old grandma always had one hanging on the back of her chair, ready to throw round her shoulders if she had to go out, or if she felt a draught. But then she was Yorkshire born and bred, and had plenty of sense.'

There was general agreement among her hearers that York-shire folk certainly knew what was what, and took sensible steps to combat their chilly climate.

The loud voice of the master of ceremonies recalled them to their tables, and Betty Bell, Dotty and hypothermia were put aside in the pursuit of fortune.

The news had even reached Miss Watson and Miss Fogerty at Barton-on-Sea.

'Sometimes I wonder if Dotty should be in a home,' said Dorothy Watson, putting down her crossword puzzle to hear the news from Agnes.

It was Isobel Shoosmith who had imparted the news in her weekly telephone conversation with her old friend.

'Oh, Dorothy,' protested Agnes, 'you know she couldn't be better looked after than she is now.'

'It's a great responsibility for Connie and Kit,' pronounced Dorothy, who was in one of her headmistressy moods, and finding the crossword somewhat difficult. She was ready for a mild argument with Agnes to add some excitement to the evening.

'And Dotty would hate to live with a lot of other old people,' continued Agnes.

'She would have to learn to make the best of it,' said Dorothy, at her most magisterial. 'We all have to come to terms with old age and disability. Look at Teddy! What an example to us all!'

Agnes felt no desire to 'look at Teddy', admirable fellow though he was, and was somewhat alarmed at his sudden introduction into the discussion. Dorothy had been so reticent about Teddy since their last visit to Thrush Green that she had earnestly hoped that Dorothy's passions had waned. But had they?

'Why, only this morning,' went on Dorothy, unaware of Agnes's reaction to Teddy's name, 'I had a terrible shooting pain under the ball of my left foot. I could hardly walk.'

'You must let me have a look when we go to bed,' said Agnes, glad to be on safer ground. 'You may have a thorn in it.'

'No, I think it's something called "Morton's Toe", or "Morton's Fork" perhaps.'

'Wasn't that something to do with taxes in Tudor times?'

'Which, dear? The Toe or the Fork?'

'Oh, the Fork without question,' said Agnes firmly.

'How erudite you are,' exclaimed Dorothy. 'Now, tell me why BAIL I has something to do with the law. Five letters.'

'ALIBI,' said little Miss Fogerty promptly.

And peace reigned again.

Carl Andersen soon set about his pleasant task of learning more about Mrs Curdle and her times.

He enjoyed meeting people, and although the serious business of the present trip was to go ahead with the great project in Scotland in which the firm of Benn, Andersen and Webbly was engaged, he found the atmosphere at Thrush Green relaxing, and his new-found friends much to his liking.

The lady with whom he had shared a table at the Bear on his earlier visit was also engaging his attention, but he had no intention of discussing that matter with anyone at Thrush Green.

He had been amused at Winnie's attempts to find out more. As she had surmised, he knew quite well how rumours fly around, and he was determined not to cause any embarrassment to the lady in question.

At the moment, she was back at her base in Chelsea, the jobs in the Woodstock area having been completed. Carl had lost no time in finding her, but found that she was now engaged on the designing of a mews flat for an up-and-coming pop star whose tastes in furnishing and general decor needed some guidance.

It was a formidable undertaking, almost as difficult as the Scottish problem was for Carl. He respected her desire for privacy whilst she was struggling, but pointed out that a little relaxation now and again, in the form of a meal out or a visit to the theatre, would assist her efforts, and she seemed glad to agree.

Meanwhile, he made another visit to the Millers at Rectory Cottages and spent a happy hour hearing about Woodstock over half a century ago, and the influx of American servicemen during the war, including of course, the handsome man who had become Carl's father. Mrs Miller's wrinkled face lit up at the remembrance.

'He was easily the best-looking man I ever saw,' she said rapturously. 'Your colouring, Carl, but even better looking.'

'Well, thank you for the compliment,' laughed Carl, 'but I know my limitations. I remember him as a fine father as well as a potential heartbreaker. Luckily for us, he never looked at anyone other than my ma, and she was a bit of a glamour-puss herself.'

Later he went to see the Henstocks, and found that Charles was in the churchyard of St John's overseeing the arrival of a load of gravel to renew the paths. His chubby face broke into a beam on seeing Carl.

'Dimity told me you were here,' said Carl. He gazed up at

the impressive spire, outlined against a clear October sky.

'Do you know, I've not been inside yet,' he told Charles.

'That must be rectified as soon as possible. But not today, I fear. I have a funeral later this morning, and we want to get this gravel laid before then.'

'Did Mrs Curdle ever come here?' Carl asked, as they watched the gravel rushing from the tip-up lorry with a mighty roar.

'I don't think so. She did have a little to do with the church at Thrush Green, and as you know, is buried there, but her fair only spent one complete day there before it moved on.'

'But surely you had a fair here too?'

'Oh, yes indeed! We have our bigger Mop Fair, and of course there are other great local fairs like St Giles' at Oxford, and the one at Abingdon. But they are held in the autumn and last for several days. Mrs Curdle's was a family affair, and much more modest.'

He turned to speak to the men, and then invited Carl to the vicarage, but he said that he had promised to call at the Fuchsia Bush for Molly Curdle.

'I've always thought,' said the rector, as they walked away from the scene of activity, 'that it would be interesting to write a history of English fairs. Have you ever thought of it?'

Carl laughed. 'I shouldn't know where to start! I'm no literary gent, you know. Steel and concrete are more in my line.'

But Charles Henstock's attention was drawn to an approaching figure, and he seemed somewhat agitated.

'Oh dear! Mrs Thurgood!' he exclaimed. 'I do so hope she isn't going to the vicarage.'

But the lady veered aside to enter the porch of one of the adjacent almshouses, and relief relaxed the vicar's countenance.

'A worthy soul,' he said hastily, 'but a troublemaker.' He looked suddenly at his companion. 'You said you called at Rectory Cottages the other day. Did you sit in the communal room?'

'I suppose so. The sitting-room place, with a conservatory.'

'Did you think it too small?'

Carl began to feel bewildered. 'Edward Young asked me the same thing. Is this something to do with Mrs Thurgood?' he asked.

'Partly. She has a bee in her bonnet about it. That's why I wanted a fresh eye on the subject. What do you think?'

Charles looked so worried that Carl was tempted to laugh, but refrained.

'Well, you must remember that I come from a country with plenty of space, and we do tend to have large rooms, I suppose. But I like smaller places, like your English cottages, and I should say that the communal room, as you call it, was just about right for those few people.'

Charles Henstock looked relieved. 'That's a comfort to know. Now, I won't keep you, but we must make a date for your visit to St John's. It is well worth seeing.'

The early part of October was clear and fresh, with that pellucid quality which is peculiar to fine days in early autumn.

Young pheasants were now strutting about the fields and woods, and occasionally stepping haughtily in front of motor cars in the country lanes, to the dismay of nervous drivers.

Harvest mice, refugees from the denuded fields, were looking for comfortable hibernation quarters in the sheds, barns and lofts of unwelcoming householders.

Gardeners were busy cutting down the dying foliage of perennials, and hustling the tender plants, such as geraniums, into the shelter of greenhouses.

The brave show of Busy Lizzies, fuchsias, petunias and lobelias which had adorned the troughs and tubs and hanging basket outside the Two Pheasants and elsewhere were now being dismantled, and tulip and hyacinth bulbs planted in their place, all with high hopes of glory in the spring, which were somewhat mitigated by the knowledge that mice, birds and other nuisances would no doubt make inroads on this bounty so generously offered.

It was on one of these gentle afternoons of mild sunshine that Connie took her refractory aunt to pick up crab-apple windfalls along the road to Nidden.

The old lady was well wrapped up, and had even submitted to wearing gloves. She was in high spirits as she sat beside Connie, who drove to the appointed place.

'I suppose I must have been coming here for crab-apples for seventy-odd years,' prattled Dotty. 'My nurse used to bring me. In those days you called her "Nurse". None of this "Nanny" nonsense. She was just fourteen when she came to work for us, and her first errand was to go to buy a feeding bottle for the new baby. That was me!'

'And how long did she stay?'

'Day and night. She lived in, up at the top of our house with me and my older brothers.'

'I really meant how many years,' explained Connie, halting to let a covey of young partridges bustle across the lane.

'Oh, heavens! She stayed in our family till she died. She went with my brother Oliver when his children came, and then she was with me and father. They died about the same time. That was some years before you married Kit.'

'She sounds a faithful soul.'

'I loved her dearly,' said Dotty. 'She taught me to knit, and to pop lime leaves with my mouth to make a really loud bang, and she could make lovely shadows on the wall by the light of the candle – rabbits and swans and Ikey-Mo, who was the local cats' meat man. She was simply wonderful, and I still miss her.'

She was beginning to sound a little tearful, something which had been occurring too frequently since her mishap, and which perturbed Connie quite a lot.

'Well, here we are,' she said cheerfully, drawing in to a farm gateway. 'Let's get the baskets.'

Dotty's spirits soon revived as she bent to collect the hard little apples on the grass verge.

Straightening up happily, she made for the gate.

'Give me a hand with this, dear,' she said, struggling with a strong snap spring.

'But we can't *trespass*!' protested Connie.

'Rubbish!' snorted Dotty. 'It's only old Bob Bennett's field, I went to kindergarten with him, and used to have to help him lace his boots. He was always an awkward lump. Still is, they tell me.'

Together they opened the gate, and went to collect the bulk of the windfalls that lay in 'the awkward lump's' property.

Dotty was enchanted at the sight. Connie, rather more conscious of trespass, only hoped that they would be un-observed.

Straightening her back, Dotty gazed across the field to the distant farmhouse.

'I remember,' she said speculatively, 'that the Bennetts always had lots of mushrooms in that field by their garden. I wonder if –?'

'No,' said Connie firmly. 'We've quite enough to cope with when we get these apples home, without stealing mushrooms as well.'

'Just as you say, Connie dear,' replied Dotty meekly. 'But these are not really Bob Bennett's. They are simply the fruits of the earth, and we are *keeping them from waste*!'

Connie stowed the heavy baskets in the car, ushered her companion into the passenger seat, and drove home with what she could only think of as 'their loot'.

Winnie and Ella, setting off for an afternoon's walk, saw Connie and Dotty driving by on the other side of Thrush Green.

'Blackberrying?' queried Winnie.

'Crab-apples, more likely,' said Ella shrewdly. 'Dotty never lets an autumn go by without raiding Bob Bennett's crab-apple tree.'

They crossed the grass to the lane leading to Nidden. Lately, the two women had seen much more of each other, for Ella now asked Winnie to check colours for her when she was engaged on much of her handwork, and Winnie had threaded many needles for her now that the other's sight was deteriorating.

Ella, in her gruff way, expressed her thanks, but Winnie brushed aside the gratitude.

'I used to read the clues for Donald's daily crossword, during the last few years of his life,' she said. 'He found newsprint trying.'

'You must miss him very much.'

'I do, of course. In fact, I wondered if I could go on without him, but one has to, and after a time one even begins to find a few small benefits.'

'Really?' Ella sounded startled at this admission, and Winnie laughed.

'Only little things! Not enough really to fill the gap completely, but I remember the relief I felt on taking down a photograph of Donald's mother, and putting it up in the attic. I felt guilty too, of course.'

'Did you dislike her? Or was Donald over-fond of her?'

'Neither really. She didn't particularly like me, but then she would never have considered anyone good enough for her Donald. I think there are quite a few mothers like that. No, it wasn't that. It was just that she was a plain woman, with a long horsy face and she looked so dreadfully disapproving in the photograph. As Donald fixed it at the head of the stairs you had to face it every time you went up.'

'You should have told him.'

'I didn't want to hurt him. Far simpler to say nothing, my dear. You learn to hold your tongue when you are married.'

'And what other small comforts did you discover?' asked Ella, who found herself fascinated by these disclosures.

'Well, now what else? Donald was a stickler for having every meal at the table, properly set, tablecloth, napkins, the lot. Even for afternoon tea. Once the poor darling had gone, I took to taking my tea into the sitting-room on a tray, and then, quite often, my supper. I can't tell you how lovely it seemed, but I still felt guilty. Childish, isn't it? But then I suppose one finds comfort in little things whatever one's circumstances.'

They had now reached the farm gate where they usually paused to have a break.

'I think I've been lucky to be single,' mused Ella. 'I don't think I should have been unselfish enough to lead a married life. Always having to consider what the other person needed, or would think, would drive me mad.'

'But you lived quite happily with Dimity,' pointed out Winnie.

'Looking back,' said Ella, 'I reckon poor old Dim did the

adjusting, and I took it all for granted. She's one of those people better off in the married state.'

'She picked the right man in Charles,' replied Winnie. 'As I did with Donald,' she added loyally.

'I don't know about you,' said Ella, 'but I reckon it's getting chilly. Come back and have a cup of tea with me. What's more, we'll have it by the fire, on a tray.'

The weather changed overnight. The mild wind which had blown from the south-west backed to the north-east and gained in strength as dawn approached. When the good folk of Thrush Green and Lulling awoke, it was to find the dead leaves bowling across the ground in a stiff breeze, and the branches above tossing vigorously.

The temperature had dropped. Harold Shoosmith decided that the time had come for the full-scale central heating to be turned on. Alan Lester, next door, was making the same decision for both his house and school, while Mr Jones, shaving in the pub bathroom, was startled to find that he 'could see his breath', and called across the landing to tell his wife so.

Nelly Piggott, hard by, was already buttoning up her winter coat preparatory to making her way down the hill to the Fuchsia Bush.

Now that she had come to terms with the fact that she was in charge of the business, in all its aspects, a wonderful strength had taken the place of her fears, and she was beginning to enjoy the feeling of power which her new status gave her.

She was the first to recognize the loyalty of the staff. Gloria and Rosa seemed to have shed some of their native lethargy, and were becoming much more enterprising. Even Irena seemed to take her more humble duties with the vegetable preparation with greater enthusiasm, and Nelly was quick to praise whenever possible.

It did not occur to her that her own energy had a lot to do

with this change in the outlook of the staff. In fact, Mrs Peters, though an excellent businesswoman, had always been a little remote in her relationship with the girls, and understandably had been even more so during the long months of her last illness at the Fuchsia Bush.

Nelly, on the other hand, the girls recognized as 'one of them'. She had the same background, the same necessity to work for a living, the same tough philosophy of 'doing as you would be done by', 'taking the rough with the smooth' and all the other homely tags which governed their way of life. They might grumble behind her back at her sharpness and bustle, but they respected her high standards and the fact that she could – and did – turn her hand to any task which cropped up.

The difficulties which had so daunted Nelly when she first heard of her inheritance had largely been solved when a competent young woman from the accountants' office was put in charge of the business side of the Fuchsia Bush. Justin Venables' wise suggestion that Miss Spooner should be consulted about the transaction had given that lady enormous gratification, and she and Nelly had parted with great goodwill.

As Nelly made her way along Lulling High Street that blustery October morning, she felt well content with the general affairs at her place of business. But one difficulty confronted her, and that she was determined to tackle that very morning.

When some years earlier Mrs Peters and other shopkeepers had approached Miss Violet with complaints about her older sister, it was all very embarrassing. The Lovelocks had been respected for all their long lives in Lulling, and no one wished them harm. Violet had tackled her duties with sense and courage, and Bertha's kleptomania had seemed to be controlled. But to Nelly's dismay she had noticed that the basket of tiny jamjars, bright as jewels, and the sort of thing which would catch the eye of any magpie or jackdaw, bird or human, was suddenly half empty after a visit from the three sisters.

Nelly had questioned Rosa.

'Oh, I expect it was that Miss Bertha,' replied Rosa nonchal-
antly, 'I think she nicks one now and again.'

'This isn't *one!*' retorted Nelly. 'It's a good half-dozen, and
we can't let it go on.'

She decided to ring the house next door at about ten o'clock.
The old ladies were not early risers, and took considerable time
dressing, as she well remembered from the days when she
worked there.

Soon after that hour, she closeted herself in the privacy of
the office and rang. Luckily, Miss Violet answered, much to
Nelly's relief. Apart from the fact that she was the only one of
the three who was not deaf, she was also the only sister who
had some sense.

With what tact she could muster Nelly explained the
problem.

'Oh dear, oh dear!' sighed Violet. 'Not again, Mrs Piggott!'

'I'm afraid so,' responded Nelly, noting that she was now
'Mrs Piggott' and not 'Nelly' to her former employers. 'Rosa
had noticed it before this, I gather, but didn't like to say
anything.'

'I shall look into it straightaway,' promised Violet, 'and come
and see you later this morning.'

The telephone was put down. Nelly returned to her kitchen,
and Violet went to her sister's bedroom.

Bertha was in her petticoat. She was sitting in front of the
mirror rubbing face cream across her wrinkled cheeks.

'I want to look through your coat pockets,' said Violet,
with commendable courage. 'Mrs Piggott next door has been
missing things.'

'Really?' said Bertha, sounding bored. 'What sort of things?'

'Little things that could be picked up easily and put in
pockets,' retorted Violet, swinging open the heavy wardrobe
door.

There were several coats hanging there, all with capacious pockets. Violet plunged her hand into the deep patch pockets of the tweed coat which Bertha frequently wore. There was a chinking of glass against glass, and Violet pulled out four small jamjars from one pocket, and three from the other.

She put them in front of her sister on the dressing-table. 'Well, Bertha?' she demanded.

'They're not mine,' said Bertha, still busy massaging her face.

'I'm well aware of that! They come from the Fuchsia Bush.'

'Then you'd better take them back,' responded Bertha.

Her off-hand manner and the assumption that Violet could

clear up any difficulties, no matter whose fault they were, infuriated Violet who normally faced life with great equanimity.

'*You* are taking those back *yourself* this time,' she told her. 'You stole them, Bertha! You are no better than a common thief, and if Nelly Piggott wants the police brought into this affair I shall back her to the hilt.'

A red flush suffused her face, and Bertha too began to look agitated.

'Someone must have put them in my pocket,' she quavered. 'I don't remember anything about it.'

'Then you will have to try and remember,' said Violet. 'The police will ask lots of questions.'

Bertha put down the jar of face cream among the tiny jamjars and bowed her head. A tear splashed among the pots.

'You wouldn't really call the police, would you, Violet? Not to your own family?'

Violet, almost in tears herself, did her best to sound firm. 'If you don't return Nelly's property, and apologize to her, I shall certainly think about the police,' she replied.

Leaving her sister to her sniffling, Violet returned to her bedroom to find a handkerchief for her own tears. How would this end, she wondered?

Just before twelve o'clock, Bertha descended the stairs, dressed in the incriminating tweed coat, and holding a small carrier bag, which chinked as she moved, and presented herself to Violet.

'Are you coming with me?' she asked in a low voice.

'Do you want me to, Bertha?'

'I think I should like a little support,' said Bertha.

Without a word, Violet fetched her own coat from the hall stand, and the two sisters made their way next door.

Nelly welcomed them as politely as ever, and ushered them into the privacy of her office, and firmly closed the door against any prying eyes.

'She's got the stuff in that bag,' observed Rosa to Gloria. 'I heard the jars rattling.'

'Would have done the old girl good to have it all thrashed out in public,' said Gloria, rather miffed at being denied a first-class row.

'Nelly's too soft by half,' agreed Rosa, and then noticed Irena peeping through the kitchen door to see what was going on.

The pair advanced upon her menacingly.

'And what do you think you're doing?' demanded Gloria.

'I saw them Lovelocks coming in,' faltered Irena who, like the rest of Lulling, knew of Bertha's little weakness.

'And what, pray, is that to do with you?' asked Rosa loftily. 'You get back to your sink, my girl, and don't poke your nose into other people's business.'

Irena retreated, and the door was closed.

'I just can't abide people *prying*,' said Gloria to Rosa, as they returned to their own territory.

'Quite right, dear,' agreed Rosa.

The sudden cold spell brought more customers than usual into the Fuchsia Bush, seeking the comfort of coffee or something more substantial. Nelly had said nothing about what had gone on behind that firmly closed door on the day of the Lovelocks' visit, much to the chagrin of her staff. However, they realized that the matter was closed, even if only temporarily.

The cold weather was to Connie's liking, for she could make sure that Dotty stayed in the warm as Dr Lovell had directed, and as there were masses of crab-apples awaiting attention, the two ladies set about the task away from the bitter wind that raked Thrush Green.

Flossie slept tranquilly in her basket by the stove, and even Bruce seemed content to stay inside out of the unkind breezes that disturbed his usual haunts.

Connie was rinsing the fruit at the sink, and Dotty busied herself cutting the small apples in half and hurling them into a gigantic preserving saucepan ready to be simmered into a fragrant pulp. Overnight, the jelly bags would drip, and the serious business of apple jelly would be on its way.

'That letter you brought me this morning,' Dotty said, 'was from poor Audrey.'

'Why "poor Audrey"? Is she ill?'

'No, no. She's worried about Lucy, her daughter. She's just got engaged.'

'And she doesn't approve?'

'Audrey seems doubtful. He's Irish, you see.'

'You and I know plenty of nice Irishmen,' Connie pointed out, lifting the last of the washed fruit from the sink. 'Look at the O'Briens! They're dears.'

'I know all that,' said Dotty testily. 'But the O'Briens have lived here for years! This man is only just over here, and has had no time to lose that Celtic roguish charm which Audrey finds so suspicious.'

'Does she think that Lucy has fallen for the roguish charm?'

'Definitely! She is most upset.'

'Well, there's not much she can do about it,' said Connie philosophically. 'Daughters usually do what they like, in the end, and I expect Audrey will come round, and fall for that roguish charm just as Lucy has.'

Carl Andersen was due to fly to Scotland at the end of the week, and invited Ben and Molly, Joan and Edward to dinner at the Bear before he departed.

He had collected quite a number of photographs and other memorabilia about Mrs Curdle, and showed some of it to his guests as they enjoyed their coffee.

'The Millers gave me these,' he said, handing over some ancient group photographs. 'I'm getting them copied. By the way, I had a look at that common room again. What worries you?'

'It isn't exactly a *worry*,' replied Edward untruthfully. 'It's just that having extended that annexe I resent the recent criticism about the need for more space.'

Joan broke in. 'Edward can't help it,' she said with a laugh. 'He's a born worrier, especially if his work is criticized.'

'I know how he feels,' said Carl. 'I'm the same.'

'It could easily be made bigger,' went on Edward thoughtfully. 'I roughed out a plan some time ago when this business cropped up.'

'You must show me sometime,' said Carl. 'I must say, I thought it looked perfectly adequate for the needs of the old folk at the moment, but I suppose a larger space would give them more seating accommodation, and there could be more room for plants and so on.'

'I can't see it coming off,' said Molly. 'Mr Henstock was talking about it the other day. He seemed a bit worried. I believe Mrs Thurgood had been at him.'

'Mrs Thurgood,' snorted Edward, 'is a public menace! She caught me outside the Fuchsia Bush not long ago, and harangued me about the matter. It was a good thing I could tell her categorically that we had no money for the project.'

Conversation turned to Carl's work in Scotland, and he and Edward became deeply engaged in technical details about stresses and strains, and the problems of frost, wind, rain and all the other weather hazards which would have to be considered when dealing with the costing of this enormous undertaking.

Ben and the women were more parochially inclined, and the affairs of Thrush Green and Lulling engaged their attention until the time came for them to part.

As they walked to the car Edward and Carl fell behind a little.

'Are you on the board of Rectory Cottages?' asked Carl.

'I'm a trustee, yes.'

They walked through the chilly darkness, and Carl spoke as they drew near to the car.

'If the money were available, would a bigger room be a good idea, do you think?'

The two men stopped, while Edward considered the question.

'Yes, I really believe it would. Looking to the future, I think it would be desirable. There's already talk of adding more residential accommodation some time, but that's way in the future.'

'I'll see you when I get back,' said Carl. 'I've enjoyed this evening so much.'

'A splendid dinner,' cried Joan, 'and a thousand thanks.'

'See you on your return,' called Ben.

The men shook hands. Carl kissed the women, and they drove off.

Later, as they prepared for bed, Molly said dreamily, 'Carl does kiss lovely!'

Ben looked startled, as he peeled off his socks. 'Better than me?'

Molly, hanging her petticoat neatly over a chair back, paused for a minute to look abstractedly across Thrush Green in darkness.

'Different, Ben. Just sort of *different*.'

November

No shade, no shine, no butterflies, no bees,
No fruit, no flowers, no leaves, no birds –
November!

Thomas Hood

It was the custom of Thrush Green to celebrate Guy Fawkes night with a roaring bonfire and a plentiful supply of fireworks.

Carl Andersen, who knew little of such things, privately thought it amazing that such a law-abiding community – or nation, for that matter – should see fit to remember one who had been about to blow up the Houses of Parliament. However, he was wise enough to hold his tongue, and simply hand over his pence to the few children who petitioned him in Lulling High Street as they pushed their guy around in an ancient pram.

Preparations had been going ahead for two or three weeks, and a splendid pile of flammable material, such as pieces of wood, small branches, cardboard boxes and the like, stood towards one end of the green, well away from Rectory Cottages and other habitations.

To be sure, it was rather unsightly, and at one time the local council had threatened to ban the bonfire altogether. At this there was such an outcry from the residents of Thrush Green, even those who had condemned the pile as an eyesore earlier, that the council withdrew its objections, and celebrations were allowed to take place.

The arrangements, by ancient custom, were in the hands of the scoutmaster and his zealous troop. Also, by ancient custom, potatoes for baking in the hot ashes were provided by the Hodge family, and the morning before Guy Fawkes Day found Percy Hodge sorting out some great beauties ready for the festivities.

His sister, Mrs Jenner from next door, had called in on her way down to the town and came upon her brother in his shed, counting potatoes as they lay in long rows on the bench.

'They look good, Perce,' she commented approvingly. 'What might they be?'

'Willjar,' said Percy.

'How do you spell it?'

'W-I-L-J-A,' said Percy, after some thought.

'I think,' said his sister, 'that you pronounce it "Veelya".'

Mrs Jenner had come across a number of foreigners during her wartime nursing, and had a smattering of various European tongues.

Percy poured brotherly scorn on such fiddle-faddle. 'If W-I-L-J-A don't spell Willjar,' he maintained, 'I'm a Dutchman.'

'Well, whatever you call 'em,' said Mrs Jenner in a conciliatory tone, 'they look as though they'll eat a treat, Perce.'

And with that she went on her way.

November had come in with grey skies and a depressing stillness. Trees dripped, and a light mist gathered overnight in the little valley by Lulling Woods and was slow to clear.

The clocks had been put back at the end of October, and now the darkness descended at about five o'clock, adding to the general murkiness of people's spirits.

The old folk at Rectory Cottages became querulous as they were obliged to spend more time indoors than they wanted.

The roads were slippery with dead leaves and general dampness. Despite good lighting in the rooms, everywhere seemed gloomy, and reading was difficult.

Jane Cartwright did her best to cheer her charges, arranging a birthday party for one old lady in the communal room, and persuading a local pianist to entertain the residents one evening. But attendance was poor on both occasions, and Jane just hoped that the dreary weather would lift, and the spirits of the little community would follow suit.

The prospect of Bonfire Night gave some cheer. There was usually a party of the old folk from the Cottages standing by the blaze, and enjoying the excitement of the fireworks.

'I hope to goodness it doesn't rain,' said Jane to her mother. 'That would be the last straw. The poor dears are so low that I'm praying for a dry starry night to cheer them up. Has Uncle Percy looked out the potatoes?'

Mrs Jenner assured her that all was well in hand, and said that, in her opinion, they would have a fine night for the celebrations.

It was usual for the more active of Jane's charges to help in providing some of the sausage rolls or sandwiches which supplemented the potatoes to enjoy round the bonfire. This had been a considerable help in raising the spirits of her little flock during the doldrums at Rectory Cottages, and Jane encouraged all their efforts.

The schoolchildren were in charge of the guy for the great night, and the question of its identity was hotly discussed. Alan Lester could remember a guy of his childhood representing Adolf Hitler which had swung from a nearby tree before hurtling to his funeral pyre amidst patriotic cheers from the war-weary onlookers.

Various names had been put forward. They included an unpopular local councillor, a school inspector who had been on a recent visit and Alan Lester himself. It seemed best, he decided as he listened to their suggestions, that a strictly impersonal guy would be a more diplomatic choice, and his decision was respected.

Two afternoons were spent happily stuffing a sack with some of Percy Hodge's straw for the torso and head, and four long stockings for arms and legs. It was the clothing of their puppet which caused the greatest anxiety.

All agreed that the pointed hat so recently worn by one of the girls, who had been to a Hallowe'en party as a witch, was perfectly in order for Guy Fawkes' headgear. Alan Lester had looked out an illustration showing costumes of the time, and considerable ingenuity was used to make Thrush Green's guy look as much like the original as possible.

The snag was the extraordinary difficulty in thrusting the straw-filled arms and legs through sleeves and trouser legs, and buttoning garments round the bulging torso. After a great deal of frustration, it was decided that he should wear a cloak which would disguise any blemishes.

The dressing-up box was ransacked and a grubby and moth-eaten cape found which had clothed Red Riding Hood in a school play some twenty years earlier.

It was agreed that it was time that this unhygienic garment was consigned to the flames, and the school guy was finally dressed to everyone's satisfaction.

It slumped on a chair at the front of the class, and far more attention was given to it, during its two-day wait for incineration, than any lesson that Alan Lester could produce.

The gloomy weather continued unabated, but to everyone's relief 5 November was no worse than the preceding days. In fact, for a brief period in the afternoon a watery sun was visible, and raised the spirits of young and old.

The festivities began at six thirty, which meant that most of the people would have had a meal after work, and could enjoy the celebrations and the extra pleasures of the snacks and Percy

Hodge's potatoes should they still have any pangs of hunger.

The children, of course, were always ready to eat. The Rectory Cottages contingent reckoned that the refreshments provided would be quite adequate for their elderly digestions, and thankfully reckoned to do without their usual supper on Bonfire Night.

The bonfire roared away. Bright sparks flew up towards the damp trees. Children capered round the crackling blaze, waving sparklers, and the guy was lowered, amidst cheers, to his fiery end.

The firework organizers included such stalwarts as Harold Shoosmith, Edward Young, Percy Hodge and Alan Lester, all capable of handling the pyrotechnics with safety, and rockets, Catherine wheels and squibs blazed into the darkness until the fire began to die down, St Andrew's clock struck nine and it was deemed fit to close the proceedings.

The old people straggled away first, becoming tired of standing on the damp grass. Parents rounded up their offspring. The scoutmaster rallied his troop for the final effort of damping down the remains of the bonfire and clearing up the litter around it.

There were many black hands and scorched faces that night, and clothes worn then would reek of wood smoke for days to come, but everyone went home that night with raised spirits.

'Better than ever,' said Alan to Harold as they helped to clear up.

'Thank God it didn't rain,' commented Edward, rubbing his hot face with a black hand. 'And your potatoes were better than ever, Percy.'

'Ah! Willjars, they were,' said Percy much gratified. 'We'll have them next year. I'll see to that!'

It was striking midnight when Harold drew back his bedroom curtains and looked out into the darkness. The night was still and damp. He remembered the rosy glow of the bonfire and smelt a whiff of wood smoke in the air.

There was something very exhilarating, thought Harold, about this mixture of the elements, fire, air and water. It had done them all good.

Greatly content, he climbed into bed.

Carl Andersen had not been present at the Guy Fawkes jollifications for he was immersed in the main purpose of his business in Scotland.

But before his departure, he had had an interesting conversation with Edward Young. He had asked Edward if he could have a private talk, and Edward had invited him to his home one evening when Joan was engaged at a reunion at her old school.

It was the cold dark night of 1 November, and the two men enjoyed the log fire at their feet, and the drinks in their hands.

Edward had wondered about this request for privacy which

Carl had mentioned. Before, he had always blown in, cheerful and informal, glad to see both Joan and Edward, and any other Thrush Green people who were present.

Perhaps, thought Edward, he wanted to discuss some point connected with the Scottish project, and felt that people generally would be bored by technical details? Perhaps there was a personal problem of health, finances, accommodation or of dealing with local or national officialdom?

The truth of the matter, when it was revealed, was a complete surprise.

Carl began by talking about his mother and Mrs Curdle.

'As you know,' he began, 'my ma felt she owed a lot to the old lady. She talked about her often, and particularly during the last months of her life. It was the reason for my coming here in the first place, and the fact that I managed to take back so many mementoes of Mrs Curdle gave my ma enormous pleasure.'

'She always had a great name here,' agreed Edward, 'and it's good to know her influence spread so far afield.'

'The thing is this,' went on Carl. 'My ma wanted me to do something practical to honour her godmother. I know you did something for Nathaniel Patten, your local missionary, some years ago, but I don't think a statue of Mrs Curdle would be quite the thing.'

'Perhaps something for the church?' suggested Edward. 'A plaque or an urn, or something of the kind, for her grave?'

Carl looked doubtful. 'I gather from Charles Henstock that the old lady was not much of a church supporter. I talked it over with Ma not long before she died, and she wanted something practical done for people living in Thrush Green.'

'A trust fund? Something like that, for people in need?'

Carl shook his head. 'As a matter of fact, you gave me the idea yourself.'

'I did?' Edward was startled.

'Yes, when you told me your worries about the annexe at Rectory Cottages. Why not make a really handsome addition to that and call it after Mrs Curdle?'

Edward was still flummoxed. 'It's a fine idea,' he said at last, 'but it would cost several thousand pounds. It's a pretty big project.'

Carl sighed. 'Look, I don't want to seem boastful, but the money doesn't matter. My old dad left a heap of dollars, and my ma had more than she ever needed when he went. Mind you, he deserved every cent he made. He worked like a Trojan for the firm and it rewarded him handsomely. My job, as I see it, is to do what my ma asked me to do, and to do it properly.'

'It does you credit,' said Edward, still bemused.

'I thought I'd broach it with you first,' continued Carl, accepting a refill to his glass, 'because we talked about the possible enlargement of that place, and because I could sound you out about how my idea might be received. What d'you think?'

'I can't think of anything more suitable as a tribute to both your generous mother and dear old Mrs Curdle,' said Edward warmly. 'What do you want me to do?'

Carl rubbed his chin thoughtfully.

'I know you are one of the trustees, but I wondered if it might be best to sound out one or two privately before a meeting. I'd like to have a word with Charles Henstock, for instance, but I'm off to Scotland tomorrow night.'

'I'd do that willingly,' offered Edward, 'if you are sure. It's a big undertaking.'

'If you do that,' said Carl rising, 'we'll take it from there when I get back.'

'We have a trustees' meeting some time at the end of the month,' said Edward. 'When do you expect to be back?'

'It all depends on the state of progress,' replied Carl. 'I must have a day or two in London as well. There's someone there I must see urgently, but I'll ring you while I'm away.'

Edward watched him stride away to his car, and then returned to his fireside. He turned over a log very carefully with the poker.

'What a shock!' he said to the dancing flames. 'But what a wonderful one!'

Ever since Dotty's escapade in Lulling Woods she had been a little more amenable about taking an afternoon rest.

This was a source of great relief to Connie and Kit, and also much appreciated by Flossie, who soon realized how comfortable it was lying on Dotty's eiderdown with her old stiff back propped against the warmth of her mistress's legs.

The two dozed for an hour or so each afternoon, much to the relief of Dr Lovell, as well as Dotty's friends and relatives, who knew what a refractory patient she had always been.

Dotty herself came to enjoy this tranquil hour of the day. Her active mind, a rag-bag of assorted thoughts from 'ships and shoes and sealing-wax' to 'cabbages and Kings', seemed to move more slowly these days, and sleep often overcame her when she sat down to rest. It was not long before she realized that her ancient bones appreciated the benison of her afternoon rest.

One grey afternoon the two old ladies composed themselves on the bed, one under the eiderdown, and the other stretched out on top. Peace reigned and neither snored, nor stirred. Only a bird chirped now and again in the still garden. At the other end of the house, Connie sat alone doing the crossword puzzle, while Kit had gone to the dentist.

It was half past two when Dotty came to her senses. Still drowsy, she lay relishing the warmth of her bed and the familiar weight of Flossie's body against her legs.

After a time, she put out a hand to feel the familiar silky head. Flossie enjoyed having her ears caressed.

But something was wrong. Something was different. In alarm, Dotty struggled up to investigate.

Flossie's weight was heavier than usual. She seemed just as peaceful, eyes closed, limbs comfortably stretched along the eiderdown, but Dotty knew at once that she had died. Gently, quietly, without stirring, Flossie's heart had stopped, and she had gone for ever.

Silently Dotty stroked Flossie's head and fondled those long silky ears which could feel nothing now. A tear or two rolled down Dotty's wrinkled cheeks and splashed upon the much-loved head.

Friends must part, thought Dotty, searching for her hand-kerchief.

A day or two after Carl's departure to Scotland, Edward called at St John's vicarage to see his old friend.

Charles Henstock was in his greenhouse, busy picking a few dead leaves from his geranium cuttings.

Edward joined him in the peaceful dampness and told him that he had a message from Carl.

'Dear fellow,' commented Charles, putting a few dead leaves to join others in a flower pot. 'I had an idea he was off about this Scottish building job.'

'He went a couple of days ago,' said Edward, 'but asked me to sound you out.'

'Sound me out?' echoed Charles. 'What about?'

Edward told him about Carl's idea of a tribute to Mrs Curdle, and his mother's wishes. Charles drew out an ancient stool from under the bench, and sat down upon it suddenly.

'But we can't possibly accept it!' he said at last. 'It would cost a fortune!'

Edward tried to explain. 'He's a very wealthy man, Charles, although he is so modest and unassuming. I feel just as you do, but he says he's determined to do what his mother would have wanted, and money is no object.'

'I really don't know what to think,' said Charles, wiping a

muddy hand across his brow, and leaving a dirty mark upon its pinkness. 'Would it be feasible to enlarge that room further? As an architect, what's your opinion?'

'Nothing simpler.'

'We should have to confer with the other trustees, of course, about this marvellous offer.'

'Naturally, but I don't think anything should be done until Carl returns. And then he should put this idea into writing, if he still feels the same way.'

'No one else knows?'

'No one. I just said that I would speak privately to you on his behalf.'

'Then we must keep silent until he is in touch again. I really am quite flabbergasted, Edward. If it goes ahead I hope you will feel able to take on the job.'

'That's for the trustees to decide,' said Edward. 'I hope they won't think I'm pushing myself forward. Not everyone seems delighted with my last effort.'

He sounded bitter, and Charles put a grubby hand on his friend's sleeve.

'You did a splendid job, and we all appreciate it. Any man in the public eye has to face the fact that he is sometimes an Aunt Sally, and I regret to say that there are unkind critics even in Thrush Green.'

'Don't I know it!'

Charles put down the flower pot, and pushed the stool back under the shelving.

'Time for coffee, Edward, and I believe Dimity has been making Welsh cakes to go with it.'

'Lead me to the kitchen,' commanded Edward, greatly cheered.

The dismal weather continued, and the people of Thrush Green and Lulling, in company with most residents in the British

Isles, were heartily sick of having the lights on all day to counteract the gloom, and of having to curtail their outdoor activities because of heavy showers.

At the village school the children were as frustrated as the old people at Rectory Cottages.

The fact that preparations for Christmas were already in progress at the school did a little to mitigate the general depression, and calendars, bookmarks and Christmas cards were being manufactured with some zest.

Of course, there were drawbacks to these preparations, and

for Alan Lester the most grievous was the revival of those noisy dances which Miss Robinson so enjoyed. The weather was too unreliable to banish the infants to the playground for their rehearsals, and Alan Lester was obliged to conduct his lessons with a background of clapping and stamping from next door which made the partition between the two rooms shudder.

The Remembrance Sunday service, with its sad splendour, took place in pouring rain, and like many thousands of villages in the land, the poppy wreath seemed to be the only glowing spot of colour against the grey wet stone of the memorial cross. It was a sorrowful time, with the glory of autumn wasted away and Christmas too far ahead to give any real cheer.

The first of the winter colds were beginning to afflict young and old alike. The talk was all about cough cures, injections against influenza, and seasonal ills.

News of Flossie's death, of course, had flown round Thrush Green very quickly, and had added to the general gloom.

As soon as Albert Piggott heard it the next morning, he was rapidly on his way, spade on shoulder, to dig the grave he had been waiting to prepare for some months. He had already chosen the site. It was towards the end of a long bed beside an old hedge where several other of Dotty's former pets had their last resting places.

He found Dotty in her kitchen stirring a large saucepan containing food for the hens. It smelt rather good, thought Albert, although he knew that the contents were only scraps from earlier meals. By the time Dotty had added bran and some poultry spice it would be fit for anyone, flesh or fowl, to eat.

He had the delicacy of feeling to prop his spade outside the back door before he entered, and Dotty welcomed him warmly, waving to a kitchen chair with an enormous wet wooden spoon.

'I've sad news for you, Albert,' said Dotty.

'Ah! I heard. Poor old Flossie! Still, she had a good life and went very peaceful, I understand.'

'That's quite right,' said Dotty with a slight sniff. She rubbed an eye with the back of her hand, and a dollop of chicken food fell to the floor, which Dotty ignored, but which was hastily consumed by Bruce who emerged from under the kitchen table.

'I brought me spade along,' said Albert, 'just in case you was needing it. I know just the place to put her if you'd like me to make a start.'

Dotty left the saucepan and came to sit down at the table. She looked earnestly at her visitor.

'Albert! You are so kind, but dear Kit insisted on burying her at once. He didn't want me to be upset. Not that I should have been. Death comes to us all.'

Albert was seriously affronted to hear of Kit's officiousness in taking over a rightful gravedigger's job, but did his best to hide his feelings.

'I daresay you was upset at the time,' said Albert, determined not to be completely thwarted of funereal misery.

'Well,' conceded Dotty honestly, 'of course I had a little weep when I realized she'd gone, but dear Bruce is being such a comfort.'

Hearing his name the little terrier wagged his stumpy white tail. His mistress bent to pat him.

'I'm sure he misses Flossie, but it seems to have made him more *responsible*. He seems to be looking after me as Flossie used to do in her heyday, the dear boy.'

'Well, he knows he's top dog now,' said Albert nastily, still smarting from Kit's impertinent hastening of Flossie's interment. 'If you don't need me to do anything I'll be getting back.'

Dotty, quite unconscious of his hurt feelings, wished him goodbye, and he retrieved his spade from outside the back door, and set off homeward.

He was not only offended, he was real hungry, he told himself. That chicken food smelt a treat.

He heard the church clock strike, and quickened his pace. The Two Pheasants would be open now.

Betty Bell brought the news of Flossie's demise to the Shoosmiths.

Isobel was much distressed on Dotty's behalf. 'Poor darling! Dotty will miss her so much. Such a faithful little dog, and so gentle.'

'She's taken it on the chin,' Betty informed her, rummaging in a kitchen drawer for a duster. 'She's a tough old party, you know, and she's got young Bruce.'

'But he's so *boisterous*,' protested Isobel. 'I wonder if Dotty can manage him.'

'He'll calm down as he gets older,' Harold assured her. 'A lot of his exuberance was simply looking for attention. I think he was always a bit jealous of Flossie.'

'You're right there,' said Betty, flapping a duster round the toast rack. 'You finished your breakfasts? Want me to wash up before I do your study? Willie Marchant's on his way, so you might get a load of letters any minute.'

'I'll do the breakfast things,' said Isobel, pushing back her chair.

'D'you know,' said Harold, 'Willie told me the most remarkable thing about his cousin Sidney. He picked up a fountain pen on Narrow Hill and it turned out to be his brother's.'

'I know,' said Betty, 'Uncle Stan told me.'

'Uncle?' queried Harold.

'Well, Willie's my cousin and Sid's another, so his dad is my Uncle Stan.'

'I might have known,' said Harold, who had never really understood the vast network of relationships in Thrush Green.

'And another thing,' said Betty, 'this makes the third.'

'Third what?'

'Death.'

'I'm not with you Betty,' confessed Harold, passing a hand across his brow.

'You know what I told you months back? That nice Mr Andersen's mum passed on in America, and Mrs Peters at the Fuchsia Bush was taken, and I said at the time, "Who's going to be third?" and it's our poor old Flossie. See, it always goes in threes, death does. D'you remember me telling you?'

'Yes,' said Harold meekly. 'I remember it well now. You are always right, Betty.'

Much gratified, she whisked off to wreak havoc in Harold's study.

Carl Andersen kept his promise and rang Edward one evening from Scotland.

'Charles was as overwhelmed as I was at your offer,' he told Carl. 'But once he got over the shock he was all in favour of your marvellous idea.'

'Good! Well, I suppose the next move is to put it to the trustees.'

Edward told him about the advisability of putting his suggestion in writing so that the committee could study it, and Carl agreed.

'I shall have to get in touch with my lawyers in the States, but they know a little about these plans, as I got their advice before I came over this time.'

'Any chance of seeing you soon?'

'In about a week's time, I hope,' said Carl. 'I've a few things to sort out here, and I shall make a stop overnight in London, but I'll give you a ring before I set off.'

'So far,' said Edward rather diffidently, 'I have only told Charles about this business, but would you want me to sound out anyone else?'

There was a brief silence, and then Carl said, 'I should rather like Harold Shoosmith's reaction. He's a wise guy, and will keep his own counsel until I get back.'

Perceptive as ever, he had guessed that Edward, always a worrier, could do with a little support under the weight of the secret with which he had been entrusted.

'I'll do that,' said Edward. 'I quite realize that the fewer people who know about it, at this early stage, the better.'

'Well,' laughed Carl, 'I've soon got to realize that any news in Thrush Green gets around pretty smartly.'

'And of its own volition,' agreed Edward. 'It's an absolute mystery, but one has to face facts. Secrets don't stay secrets for long in a village.'

'I know you'll do your best,' Carl assured him. 'I'm sorry to put a burden on you.'

'No *burden*, but an *honour*,' Edward said with emphasis. 'Come back soon, Carl. We're all missing you.'

The gloom of November's early days had lifted a little, and a watery sun began to struggle through the clouds in late morning and survived for an hour or two in the early afternoon.

This raised everyone's spirits. Alan Lester was able to recommend that rehearsals of the ear-shattering country dances could be held in the fresh air, preferably at the farthest end of the playground, and so obtained a little relief from this trouble.

Preparations were already in hand for Christmas at the school. Alan's own class was busy rehearsing the Mad Hatter's tea party and trying to find a youthful actor who could remember his words and yet might be small enough to stuff into a cardboard teapot.

Handiwork lessons were devoted to the making of Christmas gifts. Older boys were trying their hand at simple woodwork, and teapot stands, pipe racks and dolls' house tables stood at crazy angles on the shelf behind Alan's chair, and were the object of many admiring glances from the manufacturers.

Christmas catalogues were being pushed through letter-boxes, and the shops in Lulling High Street were already displaying 'Acceptable Gifts For Christmas' signs, which most people decided were much too early to heed.

Nelly Piggott at the Fuchsia Bush already had a great many delicacies made for Christmas, but they were stored out of sight, for she was one of those who deplored the too-early fever of Christmas.

'Time enough when December comes,' she told Rosa, who had suggested that it might be a good idea to start sticking blobs of cotton wool on the windows to simulate snow.

'We always done it for Mrs Peters,' she said resentfully.

'Not in November you didn't,' retorted Nelly. 'You go and give the tables a good rub up if you're short of a job, and let Christmas look after itself.'

Nelly now was in complete and happy command. Her early fears had vanished as she found that all ran smoothly under the new arrangements.

Business was brisk. There were more orders for Christmas provender than in previous years, and jars of her homemade mincemeat and Christmas puddings were carefully stored at the back. Orders for Nelly's superb mince-pies were already being noted in the order book, and if the premises had been larger she could have provided for the Christmas office parties of several local firms.

But the time for such expansion was not yet ripe. One day, Nelly mused, if things went on as prosperously as they were doing, she might think of it.

Meanwhile, she knew that she was running the business competently and with ease. It was the personal touch which her customers valued, and she was wise enough to see that this was where her strength lay.

The gold chain which hung about her neck, always concealed

by her clothes, was a constant reminder of her lost lover. Sometimes her thoughts were sad when she fingered it, but on the whole it was a source of strength.

Hadn't she overcome that grief? Hadn't she come to terms with betrayal, humiliation and loss? Wasn't she now a busy happy woman, doing the work she loved, and respected and appreciated by all Lulling?

Such thoughts often came to her as she bustled from kitchen to shop, from morning to night. Life for Nelly Piggott had never been so sweet.

Harold Shoosmith was as staggered by Edward's disclosure of Carl's plans as Charles Henstock had been. But, once over the shock, he was filled with appreciation for Carl's generosity and enthusiasm for the idea in general.

Edward explained about the letter which Carl was proposing to send to the chairman of the trustees, Charles Henstock, with a copy for each member of the committee at the meeting which was to take place very soon.

'Has Ben been told about this?' asked Harold. 'He is the closest relative.'

'Not yet,' said Edward. 'Carl particularly wants to tell him himself, once the meeting has taken place. After all, the offer may not be welcomed.'

'I can't see that happening,' commented Harold. 'Do you think it would work? Architecturally, I mean?'

'I can't see any real problem.'

'Could you do it?'

Edward looked unhappy. 'I don't want people to think I'm pushing for a job. I don't want the trustees to feel that just because I am one of them I should be handed the thing. The idea makes me cringe.'

'Naturally,' said Harold. 'Sorry I mentioned it.'

They sat in silence for a moment or two, then Harold spoke

again: 'It does seem an outstandingly generous offer, and I wonder if Carl quite realizes how much this may cost.'

'He's in a far better position than we are to judge that,' Edward pointed out. 'He's doing this sort of thing all the time. His aim is to do what his mother asked him to do. It's really as simple as that.'

'Well,' said Harold standing up, 'it's a wonderful thought, and we'll have to see how the trustees react when they read Carl's letter next week.'

The night of the meeting was cold and bright. As the eight trustees assembled, blowing on their freezing fingers, they were glad to see the blazing fire in the Cartwrights' sitting-room, which the couple had handed over for this evening's business.

They themselves did not take part in these meetings, but were kept well-informed of any decisions taken, and their own views were much welcomed by the committee.

Charles, as chairman, had wondered if the letter from Carl should be sent to each member of the committee in advance of the meeting, but had decided against it. Far better to get the initial response round the table, he felt, and so it was arranged.

Having gone smoothly through the agenda, the all-important Any Other Business brought Charles to his feet as he bustled round the table putting a copy of Carl's letter before his friends.

'We'll have a few minutes to read this to ourselves,' he said, 'and then have comments.'

The trustees applied themselves to their task diligently, and silence fell upon the little company as they read the letter before them. It said:

> *To Those Whom It May Concern*
>   *My mother, who died recently in Michigan, was the godchild of Mrs Curdle, well-known in Thrush Green. Ben Curdle, who still lives there, as you know, is her grandson.*

> *My mother loved and respected Mrs Curdle and always wanted to pay tribute to her by way of a memorial. She asked me to find out the most suitable remembrance, and this was the main reason for my visits to Thrush Green.*
>
> *I have looked and listened, and it seems to me that the most suitable tribute would be the enlargement of the present sun room at Rectory Cottages, and perhaps, if agreed, to name it 'Mrs Curdle's Room'.*
>
> *All expenses would be my concern, and I should be happy to provide this tribute to Mrs Curdle, as my mother wished.*

'Well,' gasped Mrs Thurgood, 'what an amazing letter!'

'A most generous offer!' commented Justin Venables. 'We should have to look into the legal side, of course.'

There were other comments of amazement as the letters were lowered again to the table, and the trustees looked bemusedly about them.

'I should like your comments,' said Charles.

As expected, Mrs Thurgood was the first to burst into speech.

'Well, as you know, I have always maintained that the present annexe, or "sun room" as Mr Andersen calls it, was far too small.' She turned to Edward. 'If you remember, I said as much when we had our little discussion in the High Street.'

Edward felt that 'little discussion' hardly described his capture and incarceration by a strategically placed shopping trolley, but he remained silent. It would have been a waste of breath to try to quell Mrs Thurgood.

'So,' continued that lady, 'I heartily welcome this offer.'

'Hear, hear!' came from her fellows round the table.

'It seems to me,' said Charles, 'the most wonderful gesture. I only question the expense of the project. One wonders if perhaps Carl would allow us to contribute part of the funding.'

'My daughter,' began Mrs Thurgood eagerly, 'would be very pleased to have an exhibition –'

She was cut short by Charles who interrupted her with uncharacteristic firmness.

'Not now, Mrs Thurgood! What do you all feel about this?'

Edward spoke. 'Carl mentioned this matter to me in confidence, and I did question the very considerable sum that such an undertaking would need. He was quite adamant that he wanted to meet all expenses himself, and I think he would be hurt if we suggested that we muscled in — shall we say? — on his very personal offer. He is anxious to carry out his mother's wishes, and I think we should respect that.'

There was agreement over this, and after a little more discussion and general appreciation of Carl's offer, the motion of acceptance was put and carried.

It was then that Harold made the suggestion that the Cartwrights' opinion might be sought.

'After all, they will have to cope with the building and general upheaval, and the comfort of their charges.'

'You think I should write?' queried Charles, 'and perhaps send a copy of Carl's letter?'

'What's wrong with calling 'em in now,' said Edward. 'They're only in the kitchen washing up, and we've never stood on ceremony with Jane and Bill.'

And so the Cartwrights were summoned to their own sitting-room, provided with their own chairs, and offered one of their own biscuits which were ready on a side table to eat with the coffee which came when the meeting was over.

Charles explained about the incredibly generous offer, and how pleased the trustees were. Had they any comments? Were they happy with the idea? Nothing yet had been done about replying to Mr Andersen, but he would be writing immediately on behalf of the trustees.

Bill took his wife's hand and looked at her delightedly.

Jane was starry-eyed.

'It's the best news in the world,' she said.

'She's right,' agreed Bill. 'Tell Carl when you write, that we send all our thanks and love.'

'And now,' said Jane, jumping to her feet, 'if you've nearly finished, I'll get the coffee.'

When the company emerged from Rectory Cottages, the stars were bright above, and frost was beginning to form. The grass was already crisp, and their breath billowed before them as they made their way to their cars, or on foot to nearby homes.

'Come in for a drink?' invited Harold to Edward, but the latter shook his head.

'I promised to ring Carl as soon as the meeting was over. He'll be waiting for a call.'

'He'll be delighted with the outcome, I've no doubt. What a success the meeting was! Even Mrs Thurgood was pleasant.'

'Naturally! She's got her own way again,' said Edward laughing.

'And we shan't have to have an exhibition of her daughter's ghastly daubs,' agreed Harold. 'When's Carl back, by the way?'

'Ben's fetching him the day after tomorrow.'

'Good! I've no doubt Ben will be told all about it then.'

Edward stopped suddenly beside one of the great chestnut trees near his house.

'D'you know, it was under this tree that Mrs Curdle always put her caravan. It's nice to think that her memorial will be standing so near.'

'Halfway,' mused Harold looking across the green, 'between her caravan site and her grave. I like the idea.'

'So will everyone,' said Edward heartily.

Walking alone to his own house, Harold thought that he had never seen Edward quite so happy before.

He, and all at Thrush Green, had Carl Andersen to thank for that.

December

Let joy be unconfined;

Lord Byron

A welcome change in the weather heralded the arrival of December. The weather-vanes of Lulling and Thrush Green veered to the north-east, the skies cleared and a wintry sun emerged for part of each day.

Spirits rose. Christmas shopping began in earnest, and all those loved ones in far-flung quarters of the globe were remembered with lightweight parcels sent by air mail, if they had been forgotten earlier in October, when presents should have been despatched by surface mail by prudent donors.

In Lulling High Street the Christmas decorations were being draped across the road by men balanced on long ladders.

Nelly Piggott allowed Rosa and Gloria to stick morsels of cotton-wool on the windows of the Fuchsia Bush, much to their satisfaction, and a small Christmas tree stood in a prominent position just behind the snowfall.

At Thrush Green there were more modest decorations. The Two Pheasants had a string of varied coloured lights round the door, and Mr Jones' two bay trees, one each side of the entrance, were also decked with fairy lights.

In St Andrew's church the crib stood in the chancel. Winnie had washed the figures of the nativity, as she did yearly, and she and Ella had put it all in order and set it up in its appointed place.

At the school the making of paper-chains went on apace. Jars of almond-smelling Gloy gave forth their fragrance, and paste brushes were plied with feverish zeal. Already the infants' room was criss-crossed with many-splendoured pieces of handiwork, and the fact that every now and again one link would give way and a shower of paper rings would descend upon the makers only added to the general enjoyment.

Rehearsals for the Mad Hatter's tea party and the thunderous country dances went on apace, and although Alan Lester and Miss Robinson adhered valiantly to the timetable, there was no doubt that rather less knowledge was imbibed than usual.

'Never mind,' said Alan philosophically, 'Christmas comes but once a year.'

It was at this time that more news came of Bruce's owners. They were indeed in South America and in one of those countries which did not recognize the usual international necessity for returning malefactors to the country of their origin in order to expedite justice.

Stern letters had crossed the Atlantic. Diplomats had argued. Letters from outraged readers had enlivened the columns of the local newspapers, but all was in vain.

The couple were allowed to remain in the country of their choice, living, no doubt, on their ill-gotten gains and spreading happiness among the local traders.

'It is deplorable, of course,' Dotty said to Betty Bell, 'but at least we know they won't come back.'

'Good riddance to bad rubbish!' agreed Betty.

'And in any case,' added Dotty ferociously, 'I should *never* have given Bruce back to such dreadful people. My father would have put them to rights, I can tell you!'

Carl Andersen returned, much to the pleasure of his friends, and one of his first visits was to see Ben and Molly.

Now that his plan had been accepted by the trustees, he had the freedom to discuss it openly.

Ben was much touched by this honour to his grandmother, and said so with unusual eloquence.

'It's exactly the sort of thing she would like,' he said. 'You see, she always had a soft spot for children and old people, and I think children get much more attention these days than the old folk.'

'That's right,' agreed Molly.

'What's more,' went on Ben, 'she would have known some of those folk at Rectory Cottages, and certainly some of their forebears. It's a lovely idea. We shall be very proud to have a Curdle Room.'

Edward Young had told him about the general delight expressed at the trustees' meeting.

'It is a magnificent idea of yours,' he said. 'You have no second thoughts about it? No doubts? We feel it is going to be such an expensive undertaking.'

Carl laughed. 'I've been into it all most carefully, both here and back home. It's what I dearly want to do, and to be given the go-ahead was all I wanted.'

'I'm sure you will be asked to a trustees' meeting very soon, so that they can tell you how they feel and to discuss the best way of putting the work in hand.'

'Good,' said Carl. 'And I want to involve as many Thrush Green people as possible in this affair. Ben and Molly, for instance, will be the chief guests at the opening, and I hope you will take on the job of architect.'

'*Please*,' begged Edward. 'I know it's an honour, but it must come from the trustees. I should be embarrassed to have this automatically given to me.'

'I understand,' Carl assured him. 'I'll be discreet.'

'Are you able to stay for Christmas?' asked Edward. 'Joan and I hope you'll stay here.'

'Nothing I'd like more,' said Carl, clapping him on the shoulder, 'and now I'm off to see Charles.'

The news of Carl's offer had been relayed to Barton-on-Sea by telephone from Isobel Shoosmith to her old friends.

Dorothy and Agnes discussed it with much enthusiasm.

'She was a great influence, was old Mrs Curdle,' said Dorothy. 'Everyone respected her, and this project of Carl Andersen's will get everyone's support.'

'George was a dear little boy,' responded Agnes wistfully. She often looked back to her teaching days at Thrush Green with considerable nostalgia. Dorothy, made of sterner stuff, seldom looked back. The future was what interested her, and she broached it now.

'Do you know that Eileen is contemplating moving? I don't know what Teddy feels about it, but I told her straight that I thought it *quite wrong*!'

'But surely,' quavered Agnes, 'it is their affair? And why should you think it is wrong?'

'Poor Teddy is used to his surroundings. He knows where the steps are in the house, and which way the doors open, and all those important things for a person without sight. I told Eileen so, and I didn't mince my words either.'

She thumped down a saucepan on the draining board to emphasize her resolve. The two ladies were washing up their lunch pots and pans.

Agnes was deeply disturbed. Dorothy could be so thoughtless. She might have offended Eileen. It was true that Teddy would have quite a problem in adapting to a new environment, but was it Dorothy's place to point this out?

Agnes's heart had leapt when Dorothy spoke of this proposed move. It would come as a relief to know that Teddy was safely removed from Dorothy's attentions.

She had certainly been much more restrained in her dealings

with Eileen and Teddy since Agnes had pointed out the desirability of discretion on their visit to Thrush Green earlier in the year. But this news might well inflame those feelings which Dorothy had made some effort to calm, and who knows what might happen?

'It's surely their business,' said Agnes diffidently. 'I'm sure they would have talked it over thoroughly before making such an important decision.'

'Teddy is so *unselfish*,' declared Dorothy, dropping a handful of kitchen cutlery on to the draining board with a resounding clatter. 'If Eileen wants something, then Teddy will give way to her.'

'Well, of course, they consider each other,' pointed out Agnes reasonably. 'Married couples have to make their plans jointly.'

Dorothy wrung out the dish cloth with excessive vigour. Agnes saw, with dismay, that her neck and face were getting flushed, always a bad sign.

'There's really nothing we can do,' she continued soothingly. 'In any case, I'm sure they will tell us if they do decide to move.'

Dorothy gave a gusty sigh, and folded the dish cloth with care.

'I suppose we must just be patient,' she said. 'Very irksome, I find it, but you are quite right, Agnes dear. It's just that I am so fond of Teddy – in just a *friendly* way, you understand – that I don't care to see him *exploited*.'

'I quite understand,' replied Agnes.

One frosty December morning Carl called at St John's vicarage to see his friends the Henstocks.

Dimity was busy rolling out pastry, but paused to put floury hands round his neck and give him a hearty kiss.

Charles, less demonstrative but equally delighted to see him, led him into his study.

'I'm juggling with the Christmas services for all four

parishes,' he explained, pushing a sheaf of papers to one end of his desk. 'Such a joyous festival of the Church, but *very* difficult to arrange.'

'I can imagine,' said Carl. 'I won't hold up the good work, but I just wanted a word about the trustees' meeting.'

'Of course, of course! I can't tell you how excited and grateful everyone is. We are having an emergency meeting here next week. I hope you'll be here too.'

He began to shuffle his papers.

'Somewhere I've got a letter here from the trustees thanking you,' he said with some agitation. 'Now where –?'

Carl broke in. 'I'll be there without fail. Which day is it?'

'Half past seven next Tuesday,' replied Charles. 'And we're having it here this time. You can tell us all your plans, and we can tell you how we feel about this marvellous offer.'

Carl began to tell him how anxious he was for as many Thrush Green people to be involved as possible.

'Perhaps the trustees will bear that in mind,' he said. 'There must be good builders, electricians, plumbers and the like who could tackle the job.'

'Indeed there are,' agreed Charles.

'And I should very much like Edward to be the architect,' added Carl, 'but he's very diffident about taking it on. He says it must be the trustees' decision.'

'I quite understand his natural feelings over this,' said Charles. 'I'm sure it would be the general wish that he took on the enlargement. He made an excellent job of the first stage.'

'Well, make sure you tell him that,' said Carl. 'I think he feels that he let you down by not making it bigger in the first place.'

'Oh poor Edward!' cried Charles, his face puckering with dismay. 'I'd no idea he felt like that. He has no need to reproach himself.'

'So I tell him,' replied Carl, getting up. 'Just see the message gets across. I'll see you next Tuesday then.'

The next Tuesday was as bright and clear as the days which preceded it, and, very cheerful, the good people of Lulling and Thrush Green were to be able to do their Christmas shopping without the hazards of deep puddles, dripping awnings and umbrellas.

Carl drove from Woodstock, where he had taken up his old

room, and crunched across the gravel of the vicarage drive to attend this important confrontation.

As he waited for the door to be opened he gazed at the great spire of St John's church silhouetted against a luminous sky scattered with stars.

Near by a small animal, vole, mouse or shrew, rustled among the dead leaves under the shrubs. It was very quiet, and the serenity of his surroundings calmed the slight agitation which had been with him on the short journey to this destination.

This would all be here when he had gone. When the projected new annexe had gone, for that matter. Other men, a hundred years hence, would look up at that noble spire and those eternal stars.

The door opened, and Charles welcomed him in.

The meeting began on time. Charles took the chair, and invited Carl to sit beside him. Edward sat alone at the foot of the table and the rest of the trustees were ranged along the sides.

'I have apologies from Justin Venables,' said Charles. 'He has one of his chesty colds.'

There were murmurs of sympathy for young Mr Venables, but, as Mrs Thurgood pointed out, one must face these things in one's seventies.

'Good old camphorated oil takes a lot of beating,' said Harold.

'A bit whiffy,' commented another, and the rival merits of such remedies as friar's balsam, blackcurrant lozenges, gargling with salt water, as well as such modern medicaments as Vick, Night Nurse and Benylin were being briskly discussed when Charles, who was quite used to these digressions at meetings, called them to order, and explained, although they already knew, just why they were there.

His little speech of thanks to Carl was a model of its kind, and warmly supported by all present. He responded by explaining that it was going to give him enormous pleasure to fulfil his mother's wishes, and continued by saying how much he wanted as many Thrush Green people as possible to be involved in the work.

He then paused, and Charles took up the theme.

'That is what we should all like,' he said, 'and it will involve everyone more closely with such an intimately local project. As you know, Edward here made a wonderful job of the original building, and I think it would please everyone if he were invited to take on this work.'

'I propose that,' said Mrs Thurgood promptly. 'Nobody better!'

'And I second it,' said Harold Shoosmith.

'Would you like to make a comment?' asked Charles of the silent figure at the end of the table.

Edward was looking unhappy. He raised his eyes and saw Carl's intent gaze upon him. There was silence round the table.

'Please,' said Carl gently.

Edward looked at the waiting faces, and smiled. 'If that is what you want,' he said, 'I should count it an honour to take on the job. And I promise to do my best.'

There was an audible sigh of relief. The motion was carried unanimously, and twenty minutes later Dimity appeared with glasses and the vicar's best port to celebrate.

Carl was obliged to return to his Scottish affairs the next day but had a chance to tell Edward how relieved and delighted he was at his acceptance of the work.

'I've been thinking about the design,' said Edward, 'and it seems to me that a large shallow bay with a really comfortable window seat round it would be useful as well as attractive to look at. And we must have plenty of light. It makes such a difference to old people's reading.'

Carl was relieved to see him so happily engaged, and Joan, out of her husband's earshot, told Carl how Edward's spirits had revived.

'You are a greater benefactor than you know,' she told him, 'and the news is already cheering people with the prospect of more work to do.'

She was right. Carl's present to the community was warmly welcomed, and the thought of such a practical tribute to dear old Mrs Curdle of hallowed memory pleased everyone.

Nelly Piggott, as a Thrush Green resident, had many comments made to her on the subject by customers of the Fuchsia Bush.

Christmas shopping was now in full swing, and Nelly and the staff were uncommonly busy when one morning the three Lovelock sisters made their appearance.

Instead of seating themselves at one of the tables as Nelly expected, they approached her with smiles on their wrinkled faces and hands outstretched. Bertha Lovelock, the collector of unconsidered trifles such as small pots of jam, was holding a little parcel wrapped in Christmas paper.

'Do come into the office for a minute if you can spare the time,' said Nelly, conscious of inquisitive glances from the customers and guessing, rightly, that this was an offering for herself.

They followed her obediently into the inner sanctum where so recently Bertha had made her apologies in the stern presence of her sister Violet.

'No, no. We won't sit down, Mrs Piggott. But we wanted you to have this little Christmas present with our very best wishes.'

Nelly unwrapped it with care. It was a charming little silver dish, oval in shape, called, she believed, a bonbon dish, and she remembered polishing it in days gone by when she worked for the old ladies.

'This is much too good for me,' she exclaimed, holding the pretty thing.

'Nothing is too good for you,' pronounced Bertha. 'It is a little memento of three old friends.'

Nelly was much touched. It was old, it was lovely and had been much cherished. It had cost these three old ladies a great deal to part with it.

'I can't begin to tell you how much I appreciate it. I'll always treasure it, believe me.'

'We know it is in safe hands,' said Violet.

'Do go and sit down, and let me bring you some coffee,' urged Nelly.

'No, really,' protested Ada.

'Please. It's the least I can do, to give you a cup of coffee in return for this wonderful present.'

The sisters exchanged glances.

'In that case,' said Violet inclining her head graciously, 'we should be delighted to accept such a kind offer.'

Nelly followed behind them, and summoned Rosa to fetch coffee 'and in the best cups, please'.

The Youngs were expecting Carl to come to them on Christmas Eve, and Molly and Joan were busy the day before making up a bed for him in the spare room when the telephone rang.

It was Carl. He sounded agitated, quite unlike his usual self.

'Something's cropped up,' he announced. 'Pretty serious too, I guess.'

'Are you ill? What's happened?'

'We reckon there may be a fault on site. We've got the surveyor and a whole heap of geology guys testing like crazy everywhere. The thing is, Joan, I'll just have to stay here, and I'm real sorry to miss Christmas with you.'

'I can see it can't be helped,' said Joan. 'Edward's out, but he'll be as disappointed as I am.'

'I'm sick about the whole thing, but we must get this sorted out. Luckily they don't seem to worry too much about the Christmas break up here. Something called Hogmanay next weekend or so seems to be their knocking-off time.'

'Any idea when we might see you?'

'None at the moment, but I'll keep in touch. I'll probably go straight to Woodstock if I can get away, but I can see it won't be until after Christmas now.'

They wished each other well and Carl rang off.

Sadly, Joan returned to the bedroom to tell Molly the news.

Christmas Day was bright and clear. The bells of St John's were the first to be heard, and later the answering peals from Thrush Green and the villages around were plain to hear through the frosty air.

Above St Andrew's church the rooks wheeled and cawed, as the parishioners made their way to morning service.

Winnie and Ella met at the church gate and Ella asked her if she would like a trip to Woodstock when the shops opened again after Christmas.

'I'd love to come,' said Winnie. 'Is there any particular reason?'

'That nice woman in the wool shop rang yesterday to say she had a late delivery of the wool I'm using for my rug. You know, that thick stuff I'm using for that tied-brick stitch.'

'How's it getting on?'

'Slowly. I don't really care for this coarse handiwork, but it's no good pretending I can see to do anything finer.'

Winnie was sympathetic. They entered the church, and as they knelt together to say their first private prayers Winnie thought how bravely Ella was tackling her problem of diminishing sight.

The ancient Mini which had served Ella for so many years had already been sold, and Winnie knew how much Ella missed her independence and the joy she had always felt in forays into

Lulling and the surrounding countryside. Winnie herself had never driven, for Donald had enjoyed taking the wheel and she had been more than content to be a passenger. Since his death she had become familiar with the local bus timetable, and now, it seemed, Ella had to do the same.

Charles Henstock took the service. He had already celebrated early communion at St John's at eight o'clock and Matins at ten o'clock. From there he had driven to Thrush Green's service at eleven fifteen, and rejoiced in his work.

St John's had looked splendid. The great nave had echoed to the grandeur of a full choir and an organ loud in triumphant rendering of 'Adeste fideles'. The flower ladies had excelled themselves, and swathes of greenery, branches of berried holly, great mop-headed chrysanthemums and Christmas roses added to the splendour. It was a noble church, thought Charles, nobly tended as it had been for generations, and he was proud to be the incumbent of such a fine and famous parish.

And yet, thought Charles, looking fondly about the modest interior of St Andrew's as the country voices sang 'Hark, the herald angels sing' beneath the pitch-pine rafters, there was something very endearing and very personal about this building.

It was not beautiful as St John's was beautiful. It had been built in Victoria's reign by less skilled men with less time and money. But it was the church in which Nathaniel Patten had worshipped and where that fine missionary's benefactor, the Reverend Octavius Fennel, had conducted his services just as he was doing this Christmas morning.

It was here too, at Thrush Green, thought Charles, that he had lived for a number of years, at first alone, until he had met and married his dear Dimity who had changed his life so wonderfully.

'Amen!' resounded round the church, and Charles returned to his duties, with a thankful heart.

*

Winnie Bailey and Ella Bembridge had decided to catch the bus from Thrush Green to Woodstock.

'If we catch the two o'clock,' said Winnie, 'we shall be there in good time, and after we have picked up the wool I suggest that we have a walk in Blenheim Park.'

'Good idea,' said Ella. 'I think Blenheim Palace looks at its best in winter, and it should still be light. After that we will have tea in Woodstock and catch the five o'clock back.'

The two looked forward to their outing. They had always been good friends, but since Donald's death and Dimity's departure to the vicarage at Lulling, they had seen more of each other and enjoyed their meetings.

It was dry and still, but there was no sunshine as they waited for the bus to mount the hill from Lulling. Outside the Youngs' house a bed of nerines glowed pinkly against the Cotswold stone house. In local gardens the bulbs were already pushing their noses through the soil, and winter jasmine starred the cottage walls with yellow blossom.

'Soon be spring,' said Ella cheerfully.

The bus arrived. One of the Cooke boys, who had started life in a council house along the Nidden road less than half a mile away, welcomed them aboard and took their fares. He was driver and conductor combined.

They visited the wool shop, inspected the goods, paid for them and arranged to pick up the parcel after their walk.

By now a weak shaft of sunlight was showing through the clouds, and brightening the ancient street.

Two people were crossing the road from the Bear.

'Look!' cried Winnie. 'There's Carl!'

The two came towards them. Carl was accompanied by a tall elegant woman in a long black coat with a fur collar, and a dashing little black fur hat to match.

'How lovely to see you,' said Winnie. 'We thought you were still in Scotland.'

'We arrived here late last night,' said Carl smiling. 'But let me introduce you. This is Elizabeth Winsford and we are getting married very soon.'

'What news! Congratulations Carl!' cried Winnie.

She held out her hand to the elegant stranger who was laughing at the excitement she was causing.

'And mine too,' said Ella warmly. 'This is tremendous news. All Thrush Green will rejoice with you.'

Winnie interposed anxiously, 'Unless it is a secret, of course?' She looked questioningly at Elizabeth.

'No indeed,' said the girl. 'Carl has just been telling Joan and Edward Young and we are going over there now to see them.'

'In fact,' said Carl, 'we're just slipping across to the florist to buy a belated Christmas present to take with us. Can we give you a lift back?'

But the two ladies explained about their proposed walk and the parcel waiting to be collected, and the couples parted with renewed congratulations and in high spirits.

By the next day it was common knowledge in Thrush Green, and even in Lulling, that Carl was engaged to be married. His fiancée had only been glimpsed the day before, so that descriptions of the lady varied from 'proper skinny, and all in black' (Albert Piggott), 'a real lady with furs on' (Mrs Cooke) and 'elegant, I'd say, and what a pair they'll make' (Nelly Piggott).

The use of the word 'black' in Albert Piggott's comment, was soon translated by those who had not seen the lady into conjectures about whether Carl's bride-to-be was black or white, but everyone agreed that whoever Carl had chosen would be wholeheartedly welcome in the neighbourhood.

Joan and Edward, as the first people to welcome the couple, were overjoyed and set about arranging a celebratory party as soon as possible. It had to be planned very quickly, as Carl was taking Elizabeth to America to meet his relatives. They were to be married there, which was a disappointment to Charles Henstock as well as the rest of Thrush Green. After a brief honeymoon they would return to Scotland for a short time while Carl continued with his work there.

The Saturday after the news had broken was chosen for the party, and the telephone wires buzzed from the Youngs' house to all parts of Thrush Green and Lulling. On this day Nelly Piggott was busy in the kitchen of the Fuchsia Bush filling trays with delectable tit-bits to accompany the drinks.

It was a clear dry evening when the first guests arrived at six o'clock. The stars twinkled above St Andrew's church and the bare branches of the horse-chestnut trees. Underfoot the ground was crisp. There was going to be a hard frost.

But inside all was warmth and happiness. Carl and Elizabeth stood by the Youngs to welcome, and be welcomed by, their friends.

Nelly Piggott was in Joan's kitchen supervising sizzling pans of miniature sausages, while Gloria and Rosa had volunteered, with rare enthusiasm, to act as waitresses, a tribute to Carl's charm.

About twenty or so guests made the room hum with excitement. Ben and Molly Curdle were there. Charles and Dimity Henstock, the Shoosmiths, Ella, Winnie and Jenny, the Cartwrights and a number of Carl's friends from Rectory Cottages swelled the throng.

At last the time for informal speeches and toasts arrived, and Edward gave a short, elegant and warm-hearted tribute to Carl and Elizabeth, amidst general applause.

Carl, flushed, happy and handsomer than ever, responded, his arm around Elizabeth's shoulders. He spoke movingly of his mother who had waited at Woodstock for her American to return after the war to claim her as his wife.

'That wouldn't have happened,' he said, 'but for Mrs Curdle. In fact, I shouldn't be here at all, if it were not for her advice to my mother, as some of you know. So would you raise your glasses once more, my friends, to the immortal memory of the great Mrs Curdle.'

'Mrs Curdle,' came the hearty response.

'Thank you,' said Carl when the toast had been drunk.

He smiled at Elizabeth, and added: 'As you see, we Andersens always come to Woodstock for our wives.'